Glacier Gal

—

L. Langdon

ISBN: 1494952815
ISBN-13: 9781494952815

Glacier Gal

L. Langdon

For Joan

AUTHOR'S NOTE

Instead of inventing place names and descriptions, I borrowed the real ones. Thus, the geography is reasonably accurate. In any case, I couldn't create an imaginary setting that was any prettier.

The people and situations, of course, are totally fictional.

CHAPTER 1

late April, 1969

Gerri Barton was headed toward the Pee Dee State College Library, walking silently—almost stealthily—in her rubber-soled shoes. The street lights were still burned out, and, in the deep twilight, she could barely see the ground in front of her. The State of South Carolina had higher priorities than street lights at a small, segregated college. She turned around and scanned the area behind her. There was no one in sight. She wasn't alarmed by the darkness—in fact, she was depending on it.

If she thought about it, it was actually funny—here she was, sneaking into her college library to study for her last, big final before she graduated. But, if she was caught, it would be anything *but* funny. She would get in trouble. Probably not serious trouble—she had an exemplary record—but she didn't want any stains on that record, especially now so close to graduation. The school librarian, Mrs. Blakely, however, might well lose her job. She was a high school friend of Olivia Barton, Gerri's mother, and she had given Gerri an illegal duplicate of the key to the outside door of her office.

Gerri used Mrs. Blakely's office as a secret place to study. The library's administrative offices, including Mrs. Blakely's office, were closed at this hour of the evening. Gerri could use her office with no distractions and no interruptions. She didn't do so lightly, only when she had no alternative. She was the first member of her family to attend college, and she had worked hard to do well. Money was a constant problem—she had gotten acceptances from other colleges, but Pee Dee College was only five miles from her family's farm, so she could save money by living at home. But it was hard to study at home. There were always chores to be done, and she had two younger sisters who seemed incapable of being quiet for more than two minutes at a time.

That meant that Gerri did most of her studying on campus—and the reading room of the library was the best place to concentrate for most of each semester. But as finals approached, the number of students studying in the library increased, and, along with them, the noise level increased. If Gerri studied there tonight, she would be constantly distracted.

Worse than the noise problem this week was the problem of Thurman. Thurman Saunders had been her boyfriend—she guessed that she could call him that—for the last two years. They dated, they sang together in the Pee Dee College Choir, and, last, but not least, they did homework together. Did they have a future together? She didn't know. Thurman had hinted at times that he wanted one, but nothing more. Did she *want* them to have a future together? She didn't know. He was handsome, popular, and he had a lot of big ideas. But Gerri had reservations.

He was dogmatic and intolerant of dissent. Particularly if it came from a female. And especially if it came from Gerri. Early in their relationship, Gerri had, in an informal group political discussion, disagreed with one of Thurman's statements on Black Power. Actually, she had spoken up only in favor of the non-violence espoused by Dr. King when Thurman had been praising some of the more radical groups. He told her in rather nasty tones just how reactionary and out-of-touch she was. Her brief attempt at defending herself just brought more of the same. After that, it just seemed easier to try to avoid that subject altogether. Thus, when he later mentioned that black women should support their men and not try to supplant them in the struggle, she just tried to ignore it. Though she worried about some of his attitudes, she was more than happy to delay any confrontation and keep the peace.

But it wasn't only Thurman's political and social attitudes that gave her pause. Gerri had promised her mother that she would retain her virginity until after she had graduated. That was a compromise—her mother had wanted the promise to apply until Gerri got married.

Even before Thurman knew about her promise, it had proved to be an embarrassment to Gerri. Once, when she was a freshman, Gerri had found herself in a bull session with several girls who came from some large city up north. The talk turned to sex, and Gerri, wanting to contribute to the discussion, told them about her agreement. They were scornful and amused. She had been branded as hopelessly old-fashioned, as irredeemably 'country.' They reminded her that this was the decade of free love, and that she was missing out on part of the college experience with her silly notions.

Maybe they were right—she didn't much care. For Gerri, this was more about her promise to her mother and her duty to her family. After all, they were sacrificing to pay her college expenses.

Thurman had accepted—albeit with some grumbling—Gerri's sexual limits. That was a good thing—maybe. It *would* have been a good thing if Gerri had had a healthy confidence about her attractiveness, but she did not. Therefore, she had always had this niggling doubt that he truly felt a physical attraction to her. Oh sure, he wanted her in a 'notch on his belt' sort of way—she supposed that was nearly universal with guys. But, if that was all, then what drew him to her after it was clear that she wouldn't sleep with him?

Ah, that was the nub of it, and that was a major reason for this stealthy expedition. Thurman had always been academically needy—he had demanded Gerri's help with his assignments, particularly in writing his papers. It had finally gotten to the point where Gerri felt guilty for abetting what amounted to his cheating. She was damned (morally) if she did, and damned (with Thurman) if she didn't.

Finally, a few days ago, Gerri had decided to test him. She had told him that some unspecified crisis at home would mean that she couldn't come to school at all during the period between the last class and the start of the exams. She was ever so sorry, she told him, but she would not be able to give him any help. There was no chance that Thurman would come to her home to get help—he and her mother didn't get along, and her father had made his scorn of Thurman abundantly clear.

Just in case, however, Gerri cleared the plan with her parents. Even if Thurman got desperate and called her at home, they would alibi her.

She felt horrible about this deception. In fact, she had privately promised herself that if they made it through this period—if Thurman buckled down and did the term paper that he had been bothering her about—that she would reward him handsomely. To this end, she had made a trip to the Pee Dee College Health Center. With the help of a sympathetic nurse, she had walked away with a prescription for birth control pills. The girls who had laughed at her before would have been titillated if they had known. They never would know, of course. Gerri had already learned that lesson.

She hoped that Thurman would be just as excited. Of course, if he didn't pass her test, he would never know, either. Her mother wouldn't know either way—not for a long time, anyway. Not that Gerri would be breaking her promise; she was graduating in less than two weeks, after all, but she just didn't want to have that conversation with her mother.

Gerri also hoped that she herself would be excited if this worked out. So far, she was ambivalent. She knew that feelings of guilt and obligation alone were absolutely terrible reasons for physical intimacy. Perhaps, she told herself, the excitement would come for her when the moment of truth got closer.

She sighed as she thought about this. What did Thurman see when he looked at her? She knew what she saw when she looked at herself. She saw a fit young woman, strong from a lifetime of work on the farm. She still, on more days than not, walked the five miles from her home to school, carrying whatever books and materials she needed.

What she did not see was anything resembling the popular taste in beauty. Her complexion was smooth, but her skin was dark. She didn't have the slender body and long legs to carry off the tiny mini-skirts which were so in vogue. Twiggy, she was not, and would never be. That was OK. Gerri was comfortable with her 5 foot, 5 inch frame—at least when she wasn't worried about what someone else might think of it.

So what did guys think of that frame? Gerri had heard various terms over the years, and she had her own, private translations for each. *Sexy*—of doubtful sincerity—he wants to get me in bed. *Fat*—unfair and untrue—he wants to be cruel. *Phat*—similar to 'sexy,' but trying to be slicker about it. Thurman had called her that once before he realized that Gerri wasn't going to sleep with him. He never called her that again. *Stocky*—not trying to be cruel, but certainly not what she'd consider flattering. *Chunky*—similar to 'stocky'. And *Solid*—trying to be honest without being negative. Gerri liked that last one the best, since it conjured up good personality traits as well as a physical image.

Suddenly, a noise brought Gerri back from her daydreaming. She stopped under a tree and scanned the area ahead of her. Her heart raced for a moment until she realized the noise's source. A group of students had left the library by the public entrance and were walking toward the Student Center. They were on a brightly lit walkway and they were far away. No threat to Gerri.

It was then that she realized that she had been walking slower and slower while she daydreamed. *Trying to delay this, I guess…* Smiling, she hummed a few bars of the Johnny Rivers tune, 'Secret Agent Man.' *It's a good thing that I want to teach. I'd be an awful secret agent.*

Now was her moment of truth. She took a last look around—there was nobody in sight. She left the deeper shadow under the tree and walked the last few feet to Mrs. Blakely's door. She had the key in her hand, and she was in the office in seconds. She took a deep breath to calm herself, and quietly turned on the desk lamp—invisible from the outside, thanks to the heavy blinds—and set out her books and papers.

———

An hour later, Gerri was making excellent progress on her studies when she heard voices through the vent. Mrs. Blakely had warned her of this eventuality, and had supplied the solution—a large, heavy cushion to block the vent. Gerri got up to put the cushion in place, but as she was about to do so, she realized that the voices were those of Thurman and his friend, Claude Winston.

Claude asked, "How's your paper coming? Is it done yet?"

As this was the question that Gerri most wanted answered, she moved the cushion away from the vent and listened.

"I haven't made any progress. Gerri said a couple of days ago that she had something going on at home. I think I'll ask for an extension."

Gerri was struck with an agony of conscience. *Am I being too cruel? Maybe I should go out there and help him just for a while... But he should have done at least a little on it.*

"And you haven't made any progress since then?"

Thank you, Claude.

Thurman said something that she couldn't hear, and then added: "I went to Orangeburg last night."

"You went to see Carlotta when you had a paper due?"

Who on earth is Carlotta?

"She wanted to see me." He chuckled. "Carlotta can be very persuasive."

Who the hell is Carlotta??? By this time, Gerri had abandoned all pretense of blocking the vent. Something was seriously wrong here, and she needed to know what. She set the cushion on the floor next to the vent and sat on it, eavesdropping—without shame—on their conversation.

"When are you going to tell Gerri about Carlotta? You should have done it long ago."

"I know, I know. I'll tell her soon."

"You're such a triflin' turkey. You don't want to tell her before she finishes your schoolwork."

Gerri heard Thurman make some indistinct protest, but she didn't care. All vestiges of guilt about testing Thurman—and about eavesdropping, for that matter—were banished. She was gripping the cushion so tightly that she was afraid that she might rip it. *How could I have been so trusting? So stupid?* She felt a tear slide down her cheek and rubbed it angrily. *He's not worth any tears, damn it!* She turned to the vent, and heard Claude talking again.

"Suppose Gerri finds out about Carlotta?"

"You're the only person on campus who knows. She won't find out unless she's hiding under this table." There was the scraping of a chair. "Nope, she's not there." Gerri could hear Thurman laugh.

"Just be careful. I don't know…Gerri deserves better; she's a nice girl. And she's a solid, all around person."

Thank you, again, Claude. She smiled through her tears at his use of 'solid' to describe her.

"You're right, and I like her. Geraldine's cute in her nappy-headed way. But Carlotta… Carlotta's so fine, with that bright complexion and her long, wavy hair. And you should see her long legs in one of those mini-skirts."

"Yeah, yeah. I get it. So why doesn't *she* do your paper?"

Thurman laughed suggestively. "I don't think that's her specialty. She's damn good at other things, if you know what I mean."

"I thought you told me a couple of weeks ago that this wasn't just about sex."

Gerri made a disgusted face. Here, she had been thinking that Claude was on her side—but he had known all along and said nothing. She could have a little bit of sympathy for him. He was Thurman's friend, after all. But still…

She was so preoccupied with her thoughts that she almost missed Thurman's response. "It is more than sex—although Carlotta's a hell of a lot more liberated than Gerri is. It's about adventure; about the willingness to try things. Carlotta and I are thinking about going up to New York this summer. Gerri's got her life all planned out. She's going to teach high school mathematics and settle down right here. I'll bet she'll never even leave South Carolina."

Gerri had heard enough. She didn't want to lose any more study time over Thurman's betrayal. She returned the cushion to the vent and sat back down at the desk. Maybe she would cry a few more tears after her test—in private—but she wanted her performance on that test to be up to her usual standards.

———

Much later, as she walked home from the library, Gerri allowed herself to think again about the overheard conversation. A bit to her surprise, she was already over the tears, but she needed to think. Should she have known? Were there some signs that she had ignored? She sighed in frustration.

If nothing else, his use of her full name, Geraldine, told her that he had no real respect for her. There was nothing really *wrong* with the name, but Gerri just didn't like it—just as she never cared for the crotchety great aunt that she was named after. All of her friends respected her wishes, and it was rare that she even heard that name.

She thought about Thurman's closing remarks. *Funny how some guys tried to equate being 'liberated' with giving free sex.* But his last, cruel salvo especially bothered her. She could see how Thurman might think that she lacked a sense of adventure, but it was untrue and unfair. She simply didn't have the money or the time to go on trips. And she *had* been out of South Carolina. OK, so it was only as far as North Carolina in her senior year of high school. And the part about settling down and teaching high school math: was it a crime to want to use your education? And she wasn't *that* tied to her hometown. In fact, she intended to apply for jobs at a number of school districts.

Still, she reflected, trying to put a bright face on it all, she could call herself lucky. Though she had been humiliated, it was totally in private. She didn't have to face her tormenter. Then she realized that she was kidding herself. She didn't have to face him *now*, but Pee Dee State was a small school, and she was sure to run into Thurman before the end of the semester.

She stewed about that. Only one thing was clear to her—he mustn't find out that she knew about Carlotta. The chance was too great that he would connect her knowledge with his conversation with Claude. Nothing must remotely suggest that Gerri was in the administrative offices after hours—that would lead straight to Mrs. Blakely and cost her her job.

Beyond that, however, she didn't want Thurman's pity; she didn't want to appear to be a victim, never mind that she was just that. So she would be casual, but dismissive. He might think that she was being callous, but why should she care what he thought?

———

Gerri was on cloud nine as she left her last final. There had been only one question that she was unsure about. She had asked her professor about that question after the test, and her answer had been correct. This was the test that she had snuck into the library to study for, so Mrs. Blakely's help had been valuable.

Beyond this test, and the 'A' that she now knew she would get in the course, there was the fact that her college work was over. It was hard to believe; her four years in college had gone by so quickly.

Of course, she wasn't kidding herself that life would be effortless from here on. Local schools had budget problems, and the process of racially integrating them, which was just getting started in South Carolina, promised to be stressful, to say the least. Simply put: Gerri might not get hired at all. And even if she did, the likelihood was that she would be assigned to remedial classes or to middle school— all of the interesting high school math courses would be reserved for the white teachers. But in Gerri's present mood, those problems were somewhere in the hazy future. She was in no mood to let such thoughts spoil her day.

Suddenly, her step—and her mood—faltered. *Speak of spoiling my day...* Standing on the sidewalk outside her classroom building—and obviously waiting for her—was Thurman. With him, looking somewhat uncomfortable, was Claude.

She remembered her vow. "Hello, guys," she said without stopping.

Thurman didn't let her get away that easily. "You look happy," he said. "How'd your last exam go?" The two guys fell into step beside her as she walked.

"I am happy. It went well." *Thurman is so predictable.* She waited resignedly for the other shoe to drop. It was not long in coming.

"Good, good. I'm glad for you," he said with exaggerated joviality. "I got an extension on my paper. It's due in two days"

Gerri glanced at Claude before she answered. *Was that a sympathetic look?* She wanted to scream at Thurman for the gall of his obvious hint, but she held her tongue while she forced herself to calm down. Finally, as Thurman was about to speak, she answered—ignoring the hint. "Will that be enough time for you to get it done?"

He chuckled nervously. "Well, if we work as a team the way we usually do, I think we'll be good."

This was it, then. She schooled herself to show no anger. "I don't think that's a good idea, Thurman. I've been thinking that you're leaning on me too much. I think I'll let you handle this one yourself."

"Don't say that, Baby. This'll be the last one before we graduate. We've come too far for you to back out now."

She just shook her head.

Claude spoke as Thurman was about to raise his voice. "I can't believe you, Gerri. You're not even going to give a brother a break?"

She looked at him. Any imagined sympathy was gone, as he wore an accusing expression. She knew that she could probably win his sympathy back if she explained herself, but she refused to do that. With just a quick, rueful smile to hide her anger, she looked Claude in the eye. "Now might not be the best time for Thurman, and I'm sorry about that, but I should have done this years ago."

Thurman erupted. "How could you betray... You've got a nerve. I...I just can't believe this."

Gerri just watched him as he sputtered. She felt as though she could almost read his mind. She could see him realize that any talk about betrayal would come back at him when Gerri found out about Carlotta. And she would have found out. If he hadn't told her himself, it would have come out when they talked about their future plans. So, as he swallowed his talk of betrayal, she realized bitterly that he would soon see the opportunity that this offered him.

Thurman stopped and took a deep breath. Gerri glanced again at Claude. He was glaring at her. That shook her resolve—but it didn't break it.

"OK," Thurman finally said, in a calmer voice, "If you leave me hanging like this, then we're through. I'll find someone who's more loyal."

There! He found it—the opportunity to break up without mentioning Carlotta at all. She nodded at him. "All right," she said more calmly than she felt, "I think that's best. We have very different definitions of the word 'loyal.'" *Was that too much of a hint that I know about*

Carlotta? She elaborated to make sure that it wasn't. "My definition doesn't include helping you cheat."

Now she'd thrown down the gauntlet for sure. For a minute, he looked like he wanted to hit her. She almost wished that he would— she would give as well as she got in a fight, and there were witnesses who could tell that he threw the first blow. He looked daggers at her for a moment longer, and then he visibly gathered control of himself. "Come on, Claude. Let's get away from this bitch."

Chapter 2

Gerri tensed her neck muscles against the pull of the curling iron. She had done her own hair for years now, but today her mother had insisted upon doing it for her. She had told Gerri that she wanted it to be especially nice for Gerri's graduation later today, but Gerri couldn't help but think of it as marking the end of her childhood. After today she would be a college graduate, and, nominally, an adult. Olivia was holding on to the moment by doing Gerri's hair one last time.

Gerri welcomed her new status, of course, but she couldn't help but be pessimistic about her job opportunities. So far, her apprehensions about finding a job teaching high school mathematics—especially the advanced courses that excited her—were proving justified. She had visited Mr. Harrison, the principal of the local black high school to state her interest in a teaching position, but he had not left her optimistic.

"Gerri," he had said, "I'd love to have you on my staff, but I don't even know whether I'll have a position myself. Integration is going to change everything. And I'm not calling the shots, as you can imagine. They may make me an assistant principal somewhere, or they may even put me back in a classroom. And, since they're going to send all high school students to the white school, they'll probably try to stick with the teaching staff that they have."

But now, on her graduation day, she didn't want to think any discouraging thoughts. In just a few hours… She glanced at the clock on the wall—it was getting late. "Ma, are you sure that Daddy's going to be back in time?"

"Gerri, don't you worry about him. After he lets the animals out, he'll be back here directly. He wouldn't miss your graduation for the world. But, believe it or not, the animals don't care about your graduating. They still want to be fed."

Gerri vowed to keep quiet. *It's just nerves...I know he'll be there.*

After a moment spent working in silence, Olivia picked up the thread again. "He'll be on his best behavior. He'll even shake Thurman's hand if he has to." She let a short laugh escape. "He might even smile, if I nudge him."

"Well, he will be spared that. Thurman and I are through. In fact, Thurman isn't even marching. He got an incomplete in one of his courses—and had the nerve to blame it on me."

Olivia stopped and stared at Gerri in the mirror, trying to read her expression. "You're not sorry, are you? I hope not, 'cause I'm not...and your father..."

"He'll be delighted. I know. No, I'm not sorry. It turned out that he was seeing someone else."

"That no-good excuse for a man. How'd you find out?"

"Well, that was kind of funny. You can thank Mrs. Blakely." Gerri went on to tell about the overheard conversation. "I was sad for a while," she concluded, "but I already had my doubts about him. And I found out in complete privacy, so I didn't have to look the fool."

Gerri grunted as her mother gave an especially hard tug with the iron. She hid a smile, suspecting that her mother was taking out her anger on Gerri's hair. Olivia's extra force with the iron was the product of distraction, however, not anger. She wanted to consider her next words with care.

"I'm happy that you found out that way," she finally said, "but mostly, I'm just happy that you found out. Your father and I were worried."

"Worried? Why?" Gerri didn't want to sound like her adolescent sister Marilyn, but that seemed excessive.

Olivia winced. She didn't want to have this discussion today, of all days. *How gently can I say this?* "Gerri, you are very trusting. You made excuses for Thurman so many times. When he would disappear for a weekend…"

"He was taking part in the protest marches."

"So he said. But remember the time they had a sit-in right here in town? Somehow, he couldn't take part in that one—he had to go home, I think you said. Maybe he did. But there were several other times… After a while, a person gets a little suspicious."

Gerri considered. Was she really that naïve? "But you didn't say anything before." She watched her mother in the mirror as a faint smile appeared on Olivia's face.

"Wait until you're a parent, girl. It's hard, even with you—and you're our good child."

Gerri wasn't going to defend Marilyn, her middle sister, and she knew her youngest sister—ten year old Joetta—wasn't at issue. "Rich wasn't bad—not really."

"No, he wasn't. There are worse places to be in the South, but this town still isn't an easy place for a young black man to make a life. But, let's not talk about him. Your father and I both felt the same way about Thurman; we just disagreed about what to tell you. Robert wanted to forbid you to see Thurman, and I was afraid that would just make you dig in your heels. Some things, you have to find out for yourself. All the same, that was partly why I asked you for that promise."

Gerri flushed with embarrassment to see it in that light. "I wouldn't have…" She faltered to a stop. *Would I?*

"Who knows, child?" Olivia mentally chastised herself. "I've got to quit calling you that," she chuckled, and then the smile left her face and she continued. "But it isn't just having sex. Accidents happen. I don't want to see you having to go to some back alley for an abortion. And I certainly wouldn't want to see you trapped in some bad, hasty marriage."

Gerri was surprised by Olivia's uncharacteristic bluntness. This, more than Olivia's remark about calling her 'child,' reminded Gerri that she was now an adult. She would have to think about this. To change the subject—a little—she brought up her other worry.

"I hate to admit it, but he's right about one thing. I've…" Belatedly, she realized that what she was about to say could be taken as a criticism of her parents, and as being resentful of her family's limited means. Quickly, she rephrased. "I mean, I've always known that I wanted to teach high school. I've been so busy making sure that I could reach that goal that I never had any time to travel." *Never had the money, either...* "I've never had a real adventure, and I wonder if I ever will."

Olivia put down the curling iron. "Gerri, your life is just beginning. Don't act like it's over. With all of the changes we're seeing in this country, I hope you'll have more opportunities than your father and I ever dreamed of. Watch for them, and don't be afraid to embrace them. And above all, don't listen to any of those things that Thurman said. He's not worth your time—and color struck, to boot!"

"I know, Ma. Don't pay any attention to me—I'm just on edge today."

"That's understandable, but this is your day. Make sure you enjoy it."

They were interrupted by Joetta. "Ma, Marilyn's been in the bathroom for half an hour and she won't let me in."

Olivia sighed. "Tell her to let you have the bathroom. And tell her that if she makes us late, she'll be sorry."

After Joetta had left triumphantly, Olivia shook her head. "That's the one that I worry about. Gerri, you'll do well—you'll find opportunities once you get over being nervous. Marilyn's head is so hard. She's almost done with her junior year in high school. She ought to have her head full of ideas and dreams, but all she can think of is getting a job in the candy factory, and maybe getting married."

Gerri didn't know what to say. This was a well-known subject, and her parents had even enlisted Gerri to try to talk to Marilyn. Marilyn was not, however, impressed with Gerri as a role model.

"Maybe," Olivia continued, "if she sees you get a decent job—one that actually pays something—she'll change her tune."

"I wish Rich were here. She listens to him—more than she does to me, at least."

"I wish he were here to see you march."

"So do I. I really miss him." Richard, two years older than Gerri, had joined the army to try to get some training and, frankly, to get away from the limited prospects of their hometown. He got away, all right. He was stationed thousands of miles away at Fort Lewis in Washington State, and he hadn't been home for over a year.

"You can call him tonight, if you like."

Gerri's spirits rose. "Cool! I'll tell him about my graduation. I'll try to make him feel like he saw it himself."

"Hello, ladies," Robert Barton said as he came into the house. He kissed his wife on the back of her neck. "I bet y'all thought I'd forgotten all about the graduation."

Gerri protested, "No, I didn't!" Olivia just chuckled.

"Give me a few minutes. I'll be changed and cleaned up so quickly, you won't believe it."

"See that you are," Olivia said. As he left, she had an idea. *Could we do that?* The more she thought, the more she liked it. *Yes. I'll talk to Robert about it today.*

———

Gerri's feet hurt and she was tired, but she wore a grin that wouldn't go away. Today had been her day to shine. The graduation ceremony ran long, but the speeches were inspiring. After the formal part was over, she exchanged congratulations with her classmates, as well as heartfelt promises to keep in touch. Her parents had given her a Kodak Instamatic camera as a present, and she had shot over thirty pictures. She had had her picture taken with Professor Kuznetsov, her favorite math teacher. How far she'd come: she remembered clearly walking into his class as a freshman and wondering if she'd ever be able to understand his Russian accent.

She also had a picture taken with Professor Darnell, her favorite education teacher. Gerri had always valued her as a role model. She, too—years ago—had been a double major.

There were a few students who threw Gerri accusing looks—they had apparently been fed Thurman's tale of woe. She had only one actual angry encounter. She had just finished exchanging congratulations with a fellow graduate when she heard Nadine's voice behind her.

"I hope you're proud of yourself for preventing Thurman's graduation."

She looked around, trying not to cringe. Nadine was a fellow member of the choir who had made no secret of her attraction to Thurman. "I'm not happy about that." Gerri said. "But it was his paper, not mine. You're right, though. I should have put my foot down a long time ago."

Nadine sniffed. She wanted an argument, not conciliatory remarks. "I told him that he deserved better than you, and now he knows it."

Gerri bit her tongue to avoid saying *He's all yours.* Nadine clearly didn't know about Carlotta either. "I hope it works out for him," she finally said.

After Gerri returned home, her parents threw a party in her honor. She found herself pitching in with the preparations. Olivia tried to shoo her away, but it didn't seem right to Gerri to be idle.

Now, the party was over. Gerri sat in her bedroom taking off her shoes, and thinking of Richard. He was the only one she hadn't talked to. She wondered if her mother remembered her promise. After she rested her feet, she decided, she would remind her. She lay back on the bed for a minute…

She was awakened by a knock on her door. At her sleepy acknowledgment, her parents stepped into her room. Olivia sat on the bed and, as it was a small room, Robert remained standing.

"Would you like to talk to Rich?" Olivia asked.

"Yes!" Gerri looked at the clock and groaned. "Is it too late to call him? I fell asleep."

"It's not too late—remember the time difference. He's waiting for your call."

"You've already talked to him? Why didn't you wake me earlier? I…" …*wanted to be the one to tell him about today.* But she—in the words of that repulsive TV character, Archie Bunker—stifled herself. Of course, her parents were just as excited as she was, and they had every right to tell Rich about the graduation if they wanted to.

Olivia had a knowing smile. "Don't worry; you'll be the one to tell him. We talked about something else." She glanced at Robert—as if passing the baton.

"Of course, long distance is expensive," he said with a frown, "so you shouldn't talk too long."

"I won't. I promise." How she wished that she could live a life where she didn't have to worry constantly about money.

Olivia glared at him. "Stop teasing her, Robert."

He smiled. "But you can tell him in person."

Gerri jumped up and squealed. "Rich is coming home? That's great! When will he get here?" She wished that he could have made it back today, but she wasn't about to spoil her parents' surprise.

"Nooo…" Robert said.

Olivia was getting impatient with Robert's drawing this out. "How would you like to go visit Rich for a few weeks?"

Now Gerri was truly speechless. Her jaw dropped and she just stared.

"It'd be an adventure," Robert offered.

"That's so exciting." Now, she could see the growth of this from her lament while getting her hair done. Suddenly, she was struck with guilt. "But it's too expensive. And you need me to help on the farm."

"Don't you worry about that. We'll make out all right. Rich has a buddy who's married and lives off-base. He and his wife are willing to let you stay there for three or four weeks. We'll pay your way there and give you some spending money."

The enormity of the idea overwhelmed her, and she said the first thing that occurred to her. "I've never even been on an airplane before."

"Well," Robert cautioned, "that's a bit steep for our budget. But Rich told us about a bus company that has a special excursion fare: you can go anywhere you want to for ninety days for a fixed price—one that we can afford. It'll be a long ride, but it'll get you there."

Chapter 3

Sven Halvorsen stood on his porch and looked across Gastineau Channel at the small city of Juneau, Alaska on the other side. Ignoring the raw southeast wind and the light rain, he made his plans for the days ahead. It was time to get his boat, *Glacier Gal,* in shape for the fishing season. She was a solid craft, but as with any boat, she needed care. Some things he would put off until the weather cleared up, but there was some engine maintenance that needed doing. He turned to go back inside his house. If he got down to the boat harbor soon, he could get finished and still have time to visit Rosie's book store before he went to dinner at his usual hangout, the Kash Café.

In the years since Laura's death, Sven had rebuilt his life. Some of it he planned—particularly how to spend the money from her insurance wisely—and some of it was happenstance. He would not claim to be truly happy, but he was content. Things were less stressful now, as long as he stayed away from Laura's relatives, who detested him. Her younger sister Mindy's animus was particularly hurtful, since, in his opinion, she had grown into a very capable young woman. Dining at the Kash Café, near the boat harbor, rather than at the fancier restaurants downtown helped him to avoid her. Mindy Schumacher would not dream of showing up at a fisherman's hangout.

His years now had basically two seasons: winter and summer. In the winter, he had time to paint, which he found soothing. He also spent time working on his house. This was a source of pride to him, even if he never expressed it to anyone else. He had bought some land on Douglas Island with part of the insurance money. His land was near the bridge to Juneau—and hence, near the boat harbor—but it extended well uphill from the highway. He built his home on the upper end of his property, away from any noise. He had had professional help cutting a long driveway up to the home site and framing the house. Over the years, he had finished the inside himself, learning carpentry as he went. Just this past winter, he had completed a work room, where he did his painting and stored his completed pictures.

The previous winter, he had finished off an exercise room, where he kept a set of weights, as well as a speed bag and a heavy bag. Boxing didn't appeal to him as it had in his younger days, but working with the bags was good exercise, and it could melt away stress. Of course, when the weather permitted, he could relieve stress by exercising outside. There were wonderful hiking and climbing in the Tongass National Forest which extended up the mountain behind his property.

His carpentry skills also gave him the opportunity to earn some extra money during the off season. Generally, when he accepted such work it was for a change of pace—he didn't really need the money.

But now, it was edging towards summer, his work season. By the time he got the boat ready, it would be time to go fishing. Other than the engine work, which would go quickly, he had to check his gear and paint the boat. Ironically, given his interest in art, he hated painting the boat, especially the copper painting, which was always a miserable experience. It was necessary, however. Glacier Gal would struggle through the water—costing him money in fuel—if he didn't clean the hull and apply a fresh coat of anti-fouling, copper paint.

He shook his head and went inside. He was just wasting time now. The sooner he got started, the sooner he could be browsing the shelves at the Taku Book Store. That was another of his favorite ways of relieving stress, and Rosie Craig, the store's owner and sole employee, was a trusted friend.

———

After he had his diesel engine purring, he decided to drop by Northern Marine to pick up the paint. As he entered the large marine supply store, he was hailed by Maxine MacKenzie. She had worked there since before Sven was born, and kept up with all of the news and gossip about the local fishermen.

"Hi, Sven. I heard that you finally fired Mike."

He made a face. "Yeah. He can't stay away from the bottle. I don't want anyone like that around me."

"I'm sorry to hear that he didn't work out, but it doesn't surprise me." Maxine knew Sven's own history—he had had a drinking problem himself after Laura's death. After a few months of that, he had looked himself in the mirror and hadn't liked what he had seen. He quit cold turkey. And he was determined to stay away from anything that could possibly be a negative influence.

"You know what they say about reformed drunks," he said self-deprecatingly.

"So, are you going to fish by yourself this year?"

"It's looking that way," he said, "but I wish I'd waited to fire him until *after* we finished painting the boat." He quirked a wry smile and walked over to pick out a supply of paint. When he got back to the counter, she smiled.

"You're the only guy I know who carries eight gallons of paint as if they weighed nothing."

There wasn't much to say to that; he knew he was strong. He could thank his genes for that, not any personal virtue.

After he stowed the paint in the forward cabin of Glacier Gal, he checked his watch. He had time to get to Rosie's, but he'd promised to bring her some of his completed paintings. Ah, the paintings. Of all of the facets of Sven's rebuilt life, his painting hobby was the most completely unexpected.

One morning, soon after he had stopped drinking, he was piloting Glacier Gal to one of his favorite fishing grounds. He was alone—hiring a deckhand came later—and he had a good ways to go, so time weighed heavily on his hands. As his boat came around a point, Sven was struck by a particular vista. There was a fog bank hugging the water and partially blocking the hill behind the point. In the distance, however, it was clear and there was a beautiful, sunlit view of Mt.

Fairweather, one of a number of Alaskan mountains taller than any in the 'lower 48.' On impulse, he picked up a pencil and some note paper and tried to sketch the scene. The result pleased him, so he started to look for other opportunities. Eventually, he had a sheaf of these efforts—strictly for his own satisfaction—but he wanted more.

On one of his visits to Taku Books, he had bought some books on painting and mentioned his interest. After that, Rosie had asked him about his progress and pestered him gently to show her some of his work. He didn't want to broadcast his hobby, but he *did* want to get another person's opinion. Since he trusted both Rosie's judgment and her discretion, he brought in several works—he had graduated to oils by this time—to show her. She was enthusiastic and accepted one as a gift.

Then she asked him to let her sell some on consignment. It took some time for Sven to agree to this, but he eventually did, insisting on strict anonymity. To his considerable surprise, and secret gratification, she sold a steady trickle of them. He was gradually building up a small nest egg with the proceeds. What he would do with it, he had no idea.

After swinging by his house to pick up the latest batch of paintings for Rosie, he drove downtown, parking his pickup truck in the alley behind her store. He walked around to the front entrance on Seward Street. He glanced up and down the street as he walked. An outsider would consider the older Juneau streets to be quaint. They were narrow and perched on the side of a hill. Many of the sidewalks in front of the stores had roofs to protect the pedestrians from the rain. In some places you could walk for several blocks without getting wet, except when crossing a street.

"Well, look who's here." Rosie looked up from a book she was reading and smiled. She was a tiny, bright-eyed woman who perpetually had a cigarette in her hand. Sven had estimated that she was around sixty years old.

Sven looked around. There was a single customer with her nose in a book. Sven looked at her idly, but didn't recognize her. "I've come to poke through your stock," he said to Rosie. "Any suggestions?"

"Are you going to take it out on the boat with you?"

"Yeah, so don't suggest something that I'll finish in a couple of hours."

"When are you going out? I've got a shipment coming in this week."

"That should be OK. I won't be heading out for another few days. And I've got plenty to do in the meantime."

She paused to ring up a purchase for the other customer. After Rosie and Sven were alone, she changed the subject. "Have you got any paintings for me?"

"They're in my truck behind the store."

"You and your secrecy." Rosie made an amused face. "Don't worry. I tell any customer who asks that HSSH is pronounced 'hush' and it stands for 'quiet' because the artist is a recluse and lives out in the bush. They eat that up."

Sven couldn't help but laugh. He wanted anonymity, so he signed his pictures with his initials and an extra 'H' in front: 'HSSH.' Rosie respected that, and had somehow turned it into a sales device. He was also careful in his choice of pictures to give her. Some were too personal and would give too much of a clue as to his identity. Of course, the tourists wouldn't know, but some Juneau residents would see them on display. For example, he had painted a picture of Laura from memory which he had no intention of selling. Not so much because he treasured it, but because any local person would likely guess that Sven was the painter. And who knows what Mindy's reaction to that painting would be—even if she liked it, she would be resentful that it had come from Sven. No, it was best to leave that hornet's nest untouched.

While he was thinking about this, Rosie handed him a check. "I sold all of the last batch you gave me. This is your share of the money."

Sven nodded his thanks. After he had finished his browsing, he settled on a small collection of purchases. As he left the store, he saw Mindy walking down the street. She had evidently just gotten off work. He steeled himself for some ugly remark, but she contented herself with directing a cold glare his way. Would she ever stop blaming him for Laura's death? He held no great hope for that. Especially, he thought guiltily, since she was right.

———

Sven brought his new books into the Kash Café with him. His friend Wally hadn't arrived yet, and Brian Kashimara, the restaurant's owner, was explaining to yet another new customer that the restaurant's name was an abbreviation of his—that it had nothing to do with the acceptable methods of payment. Sven didn't bother to conceal a smile. Brian must have given that explanation hundreds of times. He seemed to enjoy doing it, though. If Sven had been in Brian's place, he would have gone nuts in the first week. *I guess that's why Brian owns a restaurant and I don't.*

After he'd placed his order, Sven spread his new books out in front of him and tried to decide which he would read first. He always felt like a kid on Christmas morning when he came out of Rosie's with a bunch of books.

Wally arrived just as the waitress was serving Sven's food. "I'll have the same," Wally said to her as he slid into the booth opposite Sven. "I guess I know where you've been shopping," he added to Sven.

Sven put his books on the booth next to him and looked back at Wally. "Are you ready to go out?"

Wally made a disgusted noise. "I've got dry rot on the aft wall of my pilot house. I'll have to get that fixed first. Just what I need."

"You skipped your painting last year, didn't you?"

Wally glared at him. "Don't rub it in. I suppose you're all ready to go."

"I need to do some painting myself. Then I'll be ready. Checked out the engines today."

Sven and Wally ate a leisurely dinner, talking about everything *but* fishing. By the time Sven got home, it was dark. The rain was still falling. He looked at the lights across the channel. He liked this town. He had grown up here. But he was ready to get back out on the water.

CHAPTER 4

Gerri caught the bus in Florence two days after her graduation. In those two days, she had had hardly a moment to spare. She and her mother shopped—trying to anticipate what different clothes she might need, and trying to find them at affordable prices. She packed a small bag to carry with her and a larger duffle bag which would go in the cargo area of the bus. She was trying to travel light, since she would spend plenty of time lugging her possessions around between buses.

Her father presented her with some cash, along with urgent warnings about being careful. She cringed at what this was doing to the family budget; some day, somehow, she would pay them back for all of this.

Even Marilyn got caught up in the enthusiasm. She tagged along when Gerri went shopping, and hung close by as she packed. It was Marilyn who was the instigator of Gerri's major transformation: she argued strenuously for Gerri to wear an Afro hairdo on her trip. Gerri had certainly considered this style—a few of her classmates had adopted them, with, in Gerri's view, varying degrees of success. Gerri had been timid up to now. She had feared that an afro would look silly on her, and that she would then be unmercifully teased. The chance to experiment away from the eyes of the local girls finally convinced her to accept Marilyn's help with her hair.

The excitement was not without apprehension, though. Gerri could tell that her parents were having second thoughts about their child's—yes, Olivia slipped up and used that word several times—traveling alone, particularly through the South. They supplied Gerri with a variety of bus schedules and a road map of the United States.

Mindful of the fact that public accommodations, while subject to the new civil rights laws, were still an iffy proposition for black people in the South, Olivia handed Gerri an enormous bag of chicken and biscuits as the family saw her off.

The whole family reminded Gerri to write frequently; Olivia had quietly added that "Maybe the stories of your adventure will excite Marilyn's interest." Gerri was more than willing to write. The problem was that, after the novelty of the bus ride wore off—which happened quickly—she had little to write about.

She was able to put together enough bits and pieces to mail off a letter when the bus stopped in Kansas City: seeing the Mississippi River for the first time, seeing the St. Louis Arch, and her dawning realization of just how big the United States really was. To those remarks, she added some observations about some of the more colorful of her fellow passengers.

As the bus crossed the seemingly endless prairies of Missouri and Kansas, Gerri had plenty of time to think. She tried to anticipate what she and Rich might do together, and she wondered what her family in South Carolina was doing now. Mixed in with these were less pleasant thoughts. She wondered again whether she should have stopped helping Thurman when she did. Certainly, she wished that she had stopped years earlier—or never started. But at the last minute? Gerri couldn't make believe that he had deserved better.

In the final analysis, she took refuge in a conversation with Dr. Darnell while Gerri was taking one of her education classes. Dr. Darnell was justifying her uncompromising grading standards. "Pee Dee State College is being judged by its alumni," she had said. "While it may seem kind to let an undeserving student slide through, it would then be unkind to all of the other graduates. They will inevitably be judged more negatively by those employers who have encountered the undeserving graduate."

As the bus entered Colorado and Gerri could see mountains in the distance, she started another letter to her family. This one, mailed in Salt Lake City, had more to say about the scenery: the Rocky Mountains were indeed beautiful; the deserts were indeed desolate; but The Great Salt Lake didn't really impress her.

Gerri could hardly wait for the ride to be over, though she didn't put that in the letter. She desperately looked forward to her three week stay—which would be three weeks away from buses. In fact, she was so tired of sitting all day that she didn't care if she ever saw another bus. Her only defense was to take every opportunity to walk when there was a stopover—even if she only walked back and forth in front of the bus station.

Ironically, at the same time she took pride in getting to be—she felt—an expert traveler. She always tried to chat with the driver of the day. Some were unreceptive, but others gave her useful tips on what to see and where to eat during the stopovers. And, of course, she had her collection of maps which she spent time studying.

Now, after changing buses in Portland, she was on the final leg of her journey. She sat in the front row (the better to see forward or to ask the driver questions) next to the window on the right hand side (the better to see Mt. Rainier, which the last bus driver had said was not to be missed). She could hardly contain her excitement: she would be seeing Rich this very afternoon.

———

Gerri saw Rich waiting at the bus terminal in Tacoma when her bus pulled in. She was the first one out of the bus and yelled his name as she ran toward him. He gave a double take and started grinning as he opened his arms.

She raced into his arms and gave him a hug that had all of her pent up energy in it. "It's so good to see you, Rich."

"It's good to see you, too." His eyes slid up to her hair and his grin got wider.

"What? Does my hair look that funny?"

"No, no. It looks nice. I've always wanted to have a brother."

Gerri pushed him away and scowled. "I was afraid of this. I'll change it back tonight."

"Don't do that. It really does look nice on you."

"Sure it does. That's why you're laughing."

"No, really. That was just the surprise. You're the last person that I'd expect to go natural."

"It was Marilyn's idea. But these three weeks are supposed to be an adventure, so why not?"

The smile left his face. "We'll have to talk about your stay here. I assume you have other luggage?"

They walked to an older model car, which Rich unlocked. He saw her inquiring look. "No, it's not mine. It belongs to the people that you'll be staying with." When they were sitting in the car, he turned to her without starting it. "Their names are Mark and Ann Miller. He's a friend of mine, and they live in an apartment off base."

Gerri nodded eagerly and grinned. "I'll try to be a good guest so they won't get tired of me in the first week."

Rich winced and looked away. "Well, there's a problem with that. We're shipping out. We didn't know about it until after you had left South Carolina."

Gerri's heart plummeted. "How soon?"

"Three days." He saw her crestfallen look. "But I've got some time off. We can see a lot in three days…"

Three days! That's not an adventure. But then Gerri realized: he was trying so hard to reassure her. *I have to stop being self-centered. There's something else here…* She interrupted him. "Where are they sending you?"

She could see the skin around his mouth tighten and she dreaded his answer. "The 'Nam."

All at once, her adventure seemed trivial. "Oh, no! I don't want you to go. I hate that war!" Tears started streaming down her face and she didn't even try to dry them.

"I don't think anybody likes it."

"Do you have to go?"

"I took an oath. I'm not going to run away."

Gerri was ashamed for her last question. Now she wiped her tears. "Yes, of course. I didn't mean…" She slid over on the front bench seat to hug him. "Just stay safe. Please stay safe."

"I'll be careful. I promise." He moved to start the car. "Now let's go introduce you to the Millers."

Gerri liked the Millers. They were busy preparing for Mark's deployment, yet found the time to be very gracious hosts. Ann was a short, light brown skinned woman. She was pregnant—Gerri guessed about five months—and she was going back to live with her parents in Chicago while Mark was in Vietnam. They had done considerable packing already, but they assured Gerri that she would be no bother. The men tried their best to keep the conversation light, but Gerri could see the worry in Ann's face.

———

Gerri stood on the observation deck of the Space Needle and tried to memorize the view. This was Rich's last day. Gerri had had a wonderful time sightseeing. She had enough material for several letters home—this was at least a good start to an adventure.

The first day, Rich had taken her to see Mt. Rainier. It was a looming presence from practically anywhere in the region, but it was especially impressive when seen close up. She was flabbergasted to find out that there was still snow by the roads—in May! And not just a little. She had taken one picture on her Instamatic which showed the Millers' car, which Rich had borrowed again, parked on a mountain road. The road had been plowed and was free of snow, but at the side of the road next to the car was a vertical wall of snow, which had to be at least ten feet tall.

The second day Rich and Mark had duties to attend to, so Ann and Gerri drove to Seattle to shop. Mostly, they were window shopping, but Gerri did pick up some gifts for her family. Gerri had many exciting things to remember, including a vibrant public market seemingly in the middle of downtown and a book store that was bigger than the entire Pee Dee State college library. But the most fabulous was the Frederick & Nelson department store. It seemed to have an impossible variety of goods, and it was enormous. All of the stores in Gerri's hometown could fit comfortably into a single floor of Frederick & Nelson—and there were some nine or ten floors. She was also introduced, in a fancy eatery on the top floor, to an ice cream-like dessert called Frango that was wickedly delicious.

Now, on the last day, Rich had again been her guide. They looked at the waterfront and the busy ferry traffic, winding up here, at the end of the day, at the Space Needle.

Rich looked sideways at her. "Have you talked to Ann about a ride to the bus station tomorrow?"

"No, I might stay a little longer." Gerri stalled, "I'm going to help Ann load her U-haul." *Anything to stay off the bus.*

"But you'll be leaving soon, right? I don't want to worry about you out here by yourself. And I'm sure that the same goes for Ma and Dad."

"Mmmm." Gerri's first reaction was to get angry—to tell him that she was getting to be an expert traveler, and that three days weren't enough. But she didn't want to worry him—he had other more important things to worry about now. And, especially, she didn't want Rich to call their parents. They might demand that she return right away, and Gerri was feeling stubborn. She wasn't a child and she wanted to get all of the adventure out of this trip that she could. And stay off the transcontinental bus for as long as she could. Finally, she knew that she had to say something.

"I might stay for a little longer. I'd like to go up to Seattle and look at the Pacific Science Center again. Of course, I can't stay very long. I'll run out of money soon, so I'll certainly leave before that happens."

Rich looked skeptical, but chose not to press the point. "OK, but be careful."

———

Gerri had thought about this a lot—last night as she was trying to sleep and this morning as she helped load Ann's truck. Fortunately Rich hadn't brought up the subject again, because Gerri was more determined than ever to extend her adventure. She wondered whether she should be ashamed of her reasons. She had daydreamed during the interminable bus trip about the prospect of running into Thurman after she got back—he hadn't graduated, so he might enroll for the Fall semester—and casually mentioning that she had gone to the West

Coast over the summer. What would he think of his hurtful words in the library then?

That was petty of her, but she didn't care. Of course, 'I visited my brother' didn't sound quite so adventurous, and 'I visited my brother and had to cut the trip short because he was deployed overseas' sounded even less adventurous. No, there had to be something else that she could do.

She didn't want to worry her parents. Whatever she did, she would be sure to reassure them. And anyway, they had wanted her to have something exciting to tell Marilyn.

Gerri grunted as she picked up an especially heavy box to carry out to Ann's rented truck. "These must be books." The words sounded odd to her, and she realized that they had been largely silent all morning. After Rich and Mark had gone, there didn't seem to be much to say. The only sound came from a TV set that Ann had left on, saying that it made the apartment seem less empty.

Ann glanced at the box. "I think so." She flashed a weary grin. "You've been a lifesaver for me. I don't think that I could even lift that box."

Gerri tried to remember what her cherished map of the U.S. had shown about Chicago. All she could be sure of was that it was a long way from the state of Washington. Driving a truck alone over that route would be terrible. That wasn't her idea of an adventure, but she felt compelled to ask. "Will you be all right? That's an awfully long way to travel alone. I mean, I could…"

"Thank you ever so much, but you enjoy your vacation. There's another woman from the base who's going to ride with me and share the driving. She's going to Gary, Indiana, which is right near Chicago."

"Is there going to be space in the truck for her stuff?" Gerri had been amazed at how quickly the Millers' boxes and furniture were filling the truck.

"She doesn't have much. They sold their bulky stuff. We should have done that, too, like we sold the car. We'll plan it better next time." With that, she fell silent.

"I hope that next time Mark will be riding with you."

"I hope so," said Ann softly. Gerri wanted to say something encouraging, but couldn't think of anything that didn't sound phony.

"Tell me about your plans," said Ann after a moment. "What are you going to do for the rest of your adventure?"

"I wish I knew." Gerri had already told Ann about her bus ride.

By early afternoon, they had finished, except for the TV set. Ann handed Gerri a bottle of pop—as they called it in Washington—and they sat on the floor, all of the chairs having been loaded on the truck.

Gerri was absently watching the TV. "You know, this is the first color TV that I've ever seen."

Ann smiled. "We really couldn't afford it, but Mark had his heart set on it. Now…" She shook her head.

"It'll be waiting when he gets back," Gerri said optimistically.

As she said it, something on the screen caught her eye. It was a boat, a fairly large one, dwarfed by a wall behind it. It reminded her of the wall of snow next to the road at Rainier Park, but it was much larger. "What in the world is that?"

Ann turned up the volume. The announcer explained that this was a glacier, a river of ice, whose face was over 100 feet tall. The scene was in Glacier Bay, near Juneau, in Southeastern Alaska. They watched quietly for a minute before Ann spoke.

"It's very pretty up there. Mark was stationed in Alaska before we came here."

"Were you in Juneau?"

"No, we were in Anchorage, but we did go to Juneau once for our anniversary."

Gerri glanced at her, but Ann was raptly intent on the TV. "Was it nice?" Gerri asked.

"Oh, yes. It was gorgeous—even prettier than Anchorage—at least when it wasn't raining."

"How about the people? Umm, did you have any problems?"

"No. Everyone was very nice."

Gerri was starting to get excited. This could be just what she needed. And Ann made it sound so easy. "Was it expensive?"

"I don't know exactly; Mark took care of all that. It couldn't have been too expensive," she said with a rueful smile, "Mark was still paying for the TV set." She eyed Gerri curiously. "Are you thinking about going there?"

"Well…if I can afford it. That would be a great adventure." She didn't know how long it would take a bus to get to Juneau—her maps didn't cover Alaska—but she decided that she could stand the ride. She had enough money left to stay in a cheap hotel for a few days.

"The airline fare is not too bad."

Gerri cocked her head in puzzlement. Ann knew about her bus ticket. "Airline? Doesn't the bus line go to Juneau?"

"No, there are no roads to Juneau. You'd have to fly or take a ship."

"No roads?" Gerri couldn't quite imagine that, but she wasn't about to let anything discourage her at this point. Having pictures of a glacier to show her family… And her first airplane flight, to boot!

She came back down to earth and her shoulders slumped. "How much does it cost to fly?"

Ann gestured to the phone. "Go ahead and call a travel agent. The phone's paid for until tomorrow. I hope it works out for you. You would definitely have something to take back home with you."

When Gerri hung up the phone ten minutes later, she wore a thoughtful expression. She went to her luggage and counted her remaining stash of money, and then sat there thinking.

Ann came back from closing up the truck. "Well?"

"They have seats on tomorrow's flight. They said that the tourist rush hasn't really started for the summer. It's mostly seasonal workers going up there now." She grimaced. "That's the easy part. The money would be tight. If everything went perfectly and I found a cheap enough hotel…" She stared at the money in her hands. "Yes, I can do it."

Ann was beginning to regret her earlier enthusiasm. She remembered Rich talking about Gerri and how she could be stubborn, and she had a hunch that he would be none too happy about this. "But if everything doesn't go just right…" she cautioned, "Rich and your family would be worried."

Gerri concealed her flash of irritation. She was not going to let this slip away. Such an opportunity would probably never happen again. Saying that her family would worry was a guilt trip—and those usually worked on Gerri. But not this time. Gerri had been a dutiful daughter. She had been a dutiful sister. She had been a dutiful student. For that matter she had even been a dutiful girlfriend to Thurman, for all the good that that had done her. No, her family would not worry because they wouldn't know about it until it had already happened.

But she couldn't say that to Ann. "I'm pretty sure that I'll have enough money. I've gotten pretty good at watching my pennies on this trip. And if I need more, I'll look for one of those seasonal jobs. I don't know what they do, but I can work hard and I'm strong. Maybe I could get a job if I needed the money. And I could always swallow my pride and ask my parents to wire me some."

Ann didn't know quite how to respond, but Gerri's determination was obvious and Ann wasn't about to rain on her parade. "Well, the seasonal work is mostly fishing or cannery work, logging, and some construction work. Even though the racial climate seemed good to us, no place is perfect. Your best chance would be in something related to fishing, but I wouldn't count on it. They might not be willing to hire a woman, you know." She tried for a more positive note. "But there should be something."

Gerri's lips were set as she reached again for the phone. "I'm going to try. I want to see a glacier."

CHAPTER 5

Gerri spent most of the flight looking eagerly out the window next to her seat. She probably looked like an idiot, but she didn't care. She was actually flying—and loving it. She had thought that she might be scared, but she wasn't. Well, not much. Her heart was certainly beating fast before and during takeoff, but once they had climbed to cruising altitude, it didn't feel that much different from riding in a bus. But with a much better view.

When she heard the altitude announcement, Gerri noted it ("air pressure, cabin pressure") in a little journal that she was keeping. It was a collection of notes and ideas of things that she might use someday when teaching. Maybe the notes would be useless, but keeping them made her feel like she was somehow preparing for her teaching, even as she vacationed.

She made one half-hearted attempt to deal with her financial problems during the flight. She asked the elderly man sitting next to her if he knew of a cheap hotel in Juneau. He just raised his eyebrows, shrugged elaborately, and answered, "I have no idea. I'm from Anchorage." Gerri must have looked blank, because he added, "That's in central Alaska—600 miles away from Juneau." He grinned at Gerri's raised eyebrows. Alaska was over twice as big as Texas, she recalled, and this man, at least, seemed to take considerable pleasure in reminding others about its size.

Still, Gerri marveled at the vast scale of this country. From her home in South Carolina, 600 miles would reach almost to New York. Here, you were still within Alaska. And, his implication was clear: there were places within Alaska which were much further away than that.

Earlier, she had noticed that he was covertly eyeing her afro hairdo, and, before he had heard her voice, he had leaned over to ask her for a magazine from the seat pocket in front of her and called her 'son.' Granted, she was wearing pants and a baggy coat, and she was carrying a bag rather than an obviously feminine purse, but still... White people around here apparently weren't used to seeing an afro on a woman. Or they weren't used to seeing black people at all—Gerri had gotten a few curious looks, though thankfully nothing hostile as yet.

She reached into her bag and pulled out her letter to check it one last time. This letter was to tell her family that she was still traveling. It was also supposed to excite them about her trip and, at the same time, to reassure them of her good sense and safety. This was a difficult combination—especially since Gerri had her own doubts. She skipped over the first few pages. She didn't need to check them; they just related what she had done and seen while in Washington. She found the last page and read her final paragraphs again:

...

Still, even though it's been just great, three days is an awfully short adventure. I spent at least that much time just riding the bus to get here. So, since I have some money left, I'm taking a side trip. I'm going to Alaska!! And I'm getting my first airplane ride. In fact, I'm writing this letter as we fly. And, no, I'm not scared of flying. I was a little nervous when the airplane took off, but that's all. It felt so powerful; it was awesome.

Don't worry about me; I'm being careful and I'm watching my pennies. I'll write you soon, and I'll be back with lots of pictures. Oh! And watch your mail. I mailed a box with gifts for each of you before I left Seattle.

Love you all and see you soon,

Gerri

She put the letter back in the envelope and sealed it. It would have to do, but reading it dampened some of her excitement. Her image of herself as an expert traveler had taken quite a beating in the past 24 hours. For starters, she had grossly underestimated how much it would cost her to get to SeaTac airport from the Millers' apartment now that their car was no longer available. Then, when she went to the airline counter to buy her ticket, she got another unpleasant surprise. She had forgotten about the taxes on her fare—another extra expense.

So she was watching her pennies, all right. Watching them fly out of her wallet. The prospect of her running out of money in Juneau now seemed terrifyingly likely. She tried to shove those thoughts to the back of her mind. She would do her best to find a cheap hotel room and a cheap restaurant. And, more than ever, she would be on the lookout for some short term job. She *really* didn't want to ask her parents for more money.

Soon, the plane was approaching Juneau and the seatbelt sign came on. Gerri put her money worries aside as she looked out the window beside her. It was beautiful, but more than a little scary as they came in for a landing. There were mountains everywhere and a ribbon of water below, but she couldn't see any signs of the airport. Seattle's airport had been enormous, with runways seemingly wherever you looked. She watched the ground get closer and closer. It looked like some sort of marsh. Finally, at the last minute, there was a small runway below. They touched down and Gerri realized that she had been holding her breath. She glanced at the man beside her and saw that he was grinning at her again. She just shrugged and smiled weakly.

By the time the airport bus had dropped her off downtown, it was early evening and the narrow streets were full of office workers heading for home. The downtown area was small and nestled on the side of a hill. It was picturesque: if you looked downhill from where she stood, there was a bay and a long channel of water with mountains on either side. If you looked uphill, there was a steep mountain looming up seemingly right behind the town. The sky had a solid layer of clouds which blocked the top of that looming mountain. There was a drama to this scenery that even Seattle didn't have.

After several minutes of gawking at the view, Gerri went into the hotel that the bus driver had suggested. Five minutes later, she was back on the street, more worried than ever. If this was, as the driver had said, a reasonably priced hotel, then she'd hate to see an expensive one. She wanted to look for a cheaper one, but she didn't know where to go. She was also starving and tired of lugging her bags around.

She walked into a café that she had seen a few doors down. After standing in the doorway for a moment—nobody seemed to even notice her, let alone be bothered by her presence—she slid into a booth and looked at a menu. When a waitress appeared, Gerri closed the menu glumly and ordered a small hamburger. Even the food was expensive.

She chewed her hamburger slowly—it might have to last her for a long time—while she tried to decide what to do. If she couldn't find a cheaper hotel, maybe she could stay in a park overnight. No, on second thought, it was too cold. South Carolina in the month of May would usually have warm days and balmy nights. The temperature here in Juneau couldn't be over 60°, even in the late afternoon. The night would be even colder. Also, there had been the hint of rain in the air. No, sleeping outside was not feasible. And that didn't even address the safety issues.

While she considered her dilemma, she casually scanned the other patrons. She was the only black person in the café. *Surprise, surprise.* Most of the customers were white, but there were a few that looked like American Indians.

Gerri was distracted by the noise of an altercation in the back of the café. A slender young woman had been passing from customer to customer, briefly talking to each and handing each a sheet of paper. Her blond hair was in the long, straight style so popular with white women in recent years. A few took a pen and wrote something on the paper, but more of them shook their heads. The man that the woman was currently talking to said something in an angry tone. He then scornfully tossed her piece of paper on the floor. The woman flushed. It was obvious that she wanted to argue with him, but he turned away from her dismissively.

The woman picked up the paper and smoothed it while she tried to regain her calm. As she did so, she looked around the room. Gerri dropped her eyes. She was willing to be a spectator to this little drama, but by no means did she want to be a participant. But it was too late. The woman appeared beside Gerri's booth.

"Excuse me? Would you be willing to read and sign this petition to end the Vietnam War?"

Gerri's curiosity was aroused, but her caution was stronger. "I'm sorry, but I'm not a resident. I'm just visiting."

"You don't have to be a resident, as long as you're old enough to vote." The woman extended the paper toward Gerri.

"I'd certainly like to see the end to that war," Gerri murmured. She started reading the petition. Her heart sank. She didn't want to be part of another altercation, but she couldn't sign it as it was written. She stalled for as long as she could, and then looked up at the woman. "I'm sorry, but I can't really sign this."

Anger flared in the woman's eyes. "So you're not *really* against the war?"

"Yes, I am." Gerri said emphatically. "I hate it as much as you do, maybe more." She pointed at the paper. "It's the part about our 'murdering soldiers' that I can't support."

"Haven't you heard of the My Lai massacre?" the woman asked accusingly.

"I have." Gerri paused. In some weird flashback, this was starting to remind her of her debates with Thurman before she gave up arguing with him. Would an appeal to a middle ground work any better with this woman? She plunged ahead. "My brother just got sent to Vietnam. He didn't ask for it; he didn't want it. But he signed an oath. He's not a murderer, and I pray that he never has a commander like the one at My Lai."

The woman was momentarily silent; taken aback by Gerri's statement. Gerri pressed her advantage. "If you think of this petition as a political act, wouldn't it make sense to word it so as to get the largest coalition possible?"

The woman slid into the booth opposite Gerri and scowled at her sheet of paper. Finally, she heaved a sigh. "I don't mean that they're all murderers." She looked some more. "Maybe I should look at this again. I've just started passing it around, and I haven't been having much luck getting signatures."

"I'd be happy to sign it if it didn't criticize our soldiers."

The woman nodded and put the paper into her purse. Gerri breathed a quiet sigh of relief. Making an enemy on her first day here was the last thing she wanted.

The woman leaned back in the booth and exhaled. "So. Where are you from?"

"South Carolina."

"You're a long way from home." The woman spoke with a smile, and seemed to be genuinely interested, so Gerri ended up telling her all about her trip. At the end, she grew self-conscious about her bad planning, but she forged on.

"So I may be here for only a day. I just didn't realize how expensive everything is."

"It is," the woman agreed. "Most of the goods have to be shipped in from the states."

"The states?"

"The other states. The south 48. We haven't been a state for that long. I'll have to watch my words." She grinned. "But we're not destitute. The wages are higher as well—mostly."

"One of my ideas was to try to get a temporary job to make enough money to get back home."

The woman raised her eyebrows. "Hmm. What can you do?"

Nothing ventured… "I don't know. I'd thought of fishing."

"You know something about fishing?"

"Some." That wasn't exactly a lie. Gerri had gone fishing with Rich in the Pee Dee river. And once, years ago, a cousin took Rich and her out on the ocean. She remembered that trip because he had let her try to start the outboard motor. He didn't think that she'd be able to—it was a pull cord which required some strength—and she was delighted to have surprised him by succeeding.

The woman seemed to consider that. Finally, she shook her head. "I doubt if anyone would hire a woman. That's why we need Women's Lib."

Gerri concealed a smile. The woman was predictably supportive of liberal causes. Gerri was actually sympathetic to that idea herself, although few students at Pee Dee State had talked much about it.

She took a bite of her hamburger as she toyed with an idea. "I've had a couple of people mistake me for a guy. Maybe I could fake it." She tried to imagine how that might go. She pictured a small boat with an outboard motor. They would go out in the morning, spend the day working with fishing poles—or maybe nets—and then come back in the evening.

"You don't look male to me."

"I think that my afro throws some people off."

The woman looked skeptical. "I've heard that fishing is hard work."

"I'm strong. I've worked on a farm all of my life."

The woman shrugged. "Maybe."

"Do you know anyone who…"

Now, the woman shook her head vigorously. "I don't know anything about those people. I only know one fisherman, and I hate his guts."

Gerri's shoulders slumped. Well, it had been worth a try.

"I know where you might ask, though. There's a big marine supply store down by the boat harbor: Northern Marine. They might know something."

Gerri dug in her bag and pulled out the map of Juneau that she had picked up in the airport. The woman showed her where everything was. Gerri was surprised how small the town was. "That's easy. I can walk there."

"Carrying those bags?"

"Well, maybe not quite so easy. But I can do it." She sighed. "But not today. I guess I can go back to that hotel. I've got just about enough money for one night."

The woman drummed her fingers for a moment. "Are you willing to sleep on a couch? You can stay at my place for a few days."

"Really? Are you sure? I'd appreciate that. That's very generous of you."

"I was once in your shoes. I took a tour of South America after I finished college. I was on a tight budget. One day I made a mistake in the currency exchange rate, and I ran out of money in the middle of nowhere. A family took me in. I don't know what I would have done otherwise. Oh. By the way, what's your name?"

"Gerri Barton."

The woman grinned. "You could even use your real name if you decide to pose as a guy." She extended her hand in greeting. "Anyway, I'm pleased to meet you. My name is Mindy Schumacher."

CHAPTER 6

Gerri stepped quietly out of Mindy's apartment. It was early morning and Mindy wasn't yet awake. Gerri patted her pocket before she closed the door to make sure that she had the key Mindy had loaned her. She zipped up her coat against the wind. It was cold—maybe in the forties. Again, she was struck by the difference between Juneau and South Carolina.

But Gerri didn't care; this was just part of her adventure. She was in a good mood. She had made a new friend. They had talked for hours last night. In fact, Gerri hadn't intended to get up so early, but the sun was already high in the sky so it had seemed later.

She decided to walk downhill toward the waterfront. The sky had cleared overnight, and the air was so clear that it seemed to sparkle. She turned around and looked behind her. That looming mountain—Mt. Juneau, Mindy said—was entirely visible, and it was more impressive than ever. She shook her head in wonder. This town was prettier than a picture postcard. She would definitely be giving her new camera a workout.

As she walked, she thought about her conversation with Mindy last night. Mindy was outspoken and opinionated, but she was actually willing to listen. She didn't argue to score points or exert dominance as Thurman used to. At Mindy's request, Gerri had helped her fix the wording of her petition. That led to Gerri's telling her about all of the papers that she had written for Thurman.

Mindy had been sympathetic—and frankly scornful. Gerri got the impression that she—in addition to being a staunch supporter of

Women's Lib—had had a bad experience with some guy. Perhaps one who didn't like having anyone disagree with him. That reminded her of Thurman. He would have lasted about five minutes in a discussion with Mindy before he lost his temper and started shouting.

Mindy had also regaled Gerri with stories of her South America travels. That must have been a real adventure. What Gerri had done so far was tame by comparison. It made her more determined than ever to milk all of the excitement that she could out of this trip.

Soon, Gerri reached the end of the street. There was a wooden pier that led out to the water. She didn't see any 'no trespassing' signs, so she walked out on it. There wasn't any activity this early in the morning—just a large ship docked to her left and several small airplanes floating in the water to her right. She stared at the airplanes, fascinated. What would it be like to fly in one of those? Not anything like riding a bus, she guessed. She wondered if she could afford a trip in one of these planes. *Probably not,* she sighed and turned back up the hill toward Mindy's apartment.

Mindy was waiting when Gerri walked in the door.

"Gosh, you get up early. Where have you been?"

"I didn't realize how early it was until I was outside. The sun was up…"

Mindy grinned. "Welcome to the land of the midnight sun. It's because we're so far north."

Gerri's eyes widened. "You have midnight sun here?" *What a great addition to my adventure that would be.*

"Well, not quite. You have to go to Northern Alaska to see that. But we do have very long days in the summer."

Gerri remembered the man on the airplane. "How far do you have to go to see the midnight sun? A thousand miles or so?" She was kidding, but Mindy nodded casually.

"Probably about that."

Gerri frowned in concentration as she tried to picture the earth hanging in space with the sun's rays hitting it. That was another interesting fact for her journal. Mindy watched her dig for it in her bag.

"What's that?"

Gerri explained about the ideas that she had written down for teaching some day. "When I start teaching, I want to do a good job. Some people will be watching for me to fail. They're just starting to integrate the schools in South Carolina. I'd love to teach trigonometry, but they probably won't let me. But just in case they consider it, I don't want them to be able to say that I'm not good enough."

"'They,' meaning the white people?"

Gerri nodded, but she wasn't in the mood for a discussion right now—even with her new friend—of racial politics in the South Carolina school systems. She quickly changed the subject.

"It's beautiful outside. I was thinking about your adventure and about my adventure." She paused and gave Mindy a sly smile. "I'm really stoked." As part of their conversation, they had compared their different slang words. This was one of Mindy's—for Gerri it was the first time she had ever used it.

Mindy, not to be outdone, retorted, "Well! I wondered why you had booked out of here."

Gerri grinned. 'Book' had been one of her contributions to their slang dictionary. She considered trying to come back with another of Mindy's slang terms, but couldn't think of anything appropriate. "OK, I give up. Truce." She paused. "I've decided that I'm going to try it. I don't want to sell this adventure short."

"Try what? Oh. Groovy." Mindy returned safely to her own lexicon. "You're going to look for a job on a fishing boat?"

"Yeah. I figure that the worst that will happen is that they'll laugh at me, but then I'll just have another story to tell."

"What about the…"

"Passing as a male? I'm tempted. Do you think that's too farfetched?"

Mindy eyed Gerri speculatively. "Well, the hair will help. People won't expect a woman to wear an afro hair style around here. We'll have to do something to hide your figure, though. That's a problem that I wouldn't have." She looked down at her slender frame with a half-smile.

Gerri took courage from Mindy's enthusiasm. "I'm going to try. I'll look in the mirror after I get ready. If I look ridiculous, then maybe I'll forget it."

"This is so cool. I'll help you get ready. Let's stick it to the male chauvinist pigs."

―――

Gerri took out her city map and checked it briefly. She was more than halfway to the boat harbor area that Mindy had pointed out. It felt good to be walking briskly. Her earlier walk had been a leisurely stroll to look at the scenery; now she had a goal. She wore a baggy sweat shirt and sweat pants loaned to her by Mindy—left by a former boyfriend, Gerri gathered. Without stopping, she adjusted the band of cloth which Mindy had given her to flatten and hide her breasts. She'd have to get used to wearing it a lot if this scheme worked. She smiled as she remembered Mindy muttering about her own figure. That reminded her briefly of Carlotta. *I wonder what she looks like. Light skinned and slender, apparently.* Swiftly, she put that thought out of her mind. That was *not* the way to enjoy this vacation.

Just then, she saw a street sign that said 'Glacier Avenue.' She smiled and made a note to ask Mindy about how to see a glacier. Then the smile was wiped from her face as a car full of young, white males drove by slowly. Several of them stared curiously at her as they passed. She had been warned by her parents to avoid such cars—by running away if necessary—if the occupants seemed excessively interested. She had never known any of her friends to be accosted, but there had been some ugly incidents in the old days.

The car slowly moved out of sight and Gerri breathed a sigh of relief. Surely, things were different here. Anyway, she was supposed to be passing as a male. If they could see through her disguise from a moving car, then she didn't have much hope of fooling someone close up.

As she rounded the next corner, she could see the landmarks that Mindy had given her. There was a bridge on her left, and beside it was a harbor filled with small—and not so small—boats. Ahead of her was the sign for Northern Marine Company.

She paused and pretended to look at the window display as she went over her checklist once more. Mindy had reminded her to keep her voice pitched low to pass as male; fortunately Gerri, who sang contralto in the choir, could do that easily. More difficult was Mindy's last injunction, delivered as Gerri was about to leave. "Try not to smile," she had said, "and especially, don't grin. You have a very feminine smile." Gerri would do her best, but the 'no smile' edict certainly ate into her self-confidence.

Quit stalling. It's time. As she started to reach for the door, she noticed that her 'fro was matted. Instinctively, she raised her hand to smooth it, but stopped. *No. Only a woman would primp. A guy wouldn't care.* She converted the gesture to one of scratching her cheek. She was getting tired of this charade already.

As she entered the store, a bell tinkled in the back, announcing her. It reminded her of an unusually large hardware store. The large display area was filled with mysterious pieces of equipment, and there was a faintly spicy, not unpleasant smell in the air. *Some sort of preservative, maybe?* Gerri focused on a woman sitting at a desk working with an adding machine. She wasn't paying any attention to Gerri, or to the several other customers elsewhere in the store.

"Excuse me, Ma'am?"

"One second," the woman muttered. When she looked up, Gerri could see surprise in her eyes, but her response was courteous. "What can I do for you?"

"Do you know of any fisherman who might have a job to offer?"

Most people looking for a job went directly to the boat harbor and asked around rather than coming to Maxine at Northern Marine. Still the young fellow seemed well spoken—although his voice was odd. It had a layer of gruffness over an almost musical quality. She forced her attention to the question. "Nooo, I can't say that I do." There was Sven, of course, who had just fired Mike, but he wasn't looking for a replacement. *Still, I should give this kid a chance. You never know.* "Well, I know of one guy who might have an opening. Sven Halvorsen, on the Glacier Gal."

She was quickly sorry that she had spoken. The kid clearly had no idea what she meant. He hardly seemed like a legitimate fisherman. She kept her expression neutral as she studied the kid more carefully. He was short and androgynous in appearance, and he wore an anxious look. Maxine was secretly delighted to be able to use the word 'androg-ynous'—she had seen it in a book the previous evening and had had to look it up.

Her good mood probably influenced her. *Why should I disappoint the kid? Sven will figure it out and send him on his way.* She explained. "Sven Halvorsen is the man's name and 'Glacier Gal' is the name of his boat. Do you know your way around the boat harbor?"

"No, Ma'am."

Of course not. Maxine mentally shrugged. If Sven complained about her sending this kid, she could apologize to him then. She quickly described the location of Glacier Gal, and even drew a small map of the boat harbor for him. He thanked her and left eagerly. *Polite youngster,* she thought, *too bad he doesn't know anything about boats.*

Gerri followed the woman's directions carefully. She smiled to her-self at the name, Glacier Gal: so she would be seeing a glacier—just not a real one. Yet. She was beginning to allow herself to hope. She'd have to be alert, though. There was much that she didn't know. She could tell that the woman was disappointed at having to give her such detailed directions. She had no idea what a finger float was, but she had instructions for finding the correct one.

She walked out onto a pier, as instructed, and started down a long, gently sloped ramp. When she got to the bottom, she stopped to look at it more closely. The top of the ramp had been attached to the pier, but at the bottom, the ramp had heavy metal rollers resting on a metal track. *Why do they need such an elaborate mechanism?* She shelved that question—it was just one more thing that she didn't know, and there were more important things to think about.

She walked along the float. *OK, that was one mystery solved. They were called floats because they floated.* They consisted of sturdy, wooden planks nailed over some extremely large logs. There was a rich combi-nation of smells in the air: salt, a hint of tar or some other preservative, and something that she could only describe as marine life. It was a pleasant mix.

There were hundreds of boats in the boat harbor. Their masts, and in some cases the ropes hanging from them, looked like a strange forest.

She scanned the boats as she walked. The woman at Northern Marine had explained that the name of each of the boats was painted on each side of the bow—that was the front—as well as on the stern—that was the back. Armed with this knowledge, Gerri hoped to avoid looking like a total know-nothing.

Finally, she saw it. The boat was large—much larger than Gerri had imagined that it would be. It had at least half a dozen masts. No, she decided. Most of them were poles—maybe for fishing. Only one of them looked like Gerri's conception of a mast. It had lights and some sort of electronic apparatus at the top. There was a large area of open deck in the rear, and a hatch which, she supposed, opened to the fish storage area. She felt daunted—there was much that she would have to learn.

As she eyed the boat, a man stepped out of its forward cabin. He had several paint brushes in his hand. He was a concrete block of a man about six feet tall, with broad shoulders and a stocky torso. He looked immensely strong and well built in his faded blue tee shirt. His dark hair was short—barely longer than a crew cut—but trying to curl. He wore no jacket: this in weather that had to be in the fifties. Gerri had *her* jacket well zipped.

Gerri's heart was in her mouth. Her adventure depended on what she did now. She crossed her fingers in her pockets. Remembering to keep her voice as deep as possible, she spoke. "Excuse me, Sir."

The man—she assumed that he was Sven Halvorsen—turned toward her and scowled.

"What?"

CHAPTER 7

Gerri's steps faltered. The man had a long scar running down the side of his face and the scowl made him look fierce, and downright scary. *Maybe this isn't such a good idea.* She forced herself to be calm, and hoped that he couldn't hear her beating heart.

"I'm looking for work on a fishing boat."

Sven was in a bad mood. He had delayed the painting as long as he could. And then the latest stretch of rainy weather delayed it even more. He had a lot to do in the next two days if he was going to be able to go out on time for his first trip.

He had seen the kid walking up the float. Obviously not a local kid—maybe off the tourist boat that was in port. He didn't see any parents in sight. That was slightly strange, but Juneau was the kind of town where you could let your kid wander around on his own without worrying too much. But a job? The kid looked too young for that. Still, Sven hadn't meant to snap at him. It was Sven's own fault that he had delayed his painting—he could at least be polite to the kid.

"Come aboard and we'll talk."

Close up, the kid looked even younger. Sven wasn't about to hire a kid, even with the parents' permission. *Hell, it probably isn't even legal.* "How old are you, boy?"

Gerri fought to hide her alarm. Were southern attitudes present, even here in the far north? She forced herself to give him the benefit of the doubt. "I just turned 22. Don't call me 'boy,' Sir."

Sven belatedly recalled reading that the term of address, 'boy,' was used to show disrespect to black males of all ages in the South. *Terrific!*

I've managed to go from brusquely rude to outright offensive. Still, he wondered, wasn't it OK to use it on an obvious child? And 22 years old? That was hard to believe. He tried again.

"All right, son. I'll make you a deal. I won't call you 'boy' if you don't call me 'sir.' What's your name? My name is Sven."

Gerri felt a wave of relief wash over her—she had to work to suppress a grin. "It's a deal. My name is Gerri."

Sven eyed her skeptically. "I still don't believe you're 22, Jerry. You look about 13." He brushed the back of his knuckle across Gerri's cheek. "I'll bet you've never even shaved, have you?"

Sven had to fight to hide his reaction—he felt an almost electric jolt from the touch. This kid, Jerry, had the smoothest, softest skin Sven had ever touched. He could tell that Jerry had been shaken by the touch as well. *Is there any other way that I can offend this kid? I hope he doesn't think that I'm...*

Gerri had trouble controlling her breathing. She couldn't get the feel of Sven's finger out of her mind. His hand was rough, but his brush had been distractingly gentle. She forced herself to think.

Of course, he was right about the shaving. She wouldn't lie, but she had to say *something*—he was clearly not going to hire a 13 year old on a fishing boat. She thought briefly of showing him her South Carolina driver's license, but it gave her name as 'Geraldine,' which would end her deception—and end her chances for a job as well.

"I'm not lying, Sir—uh, Sven. I can't help the way my body is. But I'm a hard worker; I learn quickly; and I'm strong. If you give me a chance, you won't be sorry."

"Hmmm." Sven tried to decide how to politely reject the kid. *Strong, eh? He's small as well as young.* That gave Sven an idea for a test. He pointed to a pair of large, lead sinkers. "Would you mind bringing those over here?"

Gerri followed his gesture. There was a pair of grey spheres, about six inches in diameter, with some sort of braided wires sticking out of them. *Were they floats? No, they looked metallic.* Whatever they were, she wanted to look responsive—he hadn't turned her down yet, after all. She grabbed the wires, one in each hand and lifted. She grunted in surprise—the spheres hardly budged. *He tricked me!* She wouldn't give him the satisfaction of complaining. She squared her shoulders, bent her knees and held her breath as she strained. Slowly she lifted them. Once she was standing up straight, she carefully carried them to his feet, where she laid them down gently. Then she covertly rubbed her hands where the wires had cut into them.

"Thank you," he said. She did her best to look casual about it, although she thought she saw a flicker of a smile on his face.

When he remained silent, she finally couldn't stand it anymore. "That was a test, wasn't it? Did I pass?"

He couldn't help but smile. "You passed. You're stronger than you look."

Emboldened by his praise, she asked: "What are those? They're heavy."

"They are heavy. They're solid lead—about 50 pounds apiece—and they're used as sinkers, to hold the lines below the surface while I'm trolling." The kid was strong, considering his small size, and, Sven had to admit, spunky as well. He figured out that Sven had fooled him, but he didn't get angry. Sven admired that, but it just made it harder to get rid of him politely. And Sven didn't want to waste a lot of time on him; he had a long day of painting ahead of him.

That gave Sven an idea. "I don't know about a job on the boat, but if you know how to paint without making a mess, I'll pay you to help me today." If the kid was a good worker, he could make the painting go a lot faster, and it would put some money in the kid's pocket, which should satisfy him.

"Sure, I can paint. I helped paint stuff on my father's farm." Sven arched his eyebrow at that, and Gerri hastily added, "That was when I was younger—before I went to college." She didn't want him bringing up the '13 years old' thing again.

Within five minutes, she was sitting on the float painting the hull of his boat. He loaned her an old shirt to protect her clothes. It was way too big, but she appreciated the gesture. She applied herself industriously—not only was she still being tested, but hard work was in her upbringing.

It was late afternoon by the time they finished. Gerri was stiff and sore, but very satisfied with herself. Sven had been eyeing her intermittently, and she could tell that he was pleased with her work.

After they cleaned up, he handed her some money. She quickly counted it and couldn't hide her pleasure. *This is over twice as much as I would get for this job in South Carolina.* "Thank you," she said, and then tried again. "About that job…"

"I'm not so sure about that." Sven scratched his head. "But I could use your help again tomorrow—and I'll pay you at a higher rate." The kid was a willing and productive worker; he had to give him that. Sven could tell from the limited amount of conversation that took place that he didn't know much about fishing, but Sven would love to have help with the copper painting.

Gerri was disappointed that she hadn't completely won Sven over, but neither had he refused her. "Sure, I'll help. What time do you want me here?"

Now Sven's conscience bothered him. "Don't be too quick to say yes before you see what's involved. Tomorrow I'm copper painting, and that's miserable work." He saw Jerry look blank. "Walk back up the dock with me as you leave and I'll show you."

They walked back along the float in silence. When they got near the base of the ramp, Gerri stopped in shock. Everything looked different. The ramp was now steeply angled and the pier was high above them. To the side, between them and the land, where there had previously been open water, there was now solid land, stretching well above the float. She looked more closely at the ramp. *I can see that they need the rollers…but what's going on?*

Sven was watching her quizzically. "What's the matter?"

There was only one thing that she could think of, and it excited her because it was so utterly different from South Carolina—it was yet another facet of her adventure. "You must have enormous tides here. When I came down here…" She shrugged, suddenly self-conscious for revealing her ignorance.

Sven grinned. He enjoyed seeing the wheels turning in Jerry's head. The kid was sharp—and Sven was gradually being convinced that he was telling the truth. He didn't act like a 13 year old. "You're right," he said. "They're not as big as in the Bay of Fundy—or even as big as in Anchorage—but there's a big swing. And today, with the full moon, the difference between high and low tide is over twenty feet."

Gerri was silent; trying to memorize this all to think about later. *The slope of that ramp…I could make some wonderful trigonometry problems from that!*

"Anyway," Sven said, bringing her back to the present, "Glacier Gal goes up there on the grid." He pointed to the newly exposed area, which had a row of monstrous beams raised above the mud. "And we paint the hull. It's nasty work; you'll be crawling around underneath the hull in the mud. That's why I'll pay you more, but that's also why I wanted you to see what you're getting into."

Gerri didn't need to hesitate. If she said no, then her hopes of getting a job would clearly be gone. Besides, she rationalized, in a weird way, this would add to her adventure. Sometimes the most distasteful tasks made the most interesting stories later. There was just one thing…

"How do you get the boat up there? Isn't it awfully heavy?"

"Remember the tide? I come down to the harbor at high tide—around midnight—and move it over there and tie it up. Then, when the tide goes back out, it'll be sitting there waiting for us."

"May I come and help you tonight?" She was determined to ingratiate herself with him. And, of course, if he didn't give her a job, it might be her only chance to ride on the boat.

"Thanks anyway, but I don't really need the help."

"I didn't mean for money. I just want to see what it's like."

"Sure. Can you be here just before midnight?" Sven hid his amusement. He added another item to the list that he was making of Jerry's attributes: he was tenacious as well as spunky and smart. Sven was starting to realize that refusing him a job might be hard.

———

The night was magic under the soft light of the full moon. Even with the lights of the harbor, Gerri could see stars. She could also see the faint outline of the mountain behind the town in the deep indigo of the sky. She knew that she would miss the sleep later, but now she was too excited to feel it.

When she arrived at the harbor, Sven was talking to a short, older man. Sven watched her approach and when she got close, he spoke. "Here he is now, Wally."

Wally looked at her skeptically. "*This* is your ace painter?"

"Don't knock it. You complimented me on the job before you realized that I had had help. Now, come on. I know you have some old boots and rain gear that you can loan me. The kid's not dressed for copper painting and all of my clothes are too big."

Wally shot her a skeptical look and disappeared into a nearby boat. Gerri felt a sinking sense of disappointment. This was the first time that she had seen a negative reaction—at least what seemed to be— while in Juneau. *Who am I kidding? Juneau may be better than South Carolina, but it's still on the same planet.*

Sven looked acutely uncomfortable. "I apologize for Wally. I don't know what's gotten into him. He may not be the friendliest guy in the world, but that was downright rude."

"That's all right, Sir. I've seen plenty of people like that back home—and some worse."

So we're back to 'Sir.' "That doesn't make it right. I'll speak to him about it later."

Gerri didn't know how to respond, but she was saved by Wally's reappearance. He ignored Gerri and handed a bundle of clothes to Sven. "There. Make sure I get them back."

"I always do."

Wally turned and left, and Sven gestured toward his boat. He explained to Jerry how to untie the lines. He couldn't help but notice that Jerry looked somber; his earlier enthusiasm was more muted. He didn't know why Wally had gotten so cranky. *Damn Wally, anyway. Was it racial prejudice? Obviously Jerry thought so, and he made it clear that he'd seen plenty of that.* In fact, Sven realized, Jerry might be running away from just that kind of treatment.

Gerri tried to put Wally's behavior out of her mind, and to regain the sense of magic. Sven was a patient teacher. It was surely evident by now that she didn't know much about boats, but he didn't seem to be bothered by that. He showed where the boat was tied to the float, and how: the lines (don't call them ropes, he said) were wrapped around a metal object that he called a cleat. The wrapping was done in a clever figure-eight pattern which kept the lines secure by maximizing friction. When he had started the engine, he signaled to her to untie them and climb aboard.

They proceeded slowly around the harbor toward the grid area that he had pointed out before. In fact, so slowly that Gerri couldn't resist asking, "Is this as fast as you can go?"

He raised his eyebrows. "Nowhere near. If I went fast, I'd throw up a big wake, and that would annoy everyone. A lot of people live on their boats." He paused, as that reminded him of Wally. "Wally lives on his boat, for example."

"Oh." Gerri didn't want to think about Wally.

———

The painting was, as advertised, not exactly fun. Glacier Gal looked enormous as it rested with its keel across the giant beams. Gerri was thankful for Wally's boots as she stood in the mud painting. They had to work fast; the tide would come in and float the boat, hiding the hull they were painting. And work fast they did, but by the time they were done, the water was still up to her ankles.

After they had cleaned up—Gerri made sure that she left no mess on Wally's clothes—Sven paid her. Once again, she was pleasantly surprised at how much money she'd earned. But she was apprehensive: he hadn't said anything about a job on the boat. As long as he hadn't said anything, she could cling to her hopes, but she had no excuse to hang around. It was now or never. Finally, she worked up her nerve.

"Have you, um, decided about that job?"

Sven had, indeed, thought about it—more than a little. Jerry was a good worker and learned quickly. Sven still had his reservations, but he had half decided even before Wally's outburst, and after that—well, he didn't want to disappoint the kid further. But there was one issue on which Sven would not compromise. "Do you drink?"

"Alcohol? No, sir. Not at all. I wasn't brought up that way."

He seemed to like that answer, but he still frowned at her. "Remember our deal?"

Gerri nodded. "I remember, *Sven.*" It took all of her effort not to smile back. This man had such an interesting face. His scar was like an amplifier—when he scowled, it amplified the menace, but when he smiled, it gave him a rakish air which was very appealing.

"I'll give you a chance," he finally said. "I'll hire you for one trip and we'll see how it goes."

"Great. You won't be sorry."

He outlined the pay package that he would offer. Gerri wasn't sure that she completely understood it; there was a combination of wages and a small percentage of the boat's income. It sounded fair though, and Sven had proven himself to be generous so far. And anyway, she would jump at this chance just for the adventure."

"Can you be ready tomorrow morning? We'll head out around 7 a.m."

"I'll be here." Gerri was scarcely able to contain her excitement. "And by the time we come back at the end of the day, I'll try to have convinced you to keep me on."

Sven gave her a bemused look. "End of the day? This trip will take a week or two."

Gerri's jaw dropped. She hadn't expected this; would her disguise hold up for several days? What about the sleeping arrangements? How would she dress and undress? "So I sleep on board?"

Sven smiled indulgently. Yes, he'd have a lot of education to do, but it might be interesting. "Yes. There are some bunks in the front. I'll show you. You'll have them all to yourself, since I have my own cabin."

Gerri nodded in relief. That would help, and she'd just have to play the rest by ear. "I'll go pack. Is there anything special that I should bring?"

"I'll give you a list."

Back at Mindy's apartment, Gerri finally gave free rein to her excitement. "I got a job. We're leaving tomorrow morning."

"It worked? They're convinced that you're a guy?"

Gerri grinned and nodded.

"Cool. A win for Women's Lib over the male chauvinist pigs."

Gerri nodded, and then sat down as the smile left her face. Shopping. She had to get supplies. The salt air would kill her hair. *Did they even have the proper hair care products here?* Sven's list was a start, but of course he wouldn't know about the all personal supplies that she would need.

Mindy interrupted before she had much time to worry. "I have exciting news, too. I took that petition that you helped me rewrite and passed it around at work. Way more people are signing it now; I've got almost a hundred names." She went on, eagerly outlining her plans to get more names.

Gerri's mind drifted a bit. She supported Mindy and she admired her enthusiasm, but her thoughts were on the shopping. She was jerked back to the conversation by Mindy's next words.

"I'm glad for you, but I'm sorry in a way. I was hoping that you'd be able to help me go around and get more signatures."

Gerri could think of nothing that she would *less* rather do. She was struck anew by their personality differences and the incongruousness of their friendship. She settled for an all-purpose (and insincere) murmur of disappointment, and quickly turned the subject.

"Do you know where I can get some of the things on this list?"

"Hah!" Mindy took the list and glanced at it. "Now you've found my other favorite thing. Let's go shopping. I'll drive you."

Chapter 8

"Good morning, Sven."

Sven turned around at the sound of Jerry's voice and immediately started laughing. He couldn't help himself. Jerry was bent under the weight of two giant duffel bags. "It looks like you've packed enough for a whole season, not just a week or two."

Gerri didn't know what to say. She couldn't afford to enumerate everything that she had brought—it would look awfully suspicious for a male to pack hair care products and lotion. In fact, she thought with alarm, she might not even be given a private storage place. She said cautiously, "Well, I didn't know and, um, better safe than sorry. I hope there's enough space to put it all."

Sven reminded himself again not to make fun of Jerry's ignorance. "There's plenty of space. Hand the bags to me and come aboard. I'll show you where you'll be bunking."

It wasn't as bad as she had feared. She was to be in what Sven described as the fo'c's'le. It was a tiny room with two bunks (and a door that closed!) and a miniscule, built-in chest of drawers. His only admonishment was that her gear must be stored so that it couldn't fly around, even if the boat were tossing in a storm.

That sounded alarming—maybe more of an adventure than she had bargained for. She didn't want to sound like a coward, so she chose a more mundane question. "What was it that you called this room? And how do you spell it?"

He pronounced it again, and then elaborated. "It's short for 'forecastle,' I think. And it's usually spelled phonetically, with apostrophes—I'm not sure exactly how." He paused and grinned disarmingly. "See? You're not the only one that doesn't know everything."

He left her with that and she put her stuff away as best she could. Some of it would just have to stay in the duffel bags. The first drawer she tried seemed stuck. After some prodding, she discovered that one had to lift it to open it. Indeed, it turned out that all of the drawers had notches on the sliders to prevent accidental openings—they were really serious about this 'tossing in a storm' business.

After she had finished, Sven gave her a brief tour of the boat, explaining some terminology as he went. The upper cabin was dominated by the pilot house, which had a large wheel for steering and some mysterious electronic equipment. Aft of it (that is, toward the stern), and a couple of steps down, was the galley, an open area for cooking and eating. Next to that was Sven's quarters, also tiny. He wanted, he said, to be near the pilot house if anything went wrong in the middle of the night. At the rear of the galley was the door to the main deck.

Also there were some small, steep steps (more like a ladder, really) to the belowdecks area where Gerri's quarters were. Also in this area was a cramped bathroom—the 'head,' as Sven instructed her to call it. To her dismay, it consisted of just a toilet and a sink, with barely enough room to stand.

"No shower?"

"It would take too much room and use too much water. We wash at the sink, and at the end of the trip."

That reminded her. "Where does your water come from?"

"There are tanks for water and for diesel fuel. We fill them up at the beginning of each trip."

Lastly was the engine room. Sven opened the door and let her peer in. It reminded her of an unfinished basement—one could see the boat's ribs—with a very large engine taking up most of the space.

At this point, Gerri thought that they were done, but he led her back up on deck and lifted a large hatch. "This is the most important part," he said with a sly grin. "This is where we keep the fish that pay for all of the rest of it."

Gerri peered down into a cavernous chamber partially filled with crushed ice. There must have been tons of it. Sven anticipated her next question. "I loaded up with ice, water, and fuel yesterday afternoon. The ice keeps the fish fresh until we can sell it."

There was considerable equipment fastened around the deck. Sven waved at it. "You'll learn how to use this later. Don't worry; it won't happen all at once. Now let's get underway. Do you remember how to cast off the lines?"

She remembered. Soon they were headed down the channel. When they had left the harbor, he sped the boat up. Now there was a vibration that suffused everything, and the boat had a substantial wake. Gerri was beside herself with excitement. She didn't know where to look first. Then she remembered that she was getting paid for this.

"Is there anything that you'd like me to do now?"

That distracting grin again. "No, you can relax for a while."

———

Sven didn't know what to make of Jerry. From those first moments, he had tried to be helpful. Even though Sven had told him to relax, the bow and stern lines were soon neatly coiled. The kid's eyes were wide—Sven was sure that he was having a good time. But he never smiled. Even one of Sven's more outrageous puns barely elicited a twitch of Jerry's lips. Finally, Sven gave up trying to make him laugh. Who knows what motivated him?

But Sven had no complaints. The kid was a sponge. He asked a lot of questions, but Sven never had to tell him anything twice. Over the next few days Sven let him do more and more—and needed to watch him less and less.

To be sure, there were a few glitches. Jerry spent a lot of time in the head each night before turning in. Sven didn't really mind—he generally took care of his business earlier—but he thought it odd. He had asked him casually about it once and Jerry had said that he liked to clean up carefully. He seemed uncomfortable about the question, so Sven just shrugged. So maybe Jerry was a bit effeminate; so what? Sven would still take Jerry and his eccentricities any day over Mike and the bottles he used to hide in his cabin.

Jerry proved to be a picky eater as well. After Sven cooked their first meal, he asked if Sven would like him to help cook. He was trying to be polite, but he was unable to conceal his disapproval. Sven wasn't the best of cooks, but what knowledge he did have was hard-won, and he was unwilling to trust his stomach to a young, inexperienced male.

He tried to let Jerry down easily. "No, I'll take care of it. I'm used to it." He paused, amused. "You don't like my cooking?"

No, Gerri didn't like it at all. "It's OK. I just thought…"

Sven shook his head emphatically. "I'd rather not have you learn on my time. I'll bet that in your family, the females did all of the cooking. Am I right?"

Gerri sighed. *Trapped!* "You're right." *Looks like I'll be losing some weight on this trip.*

———

Gerri was learning more than she had thought possible about fishing and boating in general. She tried to remember her father's dictum: always try to be useful and try to anticipate what needs doing. This was her first completely independent job—there had always been plenty of work on the farm when she was younger—and she felt she was making a success of it.

There were good moments. Sven had taught her how to use a gaff hook—a six inch spike curved into a hook and attached firmly to a 30 inch handle—to hook the fish on their lines and lift them aboard. Once, on one of the lines she was tending, they brought up an enormous salmon. She gaffed it and pulled it smoothly onboard. Yes, it was extremely heavy, and she was relieved that she didn't falter. Or worse, lose the fish entirely. She couldn't resist glancing quickly at Sven, remembering his concern about her strength.

He had been watching and he smiled his approval. "Good work." Then he looked closer and added, "That'll bring at least $50; maybe more." Gerri looked at the fish with new appreciation.

He respected her limits, though. Another time, a halibut came to the surface on one of her lines. It was gigantic—easily over six feet long. She gaffed it, but couldn't lift it into the boat. Sven saw her struggling and quickly came to her aid. "That one's about 150 to 200 pounds."

She didn't want to seem greedy, but she had to know. "How much is that worth?"

Sven made a face. "Not as much as that big salmon. They pay a lot less for halibut. That's why we don't really try for them."

Gerri even got used to Sven's cooking, though she couldn't quite come to enjoy it. He relied heavily on opening cans, and didn't try to improve on the contents with seasoning. Since she didn't dare show her cooking ability, she made sure that she took care of all of the cleaning up.

Gerri's worst moment was on the third evening of their trip. It had been a long day. The fish had been plentiful that day and Sven and Gerri had worked longer to take advantage. It was after 9 o'clock when they finally anchored in a small cove. Gerri went below to wash up and comb out her hair. Later, after she was in her room for the night, she would finish curling her hair. She tried to hurry, since Sven had made some pointed remarks about the time she spent in the head.

When she climbed the steps to the galley, Sven wasn't there. She stepped out onto the deck and saw him standing on the gunwale, facing outward. She opened her mouth to call to him, when she realized with horror that he was calmly urinating into the water beside the boat. Her monopolization of the head had driven him to an alternate—and practical—solution. Stricken with humiliation, she swallowed her words and silently fled back into the cabin. Once there, she paused only a second to rub her shin, which she had banged against a door in her haste, and then hurried back down the steps.

She had barely scooted into her room when she heard Sven descend the steps and knock on the door of the head. "Jerry, are you still in there?"

"No, Sven, I'm in here."

She waited, practically shaking, until he finished washing his hands and went back up the stairs to the galley. Thurman would probably have thought her hilarious—he would have talked about how she had too many hang-ups, but it wasn't that. She wasn't *that* naïve. She had seen her brother naked, after all. No, it wasn't that. It was a sense of violation. Sven didn't know that she was a girl (a woman, Mindy would have reminded her), and he wouldn't have been so casual if he had known. She felt dirty, like a 'peeping Thomasina.'

When she finally got the courage to return to the galley, he was already eating. He gestured casually with his fork. "Food's in the pan. I was beginning to think that you were boycotting my cooking."

"Sorry I took so long," she said. Then, because she didn't want to have the conversation linger on his cooking, she added, "I was cleaning up. That's the one thing that's hardest to get used to—the scarcity of hot water. I'd give..." A memory flashed briefly: one of Thurman's friends saying 'my left nut.' *Was that what a guy would say? Well, not a guy that she would want to be with.* No, she wouldn't carry her deception to that level. "I'd give anything for a real bath—one with unlimited hot water."

Sven smiled. "Hmmm."

CHAPTER 9

Gerri stood on the deck of the fish buying vessel. She flexed her knees automatically to adjust for the gentle rolling of the ocean swell, silently pleased with herself for the casual way she was able to do this. Below her, visible if she leaned over the railing, was the Glacier Gal, its 40-something foot length dwarfed by the larger ship.

Her arms and shoulders were sore, but it was a satisfying soreness. She and Sven had just finished transferring their fish from the Glacier Gal's hold to oversized buckets, which were then winched up to the deck of the fish buyer to be weighed and the price calculated. While Sven and the captain of the buyer, Gary something, were chatting, waiting for the final numbers, Gerri considered her dilemma. Sven had said that he would write her a check for her share. The buyer had offered to mail it to her bank for deposit. But she didn't have a bank account. Worse, she didn't want a check in her name—that would be a dead giveaway.

At the same time, she was intensely proud of herself for the way her adventure was turning out. The amount of money that Sven had mentioned would more than pay for her entire trip. She could hardly wait to tell her parents. That was it! She turned to Sven. "I don't have a bank account. Could you make the check out to my father? I'll mail it to him with a note."

"Of course. You go write the note. I'm sure Gary has paper and envelopes that you can use."

Gary nodded. "Sure, I keep a batch of writing materials for just this sort of thing. I always have a full satchel to take to the Post Office when I get in to port." He smiled at a well-rehearsed line. "I won't even charge you the six cents for the stamp."

Gerri went into the buyer's cabin and, accepting a pen and paper, scribbled a terse account of her adventure thus far, with a promise to write a longer letter later. She addressed the envelope and then hesitated. *Mindy won't mind...* She used Mindy's address for the return address. She got an attack of nerves as she took the check and sealed the envelope—this would be her parents' first chance to share their opinion of Gerri's ad-libbed adventure. She only hoped that the money and her upbeat letter would temper any disapproval.

———

After they were underway again, Gerri daydreamed about how—she hoped—her parents would be impressed with her initiative. She even dared to imagine Thurman (somehow) receiving the news with astonishment. It wasn't that she still cared about him—she just wanted him to realize how badly he had misjudged her.

Sven interrupted her reverie. "We're going to take a detour before we get back to fishing." He looked at Gerri with a smug smile. "I think you'll like it."

"Where are we going?"

"You'll see."

Try though she might, Gerri couldn't get any further information from him. They were approaching the shore, but it wasn't a part that she recognized. Ordinarily, Sven was pleased when she showed interest in his nautical charts (don't call them maps...), but when she asked to see the one for their area, he shook his head. That just made her more curious, but she could tell by Sven's look of satisfaction that it would do no good to plead.

She looked again outside to see what she could guess. The shore here was rocky, and she could see waves breaking—highlighting the numerous rocks just below the surface of the water. She watched silently, not wanting to disturb him—these rocks could easily destroy the Glacier Gal if Sven made a false move. He slowed the boat to a crawl as he neared the shore. A tiny gap appeared, and he maneuvered the boat carefully into it.

Finally, he reached a tiny, hidden lagoon and tied the boat to a float which was little more than a couple of logs. "We have about a mile to walk."

Gerri was happy to have a chance to walk through the woods and impatient to see what was at the end of the trail. Sven was carrying a backpack that looked full. Gerri tried once more. "What's in the backpack?"

"You'll see."

Then they came out on a rocky beach. There was a shack—no, two shacks—a ways up the beach. *That must be the surprise,* she thought, but she couldn't see anything special about them. As they got closer, she could smell a faint scent of sulfur, and she thought she heard the faint burbling of a stream.

Finally, Sven stopped, put down his backpack and looked around expansively. Gerri followed his gaze. The smell was stronger, and there was a trickle of water coming out of a pipe on the beach between the shacks and the ocean. Oddly enough, it appeared to be steaming, even though the temperature was only in the sixties.

"OK, Jerry, here's your fondest wish." He gestured expansively in the direction of the shacks. "This is White Sulfur Hot Springs. All the hot water you could ever want. There's a pool inside—not large enough to swim in, but plenty large enough for several people to bathe in. I brought soap and towels. You're not the only one that is aching for a bath."

Gerri stared at him in shock as she tried to assimilate this information. *Bathe? As in undress and bathe?* Sure enough, as she stared, Sven started unbuttoning his shirt. She looked around desperately, hoping to get some inspiration—some way out. This was 'peeping Thomasina' to the tenth power.

Sven saw her dismay and misunderstood. He had already decided that the kid was shy. "Don't worry; there's nobody around. I'll bet there's not a woman within ten miles of here. Hell, there's probably not a single other *person* within ten miles."

Gerri ventured another glance at him. His shirt was entirely off and he laid it beside the backpack. She couldn't help but notice his muscular physique—but somehow appreciating it made her feel even worse. She could see no way out. With a moan, she crumpled to sit on a large rock, turning away from him and putting her hands up to frame her face and prevent her from seeing him. "I can't! I'm sorry, I just can't," she wailed.

Sven was angry now. He knew the kid was a bit weird, but this was too much. "I've gave up an afternoon of fishing and a wasted fair amount of fuel just so you could get your wish. Are you crazy?"

Gerri felt his contempt as his words lashed her. A feel of utter hopelessness descended over her. An hour ago, she had been on the top of the world. Now she felt like dirt. Sven had gone to all of this trouble to surprise her...

"I'm sorry," she repeated. In her dejection she did something which just added to her shame—she started to weep.

Sven saw the tears falling on her jeans and turned away in disgust. *Truly, a head case!* Well, he decided, at least he'd get a bath. He picked up the backpack and his shirt and walked toward the larger shack. As he got there, he turned and looked back. Then he shrugged. "I'm taking a bath—a nice long hot bath. You can sit out here and sulk if you want."

Gerri sat there after he disappeared, steeping in her misery. She frantically tried to think of something that she could say that would make this all right—to restore his good faith in her. She was surprised to realize how much that meant to her. But it was useless. There was nothing she could do to fix this up. Besides, she remembered her mother's words: one lie begets another, and that begets another, and so on. It was better to avoid going down that path in the first place.

And Sven deserved better than that. He was a kind and gentle man who had been unfailingly supportive of her. *And he can melt me with a smile...* But that didn't count, she chided herself. Could she dare to confess? That was the honorable thing to do, but would that make him even angrier? She heaved a sigh. At least he was enjoying his bath. He deserved that enjoyment, just as she deserved her unhappiness.

Sven was *not* enjoying his bath. He had been as anxious to soak and bathe as Jerry had seemed to be and, after he was inside the shack, he automatically finished undressing and slipped into the pool. But, even as he sat there soaping up, his mind roiled with anger. He replayed the last parts of the conversation over and over, looking for a rational explanation—some sort of exculpatory interpretation. Because he liked the kid. Jerry was the first deckhand whose company Sven could actually enjoy.

But now, he was rethinking that. He had no desire to be around a head case; that was barely better than being around a drunk like Mike. But most of the time Jerry seemed perfectly normal. And he was sharp. So what set him off? All of a sudden, he had a total meltdown. As soon as Sven talked about bathing—no, as soon as he started undressing—Jerry hid his face, his voice went all falsetto, and he started crying like a girl…

Something clicked into place in Sven's mind. Could Jerry be…? *That would make me the dumbest S.O.B. in all of Alaska!* He hastily finished his bath, thinking over the past week as he did so. Could he have been fooled? Jerry took forever in the head—that would fit. There had been that incident: Jerry had been taking so long using the head that Sven had gotten tired of waiting, so he had peed off the side of the boat. He had heard a noise behind him. But when he had turned around, Jerry was nowhere to be seen.

But what about that hair? Surely a girl wouldn't wear her hair like that. And what about a figure? Most women didn't have exaggerated hourglass figures like Laura, but still…thinking back, Jerry didn't seem to have much of a shape. Of course, as he (she?) said, 'I can't help the way my body is.' Then too, Jerry always wore such baggy clothes—who could tell?

All things considered, the notion that Jerry was actually female was as good as any other idea that Sven could come up with. Of course, it made Sven feel like a fool and he didn't like that one damn bit.

After Sven finished dressing and repacking the backpack, he paused in the doorway. Jerry was still sitting on the rock, head in hands. How to find out his/her real identity? And how to find out his/her underlying motive? Unless there was a convincing, benign reason for all of this, Sven wasn't going to stand for it. He used to be easygoing, but over the years, Mindy's attacks had worn down his tolerance.

He came up behind Jerry and squatted down on the rock. "What's your *real* name?"

"Gerri is my real name." She spoke barely above a whisper.

Sven glared at the back of her head. How could he have thought that was a male's voice? It was rich and melodious—and very female. He had been so distracted by Jerry's age that he assumed his voice hadn't finished changing. He shook his head in self-disgust. "What's the name on your driver's license?"

"Geraldine. But please don't call me that. I hate that name."

Sven quirked a smile at that, but it was humorless and short lived. "Let's start walking back to the boat. We've wasted enough time." He followed Gerri silently for a few minutes, feeling foolish as he pondered her masquerade. Finally, he couldn't stand the silence.

"Why? No, what made you decide to do this? Did you really think you could get away with it forever?"

"I don't know. It seemed like a good idea when we talked about it."

"We? Who is 'we'?"

"My roommate Mindy and I. She thought it would be funny to…" She stopped. She wasn't going to blame it on someone else.

Sven directed a disgusted look at the back of her head. He'd heard all that he needed to hear. Mindy was trying to make a fool of him again. She would doubtless be relating this story for months. He wanted to think about how to handle this before he spoke any more. "We'll talk about it back when we're back on the boat."

Sven didn't speak until he had maneuvered the Glacier Gal back out into the open ocean. By that time, he had decided that Jerry (Gerri, he reminded himself) probably wasn't aware of Mindy's obsession. Not that that made any difference: he still didn't like being duped, and Gerri was still guilty of that. But he wouldn't mention Mindy to Gerri. They could sort that out for themselves.

"I don't feel comfortable about having a woman on my boat," he finally said. "And, more importantly, I don't like being duped. Working with someone on a fishing boat makes for tight quarters, and I don't want someone that I can't trust completely. So here's what I'm going to do. I'm going to stop in Pelican and let you off. You can take a flight into Juneau from there and do whatever you want. Maybe you'll find another fisherman to take you on. I don't really care."

He glanced at her. She looked stricken. Unconsciously, he softened his words. "You were a good deckhand, but I just can't abide this."

"I don't have the money for an airplane ticket. I sent it all to my parents."

Damn! I refuse to accept a guilt trip. "I'll buy you a ticket to Juneau. Now, go pack up your stuff."

The little fishing town of Pelican was in sight by the time Gerri returned to the pilot house. "I left my fishing gear in the cabin. I don't want it anymore."

How could she make him feel as though he was in the wrong? "You aren't going to try to find another boat?"

Gerri didn't answer immediately. Even if she could find another fishing job, it wouldn't feel the same. Sven was larger than life to her, and she couldn't stand that she had disappointed him so. "No, I guess I'll try to scrounge enough money in Juneau to buy an airline ticket to Seattle. From there, I already have a ticket back to South Carolina." She wouldn't mention that it was a bus ticket—that would seem too much like a play for pity.

Finally, the moment came. Sven handed Gerri a ticket as the small Grumman Goose taxied up to the float. She hoisted her bag on her shoulder. "Thank you for the experience. I appreciate it. I'm sorry that I disappointed you."

Sven eased the Glacier Gal out of Pelican's harbor. He had a bad taste in his mouth. He almost wished that Gerri had gotten angry. Sven was a sucker for a woman's sorrow. Laura had never realized that. When they had argued—and it was frequently towards the end—she would immediately get angry. Her anger met his anger and brought out the worst in both of them.

He had to remind himself that he was the wronged party as the Glacier Gal steamed back out to the fishing grounds. But it wasn't satisfying. He'd only known her for a week, but the boat seemed empty without Gerri.

CHAPTER 10

Sven fished alone for the next week. No big deal—he'd done that numerous times when he was 'in between' deckhands. When the fish weren't biting, he didn't really need anybody. When they were biting, he needed the help. He had 10 lines and numerous hooks spaced out on each. They were controlled from two wells (small cockpit-like work areas), one for the lines on the port pole and one for those on the starboard pole. The wells were on opposite sides of the boat so, even with the power gurneys to bring the lines to the surface, he couldn't grab the fish off quickly enough to keep all of the lines in the water. But he worked steadily and kept long hours to make up for it.

Solitude had never been a problem. Sven had always been comfortable in his own skin. He could use his short wave radio when he had the urge to chat or to share fishing tips with other fishermen.

On this trip though, he found satisfaction to be elusive. His thoughts kept sliding back to Gerri. Had he been too hard on her? Was she really a co-conspirator to Mindy, or was she just a handy tool for Mindy's revenge? Was she going to be able to make enough money in Juneau to pay for her trip south?

He tried to tell himself that it wasn't his problem, but that fell flat. She was young and, from what she had said, was on her first long journey. There were a lot of things which could happen to a young woman travelling alone. And, though Sven didn't claim to be knowledgeable about racial issues, he was pretty sure that it would be even more dangerous for a Negro woman.

Oops, make that a black woman. He smiled as he remembered one of their many conversations during the week she was aboard. He had used the word 'Negro,' and she had—ever so gently—corrected him. Her ensuing explanation of the current preference for the term 'Black' was convincing—it wasn't meant to be hostile, she had said, but rather served two purposes. First, it was empowering to choose your own label, and, second, it represented pride in one's skin color—previously treated as an object of shame. He missed those conversations now.

Her work habits were excellent. And even when she didn't know something, she was eager to learn and she caught on quickly. With Mike...well forget him. Even without his drinking problem, Mike hadn't been a good deckhand.

It was therefore not surprising that Sven didn't stay out on the ocean on this trip. He found himself working his way back through the Inside Passage toward Juneau. As long as he was in the area, he told himself, he would sell his current catch in Juneau and, maybe, while he was in town, he would discretely reassure himself that Gerri had made it onto the plane all right.

After he had sold his fish, he tied up in his slip at the boat harbor. Surprisingly, Wally was there to meet him. Sven cocked his head in puzzlement. "Why aren't you out fishing?"

Wally scowled. "Engine's acting up. I'm waiting for parts."

"Sorry to hear that. How long?"

"Northern Marine ordered them from Seattle. They're supposed to be coming by air in the next few days."

Sven shook his head in sympathy. Days stuck in the harbor were days when you weren't making any money. And that was trouble—after all, you had only a few months of fishing to make enough to live on for a year.

Wally, though, had other things on his mind. "Where's that new deckhand of yours?"

"He turned out to be a she. I... I decided to let her go. I dropped her off in Pelican and she flew back here. I think she decided to go back South."

Wally snickered. "I knew there was something wrong about that kid."

Sven eyed him skeptically. "You mean you knew she was a female?"

Wally hesitated. He would love to claim omniscience, but... "Well, no."

"So what was wrong?" This was a little late, but Sven wanted to call him on his earlier behavior. "Maybe the dark skin was the problem?"

Wally retorted indignantly, "I ain't prejudice'. Some of my best..."

"Just shut up, Wally." Sven was tired of this. Wally was many things—fiercely loyal to his friends, a procrastinator on his boat's maintenance, and yes, a gold star, cranky curmudgeon. Was he a racist? Sven didn't know. He had a feeling that that was—for anyone, not just for Wally—a complicated question, not one that had an easy answer. He remembered one time in high school—before Laura—when he had briefly dated a Native girl. Several classmates that he had thought were friends of both of them suddenly shunned the couple. And their parents? Neither set was happy. In fact, Ellen's parents had sent her to Sitka to live. No, he couldn't analyze Wally, and he really didn't want to. But his behavior...

"Wally, I don't know what you are or aren't. But you know you were out of line when you met Gerri. You were purely rude. I don't know if you or I will ever see her again, but I better not hear about your being that rude again. You're better than that."

Wally couldn't meet his eyes. "Yeah, I guess I was a little rough on her." Then a sly smile played around the corners of his mouth. "Mike said that there was a new waitress at the Arctic Saloon—a little colored gal."

Sven frowned at him. *Who else could it be? It's not like there were a whole lot of black women in town.* He swallowed his impulse to correct Wally's inappropriate label for her. "That dive? Are you sure?"

"Mike's sure there often enough; I guess he would know. Could be this Gerri person." Wally grinned, relishing the chance to get Sven back for his earlier rebuke. "He said she had a cute little figure. One of the guys with him asked her if she wanted to make a little extra money on the side."

Almost before Wally could blink, Sven was in his face, glaring. Wally hastily raised his hands, palms out. "Whoa, buddy. Relax. I'm just telling you what he told me. Anyway, the way he tells it, she told the guy to get lost. And he had the sense not to push it."

Sven blinked and stepped back. He couldn't quite believe the force of his reaction. But Gerri didn't deserve that kind of treatment. And Sven knew that he bore part of the blame. He had left her in a financially vulnerable position. "Sorry, Wally. I…" He just shook his head. He couldn't explain his reaction to Wally if he didn't completely understand it himself.

"Sure, man. No problem." Wally was shaken. This was an unpleasant reminder of Sven's speed and power. The old catch phrase 'Toonder and Lightning' that had been popularly applied to Sven during those heady days years ago flitted through his mind. Wally didn't want any part of that—he had definitely pushed Sven too far. But how was he to know that Sven would be so defensive about her? "I didn't mean to upset you. I shouldn't have said anything."

"Yes, you should have. I want to know. I just wasn't prepared." Sven took a deep, calming breath. "She's just a kid, Wally. Granted, she misled me, but she doesn't deserve that kind of crap—from anybody."

Sven seemed to have calmed himself, so Wally dared to venture his opinion. "You know what the trouble with you is? You're stuck back in the fifties. Women nowadays think they're equal to men—so why should you talk to them all special?"

Sven looked disgusted, but at least Wally had returned to his 'normal' crankiness. "Basic politeness, Wally. That works for both men and women."

———

Sven spent the better part of the afternoon running errands and getting supplies for his next fishing trip. Thoughts of Gerri danced around in the back of his mind as he did so—her situation and his responsibility for it. Of course, he wasn't giving Mindy a free pass—after all, Mindy had probably maneuvered Gerri into her charade.

By the time he got to Rosie's—he had saved the best errand for last—he had more or less convinced himself that he should drop by the Arctic Saloon. Just to see how Gerri—assuming that she was the one that Mike had been talking about—was doing. Maybe see if she needed a loan. He knew that place well from his drinking days and he had no fond memories of it. But just to drop by—he could do that.

He wondered then whether his strategy of ignoring Mindy's hostility was wise in this situation. Should he explain his side of things to Gerri when he saw her? Bad idea. If he told her the whole story, Gerri would end up even more sympathetic to Mindy. No, he wouldn't bring up that can of worms.

As he came out of Taku Books, he stopped in his tracks and cursed his bad fortune. Mindy was walking down the street again. He seemed to have terrible luck meeting her here. He braced himself and waited. She was going to crow about Gerri's tricking her way onto his boat. *Might as well get it over with...*

To his astonishment, she said nothing. She looked surprised to see him standing there watching her, but she walked by with her customary dismissive expression. *What the hell does that mean? She's missing a chance to gloat? Not likely...*

As Sven walked up to the Arctic Saloon, he realized that he was hungry. He had made some discrete inquiries and found that Gerri's shift was over in about thirty minutes. That gave him just about enough time to eat while he waited for her to be done. He preferred both the food and the ambience of the Kash Café, but eating might help take his mind off worrying about what to say to her.

He eased into the bar. A glance told him that 'his' table in the corner was vacant. He didn't see Gerri—or any other black woman—so he sat down. He saw one of the waitresses give him a scornful expression. Samantha something-or-other. She was a friend of Mindy's, so he expected nothing else. Samantha spoke a few words to Marie, another waitress, who then shot him a worried look and started toward him. Marie was OK; she had always treated him cordially.

"Hi, Sven. I haven't seen you in here for a long time. What can I get you?"

Her subtext was clear—she had once congratulated him on the street after he had quit drinking. "Hey, Marie. Don't worry; I'm still on the wagon. Bring me a coke and a cheeseburger, please."

She smiled in relief. "Glad to hear that, Sven. I know I'm supposed to want more business, but… Coming right up."

As she left, he saw Gerri come out of the kitchen with a full tray. She wasn't looking in his direction, so he could study her at his leisure. They were right—she did have a cute little figure. She wore the standard Arctic Saloon uniform—an A-line, black dress that buttoned up the front. It was probably borrowed, as it seemed a little tight on her. It was a far cry from the baggy clothes that she had worn aboard the Glacier Gal. *Still, wouldn't I have seen some outline?*

Her hair looked the same, yet different. She was still wearing the Afro hairdo, but it looked more symmetrical and it was shinier. He had to smile at how much she had changed its look while not really making any major revisions.

Or was it his flawed perception? From the time he first realized his interest in art, and especially after Laura's death, he had devoured a variety of books on various aspects of art, vision, and perception. What he was reminded of now were the optical illusions. In particular, he remembered a picture of a goblet—which, when you looked at it a different way, became a picture of two faces. Knowing that Gerri was a woman let him see her differently. In fact, he found it hard to imagine now how he had failed to see her gender before.

Sven also studied Gerri, the person. He couldn't help but notice that she didn't seem happy. *Or is that my conscience?* She definitely looked tired. She was attracting plenty of attention from some of the male clients, which brought an unconscious scowl to Sven's face. She looked young and innocent—definitely too good for this place.

He pondered how to approach her. He now realized that—however bizarre a coincidence that would be—Mindy had no idea that he was the man that Gerri had deceived. That just increased his guilt feelings. Would Gerri be angry? All he wanted to do was check and see if she was all right and if he could help her if she wasn't.

His burger and coke arrived—with some unrequested French fries. At his questioning look, Marie smiled. "The fries are on the house. Don't tell Samantha; she wouldn't approve."

He smiled in thanks. The fries were appreciated and would be paid for—in Marie's tip instead of in his bill. He placed the money for the meal on the table and settled back to relax and eat while he waited.

But the relaxation proved impossible. He saw Gerri carry drinks to two men at a table. In spite of the relatively early hour, they had clearly been drinking for a while. Her approach to them was skittish and she attempted to keep her distance, but she wasn't far enough away. One of the men laughed and reached out to grab her leg. She wriggled free and said something sharply, which made them laugh all the more. She moved away, her back stiff with indignation.

Sven wanted to pound them into the floor, but he didn't want to embarrass Gerri. He strained to listen to their conversation. He could hear only bits and pieces, but it was more than enough. "Nigger gals have an easy attitude about sex….talk to her outside after she gets off… happen whether she likes it or not…"

Sven couldn't hear the rest. He took a deep, calming breath, pasted an insincere smile on his face and walked over to their table to have an admonitory word with them.

CHAPTER 11

One more night, Gerri reminded herself. *Just one more night.*

It wasn't that she wasn't grateful to have this job. She had been in a bad spot when she had gotten back in town. She didn't have enough money for airfare to Seattle. She hadn't had the nerve—gall might be a better word—to ask Sven for a loan. Why should he trust her? He felt betrayed by her already. But Mindy had again proved herself to be a true friend. She had made some phone calls to help Gerri find a temporary job, and she had finally gotten lucky when she contacted her friend, Samantha. One of Samantha's fellow waitresses at the Arctic Saloon had to leave for a few days because of a death in the family. They were glad to have Gerri fill in while she was gone.

It wasn't that the job was hard. Physically, it was easier than cropping tobacco or commercial fishing. Mentally, there was nothing to it. All she had to do, as Rudy, the bartender and manager put it, was to "remember the orders, don't drop any drinks, and don't piss off the customers."

The customers were a widely varied lot. Some of them were quite friendly, engaging in easy banter that she wouldn't have expected from white people back home. Some viewed Gerri, as Samantha warned her that they would, as the 'flavor of the month' and made predictable passes. Some of those had at least a veneer of good manners; others were downright crude.

Samantha's co-worker, Marie, warned Gerri that Rudy was virtually useless as protection. He said that he had a 'live and let live' attitude, but it was evident that he was mostly motivated by the money that the customers spent. Samantha had the pugnacious personality of her friend Mindy and would deflect such passes or scold the perpetrators. Marie, on the other hand, confessed to feeling very uncomfortable when faced with this behavior, and Gerri felt the same way.

As she worked, Gerri idly marveled (this job certainly left her with mental capacity to spare) that she felt such a kinship with Mindy, given their different personalities. Given more time together, perhaps Mindy would bring out Gerri's assertive side. Gerri flattered herself that she had already influenced Mindy, if only slightly, in the direction of political compromise.

In fact, in her short time in Juneau, she had met two people that she would be proud to call friends. Sven was the other one, but, of course, Gerri had spoiled that nascent friendship with her deception. Could she have done it differently? Would he have hired her knowing that she was female? She strongly doubted that. Even if he wasn't a male chauvinist pig, to use the phrase that Mindy threw around so casually, her lack of experience would have been a strike against her.

Then her eyes widened and she snapped out of her daydream. Sven, of all people, was walking into the Arctic Saloon. She was out of his line of sight, thank goodness, since she wasn't sure that she wanted to face him. Would he make a scene? Was his resentment still eating at him? She fled to the kitchen with a tray full of dirty dishes. Come to think of it, why was he even here? The food wasn't that good. Most of the customers came to drink, and she thought that Sven didn't drink. Hadn't he asked her about drinking before he had hired her?

Apparently, he attracted the notice of Marie and Samantha as well. They exchanged remarks (which Gerri strained unsuccessfully to overhear) and Marie, whose section he sat in, went to serve him. When she came back, she looked relieved. Gerri made sure to be within earshot, and heard Marie say with some satisfaction, "He ordered a coke and a cheeseburger."

Gerri continued to watch Sven out of the corner of her eye. She was just wondering whether she should at least say hello, when Rudy handed her two drinks for the customers at table number 7. Gerri groaned silently behind a carefully impassive face. Those two were among the nastiest men she had encountered since she had started here. They not only subjected her to crude sexual innuendos, but one of them—Ferret-face, she called him privately—saw fit to add racial slurs. She had made her anger clear, but it didn't seem to have any effect. She gritted her teeth. If they hassled her this time, she would go to Rudy and complain anyway. She'd refuse to serve them anymore. What she'd like to do was throw their drinks in their faces. If she did that, Rudy would probably dock her pay and charge her for the glasses. She reminded herself again: *just one more night!*

When she gave them their drinks, she stood as far away as possible. However, they had placed the empty glasses so that she had to reach over the table for them. Sure enough, Ferret-face grabbed at her leg as she did so. If she hadn't had quick reflexes, he would have had his hand up between her legs instead of just brushing her thigh. She wriggled quickly out of reach and slapped his hand. "Watch your manners, buster," she snapped.

As she stalked back to the bar, she noticed Rudy watching. He looked blissfully unconcerned. *No help there.* She had one more idea. She would wait for Samantha to come back to the kitchen. Maybe she could trade tables with her.

As she waited, she saw something that horrified her. Sven was walking over to Ferret-face's table. And he was smiling at them. Could they be friends of his? Logically, it shouldn't make any difference to her. But in reality, that would be so disillusioning. She liked Sven. It would be horrible to think that he could have friends like this. Wally was no prince, but he was nowhere near as awful as these two.

It quickly became clear, however, that it wasn't a friendly conversation. Sven's smile was a cold one, and Ferret-face's answering expression was downright ugly. After a minute of angry talk, Ferret-face pointed toward the back door. Samantha and Marie had regaled Gerri with stories that made her shudder about what had happened outside that door. It led to an alley that had, on several occasions, provided a secluded venue for some vicious brawls. Sven, to Gerri's relief, gestured arms up and palms out and shook his head. Ferret-face replied loudly and abusively. Whatever he said was too much for Sven; he turned stony faced and nodded. The two men at the table got up and all three walked out. Gerri glanced around, but no one seemed to notice. Then she saw something which horrified her even more. As the men filed through the doorway, Ferret-face—out of Sven's sight—grinned at his companion and displayed a long, wicked looking hunting knife which he had sheaved at his belt.

Heart pounding, she raced over to Rudy at the bar. Surely, he would have to do something. Call the police at least. But could they get there in time? Sven could be killed.

"Rudy! Those men are going to fight. And one of them has a knife. Call the police."

But Rudy just shrugged and dismissed her. "Don't worry. A little bit of 'Toonder and Lightning' will take care of everything. This isn't the first time there's been a brawl in the alley."

Now she seriously wondered about Rudy's sanity. *Has he been sampling his own product?* She didn't have time to psychoanalyze him now. She couldn't leave Sven to his fate. But if she walked out there alone and unprotected, then Ferret-face would come after her next.

Gerri looked around frantically for a weapon. The chairs were unwieldy. Worthless. *A bottle...*she swiftly stepped behind the bar. *Something heavy—a full bottle.*

"Hey!" Rudy barked angrily. "What the hell?"

Gerri didn't have time to reason with this fool. "I'll bring it back or I'll pay for it." *Somehow.*

Gerri followed the men with the bottle clutched by its neck. The door led to a short passage, with a storage room on one side and the door to the alley straight ahead. Rudy kept the door to the storeroom locked, but, as she hurried by, she checked it just in case. *Yup; it was locked.* She pushed on the door to the alley. It was stuck closed. She whined in frustration as she hit it with her shoulder. *He could be bleeding by now.*

She stepped back and charged at the door again. Just as she hit it, it flew open. Gerri's momentum carried her right into Sven, who was standing on the other side. He grabbed her instinctively. His awkward, but reassuring, embrace flooded her with relief.

"Are you all right? I was afraid…" Gerri peeked around him as she spoke. One man lay on the ground clutching his ribs and she heard the sound of retching from behind the trash cans.

Sven was reluctant to let her go. "I'm fine. Just a little disagreement. What are you doing out here?"

She couldn't speak at first and her heart was pounding. She took a deep breath to regain control. She glanced again at the men in the alley. "I hate violence," she muttered.

Sven laughed and held her at arm's length. He gestured to the bottle in her hand. "So. You brought that out to offer us a toast?"

That reminded her again of the knife. She ran her free hand up Sven's arm, unconsciously checking for a wound. "One of them had a knife. I thought that he might…" Belatedly, she realized what she was doing and stepped back. His arm felt like iron—and altogether too distracting.

Sven was nonplussed. He had been trying to do the right thing, but the feeling of Gerri in his arms was unexpectedly exhilarating. An errant thought floated up: *if I say something else to scare her, will she come back into my arms?* He forced it away. *Grow up, Sven!* "I'm fine," he repeated. "After he was down, I threw the knife up onto the roof. Somebody could get hurt, after all."

"No kidding," she responded weakly.

Sven got a grip on himself. "I'd like to talk to you when you get off work. May I wait?"

She stared at him blankly. "Sure," she finally said.

She spent the last twenty minutes of her shift, distractedly, with half of her mind wondering about Sven. Surely, he wasn't still angry? *No, he couldn't be. After all, wasn't he defending her virtue, as it were?* At least she assumed he had been. It would have been an amazing coincidence if the fight were over something unrelated.

Defending her virtue… She'd never had a man do that. Of course it was infinitely preferable to avoid situations where one's virtue was under attack. *But still…* It was a warm feeling.

Sven went back in to finish his food. His mind was roiling with thoughts of Gerri. He really owed her. She had spunk. She had been willing to defend him even though he had fired her. And she didn't look as if she knew the first thing about fighting. Laura would have simply watched. Hell, Laura would have brought popcorn.

And the feeling of Gerri in his arms was another thing to stew over. He felt blindsided by that. He had sworn off women after Laura's death, but his body apparently had ideas of its own. His thoughts flew back to their initial meeting when he touched her cheek while accusing her of not having shaved. In retrospect, his body hadn't been fooled then either—only his brain.

Still, he wasn't pleased with himself. It felt as though he had regressed back to his drinking days after Laura's death. Then, he had been goaded into more than one fight in that alley. Could he have handled this differently? He didn't see how. Their threat to accost Gerri while she was walking back to Mindy's... She'd be traveling on some badly lit streets; deserted at this time of night.

Mindy's! Oh, shit. Mindy would surely hear about this from Samantha. And she would definitely use this as an excuse to spread the word that he was still a no-account brawler.

The irony of it all was that Sven hated violence, too, and that was what had started his and Laura's downward slide.

———

Gerri slid into the passenger's seat of Sven's truck. He noticed that she was shivering. "Are you OK? Do you want me to turn the heat on?" It was not that cold—for Juneau—and she had on a light jacket.

"No. I guess it's just nerves. Rudy acted like nothing had happened, but..."

"That's his way. He'll probably check on them later, but if they're gone, he figures that it's not his problem." He chose not to mention that he had firsthand, previous knowledge of Rudy's habits. "Gerri, I'm sorry if I scared you. Believe it or not, I don't like violence either, but they didn't give me much choice."

Gerri took a deep breath. "Thank you for coming to my defense. They were the two nastiest people that I encountered all week."

Sven smiled at the memory. "Thank *you* for coming to *my* defense. I've never had *that* happen before."

"Well… It didn't seem fair. I couldn't just ignore it… It wasn't right." *What would I have done if Sven had been the one on the ground?* She shivered anew. "Can we not talk about it?"

Sven was more than happy to change the subject. "Actually, I came to the saloon looking for you." He paused, not knowing how to begin.

"How did you know where to find me?"

"Small town. Rumors get around." He shifted in his seat and put the truck into gear. Mindy's place was about three minutes away, and he didn't want to park out in front of it while talking to Gerri. If Mindy looked out her window, she would recognize his truck and have way too much to tell Gerri. "Do you have a few minutes, or is your room-mate looking for you?"

"I have time. Mindy's out of town."

He started to protest that, but didn't want to admit to having seen her. "Oh," he finally said.

"I think she is. She was leaving on the ferry tonight. She works for the Alaska Department of Health and she has to visit the small towns."

"Ah." That was for the best.

Sven pulled over onto a unpaved road—barely more than a track. She could see remnants of some strange equipment. Then he went around a bend and parked facing a beautiful view of nighttime Juneau across the harbor.

"What is this place?"

"They call it the rock dump. There used to be a gigantic gold mine in the mountains behind Juneau, and this is where they dumped the tailings—the rock that they dug out. It's just a place where we won't be bothered. And where there's a nice view of the city." He cut the engine and turned in his seat. "Gerri, I overreacted last week. I came to the saloon to see if you were all right. And also to apologize."

"That's all right. I can understand why you were upset. There were times when you behaved in ways that I know you wouldn't have if you had known that I was a woman." The 'peeping Thomasina' memories caused an invisible flush in her cheeks.

"Still, I overreacted." He searched for a way to change the subject. "Tell me how you came to be looking for a fishing job anyway?"

Gerri was happy to take her mind off of this evening. She found herself telling Sven all about her adventure, and how she sought to extend it after it was cut short by Rich's deployment. She even told him about how it started, with Thurman and his disparaging remarks. After all, she reminded herself, she'd never see Sven again after she left Alaska.

After she fell silent, he tapped rhythmically on his steering wheel for a few seconds. "That's pretty impressive. You have a lot of courage."

"Thank you," she said softly.

He was struck by her voice—her *real* voice. It was a beautiful voice. He almost asked how she had disguised it, but didn't want to return to that subject. He thought again about her story. "That ex-boyfriend of yours was a real idiot."

She flushed with pleasure. "Thank you."

"Do you have enough money now to get back home?"

Gerri sighed. She'd worked out this arithmetic more times than she liked. "Just about. I think so—maybe if I don't eat much on the bus."

"The bus! You're going to cross the country by bus?"

"That's how I got to Seattle. It's cheaper. And anyway, I already have the ticket. I know it'll be long…" She trailed off. She didn't want Sven to replace his 'pretty impressive' verdict with an 'are you crazy?' one.

Suddenly, Sven knew what he wanted. Perhaps he'd wanted it ever since he had seen her in the saloon and simply refused to admit it to himself. But now it made eminent sense. "Why don't you stay for a few more weeks? Come back on the Glacier Gal. You'll make more than enough to fly back home."

"You'd accept me back? After all this?"

"Yes. I told you that I made a mistake. You're a good worker…and good company."

Gerri's breath caught. This was a chance to redeem herself—to show Sven that she was worthy of his confidence. And a chance to complete her adventure. But to make a promise…she didn't want to disappoint him again.

Sven took her thoughtful silence as indecision. "I'll give you a better title," he smiled, "You can be First Mate."

Gerri stared at him in wonderment. *Wouldn't that be something to brag about.*

Sven saw her shock. *Could she have thought...the last thing Gerri needs is some more innuendos from a male!* "I mean," he said hastily, blushing furiously, "That's a nautical term. It means the second in command of a vessel."

Even in the dim light from the dashboard, Gerri could see the color in his face. For some reason, she found his embarrassment endearing. "I'm honored, sir. And I accept." With that she grinned and snapped off a salute.

"It's a deal. But you have to promise not to salute. Especially around Wally."

Her excitement sparked a playfulness that Gerri scarcely knew she had. "I promise never to do that..." She watched him nod, and then grinned. "Unless I want to annoy you."

Sven sat in his truck and watched until Gerri was in the building with the door latched behind her. Then he drove slowly back to the boat harbor. He had much to think about.

He had apparently appointed himself to be Gerri's protector. He hadn't told her about the overheard conversation suggesting that the two drunks had planned to accost her after work. He didn't want to upset her. Anyway, they would have their hands full tonight with the basics—like walking and keeping food down. Tomorrow, they would sober up and realize what a rotten idea the whole thing had been.

How would Gerri feel about his protectiveness? Sven didn't pretend to have a handle on the women's lib thing, but he was pretty sure that that subject should be broached much later, if ever.

Did he have any regrets? No, not at all. Gerri had a very appealing combination of courage, spunk, and sweet innocence that Sven found irresistible. Yes, he would watch over her and help her have the best adventure possible.

CHAPTER 12

Gerri eased her way cautiously down the ramp to the floats of the boat harbor. She was carrying a full shopping bag in each hand, and she was wearing a backpack that contained her personal effects. It was low tide and the ramp was steep this morning. When she reached the bottom, she couldn't resist turning around to look back up. For some reason, that ramp tickled her fancy. A reminder of the 'otherness' of Juneau, perhaps.

When she resumed her walk, she almost bumped into Wally. "Good morning, Wally," she said, hoping for a friendly response this time.

He muttered a greeting, and cocked his head. "Are you back on the Glacier Gal?"

She nodded and grinned.

"Hmmph," he said in mild surprise, and walked on.

She pondered that as she approached Sven's boat. *Was that a friendly response? A little*, she hoped.

She could see Sven now, making things shipshape on the Glacier Gal. He was carrying two of those lead sinkers, seemingly without effort. Seeing his strength reminded her again of last night. *My knight in shining armor.* She didn't approve of the violence. And she accepted Sven's word that he didn't either. But the evident ruthless efficiency he showed in dispatching the two men made her wonder.

That hadn't, however, stopped her from dreaming about Sven when she finally fell asleep. She remembered bits and pieces—most of it embarrassing. She had been in his arms on the Glacier Gal, and was explaining to him that she was on birth control pills even though she was a virgin. That was one dream that she would never tell anybody about, ever!

He looked up and saw her. He gave a little wave and grinned, and she felt an involuntary flutter in her chest. He hopped over the gunwale of the boat and started toward her with hands extended to take her shopping bags.

When he caught sight of Gerri, Sven couldn't suppress an irrational feeling of relief and excitement. He had spent much of the night imagining reasons why she might change her mind. When their eyes met, she flashed him a brilliant smile and his jaw almost dropped. *That* was a smile that she hadn't shared even once during their first trip. It was the kind of winsome smile that made a guy want to grin foolishly in response. And dimples! It was almost unfair. He wondered if she knew its impact. *If I had seen that smile, I would have known right away...*

Sven also noticed that the baggy sweats that she had previously worn on the boat were gone. In their place, she wore a sweater and jeans. *Yes, definitely a cute little figure...*

He found his tongue. "Welcome back, sailor." *Am I grinning like an idiot or what?* Suddenly self-conscious, he stepped back onto the boat with her shopping bags and asked over his shoulder, "Do you want me to put these on your bunk?"

"Uh, no." This was the part that Gerri was uncertain about. Would Sven still be touchy about the cooking? "That goes in the kitch... uh, galley. It's food—some fresh produce, actually."

He put the sacks on the table and turned to look at her.

Is he angry? Or just puzzled? She took a breath. "I was hoping...I thought that if I'm the First Mate, I should take on some new duties— like cooking." She looked at him hopefully.

Sven's eyes opened wide. He'd never thought of this perk when he offered her the job back. "You can cook?" *That was dumb! Of course she can.*

"Yes I can." Gerri gave him a sly smile. "You see, in my family, the females did all of the cooking."

Sven stared. Then he chuckled. Then he laughed out loud, which started Gerri laughing as well. Finally, they fell silent and stared at each other, smiling. Sven shook his head. "You must have been ticked off when I said that."

"Not at you. I felt trapped, and I knew it was my own darn fault."

"Well, I'm delighted. You've got yourself a new duty. Wait. Can you cook on an oil stove?"

"You name it; we've had it on the farm. I've even cooked on a wood stove."

Sven made a bowing gesture. "Goddess of the galley. And I'll help with the cleanup."

Almost before she knew it, they were underway. Sven had evidently been waiting for her. "OK, let's go," he had said after he had started the engine and studied the dials for a few seconds. That, and a nod toward the mooring lines, had been all the direction that she needed. She was proud of that. She cast off the lines quickly and he eased out of the slip. After they were out of the boat harbor, he brought the Glacier Gal up to cruising speed, and Gerri eagerly took in the vista off the port side— the city of Juneau, nestled tidily between the ocean and the mountains.

Suddenly, she realized what she was missing. She raced down to her bunk and got her Instamatic. Her family would never believe how beautiful this town was without pictures to prove it. Gerri wouldn't have believed it herself, if she hadn't seen it. She hadn't used the camera on their first trip out—there was too much to learn and she was concentrating too much on playing her 'male' role. Making up for lost time, she snapped several pictures.

She glanced at Sven as she returned the camera. He was smiling, but he seemed distracted and thoughtful. *I hope he isn't having second thoughts about this.* As she climbed the ladder back up to the pilot house, she tried to think of what she might say to reassure him, but she came up blank.

Gerri's joy was contagious. Her happiness made Sven happy. It was such a simple thing, but precious. He couldn't remember the last time this had happened to him. Maybe during the early months with Laura? Possibly, but not the same.

He wanted to keep this mood alive, but there was an issue festering in the back of his mind. And he wanted to get that issue out of the way even more. When Gerri came back to the pilot house, he asked, "Did you see Wally on your way to the boat?"

He already knew the answer. Unless Wally had learned how to fly, she had to have passed him on her way down the float.

"Yes, I did."

"Was he…" Sven hadn't quite worked out how to phrase this. "Was he polite?"

She considered her answer. "Sort of. I'd say yes; at least he was much nicer than he was the last time."

"Good." Sven exhaled the breath that he'd been holding unconsciously. "I talked to him. I think he'll come around." Gerri watched him solemnly. "I'll be honest with you. I don't know what his problem was." He shrugged. "I don't pretend to understand what makes people tick. But even on his good days, he's sort of…"

"Grumpy? Irascible? Surly?" Gerri grinned. "Just kidding." And she was kidding—sort of. A franker analysis on her part would have added 'racially prejudiced' at the front of the list. But that wasn't Sven's fault, and she didn't want to make him feel bad.

Sven laughed, relieved at her lighthearted response. "All of those, probably. But I can tell you that he's basically a good guy after you get to know him."

After they were a couple of hours out of Juneau, Gerri disappeared into the galley, where she was stowing the extra food and, to Sven's eager anticipation, beginning to prepare their first meal. He gazed idly around. The sky was covered with a high deck of clouds, but there was no rain. The clouds tended to mute the colors: the near hills were dark green, fading to blue, and ultimately to a pearly gray as they receded into the distance. The water, too, was blue gray.

He had the urge to draw, but he didn't see a likely subject. *Just as well,* he thought. Both drawing and painting were private activities for him. He wasn't ready to share them with Gerri.

His usual practice was to make pencil or charcoal sketches of whatever took his fancy while on the Glacier Gal. He rarely did any actual painting on the boat. It was too much trouble, to juggle his paints on the boat, and, in any case, he was too busy fishing. He did his painting at home, after the fishing season was over, frequently using his sketches to jog his memory.

Then, in the corner of his eye, he saw a flash of motion close to the boat. "Gerri, can you come up here?"

Gerri stepped forward from the galley and looked around. She tried to make it a test of her nautical skills to see what had caught Sven's attention, but she couldn't see anything unusual.

Sven gestured to the door on the side of the pilot house. "Go out on deck at the bow and look down at the water."

She paused to grab a light jacket—this wasn't South Carolina. Sven watched her as she worked her way to the bow and stared down. He was hyper-conscious of her form as she bent over. Was she wearing different clothes? Or was it just that the blinders had been removed from his eyes? Her jeans pulled taut as she bent.

Laura had always been proud of her hourglass figure—and justifiably so. But, Sven now realized, she never really had much of a bottom. Hips, yes, but her butt was flat. Gerri, on the other hand, had a delightfully round and firm looking bottom. Sven found himself wondering what it would be like to cup it in his hands. He was just about to feel guilty about his inappropriate thoughts, when Gerri jerked upright.

Gerri turned back to look at him with a shocked and delighted expression. Sven checked briefly—there was nothing dangerous in the Glacier Gal's path, so he engaged the automatic pilot and headed up to join her.

"What are they? They're beautiful."

"Porpoises. You see them every once in a while."

"What are they doing?"

"Just playing. I don't know whether we're part of the game or whether we're just a handy prop in a game of 'zoom the boat.'"

Gerri was silent, and they both watched. Several times a minute, a porpoise would streak by the boat, just skimming the edge of the bow wave no more than two feet away from the boat. They were impressive creatures, easily seven to eight feet long.

"Actually, I have them trained just to give you a show."

She grinned at him. "You lie."

He grinned back and nodded. "Yup."

But Sven had taken away one valuable idea. That evening, after they had anchored and eaten, in the privacy of his cabin, he set out to capture Gerri on paper. By the time he finally turned in, he had several drawings that he liked. There was one of Gerri squatting in the mud, with a paint brush in her hand and the hull of the Glacier Gal above her. Even better—one he would definitely keep for himself—was a picture of her in the pilot house, eyes wide and intent, lips pursed in concentration, as she guided the boat. His favorite, which he would not only keep, but make into an oil painting after the fishing season was over, was inspired by her encounter with the porpoises. It had her on the front deck, head thrown slightly back and laughing—sharing her joy with the viewer of the picture.

He affixed his mark, 'HSSH,' on those that he intended to keep and carefully stored them away.

Chapter 13

Several days later, Sven was awakened by the sound of singing. He lay there trying to make sense of this. He had shown her the Zenith Transoceanic radio that he kept in the pilot house. It was a multi-band radio which could easily bring in broadcast stations from the 'lower 48' states at night. At this time of day, the best one could hope for was one of the Juneau stations. He lay there listening. She had apparently taken it out onto the back deck. That was fine with him—the batteries were fresh.

The only thing that he had worried about—selfishly—when he showed her the radio was the prospect that she might choose music which he would hate. This song, however, was very pleasant, even haunting.

He glanced at his watch and made a disgusted noise. He had been up late drawing and he had overslept. He stumbled out of his cabin and splashed some water on his face before he went on deck. He didn't want to look like a total savage in front of Gerri.

Gerri was surprised that Sven hadn't been up and at it long before now. He normally had the Glacier Gal moving before dawn. On the other hand, she couldn't be too shocked at his sleeping late. He had been working late in his cabin recently. She was curious about what he was doing, but it seemed rude to ask. He was very willing—almost eager—to instruct her in anything having to do with fishing, so she assumed that it was a private relaxation time for him. He probably got sick of her by the end of the day.

This morning was unusually gorgeous. The sun was just coming up, and the water in the cove where they had anchored was like glass.

She thought she saw an eagle soaring over the edge of the tree line where the forest met the beach. It was just so lovely, and she was just so happy to be here to see it that she channeled her choir experience and just started singing. She stopped singing as she heard Sven's voice.

"Was that you? I thought it was the radio."

Gerri watched Sven stepping out of the cabin. He had obviously just awakened, but other than his sleep filled eyes, he looked fresh and alert. He also looked incredibly attractive. He had a quizzical smile, which, as usual, made her want to sigh. He wore a T-shirt which was slightly too small, emphasizing his muscular frame. She tried to avoid staring. An errant thought, quickly squashed: *if I had grown up here and he was my boyfriend I would have had a hard time keeping my promise to my mother...* She gathered her wits.

"I'm sorry. Did I wake you up?"

"No. Well, sort of, but I'm glad you did. I overslept. You have a beautiful voice." He wished now that he had stayed inside and listened. As he was about to ask her to continue, she interrupted.

She pointed to the shore. "Do we have time for me to take a walk?"

"On the beach?"

"Or in the woods. I just like to walk, and it might be fun to explore a bit."

He looked at the shoreline and then at his watch. "Sure, why not? We've been going hard for the past few days." His lips twitched in private amusement as he turned away to get the Glacier Gal's skiff down from its rack. His easy acceptance had more to do with her sweet look of entreaty than any burning desire on his part to explore the beach.

After Gerri had climbed into the skiff, he handed her the oars. "The outboard motor is too noisy for such a peaceful morning. I'll teach you how to row."

As usual, Gerri was a quick study. Everything went well until she decided that she was an expert and started to act like a speed demon. Quickly, she was on her back in the bottom of the skiff, and Sven was doused with a splash from an errant oar.

He laughed—he had seen that coming, but not in time to stop her. "Are you OK? Do you know what happened?"

"I'm OK, except for my pride. One oar kind of missed the water, so it splashed you and, because I was pulling on it so hard, the lack of resistance made me fly backwards onto my butt." She laughed shame-facedly. "How embarrassing."

"Don't worry about it—it happens. It's called catching a crab. You're doing fine, overall. Just concentrate on getting your stroke down pat, and worry about your speed later."

Sven wondered whether he should say more. He'd noticed this tendency in her before. Gerri caught on to things quickly, but she was so eager to do well that she sometimes rushed a little too much, forgetting about Murphy's Law. He decided not to belabor the point—her embarrassment would help to teach her the lesson.

She guided them to the beach with no further mishaps and they scrambled out of the skiff. Sven grabbed one side. "Get the other side and we'll carry it away from the water."

Gerri gave him a puzzled look as she complied. They were about fifty feet away from the shore when he stopped. "This should be enough."

She looked back at the water. *Why so far?* The only thing she could think of was the rising tide. *But so far?* Sven watched her puzzle it out—he was coming to enjoy seeing the wheels turn in her head.

Gerri glanced up and saw him watching her. *Uh, Oh! Now it's a challenge.* She thought about the tide. It might rise… What? Maybe a foot while they were walking. *But the beach is flat! And the angle…* She had it now. "This beach is very flat—unlike a lot of them which are steeper. So as the tide comes in the water will cover it quickly." She grinned triumphantly. "Right?"

"You got it."

She looked back at the shore. "This will be perfect for my journal," she murmured, thoughtfully.

"What journal?"

Gerri grimaced. She hadn't meant to say that out loud. "I'm keeping a journal with ideas for teaching. I want to be an extra-good teacher."

"You'll be a great teacher. I'm sure they'll love you."

Gerri didn't really want to discuss this. They had talked politics, but this was so personal. Then, too, she liked to have Sven admire her, so confessing weakness was anathema. But refusing to talk when he was so obviously interested seemed unpleasant as well.

Sven could see that Gerri was uncomfortable. "Come on. Let's walk down the beach as we talk." It might be easier to talk while walking. She could pause—or stop talking altogether—without so much self-consciousness.

"Well, it's complicated. They're starting to desegregate the schools in South Carolina. It's going to be stressful for everybody. They're closing the black high school, so if I'm able to get a job—which is by no means certain—it will be in a tense atmosphere. And I don't know how to say this diplomatically, but many of the white teachers and staff will be expecting someone like me to fail. Some of them will *want* me to fail. Any time I make a mistake in the classroom, someone will whisper about it."

"But every teacher makes mistakes. One of my favorite math teachers even did that on purpose occasionally. She said it was good for us to find a mistake in someone's reasoning."

"I think that's true. But you're talking about an atmosphere of mutual respect. I won't have that, I'm afraid."

Sven made a growling noise. "I don't know what to say. It frustrates me that I can't do anything to help."

Gerri smiled. "Nobody can. I can only hope that we get through these times. And I can only try to be as good as possible." She linked her arm through his and squeezed him to her as they walked. "But it's sweet of you to say that. I appreciate it."

This reminded Sven of the episode in the bar. He liked the feeling of Gerri brushing against him. He liked it way too much. He was at war with himself. One part of him wanted to stop and give her a *real* hug. The other part reminded him that he shouldn't be thinking that—she was a kid, and she was his employee, for crying out loud. Women's Lib—to the extent that he understood it—would consider that to be taking advantage of her. He made a note to ask her about that at some safe, later date.

As they walked along, Gerri could feel the tenseness in his arm. She didn't want him upset, but it made her feel good that he again wanted to protect her, even though he couldn't do so this time. Better to change the subject. There would be plenty of time to be depressed come autumn—and she hadn't even gotten to the part about whether she could even get a high school job. When she saw a chance to change the subject, she took it eagerly.

"What was that? I just saw a stream of water squirt up from the sand."

"That's a clam. Some people go out with shovels and dig them up."

Talk turned to their plans for the day—neither of them wanted to return to the earlier subject. And when they had finally returned to the skiff, the water's edge was no more than fifteen feet away. Gerri looked at Sven in surprise. "Wow! The tide really came in quickly. What's the fastest that it can be?"

"There are places where the Glacier Gal can't outrun it—places that look like river rapids when the tide is moving. I'll show you one before the summer is over."

"How about a glacier? Before I came to Juneau, I decided that I wanted to see a glacier as part of my adventure."

He looked at her in surprise. "There are lots of glaciers around. I'll make sure that you see one. But there's one that we can walk right up to just out the road from Juneau."

"Out the road?" That phrase didn't quite sound right.

"Yeah, about fifteen miles or so." She still looked puzzled. "You know that there's no way to drive into Juneau. The farthest you can drive from downtown is about 30 or 40 miles. The major road is Glacier Highway. So when you drive away from the city on Glacier Highway, we say that you're going 'out the road.'"

"You mean the road just ends?" No major road in South Carolina just ended. They went somewhere or they merged into another road.

Sven nodded. "That's right. There's a guardrail at the end. Beyond the guardrail is just forest—wilderness. I'll show you that, too, though it's not really much to see."

Gerri had to digest this. In many ways, Juneau seemed like a normal town. Then there would be something completely unexpected to remind her that Alaska was a very different place.

———

On the way back, Gerri rowed with concentration and care—she refused to have another rowing mishap. Once they were back aboard, Sven started up the engine and pulled the anchor immediately. Now it was time to go to work.

As they motored along, Gerri kept her eye on Sven. The way he chose where to put down the fishing lines seemed like magic—or at least mysterious. It had something to do with the tide, the current, whatever he could glean from the fathometer, and even what birds were feeding nearby. When she had asked about it, he was uncharacteristically at a loss for words. But whatever he did, it seemed to work. It was rare that they weren't busy.

Gerri had had a question rolling around in her mind since the morning. "You mentioned the radio this morning. It seems as though you haven't used it much this trip. Not the one with the radio stations, the one you talk on."

"I guess I haven't. Normally I use it to get weather forecasts or to talk to other fishermen—about where fish are biting or just to chat. Now I have you to chat with, and we're finding plenty of fish on our own." He watched her nod, but that gave him an idea and he turned the shortwave radio on. "I'll let you do the talking."

Gerri was intrigued, but... "What would I say?"

Sven gave some quick instructions and suggested that she try to get Wally to see if his engine had been fixed. "Just ask for Wally, aboard the Meanie."

Gerri took the mike. "Is that really the name of his boat?"

"That's just Wally's sense of humor. He says the boat is mean to him."

Gerri hesitated briefly. *Would Wally be hostile over the air?* She shrugged inwardly and opened the mike. "This is Gerri aboard the Glacier Gal, looking for Wally on the Meanie. Are you there, Wally? Over."

She didn't hear anything from Wally, but another boat quickly replied. "Glacier Gal, this is the Betty J. You working for Sven?"

"Yes I am. He's got me on the radio."

"Tell him to make that permanent. You sure sound nicer than he does."

Another voice cut in. "Glacier Gal, where are you? Nothing's biting for me. Maybe I'll try my luck where you are."

Sven stopped her and murmured instructions.

"Sven says to tell you that we're heading toward Pelican. He'd rather not be more specific."

"Not fair. He's a highliner. He's supposed to tell us poor mortals where they're biting."

The first voice cut back in. *Who said these fishermen didn't gossip?* "Just keep talking, Gerri. We'll each get a bearing with our RDF and find you that way."

Gerri looked to Sven. "I didn't understand any of that."

"A highliner is someone who consistently catches more fish than other people. An RDF is a radio direction finder. If two different boats get our bearing from their positions, they can draw lines on a chart from their locations. Where the lines cross is where we are. But he's just kidding."

Now, a new voice came on. "This is Ace Artin on the Smoothie. I'm an old friend of Sven's. Don't listen to them. You have such a lovely voice; I can't believe you're wasting your time on Sven's boat. Come work for me—I'll beat whatever he's paying you."

Gerri rolled her eyes. "You're very kind, but I'm happy here."

Ace responded immediately. "You say you're heading for Pelican. Are you going to be there tomorrow night?"

Sven nodded. "Yes," Gerri said.

"They're having a town dance. Come on out. I'd love to meet you, and I'll show you a few steps. You'll have fun, and it'll let you get away from that old guy for a while."

But I don't want to get away from Sven...but a dance sounds interesting... She looked at Sven for guidance, but he was staring out the window of the pilot house with a scowl worse than the one he had worn when she first met him. *Not the time to ask...* "Thank you. I don't know if I can, but I'll keep it in mind."

Sven put his hand out for the mike. But when she handed it to him, he didn't talk—he put it back in its holder and snapped the radio off. *Ace fancies himself to be such a damn smooth operator.* Sven hated the idea of him getting his hands on Gerri. *Like it's my choice...* "I can't stand the guy. He tries to be a ladies' man. He's got a nerve—he's older than I am."

"You're not that old."

Sven didn't know how to take that. Was she defending him or defending Ace. "Just so you know, he gave himself that nickname." Yes, he knew that was petty, but it had just slipped out.

"Pelican's such a little teeny town," Gerri said cautiously, "A town dance sounds interesting." Sven gave her an annoyed look.

She was puzzled by his hostility. "He said you were friends—or you used to be," she coaxed. "How long have you disliked him?"

Sven sighed. He knew he was out of line here. In fact, he was behaving like an ass. Finally, he gave up—there was no way he could climb out of this hole with his dignity intact. He turned and said with a rueful grin, "For about five minutes. Ever since he started being fresh with you." He searched her face. "Would you really like to go to that dance?"

"For a little while, maybe. If you go with me."

That brought a smile back to his face. "OK, it's a deal."

Later that night, after they had anchored and turned in, Sven found himself brooding, unable to sleep. What had caused him to be so childish when Ace had been talking to Gerri. Was he really trying to protect her? She was young and inexperienced, so that would be understandable—in some sense, Sven had taken responsibility for her.

But he feared that that explanation was an evasion. He wanted Gerri for himself. He had to control that impulse—she was adorable, yes, but barely out of college. Her adventure should not include getting seduced by her boss, especially since he had so spectacularly failed the only woman that he had ever been truly close to.

CHAPTER 14

Gerri checked her watch. She still had time. They had arrived in Pelican early in the afternoon and sold their catch at the Pelican Cold Storage quickly, so she had no excuses. She didn't want to be a stereotypical female; taking forever to get ready for the dance.

But she did want to make special preparations. She was enjoying her time on the Glacier Gal, but, though she didn't consider herself a girly girl, it was still nice to have the chance to dress up a little and to feel feminine. And especially to look feminine for Sven. *There, I've admitted it.* That was silly, of course, but harmless. Sven was her constant companion lately, and he just happened to be one of the most virile men that she had ever encountered.

Her mother—and others—would harp to her about such dangerous thoughts, but Gerri knew better. Nothing would come of it and she would be returning home in a few weeks. Besides, she felt comfortable around him. He didn't ignore the fact that she was black, but he didn't seem to find it freighted with significance. It was like her being from South Carolina—just another part of who she was. And once they got past her gender deception, she felt an easy acceptance from him. And she valued that very much.

After washing up in the head—one of the few things she disliked about the boat—she returned to her cabin. Her special preparations for the dance had two parts. The first was to change her hairdo. She had come to like her afro for everyday wear. But tonight, she wanted to look more clearly feminine. She didn't have the time or the desire to do a major overhaul, but since her hair had grown out a bit, she was able to pull it back into an afro puff.

She stared at the result in her small hand mirror. Would Sven like it? She hoped so. She thought it looked decent. It occurred to her to wonder what the other people at this dance would think of her, but as long as no one was nasty, she really didn't care.

The second part of her special preparations was a dress. For this, she could thank her mother—and she vowed to do so profusely in her next letter. Gerri—who was accustomed to being a blue jeans girl in college—had been incredulous when Olivia had insisted that she pack a dress: "You never know where Rich might take you. Why not be prepared? Besides, you like this dress—and it sheds wrinkles very well."

Of course, her mother could never have imagined this occasion, but her foresight was much appreciated. And Gerri had helped with the wrinkles by pressing the dress under her suitcase in her cabin.

Finally, she was ready. With one last look in her hand mirror, she went looking for Sven.

Sven had a bad case of nerves. He had finished cleaning up the galley—his gratefully accepted duty now that Gerri was doing the bulk of the cooking. He tried reading, but he couldn't concentrate. Drawing was out of the question for the same reason. He couldn't do any busywork out on deck because he didn't want to soil his only presentable shirt and slacks. Out of desperation, he puttered around in the pilot house, arranging things that were already arranged. It wasn't as though Gerri was late. He glanced again at his watch. She should be out in a few minutes. He decided to go out and check the moorings.

He hadn't been this nervous on a date (*it's not a date*, he unconvincingly told himself) since high school. He wasn't worried about Gerri—not exactly. And, in spite of his behavior the day before, he didn't dislike Ace. But he wouldn't trust Ace with a woman. And especially not a woman that Sven cared about. He refused to analyze precisely what 'cared about' meant, but he knew that Gerri fit firmly into that category.

What if Gerri was fascinated with Ace? What if Ace offered to show her his boat? But Gerri had wanted Sven to come with her to the dance, so maybe he was worrying too much. Easy to say…

Lost in his worries, Sven didn't hear Gerri come out on deck.

"I'm ready if you are," she said shyly. She stood still, waiting for his reply, but waiting—and hoping—more for his reaction.

Sven didn't have a reply. He didn't have any words at all. Gerri stood on the back deck, which was above the level of the float, so that it was as if she was on a pedestal. She wore a bright, summer dress with a demure, square-cut neckline. It had a profusion of bright white, yellow and green, and it ended about six inches above her knees. She looked ravishing. Sven didn't know where to look first. Her hair: she had a different style—a bun, but a curly one. It managed to look impishly cute, while simultaneously making her look young and innocent—as if Sven needed to be reminded of her youth. Her legs: he'd never actually seen them before, so they got extra attention. They were trim, curvy, and well muscled. Thanks to all of the walking that she did, Sven supposed.

In fact, her whole body was trim and curvy. Everything was in nice proportion. Laura was top heavy—that was one of her claims to fame, an attribute that she had hoped would get her to Hollywood. Gerri didn't catch your eye in a 'Wow, look at the size of those…' way. With Gerri, everything fit together perfectly. The artist in Sven itched to draw her as she was right now. The male in him had a different itch… he suppressed it ruthlessly.

His wits came back to him. *How long have I been standing and staring?* He probably didn't even want to know. "You look beautiful," he said huskily, "just beautiful."

Gerri had considered wearing a light sweater—the evening was cool, as usual. She had decided against it because she wanted Sven to see her in the dress without extras. Now she didn't need the sweater; she felt warm from the approval in his eyes. It was everything that she had allowed herself to hope for.

And Sven himself was mighty easy on the eyes. He, too, had evidently had some nice clothes stashed away. While he was studying her, she had allowed herself the same privilege. He wore a pale blue, long-sleeved dress shirt with the sleeves folded below his elbows. Both shirt and slacks fit more snugly than his usual daily garb. In fact, they almost looked tailored, though Gerri would never believe that they were. *If I stand here any longer, he'll know I'm posing.* "You look very nice yourself," she said. She glanced down. The Glacier Gal's gunwale was high enough to make a graceful disembarkation difficult in this short dress. She angled sideways, preparing to scissor over with minimum indecency.

"Wait," said Sven, approaching with his hands outstretched. "That dress is lovely, but it's not meant for climbing around a boat. May I?" Before she knew it, he put his hands on her waist and lifted her gently, but quickly, over and onto the float.

"Thank you," she said shyly. That had been completely unexpected. But she liked it. The feeling of effortless levitation was seductive and left her wanting more contact with him. As they started to walk, she indulged this by leaning into him a bit, as if she were cold. Sven took the hint (or opportunity) and put his arm around her shoulder as they walked.

The town of Pelican, she mused as they walked, was strange indeed. No, 'strange' wasn't quite right. Exotic, maybe? It was barely a town. A hamlet, maybe? A settlement? It was perched between the water and one of the typical steep mountains of Alaska. There were no streets, per se. Rather there was a boardwalk running along the shore from one end of the town to the other. Most of the buildings were connected to this boardwalk, and rose on stilts over the shore. Gerri had been told that the town actually had a car—a tiny thing called a Crosley—but she had never seen it.

At one end of this defining boardwalk was the Pelican Cold Storage, the largest building in Pelican, and the town's primary economic engine. In its heyday, Sven had told her, it processed millions of pounds of fish per season. The dance was being held in a building at the other end of the boardwalk, perhaps a half mile away.

Their walk became a sort of a promenade, with occasional greetings called out to Sven and numerous curious looks directed at her. A number of the people walking seemed to be heading to the dance. As

Sven had said earlier, it wasn't like there were many other things going on in Pelican this evening.

She tried to imagine, as she scanned the various faces, which one might turn out to be Ace Artin. She had mixed feelings about meeting him. On the one hand, she was glad to have found out from him about the dance. It was a great excuse to dress up for Sven (she could admit that in the privacy of her thoughts). On the other hand, Ace sounded like somewhat of a wolf, which didn't interest Gerri at all. It was likely moot, since Gerri would clearly be nothing like what Ace expected.

Sven saw him first. His arm unconsciously tightened around Gerri's shoulder. She glanced up at him, saw the frown, and followed his gaze. The man approaching with a wide smile was reasonably nice looking—white, of course—and a few inches shorter than Sven. Gerri had just time enough to be bemused by his hair before he reached them. *Does anyone still wear a ducktail?*

"Hi, I'm Ace. Gerri, I presume? Aren't you a pretty sight?" He pumped her hand. "Sven, old man," he added jovially, "You decided to come out tonight, too, huh?" Sven was not known for attending these events.

"Hello, Ace." Sven was polite, but Gerri could tell that his heart wasn't in it.

"I've got a friend holding a table for us. Let's go in before he gets impatient."

Once inside, they approached a table near the dance floor. A man seated there was watching them with great interest—and more than a little amusement. He was just a shade taller than Gerri and stocky. He was an American Indian (*oops, make that a Native*, thought Gerri remembering the local term). Sven grabbed an extra chair and Ace introduced them both.

"Gerri, Sven, this is Edwin John, captain of the E 'n E."

Sven nodded. "Seiner, right? I've seen it. It's a nice looking boat."

As Sven and Edwin chatted, Ace reconsidered his strategy. He had not expected Sven's presence, and wasn't sure whether his plans for Gerri were scuttled. He decided to be an optimist. "Gerri? May I get you a drink?"

She glanced at Sven. "Thank you. Nothing alcoholic—do they have pop?" She took a quiet pride in remembering the local name for soft drinks.

As Ace and Sven went to get drinks, Edwin turned to Gerri with a look of amusement. "I don't think Ace was planning on having Sven here with you. Are you and Sven a couple?"

Gerri opened her mouth and then, smiling shyly, reconsidered her words before she spoke them. "No, not really—not exactly. We've known each other for only a few weeks." Honesty bade that she say no, but it pleased her to leave a little ambiguity in her answer.

Edwin suppressed a grin. Unless he was misreading the signals, Sven was looking mighty possessive. For safety, he changed the subject. "Did you just recently move to Alaska?"

"I'm just visiting." Gerri found herself describing once again her trip and her improbable encounter with Sven, leaving out only the part where she posed as a male. That, at best, would have resulted in her being teased, and possibly Sven as well.

The two men returned with pop for all and, as they settled in, Edwin turned his attention to Sven. "Sven, Ellen says to tell you hello."

Sven looked startled. "Ellen Ward?"

"Ellen Ward John now." He paused and looked around the table for effect. Gerri was beginning to get the feeling that Edwin loved being just slightly outrageous. "I want to thank you for dating her in high school."

"Thank me? Why? She probably wishes that she had never met me." Now Gerri was listening with rapt attention.

"Nah, she doesn't hold it against you. She was pretty mad at her father for a while. But you did me a good turn. If he hadn't shipped her to Sitka to get her away from you, I wouldn't have met her," he said laughingly.

Gerri was eager to hear more details, but just then some music started playing. Ace immediately asked her to dance. Gerri didn't want to refuse, so she compromised by leaning over as she got up, squeezing Sven's forearm, and whispering: "Back soon. You're next." in Sven's ear. She would get the story about Sven and Ellen later.

She never got to hear that story. When Ace's dance had finished, Sven was right there to ask her for the next. Between the two of them, Gerri got little rest. Sven warned her that he couldn't dance any of the 'new' dances, but he did an enthusiastic and very presentable jitterbug.

On one of the slow dances, Ace—perhaps impatient with his progress with Gerri—held her in a tight, barely moving embrace. She tried to keep a little distance, but it was difficult without making a scene. After a few seconds of this, Sven appeared by their side to cut in. Ace glared at him, but gave up his place without any verbal fireworks. To her disappointment, Sven didn't try to duplicate that embrace.

When they returned to the table, Ace bent toward Gerri and spoke softly. "Sven seems to think you're his alone. Is that true? Did I get the wrong idea?"

That was the second time Gerri had been asked about her relationship with Sven, and she didn't know any better how to answer. She gave a strategic answer to let Ace down easily. "Maybe. I mean, we're still new to each other, but we're…um…exploring the situation. Please don't tell Sven I said that." *Because I'd die of embarrassment!*

Ace glanced at Sven, who was talking to Edwin. "I won't say a word. He doesn't need the encouragement." In a louder voice, he added, "If you folks will excuse me, I see someone I know. Gerri, if I don't get back, it was nice meeting you, and I had fun dancing with you."

Sven left as well, to get refills on their drinks, leaving Gerri at the table with Edwin. She fanned herself. "It's warm in here."

"You'll cool off now that you finally have a chance to rest. I think that Ace finally realized that Sven wasn't going to let you get away from him."

Gerri looked at his amused expression and gave a small shrug and a smile. "I don't know about that, but I'm enjoying myself." She decided to give Edwin some of his own teasing medicine. With an innocent smile, she asked, "Tell me about yourself. How does your wife feel about your going to a dance without her?"

If she thought that she was going to discomfit him, she was wrong. He threw his head back and laughed. "She knows why I'm here, and she's fine with it." He looked around conspiratorially and bent his head close. "I'm here on a secret mission—actually two secret missions, but she only knows about one." He paused to gauge his effect on Gerri. "I'm here as a baby sitter. We're going out tomorrow, and I don't want to have anyone on my crew hung over."

Gerri knew she was being good naturedly baited, but she couldn't resist. "That's the one she knows about?"

"Right." He paused and twirled his glass. "And, of course, I'm here to gather gossip and report back to her. She'd never forgive me if I didn't do that."

Gerri looked around. "She knows the people here?"

He shook his head and pointed at Gerri. "The gossip is about you guys. She'll be curious about how Sven is doing. He's..." His voice trailed off, as if he was sorry he had spoken. "Sven has had some tough times in his life. Ellen will be glad to hear that he has a lady friend after all of these years."

"Tough times? You mean when he dated Ellen?"

"No, No. That was nothing. What I'm talking about was later."

Gerri made encouraging motions with her hands. "Come on, tell me. The suspense is killing me."

Edwin smiled apologetically. "Sorry. What I know is third hand." He cast a look toward the concession area. Sven was heading back with drinks in his hands. "It's not really my story to tell. According to Ellen, he's a very polarizing person—some people hate him and others think that he's a great guy." He glanced toward the concession area. Sven was almost in earshot. Edwin added quickly, "Ellen is definitely in the latter group."

"So am I," Gerri added in a considerable understatement. She was already making plans to get more information. *From whom? Mindy? Wally? Or Sven himself?*

"You two look like you're plotting something."

Gerri started to reassure him, but Edwin spoke first. "If you two are ever in Hoonah—that's where we live now—Ellen will insist that both of you come for dinner."

Sven cocked his head in puzzlement. "You talked to her?"

Another chuckle from Edwin. "I don't have to talk to her. We know each other well. In fact, I knew from the moment I heard your radio conversation with Ace yesterday that she would expect me to ask."

Now Gerri wondered if she'd missed something important yesterday. "Were you on the radio? I didn't recognize your voice."

"I didn't say anything—didn't have anything *to* say. Sometimes you can learn more by listening than by talking."

Gerri smiled wryly, picturing herself huddling by the vent in the Pee Dee State college library. "That's certainly true."

After the dance, Gerri and Sven walked slowly back to the boat. Neither one wanted this evening to end. Gerri shivered a bit and Sven again put his arm around her. She allowed herself a small, secret smile of satisfaction—that was exactly what she'd hoped he would do. And she hadn't even faked the shiver. The temperature had dipped into the fifties—Gerri had learned by now that 'a warm summer evening' didn't mean the same thing to an Alaskan as it did to a South Carolinian.

Gerri was energized by what she had heard from Edwin. She had already been fascinated by Sven, but now he had an added aura of mystery—even tragedy—that she yearned to penetrate. *I can start with Ellen…*

"Tell me about you and Ellen."

Sven was startled by the question. *Was this a proprietary interest?* He dismissed that quickly—in his dreams, and illicit dreams at that. "There's nothing to tell. Edwin pretty much said it all. Her father moved her to a Native school in Sitka. I'm glad that things turned out well for her. Edwin seems like a nice guy."

"Were you unhappy?"

He looked at her. "Unhappy as in heartbroken? No. We'd only been on a couple of dates. I don't even know if anything would have developed. Unhappy as in pissed? Yes. We both were angry at our parents. She for being uprooted, and me for…" He paused.

After a minute of silence, Gerri glanced at him. He saw her out of the corner of his eye. "You know how at some point in life, you find out that your parents are just ordinary people? And not necessarily very nice ones? That was that point for me."

"They objected to your dating a Native girl?"

"Yes. Vehemently." *And not in polite terms.* "I mean, Juneau is nothing like the South. But at that time—ten years ago or so—there was a color line. It wasn't that people were nasty: just that certain things weren't done. It depended on the person. My parents, to my surprise and disillusionment, had a problem with, um, mixing."

Gerri could imagine this all too well, but didn't want to seem to be criticizing his parents. "Are they… Have they changed?"

"I doubt it. I don't know. They're not in my life now. In fact, they don't even live in Alaska anymore."

"All that because you dated Ellen?"

Sven sighed. This conversation was getting out of control. "No. There were some other things that happened later." Gerri was silently waiting, Sven sensed, for him to elaborate. "I'd rather not talk about those things now," he said.

Gerri gave him a squeeze. "I understand. And I'm sorry. I guess I'm lucky. I haven't been disillusioned by my parents. I hope I never am."

They had arrived back at the boat. "I had a wonderful time," Gerri said. "I hope I didn't spoil it at the end with my questions."

Sven took her in his arms and held her. After a moment, he whispered in her ear. "I had a great time, too. In fact, I almost forgive Ace for trying to make time with you."

Gerri laughed against his chest. "Poor Ace. All of his wonderful plans, gone to naught."

"Don't worry about him. I'm sure he found somebody more…tractable." He stepped back and looked at her. She stared back, her big eyes intent and a small smile playing on her lips. *And in a minute, I'll be as bad as he was.* He lifted her gently over the gunwale to the deck. "We need to start early tomorrow. Let's turn in."

CHAPTER 15

Gerri wasn't able to make much progress in solving the mystery of Sven's past. Three days later, she knew nothing new. They had been fishing long hours and falling into their beds exhausted at the end of each day. It never seemed to be the right time to bring up the subject.

Gerri had no cause for complaint, though. The fishing was good. She was learning to estimate the catch and, more to the point, estimate her share of the profits. That was telling her that she had another size-able check coming to her at the end of this trip. At Sven's suggestion, she was going to open a checking account at a Juneau bank when they next came into port.

She smiled in satisfaction as she lay in her berth. Who could have believed that her very first checking account would be a whole conti-nent away from South Carolina? Who could have believed how much money she would be depositing in it? She could hardly wait to tell her parents about this in her next letter.

That reminded her—she should have a letter from home by now, waiting at Mindy's. This summer was turning into such a wonder-ful adventure. She just hoped that her parents weren't upset with the changes she had made to her plans. She mentally started composing her next letter. As always, she would accentuate the positive and be reassuring.

She would mention the money, of course. She would mention all the interesting people that she had met. She would mention that she was still looking forward to seeing a glacier. She would mention the town dance and thank her mother for insisting that Gerri bring the dress. She would *not* mention—she grinned briefly in the dark—that she had spent the dance with two white men competing—politely, but tenaciously—for her company.

That guided her thoughts to her relationship to Sven. She had to admit that she had a crush on him. If he were black and lived in South Carolina, she would very much want to date him. But he was neither. Still, she thought that he liked her as well. Didn't he say that she looked beautiful? She remembered that well, having played that scene back in her mind more than once.

None of this would be mentioned in her letter. Her parents would be alarmed, of course, especially in light of the fact that she and Sven were alone together much of the time. She didn't feel threatened in the least, however. Sven was courtly and maybe even a little shy. She almost wished that he would show a more aggressive interest.

The atmosphere between them had changed since the dance, however. She felt more of a physical awareness toward him, and she thought that he shared that feeling. He still respected her, but he now teased her occasionally. Not in the nasty way that some young males affected, but affectionately. He had started demonstrating a predilection for puns. He seemed happy when she reacted, even if it were just to roll her eyes at him and groan.

———

The next day, they stopped fishing a little early. The weather was nasty, which, alone, would not have stopped Sven, but the Glacier Gal's fathometer went on the fritz. This instrument was vital. It measured the water's depth beneath the boat and helped Sven decide, according to his usual magic, where to fish. The next morning, he announced, they would return to Juneau to get it repaired.

Gerri started preparing the evening meal as soon as they anchored. She decided to probe Sven's past while they ate. She wasn't sure just how to approach it; the things she was most interested in—courtesy of Edwin—were probably what Sven least wanted to talk about. She would start with general questions about his past and hope for the best.

"So," she said as they sat to eat, "What was it like, being in high school in Juneau?"

Sven looked at her with a half smile. She had hardly put any food in her mouth. "Wow. We just sat down. You must have been saving that up to ask."

He was right, of course, but she wouldn't admit it. She shrugged. "Not exactly. We don't get much of a chance to talk in the evenings. You get tired of me and disappear in your cabin." She wanted to kick herself. That had come out sounding like she was whining.

"No," he said, shaking his head emphatically, "I don't get tired of you. Not ever." He paused, knowing that he should give her a better explanation. He didn't want to share his painting with anyone—Rosie Craig excepted—but if he were to do so, Gerri would be the one. Another reason to tell her occurred to him—he hated to be a coward, but this would take Gerri's mind off asking him about high school.

Gerri watched him as he sat thinking and wondered whether he would say more—whether it would be polite to press him.

She saw him come to a decision. "Can you keep a secret? Only one other person knows about this."

She started to joke, but he looked very serious. "Yes. Anyway, I don't know anyone to talk to here except you and Mindy. Am I supposed to keep the secret from my family in South Carolina as well?"

He looked at her intently. "I don't care about the people in South Carolina, but, yes, keep it from your roommate as well."

"Well, as long as it's not..." She didn't know how to say it, but open ended promises made her nervous.

"Don't worry; it's nothing harmful."

"OK, I promise."

He took a breath. Whatever this was, Gerri reflected, it was important to him. He seemed finally to come to a decision. "After we're done eating, I'll show you what I've been doing in my cabin at night."

Curiosity was eating at Gerri, but Sven seemed to be in no hurry. He finished cleaning up the galley, taking special care to have the table clean and dry.

"Wait here," he said. "I'll be right back." Now that he had committed to showing Gerri his drawings, he was nervous. He realized that her opinion was inordinately important to him. He returned with a sheaf of papers, laid them down in front of her, and then sat down beside her.

Gerri glanced at him for approval and he gestured toward the sheaf without saying a word. She picked the papers up and started looking. As she did so, her mood went from bemused to astonished to fascinated. They were a collection of drawings. The styles varied widely; from clever caricatures almost like comics to finely detailed scenery pictures to portraits. They had one thing in common. They spoke to her. They drew her in and demanded her attention.

"Sven, these are wonderful. You're very good at this. Some of them I don't even want to give back."

Sven exhaled—unobtrusively, he hoped. He had been hanging anxiously, caring about her opinion more than he wanted to admit. "Keep going," he said, "There are more." Even though he affected a casual air, he had chosen which ones to show her—and which not to show her—with great care. And she hadn't gotten to the most important ones yet.

Gerri continued looking. Then, she came to one that made her laugh out loud. It showed Wally standing on the deck of his boat. His face was screwed up in a frown. "You surely captured Wally. Has he seen this?"

"No. Remember? Only one other person knows that I do this. Keep going."

Gerri cycled through several more pictures. Then came one that made her gasp. It was a picture of her on the front deck of the Glacier Gal, with her head thrown back, laughing delightedly. "This was when I saw the porpoise, wasn't it?"

"It was. Do you like it?"

"I love it. But..." She squirmed. "It's too beautiful. I don't think I'm that beautiful."

Sven grinned with equal parts amusement and relief. "That's how I see you. The artist gets to exercise his judgment."

She continued. Next was a picture of Gerri on the float, heavily laden with all of her luggage. *I guess it did look like I was carrying everything I owned.*

The last picture was also of Gerri. She was carrying a fifty pound lead sinker in each hand, with the strain showing on her face—overlaid by an almost smug expression of triumph. That made her laugh. "That's good. Did I really look that self-satisfied?"

"Yes, but you earned the right."

Gerri started going through the drawings again. She wanted to ask for some, but actively soliciting a gift seemed to be poor manners at best. Then she noticed a common feature. "All of them have this little design in the corner. Is that a secret code or something?"

"Or something. That serves as my signature. Yes, it's deliberately obscure. Remember that this is a secret, and I'd like it to stay that way."

Gerri squinted. "They don't even look like letters."

"They are—two 'S's overlapping with an 'H.' My initials. And an extra 'H' on the front for symmetry and additional obscurity."

"HSSH. Hmmm." This didn't exactly qualify as solving the mystery of Sven's past, but she'd take what she could get, when she could get it. "So what's your middle name?"

"Sven."

She twisted her lips as she studied his amused expression. Once again, she was struck by how good he looked with that rakish grin. She jerked herself back to the matter at hand. "Then what's your first name?"

"Sidney." His grin got bigger as he added in perfect falsetto. "But please don't call me that. I hate that name."

Gerri hissed in disgust, and then jerked sideways in her seat to nudge his shoulder sharply with hers. "OK, funny man." As she thought about it a bit more, she shuddered. "That day at White Sulfur Hot Springs is not my favorite memory."

"Mine either. But that's all it is—just a memory. Don't worry about it."

"I'm so thankful that you didn't draw me like that." She glanced at him sharply. "Or did you?"

"No, I didn't. I'm selfish. I draw you as I want to remember you."
...and because I find you fascinating.

Gerri didn't know how to react to that. She was warmed by his apparent vision of her, but the 'remember you' part reminded her unpleasantly of the fact that her time with Sven must end.

He interrupted her reverie. "Would you like copies of some of these? I want to keep the originals to paint from."

Surprises and more surprises! "You paint too?" Gerri looked around the galley as if she expected to see some paintings pop out.

"Yes, but not here on the boat. I'm too busy and it's too hard to store my supplies. I paint at home during the winter. And sometimes I use these sketches to keep my memory sharp."

"I'd love to see some of your paintings some time."

He nodded. "We can do that."

"Who's the other person that knows about your painting?"

"Rosie Craig. She runs a book store in Juneau. I'm in there a lot, and I've bought a bunch of books on painting and on visual perception. So she knows about my interest. She even has a few of my paintings."

"A book store!" This opened up whole new exciting possibilities for Gerri. For practically the first time in her life, Gerri had some time to read for pleasure, a book store where she could be just a regular customer—without worrying about the strictures of segregation, and, last but not least, enough money to spend for pleasure. "Tell me where it is. I'd like to visit it."

Sven gave her directions, and then added: "We'll probably be in town for a few days until the fathometer is fixed."

They had another early start the next morning. By this time, both of them were eager to reach port. Gerri was at the helm (steering the boat, she would have said a month ago) when she saw the sun glint off an iceberg dead ahead. She had seen a number of icebergs in the distance, but, with their present heading, they would pass very close to this one. She was reaching for the binoculars as Sven came in from the back deck. He squinted at it briefly and grunted. "An iceberg. A big one. Don't hit it."

She turned and saw him grinning at her. "I think I will, just to surprise you."

"That would get us an unexpected and very uncomfortable swim. That reminds me. You haven't gone swimming yet. We'll stop and do that some time, just so you can see what the water's like."

"I know what it's like: freezing. Brrr! No, thank you." She thought for a minute. "Do you ever go swimming? Really?"

"Occasionally. More when I was a kid. Last year some lines got wrapped around the prop and I went down to clear them."

"How can you stand it?"

"Mind over matter, I guess. The water's about 50 degrees in the summer. The first few seconds are rough. Then I have about 20 minutes to stay in before I get so cold that my muscles won't work right. But you're right. You won't find many tourists swimming."

Gerri watched the iceberg as they got closer. She realized that it dwarfed the boat. Hitting it would be as deadly as hitting a rock. "I'd like to take a picture as we go by."

"Good idea. I'll take the wheel while you get your camera."

When she got back, he had brought the Glacier Gal to a stop several yards away from the berg. The boat rocked gently in its own wake. Gerri took several pictures and then got up her nerve. "Would you stand over there?" She asked, "I'd like to take a picture of you with the iceberg in the background."

Sven obliged, muttering about breaking the camera. After she had several of him—she hoped that he didn't realize that some of the close ups of him barely showed the iceberg—he took the camera and took some shots of her.

Sven was delighted at this opportunity and had every intention of asking her for some of the pictures of her. He had every faith in his ability to capture her in painting and drawings, but this provided a different look. He was hungry for all of the remembrances that he could get.

When he had taken several of her (some of which he intended to use to create paintings in the upcoming winter), he handed the camera back to her. "How about a picture of you on the iceberg itself?"

"Are you serious?" But she allowed herself to be persuaded. He maneuvered the boat to within inches of the iceberg, and they used a pike pole about ten feet long to hold themselves in place and to steady her. "Won't I slip? It is ice, after all."

"Step carefully and use the pole for balance and you'll be OK. The surface is rough and you'll find footholds."

Finally, they left the berg behind. Gerri could hardly wait to get these pictures developed. *Wait until my family sees these!* But an iceberg, she remembered, is only a little piece flaked off of a glacier. "This makes me want to see a glacier even more."

Sven was not about to pass up this chance. He had thought—unhappily—about the fact that he had no reason to see Gerri until they were leaving Juneau. "I'll be glad to take you while we're in town."

"Really? I'd love that. Thank you." Not only would she get to see a glacier, but she'd get to spend time with Sven away from the boat. "How close will we be able to get to it?"

"How close do you want to get? I can put you inside it if you want."

"What does that mean?"

But Sven was back into his role as a man of mystery. "You'll see." Gerri vowed that this expedition would turn out better than his last surprise at White Sulfur Hot Springs.

As they approached Juneau, Gerri was again at the helm. Sven was training her in all aspects of seamanship, which she loved. As they came close to the city, she found herself stealing looks at the mountains surrounding the town. *What a beautiful setting...I'll never get tired of seeing it.*

"Turn to the starboard, helmsman," Sven said with a smile. "I want to get fuel before we tie up at the float."

As Gerri dutifully headed toward the Union Oil dock, Sven reconsidered his words. "I don't know about this Women's Lib stuff. Do I have to call you the helmsperson?"

Gerri laughed. "Don't do it on my account. I can think of better places to put my Women's Lib energy." She cut the throttle. *Approach slowly...*

"Good work," Sven replied. "I was just about to tell you to do that."

After they had topped off their fuel tank, it was just a short jaunt to the boat harbor. As they approached the boat harbor, Sven took the helm and Gerri kept an eye out for Wally. He was to meet them and catch a ride with Sven when he took the fathometer in for repair. He wasn't there when they docked, so she jumped onto the dock and secured the Glacier Gal, bow and stern. Only then did she see him walking down the float.

Another boat had followed them in and was docking in the berth next to them, but it was going too fast and was about to crunch into the dock. Gerri was proud of her competence—docking at the oil dock and efficiently tying the boat in just now. For some perverse reason, she wanted to impress Wally to win his respect. She braced herself against a piling and prepared to shove against the newly arriving boat to lessen its impending collision against the dock.

Just as it was about to come within reach, however, Sven appeared by her side. "Watch out," he said sharply. "Step aside."

Obediently, she moved, but complained, "I had it."

Sven pushed against the oncoming boat. Gerri's eyes widened when she saw how much effort he was expending. His arm muscles corded powerfully under his tee shirt and she heard him grunt with the strain. *If he had to work that hard...* Even he didn't completely stop the boat—he stepped aside at the last second and let it thud into the piling.

"At least, I thought I had it," she conceded. "It really wasn't moving very fast."

Sven nodded. "Small velocity, but a very large mass. Momentum is mass times velocity, if I remember correctly."

Gerri considered that. "I remember that now," she said quietly. If she taught physics instead of mathematics, this would have been a great example to use in class.

"I was afraid that you'd get squashed between the boat and the piling."

Wally had arrived and was listening to this conversation. Gerri realized that in her efforts to look competent, she had achieved the opposite. "I'm sorry," she said ruefully, "I'd hate to be remembered for shouting 'Oh no! Momentum!' just as I was being squashed."

Sven grinned mischievously. "Don't worry about it. And besides, nobody ever remembers someone's dying words anyway."

"What do you mean?"

His grin turned sly. "Because, by definition, they're just mentioned in passing."

Gerri giggled—she couldn't help herself. *'In passing?' He got me again.* Then she shoved Sven—hard—while still giggling.

"Hey, what was that for?" He neutralized her shove by gathering her in his arms.

"Because you made me laugh at something terrible!" But she was in no hurry to get out of his arms.

CHAPTER 16

Gerri left quickly, on her way to Mindy's apartment. Mindy would still be at work, but Gerri could get some of her laundry out of the way while she waited for her to get home. But, especially, she wanted to check her mail. Even though she was having the time of her life, she missed her family. And maybe the letter would include some news from Rich.

It felt good to fall into the rhythm of walking again. She and Sven walked along the beaches frequently now, but there was nothing like walking on a sidewalk to stretch out and set a fast pace. As she walked, she let her mind drift. She had already admired Sven, and she was delighted that he was becoming more relaxed and open around her. Of course, that meant that she was subjected to his awful puns, but they were kind of fun in their very awfulness.

And again—she was doing this too often lately—she imagined living in a world without racial overtones. Would Sven consider dating her? She knew that she felt good around him, and she would certainly accept if he asked.

And then there was Wally. She couldn't figure him out. When she and Sven had finished their brief horseplay at the dock just now, she had caught Wally looking at her intently. Was it a hostile look? No, she didn't think so. But neither was it a friendly look. It was…assessing. Well, she wouldn't worry about Wally. As long as Sven liked her, that was enough.

And Mindy, she remembered. She wanted Mindy to like her as well. She would definitely spend time with her. Maybe she could help with Mindy's political activities. She would ask.

As soon as she got to Mindy's apartment, she dropped her load on the floor and eagerly looked around. As Gerri had expected, Mindy wasn't home. Even if she was not travelling for her job, she would have left for work already.

She found what she wanted prominently displayed on Mindy's catch-all shelf. The letter was postmarked a week ago. For just a second, she stared at it, grinning, as she took in her mother's handwriting. Then, the apprehension started seeping in. Would they disapprove? Would they scold her for such a dramatic deviation from their plan?

She tore it open carefully—for some reason she wanted to be able to save the envelope—and started to read.

Dear Gerri,

Well! You surely know how to astonish us. You could probably hear our jaws hitting the floor all the way up in Alaska. Alaska!! We've hardly been able to stop talking about it. You can stop worrying about exciting Marilyn's interest. She and Joetta have been telling all of their friends about their big sister—the world traveler. And the size of the check you sent had Marilyn's eyes popping out of her head.

Your father and I are a little worried about you, though. It can be a big, ugly world out there. Just remember that. I know, I know. You've met some very nice people. But not everybody is like that. We talked (after the kids went to bed) about you. Don't tell him I said so, but at first he wanted to insist that you come back immediately. But we know (even if we forget sometimes) that you are grown. And apparently, you're not spending our money anymore—rich girl!

We'll save the money you sent and give it back to you when you come home. Don't worry about paying us back for the trip; that was our graduation present to you.

Speaking of presents, please send us some pictures. You've told us how beautiful it is up there, and I hope you've been using that new camera of yours.

Have you seen a glacier yet? I hope you do. They seem unreal to all of us. Maybe a picture of you standing in front of one will convince us that they really exist. (ha, ha)

We got a letter from Rich. He's stationed at some big base and he hasn't had to go out into the jungle yet. So that's good. It's hard to get used to my kids being scattered all over the world. Who would have believed this even six months ago?

Mr. Harrison came by the other day. As we had feared, he is no longer a principal, but he does work at the integrated high school. He's looking out for you, but he warns you that you won't be able to teach high school math—at least not at first. These are difficult times for him (and for all of us), but we hope that things will get better in time.

Love,

Ma, Dad, and your sisters

P.S. Pictures, pictures, send pictures! Not just of the lovely scenery, but of these people you talk about.

P.P.S. Do you remember our talk on your graduation day? I told you to watch for opportunities for adventure and to embrace them. Well, I can't help but laugh: you certainly listened to your old Ma, didn't you?

Gerri leaned back, blinking tears as she smiled. This letter reminded her of how much she missed her family. Even beyond the distances involved, she had never been away from home for this long in her life.

And they weren't angry—at least not seriously so. She read the letter through again and reluctantly folded it up. Pictures—yes she could do that. Mindy would certainly pose for pictures. Sven? Gerri would try to get more pictures of him. Maybe when he showed her the glacier. This would give her a good excuse.

Finally, she stood up and stretched. She had plenty to do today, and she wanted to do it all before Mindy got home, so she could tell her about her experiences.

————

As they lifted Sven's fathometer out of its mounting, Sven could tell that Wally was itching to speak. Sven rested it on the gunwale and looked at Wally questioningly. They knew each other well enough that it was unnecessary to say anything.

"What's up with you and the girl? You seem pretty cozy."

Sven glared at him. *He damn well knows her name.* "You mean Gerri?"

Wally actively cultivated his curmudgeonly persona. And he was not averse to yanking Sven's chain. But he wanted to make a serious point, and antagonizing Sven wasn't going to help him do it. He nodded shamefacedly. "Yeah, Gerri. Look, I've got nothing against her. She seems like an OK person, and from what you say, she's learned the basics of seamanship pretty quickly, umm…" He turned involuntarily toward the piling that Gerri had just braced against, but turned back immediately. Sven knew that she'd made a mistake—misjudging the momentum of the oncoming boat—and Wally didn't want to get sidetracked. "It's just that she's got you pretty fond of her. I don't want to see you hornswoggled again."

Sven didn't know whether to laugh or scowl. "That's wrong in so many ways. First, if you're talking about Laura…"

"Bingo."

"That was a disaster; I don't deny it. But I don't think Laura was faking her affection—at least not entirely."

"We've had this discussion before. We disagree, but I'm not trying to rub salt in your wounds. You said 'first.' Is there a second point?"

"Yes. I meant what I said years ago. I've carved out a reasonable life for myself, and I'm not looking to add a woman to that life. Gerri's not looking for romance either. She's a kid—just out of college—and she's having the adventure of her life. And I admire her. Can you imagine how much courage it must have taken to just take off like that? She had never travelled before in her life."

"Maybe you don't have to be looking for romance. She acts like she likes you. And you…" Wally trailed off with a shrug. Sven's personality had changed when Laura died. When he was young, he had been cheerful and had displayed a quirky, somewhat offbeat way of viewing the world that manifested itself frequently in rather outrageous puns. After her death, he had closed up, abandoning such humor entirely. Sven's affection for Gerri was palpably obvious from both his pun and their horseplay when they docked, but pointing that out would only make him angry.

"Well *nobody* is looking, you can set your mind at ease. And she's not interested in me that way." Sven ruthlessly suppressed the flash of pleasure that the prospect of her interest provoked. "She's a college graduate, bright as a penny, pretty as the dickens, and very sweet natured. She'll find some college guy back in South Carolina. She wouldn't settle for an old, broken down fisherman."

That last statement had done nothing to reassure Wally, but pointing it out would be worthless. He nodded. "Let's get your fathometer."

Sven was grateful that the inquisition was over, but he couldn't resist. "There is a third point."

Wally eyed him warily. "Oh?"

He grinned. "Yes. We've got to get you up to Taku Books and buy you some new Westerns. You have to be the only guy in the last fifty years who has used the word 'hornswoggled.'"

After he had delivered the malfunctioning fathometer to the repair shop and dropped Wally off, Sven turned his thoughts back to their conversation. The very fact that Wally had been at least nominally polite signaled to Sven that he was seriously concerned.

Sven sighed. He really didn't want to think about this. Was he encouraging an inappropriate relationship with Gerri? No, he told himself. He was fond of her—probably too fond of her. But that was his problem and any grief would be only his. He thought about how much willpower it had cost him during the last slow dance in Pelican not to pull her close, cup her behind in his hands, and just stand there swaying. And when they'd gotten back to the boat, he'd wanted nothing more than to take her in his arms and carry her to his cabin. He was human, after all.

But he had not—and would not—take advantage of her, even if that were possible. He was her boss and her mentor, as well as being considerably older than she. He couldn't help but wonder how his life might have been different if Gerri had grown up with him, before his life went off the rails. He shook his head irritably. Those thoughts were pointless. He would, he vowed, protect her and help her to have the best adventure ever. He wanted her to remember him fondly.

Then, another ugly thought intruded. Mindy. That was a ticking time bomb. Eventually, Gerri was going to say something to Mindy—some casual remark which would lead Mindy to put two and two together. He'd be lucky if Gerri would even speak to him after Mindy got through with her.

———

Gerri smiled happily as she left the bank. She now had her first checking account. And what an exotic one! She tried to imagine people's reactions as she ever so casually wrote one in the grocery store back home—the little one owned by the black couple. The bigger stores—the white owned—might refuse to accept a check from her on a bank in Juneau, Alaska. So be it—they would just lose her business. Of course, her checks wouldn't be printed for a couple of weeks yet, but that was OK. She had kept some cash for miscellaneous expenses, like the book store, which she was now approaching.

The small woman sitting behind a table in the back of Taku Books dragged on a cigarette and gave Gerri a curious look as she entered the store. Evidently, Gerri passed muster, and the woman spoke. "Good morning. May I help you with anything?"

"Thank you, but I'll just browse for a bit."

Gerri picked out several cheap pocket books—she didn't intend to let her money burn a hole in her pocket too soon—and then she settled in to look at the hardbacks. She chose a couple—a history of Alaska that she told herself she would read someday and a used book—an old one—called 'Travels in Alaska.' That one sounded particularly interesting. The author was an explorer who had done considerable walking in the wilderness of Southeast Alaska many years ago. Maybe she would get some ideas for walks.

As Gerri browsed, she heard the front door start to open and then stop. When she looked up, there was a frail looking woman who was evidently having trouble pushing the door. Gerri quickly moved to the door and held it open for her.

"Thank you," the woman said as she stepped into the store. Gerri could hear the rasp of her breath as she passed her.

The woman behind the table—Rosie Craig, Sven had told her—greeted the new arrival as an old friend. "Hello, Mrs. Kallek. I'm glad you could make it. Your book came in." She rang up Gerri's purchases as Mrs. Kallek sank into a chair with a sigh.

After Gerri paid her, Ms. Craig pulled a book from under the counter and handed it to Mrs. Kallek. "There you are. Fresh from the lower 48: a brand new copy of 'Men of Mathematics' for you and your students."

Gerri's ears perked up at that. She had actually read that book in school. *Was Mrs. Kallek a teacher?* She didn't want to butt into their conversation, but she dawdled rather than leaving the store immediately.

"I've been looking forward to it," said Mrs. Kallek. "Now all I need is a book on women in mathematics."

"Women in mathematics?" Ms. Craig chuckled as she spoke. "Are there any?"

"Oh, heavens yes. But try telling that to my female high school students."

Gerri couldn't stand it anymore. Rude or not, she murmured as she opened the door to leave: "Emmy Noether; Julia Robinson—among many others." Instantly, she blushed at her temerity, but Mrs. Kallek was delighted.

"Good for you, young lady. See," she turned to Ms. Craig, "There are plenty of women in mathematics. They just aren't well-known."

Gerri smiled a farewell and left hastily. In the South, she would have been considered rude—or even uppity—for interrupting her elders' conversation, but Mrs. Kallek seemed not to have minded at all. As she walked up the street, she was burning with curiosity about Mrs. Kallek. She would love to talk to her about teaching, but she hadn't had the courage to ask.

Before she had gone a block, she changed her mind. Mrs. Kallek had seemed very nice. Why shouldn't Gerri talk to her? She had to remember that she was an adult now. And this wasn't the South. One teacher—well almost a teacher—talking to another: why not?

Mrs. Kallek had left the store, but she was walking slowly and Gerri caught up to her quickly.

"Excuse me," Gerri said. Then she stopped. She realized that she didn't know what to say that wouldn't make her seem silly. *'I just wanted to say hello to a real teacher.'* or maybe *'What's it like being a teacher here?'*

She needn't have worried. Mrs. Kallek beamed at her. "There you are. You ran away so quickly that I didn't get a chance to talk to you." She shifted her book and extended her hand. "I'm Helen Kallek and, as you probably gathered, I teach math at Juneau-Douglas High School."

"I'm Gerri Barton. I'm not a teacher yet, but I just graduated from college and I hope to teach high school math when I get back home."

"And home is?"

"South Carolina."

"Oh, my. You're a long ways away. How did you end up here?"

They walked slowly as they talked, and Gerri found herself explaining about her adventure, her hopes, and even about her journal of teaching ideas. Mrs. Kallek confessed that she had taught for 47 years. Finally, Mrs. Kallek stopped in front of an office building. "I have a doctor's appointment in here, so I'll have to go, but I'd love to talk to you some more. And I'd love to see that journal of yours."

"I'd be happy to show it to you. Maybe you can tell me if some of my ideas don't make sense."

Mrs. Kallek smiled mischievously. "Or maybe I can steal some of your ideas for myself. Can you come to Taku Books tomorrow morning? About 11?"

Gerri was nodding almost before the question was out. They said their goodbyes and Gerri was on her way. She had thought that she was in a good mood before the bookstore, but she was even more excited now. She had so much to look forward to. She would talk to Mindy tonight and maybe help her with her petition. Sven would take her to see a glacier the day after tomorrow. And now, she would get a chance to trade notes with an experienced teacher—one who seemed to value Gerri's opinions. She felt like she was walking on air.

CHAPTER 17

Gerri decided to share her good mood: she would cook a dinner for Mindy and to celebrate her own return. After stopping at the grocery for supplies, she hurried back to the apartment. She could just about have the meal on the table when Mindy got home from work.

Mindy came in as Gerri was finishing up. "You're back, sailor! Something smells really good in here."

"Meatloaf and string beans. They'll be ready in about ten minutes, if you're interested. How have you been?"

"Busy. You certainly are a bundle of energy for someone just back in town."

"I'm just in a really good mood, so I decided that you wouldn't mind if I cooked."

"Mind? Are you kidding? So what put you in such a good mood?"

"Well, the latest thing… Do you know a Mrs. Kallek?"

"The math teacher? Sure. She's nice. I liked her."

"Me, too."

"How did you run into her?"

"I met her in Taku Books and we talked." Gerri decided to leave out the part about her initial loss of nerve. "She was very nice and very interesting. She wants to see the journal that I've been keeping, so I'm going to see her again tomorrow."

"That's nice."

Gerri could tell that Mindy didn't feel her level of enthusiasm. "It's very gratifying to have someone who's as experienced as she is take me seriously and take an interest in me."

"I can understand that." Now Mindy remembered the insecurities that Gerri had confessed to earlier. "I think that she would appreciate someone who's as dedicated as you."

"I hope so. That would mean a lot to me." Gerri turned off the final burner on the stove. "Tell me about her."

"I've heard that she's been sick lately, but she used to be really something." As they ate, Mindy shared several anecdotes, including one very embarrassing one involving her unsuccessful attempt to sneak a late assignment onto Mrs. Kallek's desk after hours. "You better not tell anyone about that or I'll never forgive you."

Gerri grinned. "I promise. What did she do to you when she caught you coming out of her room?"

"She didn't *do* anything, but she didn't have to. I've never been more humiliated in my life. We talked about it and about responsibility. I'd never done anything like that before and I never did again. Laura could get away with all kinds of stuff by sweet-talking someone and looking innocent, but I couldn't. I was afraid to try."

"I'm like you. It's too easy to imagine how disappointed my parents would be."

"Delicious," Mindy said as they finished and gather up the dishes. "My turn next time."

"Sounds good to me."

Mindy washed the dishes as Gerri dried them. She remembered Gerri's opening remarks. "You said 'the latest thing.' What other adventures have you had?"

"I opened my first checking account today. And I got paid, so I actually had some money to put in it. I can hardly wait to show off my Alaskan checks when I get back home."

"Cool. That should surprise them."

"And I have time to help you with your political work—for a couple of days, at least."

That got Mindy's attention. "That's great. I've got another paper for you to edit, if it's all right. That boyfriend of yours was a jerk, but I thank him for helping you hone your writing skills."

"There must be more painless ways of getting those skills, but you're right. I'm glad I have them, one way or the other."

Mindy sat down and watched as Gerri put the last of the dishes away. "Oh, one more thing," Gerri added. "Last, but not least, I'm going to get to see a glacier. Sven is going to take me out to Mendenhall Glacier the day after tomorrow. So I'll have that part of my adventure."

As she closed the cabinet, Gerri sensed that something was different. It was almost as if the air had changed—gotten thicker and more laden with tension. She glanced over her shoulder and saw Mindy staring at her with horror. Her face was pale.

"Sven? You mean Sven Halvorsen? Is he the fisherman you work for?"

"Yes, do you know him?" Too late, Gerri remembered Mindy's words weeks ago: 'I only know one fisherman, and I hate his guts.' Now she didn't know what to say in the face of Mindy's rancor. It didn't matter. Mindy wasn't waiting for Gerri to talk anyway.

"I hate him. He's a monster."

Gerri slowly sat down opposite her. Mindy was literally wringing her hands in her distress. "Why?" Gerri started to ask. "What on earth happened?"

Mindy took a deep breath and sat down opposite Gerri. "It's a long story, but he killed my sister. And that destroyed my family."

"I'm so sorry. Please tell me about it." Gerri desperately wanted some information to reconcile this view of Sven with her impression: a soft-spoken, gentle man who had been unfailingly good to her.

"Laura and Sven were high school sweethearts," Mindy explained. "They were a beautiful couple. Sure, I'm prejudiced, but Laura was so glamorous. And all of the girls thought that Sven was so cute. They…" Gerri got the impression that Mindy was choosing her words carefully. "They got married in their senior year. They had big plans—Laura was going to be a movie star and Sven was going to be a boxer. They both could have been famous.

"After they were married, Sven changed his mind. Laura felt that she'd been betrayed. He wouldn't budge and they started fighting all of the time." Mindy stared at her lap. "One night they went for a drive out the road. He wrecked the car and Laura was killed. She was four months pregnant." Mindy smiled bitterly, "He had only minor injuries. That's how he got that scar."

"That's tragic. And your family…"

"My mother was devastated. She had shared Laura's dreams—and to just have them yanked away…" She paused again. "Afterward, he was horrible to my parents…" Her voice trailed away.

Gerri was stunned. She felt bombarded by Mindy's words and the force of her emotions. She wanted to express her sympathy, but she wasn't ready to join Mindy in trashing Sven—she wanted to think about this. "I had no idea," she ventured. "He's been completely proper around me."

Mindy seemed to focus on Gerri for the first time since her outburst. She patted Gerri's hand. "I'm sorry. None of this was your fault. You couldn't have known." She stood up. "Let's go into the living room."

But the mood of the evening was pretty much spoiled. Mindy tried to project a cheerful air, but she couldn't seem to help throwing a few more shots at Sven.

According to Mindy, Sven had profited from Laura's death. Laura and Sven each had life insurance policies, purchased after they got married. Sven had refused to help Laura's family with some of their debts, resulting from help that they had given Laura.

Then she delivered the allegation that shook Gerri the most. "He's violent, you know. He used to get in fights down at the Arctic Saloon—still does now and then."

Gerri started to speak up and defend him, but she stopped. Maybe Sven's almost casual destruction of her tormenters was normal for him. Maybe his protestations of non-violence were just talk. Gerri didn't say anything. She just wanted to think about Mindy's revelations and the Sven that she had come to know.

———

The next morning, Mindy apologized for her outburst—without retracting anything that she had said about Sven. "I don't want you to think that I blame you. You'd be crazy to refuse a job that pays the kind of money you're getting. Just be careful. I know you're not going to get attracted to him, but he can be very charming."

Gerri knew full well that she was already attracted to him, but she certainly wasn't going to share that. "So far, he's been a good person to work for. But I'll be careful." She felt ashamed for that restrained, limited defense of Sven. But she didn't want to discuss it any more.

Gerri got to Taku Books before Mrs. Kallek did, so she took the opportunity to browse some more. As she wandered around, she suddenly did a double take. There were two pictures of Sven's—complete with his cryptic 'signature'—hanging on the wall. Her eyes widened at the discretely displayed prices. His paintings must be popular, indeed.

Rosie Craig had been watching her, Gerri realized. Not in a suspicious way, but in the 'what can I sell you?' way to be expected of a good shopkeeper. When she saw Gerri's interest in the pictures, she spoke up. "That's an Alaskan artist—very popular. He lives out in the bush and is very reclusive. To keep his privacy, he calls himself Hush, spelled 'HSSH,' rather than putting his name on them."

Gerri couldn't help herself. She giggled. *So that's how they explain it!* A look of surprised irritation crossed Ms. Craig's face. "I'm sorry," said Gerri, making a placating gesture. "I knew that his identity was a secret, but Sven didn't tell me that there was a cover story."

Ms. Craig's eyebrows rose and her look of irritation was replaced by one of astonishment. Sven had kept his secret for years, showing no interest whatsoever in sharing it with anybody else. Who was this woman that he seemed to have confided in? And who seemed to have intrigued Mrs. Kallek?

"I work for him on the Glacier Gal. And he showed me some of his drawings. He's very good. But this is the first time I've seen one of his paintings."

"He must have a great deal of trust in you."

"I hope so. I…" Gerri flushed in embarrassment. She hadn't shown much trust in Sven when Mindy was attacking him. "He's a very interesting man." *Am I shameless enough to try to get some information out of Ms. Craig?*

"He is, indeed." Ms. Craig looked at Gerri speculatively. "Are you aware that he's a widower?"

"Yes, but I don't know what happened. It must have been very tragic."

"The whole marriage was tragic. It never should have happened. They were just kids and they weren't suited to each other at all."

It was plain that Ms. Craig was considering how much to tell Gerri, but while she paused, Mrs. Kallek arrived and, to Gerri's frustration, the moment was lost.

———

Sven was waiting on the Glacier Gal well before Gerri was supposed to meet him. He had taken care of a few minor chores, but now he was reduced to waiting restlessly—practically pacing—waiting for her. It had been two days—or nearly so—since they had arrived in town and she had hastily disappeared with her laundry. He could understand that. He had done laundry and a number of other chores around his house in the time since then. As long as they were stuck waiting for his fathometer, he tried to at least be useful. When something like this happened, he was generally philosophical about the delay.

Not so this time. He started being edgy and restless practically from the moment she walked away. In some ways, it was worse than his discontent during the week he had fished alone after sending her away in Pelican. By now, he had become constantly, and dangerously, aware of her attractiveness. He hadn't felt this attraction since Laura. But this was different than that. What he had felt for Laura, he could now admit, was simple lust. With Gerri, he had all of the same urges. But in addition, he took pleasure in her simple presence—a conversation; a shared chore. This was OK as long as he didn't lose control and try to take advantage of her affection. Her youthful innocence both charmed him and served as a reminder to behave.

But the skeletons in his past hung over even this relationship. Inevitably, Gerri would mention his name to Mindy, who would tell her just what a terrible person Sven was. He had had this happen before, but never with anyone who mattered to him as Gerri did.

Always before, he could shrug it off—if someone wanted to dislike him, he would accept it and avoid that person.

He found himself wanting to explain to her his side of the story—as weak as it was—and hope for her approval. Of course, her probable rejection would be all the more painful if he pled with her. And, in truth, he wouldn't want to create a conflict between Gerri and Mindy. Gerri had made it clear that she considered Mindy to be a true friend. And Sven found that unsurprising. For all of her confrontational nature, Mindy would be a loyal friend. Surely Gerri deserved to have a lasting friendship come from her adventure. And it was merely Sven's selfishness that made him hope to become Gerri's second lasting friend.

As Gerri walked to her meeting with Sven, she pondered the surprises of the previous evening. Mindy and she had gone out to talk to people and try to get signatures on their anti-war petition. Unexpectedly, Gerri had enjoyed herself. People were receptive and friendly and many signed the petition.

They seemed fascinated by Gerri and Mindy as well. The contrast between them seemed to intrigue people: Mindy was the elegant blonde, still dressed for work. Gerri was black, wearing an afro (still an unusual hairdo) and dressed neatly but casually. 'Salt and pepper,' one man had said with a smile. Another man, after signing the petition, confessed that 'I like your accent' to Gerri. When she had eyed him warily—when people teased her about her accent, she frequently felt patronized—he had hastily added, 'It's not that strong; I guess you just have a nice voice.'

The evening was a success also because it took her mind off Sven. Now as Gerri got close to the boat harbor, she wondered how to face him. Should she pretend as though she knew nothing? Should she ask him for his side of the story? Or would it be too painful for him to discuss? She was still dithering when she arrived at the Glacier Gal's float.

"Good morning. Sorry I'm late."

"That's OK, I was…" Sven tried to hide his relief, but he couldn't think of anything to say that sounded suitably casual. "…just puttering," he finished weakly. He stepped onto the float. "Let's get started."

As they walked toward his truck, Gerri studied him surreptitiously. She thought she saw signs of strain on his face. *Maybe there had been a delay with the fathometer.* "Is everything OK?" she asked.

He looked at her. Suddenly, she couldn't meet his eyes. She became very interested in the ground in front of her. "Is the fathometer going to be ready on time?"

"Yes." Her obvious discomfort could have only one cause. "Mindy found out who you were working for?"

Gerri nodded.

Sven heaved a sigh. "And told you all about me?"

"Yes, she's pretty upset about her sister."

They paused beside the truck. "Do you want to call this off? Do you want to quit working for me?"

"No to both of those. But I'd like to hear your side, if you want to tell me."

"Let's drive as we talk." He was silent for a couple of minutes until they reached the highway. Finally, he spoke with a resigned air. "I won't ask what she said—I've heard it all before. The thing is, she's mostly right about the accident. I was driving. Laura and I were arguing—it seemed like we argued all of the time toward the end. We hit something on the road and the car flipped. Laura was killed." He made a face. "I was lucky, they said. That was a very loose definition of luck."

"It must have been horrible."

He said nothing. Gerri could practically see him reliving the experience. She was prying, but she couldn't help herself. "She said that you refused to help her family afterwards."

"Help? That's a joke. Laura's mother—who's one of the most unpleasant people I've ever met—came to me and *demanded* that I split the insurance money with her. She already hated me, but I...uh... said some things back to her which made it worse. I had been drinking when she accosted me, and I guess that loosened my tongue. They were things that I'd wanted to say for a long time. I found her demand offensive—they hadn't done anything to support us. I was still in school, but I took a job in the evenings after we got married."

Gerri felt guilty about focusing on a side issue, but she couldn't help asking. "You were drinking? But I thought you hated that. Didn't you ask me about that before you hired me?"

"I did ask and I do hate it. I had a real drinking problem for a few months after the accident—spent a lot of time in the Arctic Saloon." He paused for a rueful shake of his head. "I'm not proud of that time. I swore that I'd never go back to that place." He flashed Gerri a quick, rueful grin. "The time I came in looking for you was my first time in there in years. Since I've been on the wagon, I don't even like to be around drinkers."

"I'm glad you don't drink." Gerri had many more questions (*What did Laura look like? Why did you get married so young?*), but Sven was clearly not enjoying this, and it seemed like bad manners to pry any more.

After a few inconsequential remarks about the approaching glacier, he returned once to the subject. "I just want to say one more thing. Mindy's a good person. She has anger in her—about me, among other things—but she's way nicer than Laura ever was. I sometimes wonder how she could have come out of that family. The family, I see now, was always oriented around Laura and her ambitions—or maybe I should say her mother's ambitions for her—and Mindy was the dutiful child."

"She's been a good friend to me."

"I would expect her to be." Sven fell silent and Gerri stole a look at his expression. It was somber and closed—definitely not one to invite any more questions.

Finally, he spoke again. "Let's go see the glacier."

CHAPTER 18

The drive to the glacier reminded Gerri of how close Juneau was to true wilderness. The last couple of miles to the Visitor's Center were unpaved, reminding her of some of the back roads back home. The Visitor's Center was a modest sized, attractive building, generously supplied with picture windows facing the glacier.

The glacier itself was like a frozen river, caught in the act of tumbling down a valley with steep mountains on either side. The front of the glacier settled into a lake, perhaps a half mile from where Gerri stood. Its color was predominately white, with hints of blue and brown. The latter color, Sven told her, was from the soil that the glacier had scraped from the mountains as it flowed.

"It's beautiful, Sven," she declared, when she finally returned the binoculars that he had loaned her.

"There's more," he said enigmatically. "I'm counting on the fact that you like to walk," he said as they returned to the car.

As they drove—around the lake, as it turned out—Sven gave her a quick tutorial in glaciers. All of the ground that they were driving on—even miles from the glacier—had been pushed down the mountain, over the course of eons, by the glacier.

"Now we walk," he said as they parked. "You got the panoramic view at the Visitor's Center. Now you'll get the close-up."

Gerri was happy to have an excuse to walk, but she soon realized that this was different from walking in South Carolina. "Let's rest for a minute," she panted. "I'm not used to hills like this."

Sven quirked a brief smile and then resumed his serious expression as they restarted their climb.

Soon, they came over a rise and saw the glacier stretched out below them. It was much closer now and looked much larger. Sven started down toward the glacier's side.

"Sven, wait." She snapped several pictures, including some of Sven posing, smiling with the glacier as a backdrop. Then he took some of Gerri. Finally, they started down the steep slope to the glacier itself.

"Wow!" Gerri truly began to appreciate the scale. The ice was jagged and irregular, but even at the edge, it was at least 50 feet thick. And it was thicker in the middle, Sven assured her.

Sven knocked off a piece and handed it to her. "Here, chew on this. You can say that you've tasted thousand year old ice."

They walked uphill along the edge of the glacier. It felt like a canyon—the slope of the hill rose up on their left, and the glacier rose even more steeply on their right. After a few minutes, Sven stopped.

"This is as far as we go." He gestured ahead. "Walk in there."

Gerri stepped into a cave. The ground was rock, but the roof and sides were ice. As she walked in, the quality of the light changed. Less light came from the mouth of the cave, but the very ice glowed. She looked around in wonder. As the sunlight passed through the many feet of ice above her, it took on a rich, breathtaking blue color. She looked back at Sven, who was taking pictures of her with her camera. It was a moment before she found her tongue.

"Oh, Sven. This is magical. It's the most beautiful thing I've ever seen."

He entered the cave with her, shielding the camera from the drips of water falling from the roof. He nodded and she saw a small smile of satisfaction. But he was still so solemn. Ever since the conversation about his wife's death, Gerri realized, he had taken little joy in their outing.

Gerri impulsively stepped forward and hugged him. "Thank you so much, Sven. You've been so wonderful to me." As she stood in his arms and looked up at him, she caught him staring at her lips. It just seemed right to her to stretch up a bit...

Sven was having trouble accepting her enthusiastic hug calmly. Whenever he touched her, he wanted *more*. He couldn't help but watch her lips and think of how good they would taste. When she brushed his lips with hers, he stopped trying to be virtuous. He tightened the embrace and deepened their kiss. Gerri made a small noise of surprise, but she returned his kiss eagerly. Her tongue darted out and touched his lips, making Sven growl under his breath. His hands moved up and down her back, and he started thinking of where they might sit down to continue this.

As he shifted position, they came under a trickle of water—freezing cold from seeping down through a crack in the ice. Gerri gasped and jerked back. She stared at him in astonishment, and then looked up and laughed. "I guess we should expect that from a glacier." Then she looked at him, still smiling, but not speaking. Sven started to realize what he had been about to do. He was still finding words to apologize when Gerri grinned and put her fingers to his lips.

"My adventure is just getting better. Do you realize that I might be the only girl in all of South Carolina who's been kissed inside a glacier?"

He had to laugh with her. Her laughter always gladdened his heart. In fact, he already had some ideas about more drawings of her. Besides, since she was obviously not offended by that kiss, he would put any misgivings aside.

———

Gerri would have liked to have stayed there all day, hiking further up the mountain; exploring and just enjoying Sven's company. But the weather was worsening. The sun clouded over; the wind picked up; and the temperature dropped. There was the threat of rain—and if there was anything that Gerri had learned in her stay, it was that Juneau had a tendency to make good on such threats.

They were almost trotting down the hill, trying to beat the rain, when Sven called for a rest stop. "Let's rest for a few minutes and grab a bite to eat. We have time."

"You need to rest?" Gerri teased. "I could run *down*hill all day."

"You'd be surprised," Sven said as he took two U-No candy bars out of his pack and handed one to her. "You feel fine now, but you'll feel it here tomorrow." He gestured to the fronts of his thighs.

"We'll see," said Gerri as she hungrily attacked the candy. "Ummm. I'm lucky they don't have these in South Carolina. I'd be even fatter than I am already." Instantly, she regretted her unguarded words—she didn't want to call Sven's attention to her deficiencies.

But he just snorted. After a minute, he elaborated. "That's ridiculous. You're not a bit fat. In fact, you're very nicely proportioned, if you don't mind my saying so. And with all of the exercise you get, that's not likely to change."

If I don't mind? Are you kidding? But she merely beamed and said, "No, of course I don't mind. Thank you." *Would Thurman have come up with such a courtly compliment? Not likely.*

Sven stared at her. When Gerri's dimples were blazing at full wattage, he had to be very careful, lest he do something foolish. It was bad enough that he couldn't stop thinking about that kiss. He made a show of checking his watch. "We should get started again," he said. He took her candy wrapper and stuffed both of them into his pack.

Gerri sensed his shy embarrassment, and she smiled secretly as they continued down the hill at a slower pace. She liked how Sven could make her feel appreciated without making her feel like prey.

Searching for a neutral topic of conversation, she looked at the valley in front of them as well as the water and the mountains beyond. "Look, it's already raining on that island. We'd better hurry."

"Douglas Island," Sven supplied helpfully. "That rain will be here in half an hour, but we'll be back at the truck in plenty of time."

"Look how pretty it is. Maybe I'll take a picture."

Sven considered the scene for a moment. "I think you'd be disappointed. The clouds and the mist would wash out all of the color. You'd need an expensive camera and special filters to increase the contrast."

"Oh." Gerri thought about that. Her remark had been offhand and she hadn't expected such a technical answer. It shouldn't have surprised her—Sven was a painter and painting was similar to photography. "Did you ever think about trying photography instead of painting?"

"Nooo…" He paused. That answer was easy, but his reasons were a bit harder to express. "I like the challenge of capturing a scene just the way I want it through my own skill. Without any extra equipment and without the extra step of film development. It's more work, but…" He shrugged.

Gerri thought of that sketch that he had made of her when she'd just seen the porpoises. Would the camera have made her look as good? Probably not. She certainly wasn't complaining. "I saw a couple of your paintings in Taku Books. They were very nice. I'd love to see some more."

Sven looked at his watch again. *Could we swing by my house? No, I'd want to clean it up first.* But before he could say anything, Gerri piped up again.

"But I can't do it today. I promised Mindy that I'd go to a political rally with her tonight. She'll worry if I'm late."

Sven shot her a disgusted look. "Of course: in the hands of the malevolent monster."

"I'm sorry. She…"

"That's all right, don't worry about it. I was just blowing off steam."

"Have you ever tried explaining your point of view to Mindy?"

"No. And don't you try either."

Gerri had been considering just that. There were still things that she didn't know about Sven—the violence thing came to mind—but she was convinced that he was not as bad as Mindy thought. But still… he was so adamant. "Why not?"

"I don't want to come between you and Mindy. But I also don't want to come between Mindy and her family."

"Why would that happen?"

Sven grimaced and shook his head. "Mindy's mother is possessed by her hatred of me. Her whole life revolved around Laura's ambitions, and I took that away from her. If Mindy started defending me, her mother would go spastic. It would tear their family apart. It's best to leave well enough alone."

Gerri started to object, but one glance at Sven's expression stopped her. And in case his expression wasn't clear, he quickly changed the subject. "Let's walk faster—that rain is moving this way quickly."

She considered her impulse as they hurried toward the truck. She had no business talking about this obviously sensitive subject. They, after all, had lived through the terrible experience and had lived with the aftermath in the years since. She, however, quite literally didn't know what she was talking about.

But it saddened her. These two people—each of whom had proved to be a wonderful friend—were locked into perpetual strife. But she would be gone soon. She decided to enjoy the company of each of them for the few remaining weeks of her adventure.

———

"You went *inside* the glacier? I've never been on that trail."

"I can take you there next time I'm in town."

"That's a turnabout—you showing me around. But yes, I'd like that."

Gerri had told Mindy about her glacier trip, being careful to downplay Sven's role. In her telling, he was reduced to little more than a chauffeur. She would have loved to say more. She wanted a confidant with whom she could talk about the kiss that she and Sven had shared. But not Mindy. In fact, she couldn't think of anyone whom she could tell. Not her mother, whose immediate response would be "Isn't he white?" Gerri sighed. That part of her adventure would just remain her secret.

The next morning, Gerri went to the grocery early to shop for their next trip. Mindy volunteered to drive her before going to work.

As they unloaded the groceries onto the dock, Mindy asked nervously, "Do you need help carrying them to the boat?" But Gerri knew that Mindy would rather avoid running into Sven.

"No, I'm fine. I'll just take two or three loads. You go ahead and get to work."

They hugged goodbye and Gerri watched Mindy's car disappear down the street. She turned to pick up her first load and almost ran into Wally, who was coming up the ramp from the floats.

He gave her a strange look and gestured toward Mindy's car. "You know her?"

"Yes, we're friends. I met her the first day I came to Juneau. I stay with her when I'm not out on the Glacier Gal."

Wally made a face. He didn't like this one damn bit. In his opinion, Gerri was leading Sven around by the nose. And Mindy would say or do anything to make Sven's life miserable. *So what are they cooking up?* "So what's going on? Does Sven know about this?"

Was everybody worried about this feud? "Yes, he knows. And yes, I know that they don't get along."

Now there's an understatement! "Did she put you up to asking him for a job? You know you can't trust anything she says."

"Sven admitted that much of what she said was true." *Can I get Wally's side of this without making him angry?*

"He is too damn agreeable for his own good. I guarantee that someone's up to something."

Gerri's eyes widened as she realized what Wally was insinuating. "I beg your pardon, *Mr. Trager.* If you're implying that I would let Mindy use me to hurt Sven, then you owe me an apology. I would never hurt him. Never."

Wally just stared back. He had never seen Gerri angry. He couldn't help but be impressed by her fire. Belatedly, he remembered Sven's telling him about the Arctic Saloon episode: Gerri had been ready to wade into the fight, brandishing a champagne bottle. He then remembered their horseplay at the dock. The affection that they showed then was not one-sided. He took a deep breath to gird himself for an unpleasant duty—Damn, but he hated apologizing.

"I'm sorry," he offered grudgingly, "I didn't mean that you would help her. She might be planning something behind your back."

"OK, but I don't think so. She just found out two days ago, and she knows I need the money that I get from working on the Glacier Gal."

Wally stared off into the distance, deep in thought. He looked unconvinced.

"Look," Gerri entreated. "I didn't ask to get into the middle of something like this. I really like Mindy, and I like Sven at least as much." *Maybe too much...* "And his wife's death sounds tragic, but that shouldn't cause a feud that lasts for years. Maybe you could explain it to me a bit?" She looked at him hopefully.

Wally looked at her thoughtfully. Then he looked around and pointed to a wooden bench. "Put down those groceries for a minute and let's sit."

When they had settled onto the bench, he started in. "The Schumachers were an ambitious bunch, and it all revolved around Laura. Her mother was grooming her to be a movie star. The odds against something like that were high, of course, but they were determined. They sent her to Seattle for acting lessons a couple of times..." He paused and shrugged.

"Who knows; she might have had a chance. She was real pretty—in a flashy way. Pinup pretty, if you know what I mean."

Gerri nodded, but felt a stab of hurt. *If that was what Sven was used to...*

"This was before Sven was even in the picture, mind you.

"Then all of the fuss about boxing happened." He glanced at Gerri inquiringly, but she just shrugged and shook her head.

"He went on a shopping trip to Seattle with his parents when he was sixteen. He wasn't getting along too well with them, but that's another story. They pretty much left him on his own while they were shopping. One day he wandered into a boxing gym.

"Somehow, he convinced the proprietors to let him try his hand. They probably figured 'what the hell;' I mean, he looked as strong as an ox even then and if he got a little beat up, well, no skin off their noses.

"Only, it was he who did the beating. He was a natural, I guess. He came back to Juneau saying that he wanted to be a boxer. We didn't think too much of it—I mean kids change their minds about what they want to be all of the time."

Wally shook his head. "Then things got crazy. A few weeks later, a boxing promoter breezed into town. He tried—hard—to talk Sven and his parents into signing a contract. But he didn't leave it at that. He threw a lot of money around and he talked to the local newspaper about how Sven could be the next Ingemar Johansson." He stopped and looked at Gerri significantly.

She realized that she was supposed to be impressed, but she couldn't oblige. "I'm sorry, but I don't know who that is."

Wally made a resigned noise. "Not a boxing fan. OK. He was the heavyweight champion of the world during part of that time. You know: 'toonder and lightning?' That's how Johansson described his right fist."

Now, Gerri remembered the bartender's cryptic phrase at the Arctic Saloon. She raised her eyebrows and nodded slowly. "I see. And 'toonder' means…thunder?"

Wally looked satisfied at her reaction. "Yes. Swedish accent. Johansson was from Sweden."

"How did Sven handle all of that?"

"Pretty well, for a sixteen year old. He didn't sign a contract, but he did make a couple more trips—paid for by the promoter—to Seattle to work out in that gym."

"Meanwhile, thanks to the articles in the newspaper, Sven was a big man in town. People started calling him 'toonder and lightning.'" Wally stopped and sighed. "That's when the Schumachers got involved."

"All of them?"

"Well, not Mindy, of course. She was just a kid. But the parents? Yeah. At least the mother. Laura never did much of anything without her mother's approval. Anyway, Laura started making a big play for Sven. And she was the big deal in high school, so she certainly caught his attention. Next thing you know…"

"They fell in love that fast?"

That caused Wally to briefly look askance at her. "I wouldn't know about that. She got pregnant. The Schumachers talked about sending her to Seattle for an abortion. Not public talk—Sven told me this. But Sven was determined to do the right thing, which to him meant marrying her."

"So they weren't in love?" Gerri hated herself for caring about the answer, but Wally just shrugged.

"Who knows? Sven said all of the right things, but I think he could feel the weight of all of this hanging around his neck."

They both sat quietly for a time. Gerri broke the silence. "Was that why he decided not to be a boxer? Because of his marital responsibilities?"

"I don't know why. He didn't tell me. I don't think he told anybody. It was a few weeks later, after one of his trips to Seattle. He just announced that he wasn't going to box any more, and he wouldn't talk about it any more.

"The Schumachers were livid. He was to have been Laura's means of getting noticed by Hollywood. That pretty much sent the marriage down the drain."

"I can imagine. One minute you're married to a man destined for fame. The next minute you're married to a small town guy who intends to become a fisherman."

Wally scowled. "Are you saying you sympathize with her?"

"No, not a bit. I don't think that's a good reason for getting married. When I marry, it'll be for love."

Wally looked down towards the floats, and then stood up. "I see Sven coming this way. He's probably looking for you." He reached for one of her bags. "They have carts at the foot of the ramp. I'll help you carry these down."

At the bottom, just before Sven came into earshot, Wally leaned in close to Gerri. "I told you this in confidence. You won't say anything, will you?"

"I won't say anything. I promise."

After they had stowed the groceries in the galley of the Glacier Gal, Sven turned to Gerri. "Wally was helping you?"

She grinned. "Helpful and cordial, both."

Sven shook his head and smiled. "Will wonders never cease?"

CHAPTER 19

Gerri was tired, but her day's work was not over. She and Sven had been out for two weeks, but had agreed to keep going because the fishing was so good. Today, they had fished until a rising storm had forced them to seek an anchorage. They were about an hour away from a safe cove, but it would be a tough hour.

She was at the helm while Sven was trying to fix the suddenly recalcitrant galley stove. She liked steering the boat—the sense of responsibility and, maybe, power. Some days it was easy. When the water was calm, one just had to maintain the heading and watch for logs and other hazards. The biggest danger was being lulled into inattention.

On days like today, though, being the helmsman was hard work. The clouds were dark and the rain, lashed by a strong wind, was beating against the windows of the pilot house. The waves were large and getting larger. Some were breaking over the Glacier Gal's bow and cascading against the pilot house. At Sven's direction, Gerri had throttled the engine back below normal cruising speed, but the boat was still tossing around. They were quartering into the prevailing sea, which meant that the waves were coming at them at an angle of 45° off the bow. So each wave not only pitched the boat around, but tried to push it off course.

She glanced back into the galley to try to judge Sven's progress. Even though she wasn't cooking now, they needed that stove. It provided the warmth for the boat, and the storm-borne wind was cold and raw.

And the cooking was important as well; they were both hungry. In nicer weather—and with a functioning stove—she would start the cooking now so that they could eat immediately after anchoring. Cooking on a boat in anything but the calmest water was an experience in itself. As with everything else on the boat, the galley was designed for the weather. There were small railings on the stove and all of the counters, and all of the cabinet doors had latches which she had learned to use at all times.

She smiled as she imagined telling her mother about the adventure of cooking in these conditions. But her smile was short-lived—she wouldn't attempt cooking in *this* storm. Today she would wait until they had safely anchored. She was not about to risk a pot of boiling water sent flying by a gigantic wave.

She felt Sven's hands on her shoulders and she leaned back against him. She hadn't heard him over the engine noise, but it seemed as though she could tell when he was near. He leaned close and spoke into her ear.

"How are you doing?"

"I'm doing fine. I think the waves are getting worse." He massaged her shoulders. "Oh, that feels good. Don't stop." She hadn't realized how tense her shoulders had gotten.

As he continued his massage, Gerri thought about the last two weeks. The 'glacier kiss' had not been repeated, but there had been small expressions of intimate affection more and more frequently from each of them. She was willing to admit, to herself at least, that she had a large crush on Sven. *And what's wrong with that?* There was no safer place to have it—far from the racial turmoil of South Carolina: thousands of miles from the disapproving eyes of family, friends, and future coworkers. When she returned home, all of this would exist only in her memories.

And what of Sven? Her feminine instincts told her that he was attracted to her as well. Ironically, she was surer of his affection than she ever had been of Thurman's, in spite of the fact that Sven had made no overt passes at her. Was he shy? Or reluctant to get involved with a black woman? Or reluctant to get involved with someone who was leaving so soon? She would love to encourage him subtly. For the first, and probably only, time in her life, she thought with amusement that she would welcome the advice of those sophisticated, big city girls who used to tease her in college.

As Gerri luxuriated under Sven's hands, it occurred to her that she should say something about the business of the day. "I set our course a few degrees to the starboard. We're well out from the point and the chart doesn't show any reefs, so I thought we could begin to turn around it."

"Hmmm." Sven had noticed. He had detected the difference in the motion of the boat. In fact, this was the main reason that he had left the galley. "But don't change any further. In weather like this, we can't make a curved path around the point. We want to stay out of the trough at all costs. Instead of our path being a circular arc, we want it to be two straight lines with a sharp angle where we turn." He gestured with his hands.

Gerri considered that. The 'trough' was the dreaded configuration where the waves hit the boat directly from the side. It caused the boat to roll violently—or even capsize, if the waves were large enough. She had learned a lot about seamanship but, she realized, there was much left to learn. She nodded. "Sorry, I didn't think of that." She looked for a way to change the subject. "Did you finish with the stove?"

Sven grunted. "No. I think the fuel line is fouled. Must have been some dirt in the tank and the rocking of the boat stirred it up. I'll go back now and clear it out. I was hoping to avoid that 'cause it's so cramped behind the stove."

"Do you want me to do it? I'm smaller."

He paused. He had had a second reason for coming up to the pilot house to check on her. One that he didn't want to tell her about. One of the things that had delighted him thus far about Gerri's adaptation to boating was her freedom from seasickness. She had felt queasy only once, when they had been out on the ocean on a fairly windy day. Sven had made sure that she was kept busy and that she stayed in the fresh air, and her queasiness eventually dissipated.

He was under no illusion that she could control motion sickness, or that he could control it for her. But the fonder of her that he got, the more he wanted everything to be perfect for her during her 'adventure.' He wished that he had picked up some medicine, just to keep on hand, for today's storm would be the toughest test by far.

In the long run, most people's bodies grew accustomed to the motion. But not everybody—and the adjustment process could be miserable. He remembered a friend who had loved boating until he experienced his first really rough weather. He never again wanted to set foot on a boat.

Without the medicine, Sven had only a few heuristics that he thought helped: keep your mind off your queasiness and stay in as much fresh air as possible. In keeping with this, he didn't want Gerri to be crawling around amidst the oil fumes behind the stove.

Finally, he gave the only excuse he could think of. "No, it's dirty back there. I'd rather be the one to get filthy." It was awkward because her idea made a lot of sense, and if he told her his real reasons, she would insist on trying anyway. To forestall an argument, he added, "Let me go back to the galley and get this over with." He patted her on the shoulder and returned to his stove repairs.

As he settled in behind the stove, he thought again—Gerri was turning into an excellent crew member. No, she was *already* an excellent crew member. Sven couldn't think of anyone else of her experience that he would entrust the Glacier Gal to in this weather, even though he was trying to keep a close eye on her.

But that was the one thing about her that he found troubling. Her strength was potentially her weakness. She showed a lot of initiative. Sometimes too much. Her change of the boat's heading just now was not serious; she would have realized it quickly if she had turned further and the motion of the boat had become too violent. But the outcomes of her well-meaning decisions weren't always so benign. She could have gotten seriously hurt, for example, when she tried to fend off that piling in the boat harbor.

He needed to talk to her about this. The Alaskan wilderness was full of things which could kill a person and Gerri didn't yet appreciate that. He should have talked to her already, and to his disgust, he knew exactly why he had been putting it off—he treasured their affectionate relationship, and he was reluctant to appear as a disciplinarian. *There's no fool like an old fool.*

Even that description—affectionate relationship—was an evasion. She was driving him nuts. He was constantly looking for excuses to touch her—and heaven knows, he wanted more than a touch. But he wouldn't violate her trust. She was just a kid. Besides, he was her boss and he refused to take advantage of that relationship. And he was still replaying that kiss in his mind. He wondered, not for the first time, how he would have reacted if there had been someone like Gerri when he was in high school. Would he have had the sense to resist Laura's blandishments then? He thought so, but he was honest enough to have some doubts.

He was older and wiser now. Gerri was the kind of girl—or make that the kind of woman, as the libbers would remind him—that any guy would be lucky to have. Not that it mattered. She would be going back to South Carolina soon and she would undoubtedly do better than some old fisherman. He sighed and reached behind the stove.

As Sven left the pilot house, Gerri briefly glared at his retreating back. It was his boat and he could do what he wanted. But, *really.* 'I don't want you to get dirty' was such a dumb excuse. What did he think she got every day while baiting hooks or hauling fish off the lines?

The thing that really bothered her was that she was coming to revel in their partnership—she loved the feeling of working smoothly with a man whose company she enjoyed. A man whom she admired. A man whom she found attractive—too attractive. This aspect of her summer had been an education. She now knew what she wanted to look for in a husband—and knew that Thurman would never have been right for her.

Sven, of course, was unattainable. He would never want to live in South Carolina. Nor would that be viable for Gerri. An interracial relationship would, at best, be a source of constant whispers, and at worst, a source of constant harassment. Better to be realistic—her attraction to Sven was just one more part of what was turning into a most wonderful adventure.

While Gerri was thinking about this, she still had to concentrate on guiding the boat. That was almost a full-time task, as the storm seemed to be getting worse. She could hear the howling of the wind, punctuated by the crashing of the waves over the bow. Suddenly, she became aware of another sound added to the mix. It took her a minute, but she finally realized that something was loose; rolling around on the deck.

Leaving the wheel for just a moment, she cracked open the side door of the pilot house and leaned out. At first, she saw nothing. Then it rolled into view. Sven had several five gallon buckets, originally containing paint, which he had cleaned out and used to store odds and ends. One of those had come loose from its fastenings. Its top was closed tightly, so at least whatever was in it wouldn't spill out. She was tempted to let it roll around, but the bucket could damage something as it tumbled around the deck. Or if it went overboard, Sven would have to replace its contents, and some of the tools he kept in these buckets were expensive.

Gerri came back inside and checked her heading as she tried to decide what to do. She craned her neck to look back at Sven. He was sprawled on the floor of the galley with his head and shoulders behind the stove. She really didn't want to bother him every time some little issue came up. But she knew that the boat wouldn't steer itself in this weather. The waves and the wind would push the bow to the right—to starboard.

But she had an idea. If she changed the heading to the left to compensate for that, it would buy her a few seconds. Then, if she was very fast… She stuck her head outside again. *I can do this.* She visualized it—step out onto the deck, take three quick steps and grab the bucket. She would simply bring it inside the pilot house—she certainly didn't want to take the extra time to fasten it on deck in the storm. She could almost imagine explaining her reasoning proudly to Sven over dinner and Sven nodding his approval and smiling.

She shook her head to clear those silly thoughts away. *Time to get this done.* After steering the boat left a few degrees, she took a deep breath and opened the door. One quick glance around, and then she stepped outside. The wind caught her instantly and she shivered. One more reason to do this quickly—she wasn't dressed for this weather.

Quickly she reached the bucket and bent over to grab it. Just then the boat lurched and the bucket skittered out of her reach. With a grunt of disgust, she caught up to it and reached for it again. As she did so, she heard a crashing sound behind her. She turned around to see what it was and her jaw dropped. The largest wave that she'd ever seen was crashing over the bow and surging toward her. She opened her mouth to scream, but the wave hit her and knocked her backwards before she could get a sound out. It picked her up effortlessly and carried her to the side of the boat. She tried to grab a railing, but the wave was too powerful. She briefly registered the scrape of her calves against the gunwale and then she was overboard—submerged in the frigid ocean—with the Glacier Gal steadily pulling away from her.

CHAPTER 20

Sven bit back an oath as a particularly abrupt roll of the boat pushed him against the stove. *Why am I doing this now—in this weather?* But he knew exactly why, and it was a lousy reason. He wanted to be able to relax with Gerri in the galley after they anchored. They were both tired, but he knew that Gerri would insist on cooking before she would relax. He wanted to have the stove ready so that her day wouldn't be any longer than it had to be.

But that wasn't necessary. They could grab sandwiches, wolf them down, fall into their respective bunks, and get some overdue rest. But that would eliminate the togetherness that he was looking forward to. So here he was, fooling with the stove during the worst storm of the season—and leaving Gerri to handle the boat alone.

Another roll of the boat—the worst yet—caused his wrench to slide out of his reach. *Screw it!* He'd do the stove later; he should be with Gerri in the pilot house now. He started sliding out from behind the stove.

Walking was difficult. Sven braced himself against the wall as he hurried through the short passageway from the galley to the pilot house. He couldn't see Gerri from his angle, but he saw a giant wave crash across the front deck as the Glacier Gal buried its bow in the water and felt the boat shudder as the bow fought its way back up. He sped up; Gerri's training didn't cover anything like this.

As he stepped into the pilot house, he stopped, astonished. Gerri was not there. Almost automatically, he checked the heading, and then looked around. The door to the side deck was ajar. *Now why the hell would she go outside?* She must have had some reason—some notion that something needed fixing. Now he was starting to get scared.

He stuck his head out and looked around, ducking back briefly as another wave swept across the deck. She was nowhere to be seen. She wouldn't have gone to the back deck—if she'd wanted to do that, she would have come through the galley. Panic started clutching at his gut. There was only one place she could be—overboard!

He jerked back inside. There was a little voice moaning in the back of his brain: *Not Gerri! I can't lose Gerri!* He willed himself to ignore the voice, and his hands flowed over the controls by instinct. Within seconds, he had cut the power to just above idle, spun the wheel hard over to turn back in the direction from which they'd come, and turned on all of the outside flood lights. He heard something crash in the galley as the boat rolled heavily in the trough, but he ignored it; that was unimportant now. He quickly grabbed a portable spotlight and stepped out on deck, leaving the boat to wallow in its new heading.

He knew that he had to find Gerri fast, before she succumbed to hypothermia. But he had no way of knowing how long ago she had gone over. He tried to calculate, but it was hard to think straight. He couldn't have left her more than two minutes ago—maybe three. But still, even at its reduced speed, the boat had been making perhaps eight or nine feet per second. That meant that she could be hundreds of feet away—maybe up to a quarter mile.

Sven played the spotlight around, but all he saw in the approaching darkness was the occasional glint of a whitecap. The raw wind tore at his shirtsleeves, but he didn't even feel it. The cold that he felt was deeper—in his heart. He tried to fight the sense of hopelessness. *I won't give up, no matter what. If I have to search until I run out of fuel... If I have to search all night...*

———

Gerri surfaced and shook her head to clear her eyes. She could see the boat when she was on the top of a wave, but it seemed distant. When she was in the trough between two waves, she couldn't see anything. She tried to figure out what to do. While she treaded water, she slowly turned. She couldn't see anything but the wind-whipped waves. She looked again for the Glacier Gal. It seemed to be even further away.

Now that the initial shock was wearing off, she was starting to feel cold. Very cold. Sven had mentioned the dangers of hypothermia, but Gerri didn't remember what he had said about the symptoms. She did remember his saying that a person would last only a few minutes in this cold water. And she realized with a sinking heart that Sven probably didn't even know that she was overboard.

She refused to give up. She thought about her family that she so longed to see again. She thought about Sven… But what to do? She could never catch the boat. Could she reach shore? Not likely. She remembered from checking the chart in the pilot house that it was about a half mile away. She didn't know whether she could swim that far even on a good day. And she could already feel her muscles stiffening in the cold—it was getting hard to even tread water.

Gerri looked around. The Glacier Gal was almost invisible—she could just see the light on the mast from the top of a wave. She turned again toward where the shore should be. The tree line was now visible—barely—through the low clouds. Then she noticed, incongruously, that the bucket was bobbing in the water about ten yards away. She had thought that it would sink, but evidently—after all of her trouble—Sven didn't have enough in it to make it sink. And, just as important, he had sealed the top of the bucket tightly.

But if it was floating, then she could use it as a makeshift life ring. She was too chilled to get excited. In fact she was fighting the urge to simply relax and let go, but she forced herself to swim toward the bucket. At first, she wasn't making any progress. *If I can't even swim ten yards, how can I expect to reach the shore?* Then she realized that the wind was blowing the bucket away from her. *I can do this—just a few strong strokes.* She thought of her family again. She thought of her brother Rich's teaching her to swim in a creek near their farm. At the time, she complained incessantly about her hair, but now she was thankful that Rich had persevered. She thought again of Sven and how she wanted to get to know him better. Somehow, she used these thoughts to find a burst of strength and reach the bucket.

When she finally reached it, she barely had the strength to grab it and hang on. But how could she get to shore? She decided to start kicking, but she couldn't make her legs follow her orders. When she was on top of the next wave, she saw a flash out of the corner of her eye.

The Glacier Gal had turned and was heading back this way, lit up like a Christmas tree. She felt a faint surge of hope as she watched. Maybe Sven would see her here. Then she realized that the boat wasn't heading precisely toward her. It would pass her about fifty yards away. Could he see her from such a distance? It would be hard. If only she had a light.

The boat was moving slowly, and she saw Sven on deck playing a spotlight over the surface of the water, but while she watched, he moved out of sight to check the other side. In a few minutes, the boat would be abreast of her. But she would be just a speck in the ocean, visible only when she was at the height of a wave. Could she shout? She barely had the strength to breathe, and she knew she couldn't be heard over the wind and waves.

Now he was back on her side of the boat. The spotlight passed over her briefly and then moved on. Gerri had an idea, borne of desperation. The bottom of the bucket was shiny metal. Maybe if she could orient it just right...

Sven played the spotlight ceaselessly. The boat should, he calculated, be close to where she went overboard, but he didn't see anything. Of course, if she started swimming for shore. No, he didn't think she would do that. On the other hand, if she had sunk... He stifled that thought. One more sweep of the spotlight and he would go back to check the other side.

There! Was that a flash of light in the beam of his light? He looked again and saw nothing but the dark water. He sighed at his brief, false hope.

Wait! He saw the flash again. There was something bright out there in the water. It was one of his jury-rigged containers, facing just right to reflect his light. He squinted and saw Gerri clinging to the bucket! A great flood of relief washed over him. Thank heavens. But they weren't out of the woods yet—or the water, as he thought in his new, giddy mood.

He waved and shouted. "Hang on, Gerri. I'll be there in a minute." He thought he saw her hand move in a weak acknowledgement.

It took only a moment for Sven to maneuver the boat close to Gerri, but it seemed like forever. Her arms wanted to let go, but she clung tightly to the bucket. When he was just a few feet away, he tossed a coiled line which practically slapped her in the face.

"Grab it and pull yourself to the boat."

"I don't think I have the strength. My muscles won't work right." She was afraid to let go of the bucket.

He frowned in concern—that was a classic symptom of hypothermia. "Then just wrap the line around your wrists and hold it as best you can. I'll pull you in."

Finally—gloriously—she was within reach and Sven grabbed her hand. "Let go of the bucket and I'll pull you aboard."

Gerri shook her head stubbornly. "I'm not losing this bucket. It caused all of this trouble in the first place."

Sven had to smile at her stubbornness, if not her good sense. He grabbed the bucket with his other hand and threw it behind him on the deck. Then he lifted Gerri aboard.

"You're strong," she said groggily.

Sven took her in his arms and squeezed. "I'm so pumped up, that I could probably lift the boat. Oh Gerri, I was so scared."

She laughed weakly. "*You* were scared..." A spasm of shivering wracked her body.

He carried her quickly inside, trying to figure out what to do. He couldn't ignore the storm—he had to give his attention to navigating the boat around the point and into the safe anchorage. Meanwhile, the stove still wasn't working and it was cold even inside the cabin. It would be even colder down in the fo'c's'le. He paused to adjust the boat's heading quickly and carried Gerri to his room.

"You need to get out of those clothes. I'll put a T-shirt on the bed. Can you change and bunk in here? It'll be warmer than your bunk down below."

"I'll try." He could hardly hear her.

"I have to get back to the pilot house. I'll check on you as soon as I can."

This time she just nodded.

————

Sven didn't know how he managed to get the boat to the anchorage. Navigating in the storm demanded his full attention, but his thoughts were on Gerri. Was she all right? Would his rather thin blanket be enough to restore her body heat? Was she still in danger?

As soon as the boat was anchored safely out of the storm, he raced back to his cabin. He opened the door cautiously, worried that Gerri might still be undressing, but she was in the bed. The blanket was pulled up so that only her face was showing. He knelt on the floor beside her. "Are you all right? Can I get you anything?"

Her response was so weak that he could barely hear. "Cold."

Sven, like most Alaskan outdoorsmen, had more than a little acquaintance with hypothermia. He laid his hand against her forehead. She felt scarily cold. *But that's not under the blanket,* he thought hopefully. He snaked his hand beneath the blanket. She had her arms folded tightly around her chest and her back and arms didn't feel any warmer. He was starting to get scared again. Time was important here. He jumped to his feet. "I'll be right back."

He hurried to the galley and quickly assessed the stove. His heart sank. The crashing noise that he had heard earlier when turning the boat apparently had been his tools as well as the loose parts of the stove. He glanced around hastily, but realized that he was kidding himself: Fixing the stove would not be quick. He had only one idea left.

"Gerri," he said, stripping his clothes off as he spoke, "I'm going to lie down with you to try to warm you up." Incongruously, he worried that she would misinterpret his motives, but she barely seemed to react. Probably just a reflection of his own thoughts, he realized. But there was no need to worry—he was firmly focused on saving Gerri's life.

Maybe later—much later—he would sigh over the silken feel of her skin. But not now.

He slid in behind her on the small bunk and spooned with her, trying for the greatest area of contact between them. He alternated between holding her tightly to him and rubbing her arms to generate friction. Occasionally, he moved an arm down and rubbed her hip and thigh, but that severely tested his resolve to behave impeccably—he quickly realized that she was wearing nothing besides his T-shirt.

After what seemed like a very long time, Gerri's shivering lessened and her breathing became more relaxed. Sven didn't stop stroking and holding her, though. He didn't want to take any chances with her recovery. And, in any case, sleep eluded him for most of the night.

CHAPTER 21

Gerri woke gradually and felt as if she was in a different world. All signs of the storm were gone. The sun was peeking through the window and the sea was calm. She could hear the faint cry of some seagulls in the distance, but otherwise, all was quiet.

She could remember the horrific events of the previous night, but to her faint surprise, the memory had remoteness—as if it had happened to someone else. Instead, Gerri felt warm and secure. Without moving, she eyed Sven's arm which was still draped over her. He looked powerful even in repose. She took an intense satisfaction at his slumberous embrace. She almost wriggled with pleasure, but she didn't want to wake him yet.

Would he be angry? Surely she deserved it. Going out to get the bucket without telling him—and leaving the helm to do so—was irresponsible. She could see that now. If he hadn't somehow sensed that something was wrong... *How did he do that so quickly?* And if he hadn't seen her in the water... But he had seen her. *Maybe my bucket mirror worked.* And he had rescued her. For the second time, he had rescued her. She smiled. *My hero!* That sounded trite, but it was true. Right now, there was nowhere else she wanted to be but in Sven's arms.

But after a few more minutes, Gerri got restless. Sven had provided comfort and warmth all night, but now she wanted more. She wanted to continue from where the glacier kiss had left off. Gerri thought about where she was and what that meant. But she didn't hesitate. She didn't pretend to be experienced in the ways of sex, but she was utterly sure. This was the right time. And this was the right man. She squirmed around from the spooning position so that she could embrace him properly.

Sven lay in bed in a pleasantly lethargic state. He was in no hurry to get up. It had been the wee hours of the morning before he had been confident enough about Gerri's recovery to allow himself the luxury of sleep. Now, however, she felt warm and her breathing was normal.

In fact, she felt wonderful. He would have been in a state of bliss about her relaxing in his arms, except for one little problem. Well, not so little—that was the problem. His morning erection—normally unobtrusive and quick to disappear when he got up—was magnified a hundredfold by Gerri's presence. He had kept a slight distance between their lower bodies to avoid offending her. And he was prepared to get up quickly when she awakened, but he hoped to put that off for a while. It simply felt too good to lie here embracing her.

Suddenly the status quo was upset. Gerri started moving and turning in his arms. He tried to make his arms unwind, but she quickly put her arms around him and held him close. She was indeed strong, he thought in passing. And he was weak. She made him weak.

She smiled shyly. "Good morning, my hero."

Some remote corner of Sven's brain wanted him to be a gentleman, but his body rebelled against the very idea. The least he could do was to pretend some kind of normalcy. "Good morning. How do you feel?"

"I feel wonderful, thank you." She wriggled against him.

Sven groaned. She felt wonderful, all right. In a minute, his state would be obvious, but he didn't have the will to disengage. 'Consenting adults,' he told himself and shoved the 'gentleman' instinct out of his head. He looked her in her beautiful eyes as his lips brushed hers.

Gerri's smile transformed from shyness to satisfaction. She had been right. Sven wanted her as much as she wanted him. She would worry about the outside world later—everything she wanted now was right here. The kiss turned hungry as she ground against him.

Sven growled in inarticulate pleasure as he probed her lips with his tongue. Gerri opened her mouth to receive it, meeting it with her own in a dancing duel. She shivered as Sven's hands stroked her back and moved to her sides. He moved his caresses slowly up her sides under her shirt until he was able to tease her nipples lightly with his thumbs.

Suddenly, he became impatient. Abruptly, he grabbed her shirt and started to tug it over her head. There was a ripping sound. "Damn," he said, hoping that Gerri wouldn't be put off by his eagerness. She just giggled as he settled for rucking the shirt up under her arms

Gerri had a fleeting thought: as bad as she had felt last night, she was now glad that she had not had the strength to put on more than the borrowed shirt. Which led her to another thought: she could clearly feel Sven's arousal, but it was constrained by his shorts. That would not do. She tried to grab them by the waistband and remove them, but, made clumsy by the continuing distraction of his hands, she could not remove them.

Sven was lost in his own tsunami of sensation. Gerri felt as good as his illicit imagination had predicted. Her breasts were a nice handful. Not pendulous pillows like Laura's, but firm and—in his opinion—in perfect proportion, just like the rest of her. He broke the kiss and buried his face in her neck. She even smelled good—faintly of salt from her inadvertent swim combined with the pleasant smell that could only be described 'Gerri-esque.'

His blissful exploration of her body was interrupted by her grunt of annoyance. She was trying to pull his underwear off with no success. He was immensely flattered, but couldn't help but chuckle.

She looked at him with mock severity and complained, "It's not fair. You have more clothes on than I do." Then she giggled at her boldness.

He grinned back. "You modern women are such a caution."

That earned him a blow in the shoulder with the heel of her hand and another giggle. "I'll caution *you*, mister."

"Allow me, please." He shifted his weight and slipped his shorts off. He considered stripping both of them completely, but his hunger was matched by that in her eyes—he couldn't wait any longer. Slowly—almost reverently—he put his lips to work on her left nipple and slipped one of his hands down to stroke the moistness between her thighs.

Gerri didn't claim to be an expert at this, but she wondered: was it supposed to feel this good before he was actually inside of her? She could feel the sensations spiraling out of control. Was there such a thing as premature ejaculation for women? The question became moot as she shattered, making a noise between a moan and a scream of primal satisfaction.

She hardly stopped for breath. Deciding that she didn't want to take a chance on disappointing him, she rolled onto her back, pulling Sven with her. "Please," she said, "Let's do it now."

Sven had never felt this out-of-control. And Gerri was already moist and ready. Finesse could wait for another time. He slotted himself and pushed.

There was a momentary resistance and a sharp intake of breath from Gerri. Before he could think about the implications of this, Gerri gyrated her hips and made an impatient noise. Rational thought was beyond him.

Gerri felt the momentary pain, but it wasn't as bad as she had been led to believe and it soon dissipated and she instinctively moved with Sven as he stroked powerfully into her.

In what seemed like only a minute, she felt another rising wave of tension and excitement. This was made more intense by Sven's ragged breathing. She was completely attuned to his body—she felt him tense up and jerk inside of her. That pushed her over some cliff, and she found herself in another orgasm, even stronger than the first.

She knew that before long, she would be analyzing this whole experience in her mind, but now all she could think of was catching her breath. Sven rolled off of her with a grunt and lay by her side with one arm partly splayed over her and the other folded over his head.

She turned toward him and brushed her hand across his chest. She wasn't sure what to say, but... *If sex is always this good... Wow!*

Sven groaned, "Gerri, I had no idea. I'm so sorry." He shook his head.

Gerri's smile froze. *Please, please, don't let him be disappointed.* "Well, I'm not sorry," she ventured. Working up her courage, she asked, "Was it not good? I mean..."

He snorted. "It was fantastic. If it had been any better, I probably would have had a heart attack. But I didn't think about the consequences. I didn't mean to put you at risk; I shouldn't have just bulled ahead."

Sven cursed himself silently. *Have I learned nothing since high school?* He had already screwed up Laura's life—and his own—by recklessly getting her pregnant. He couldn't bear it if he did this to Gerri as well. Which was ironic, since he found it easy—frighteningly and excitedly easy—to imagine doing the right thing by Gerri. A marriage to Gerri, even if it was forced by pregnancy, was much more pleasant to contemplate than his marriage to Laura.

But that was easy for him to say. Gerri's plans for her life certainly didn't include getting knocked up by someone that she'd probably never see after this summer. And the fact that she was a virgin knocked him for a loop. Bottom line: he had wanted her so badly that he never stopped to consider what he was doing. To make it worse, she was in an emotionally vulnerable state after her close call last night. Had she not been so, this would probably never have happened. Or if he'd given her time to think…

Gerri had no idea how to respond. *He said that he enjoyed it; is it the idea of commitment that worries him?* She wanted to defuse that—if Sven became uncomfortable around her she would be devastated. She forced herself to smile and answer lightheartedly.

"Don't worry about consequences. I don't expect any. Sven, don't you understand?" She looked at him beseechingly, "You're part of my adventure."

Sven was struck dumb—first by utter surprise, and then by the ridiculous irony of the situation. Commitment-free sex was supposed to be a male fantasy, not a female one. The women's libbers would probably find this to be a delightful turnabout. He would not have guessed that Gerri would be into casual sex, but maybe he didn't know her as well as he hoped he did.

Still, it hurt. He couldn't hide from it now—Gerri meant a lot to him. And some part of him had hoped that she felt the same way about him. But it was her choice. From what he had read about women's lib, they had some legitimate points. He couldn't *demand* that she care for him. She hadn't promised him anything. If he complained now, he would just spoil what little there was of their relationship. Disappointment or no, he couldn't stand to do that.

Then, there was the elephant in the room. The thing that she apparently hadn't considered. "I had no idea that you were a virgin. I didn't use any protection. What if you get pregnant?"

She made a dismissive gesture. "Don't worry about that. I'm on the pill."

"A virgin on the pill?"

Gerri agonized. She had no desire to explain her gullibility with respect to Thurman. "It's complicated."

Sven shook his head. "Never mind. It's none of my business." It was time to salvage whatever he could of their affectionate relationship. Never mind that for him, it had become more than that. He'd deal with that later when Gerri had gone back home.

He swallowed his disappointment and pasted on what he hoped was a carefree smile. "I'm honored to be part of your adventure. And I meant it when I said that this morning was wonderful."

———

Breakfast was almost nonexistent; only a few leftovers that they ate while steaming out to the fishing grounds. They stood in the pilot house eating, Sven at the wheel and Gerri watching the shore. Gerri tried to think of some way of bringing up the subject of their lovemaking—or maybe she didn't dare call it that. The subject of their sex might be more honest. Regardless of his supportive words, Sven had seemed utterly dismayed by what had happened.

Failing to come up with a graceful segue into that subject, she made some inconsequential remarks, but Sven didn't seem interested in responding. She looked at him, trying to read his expression. He caught her looking and stared back for a few seconds before smiling at her.

"A penny for your thoughts," he said. Sven was highly conscious of the fact that they had to talk about Gerri's accident and how to avoid a recurrence. Sven didn't want to be the one to bring it up—the last thing that he wanted was to scold her. She'd been through enough. And he didn't want to slide out of the partner role into the teacher/ boss role.

Gerri sighed. "I was just thinking about last night," she lied. "I was pretty stupid. I wouldn't blame you if you wanted to fire me."

Sven shook his head vigorously. "No, not at all. Everybody makes mistakes. Yours was a serious one, but you make fewer than most. I mean that. I would like you to tell me what happened, though."

Gerri summarized the events surrounding her fall overboard. She repeated the reasoning she had used to convince herself that she could grab the bucket safely, but she did not spare herself. The only thing she left out was her daydream about how Sven would be proud of her planning—if he was already nervous about commitment, letting him realize that she had a schoolgirl crush on him would only make him more uncomfortable.

When she finished, Sven didn't say anything for a long time. His eyes were scanning the water around them, and Gerri knew from experience that, even while concentrating on another subject, he was constantly evaluating likely fishing spots. She admired that ability—it was one of those things that made him a highliner. But right now, she wanted to shake him. She needed to hear something, even though she knew that it would be scathing.

Sven finally nodded. "OK," he said tentatively. Gerri let out the breath that she had been holding. "I can understand what you were thinking." She knew that there was a 'but' coming and waited anxiously. "And once you were in the water, grabbing onto that bucket was a good idea. Using it for a mirror was an even better idea. I don't honestly know if I would have thought of that."

Gerri opened her mouth to hurry him along—she wanted him to get to the bad part that she knew was coming. He shook his head imperceptibly and raised a finger to quiet her.

"Your first mistake was assuming that I couldn't be interrupted. Your second one—perhaps more fundamental—was not being suffi- ciently paranoid. I don't mean to be melodramatic, but the sea has a lot of ways to surprise you—and a lot of ways to kill you. Always think about what could go wrong."

Gerri nodded, relieved that Sven hadn't been as critical as she feared. "I get it. Anticipate the risks, so that you can eliminate them."

Sven rocked his head from side to side. "That's the idea, but you'll never eliminate them entirely. Let me tell you a story.

"A lot of people fish alone. I sometimes do myself. A few years back, there was someone who was called in to the Coast Guard as being overdue. So they mounted a search—with both planes and ships. They finally found his boat. It was empty and out of fuel, but they never found him."

Gerri felt a chill. "So what had happened?"

"Nobody knows for sure. Most likely he fell overboard for some reason and couldn't get back to his boat. Even trolling speed is faster than most people can swim."

"And he couldn't get to shore?" Gerri remembered her desperate hope that she could swim to shore.

"No. No chance. He was miles from shore."

As Gerri thought about that terrifying scenario, Sven checked the depth sounder and throttled the boat down. This was the signal that he had found a likely spot for fishing. Gerri jumped up, ready to start letting out the fishing gear. "Do you want me out on deck getting ready?"

Sven reached out and took her arm to keep her from leaving. "Wait a minute. We're not done discussing this yet."

Gerri looked at him apprehensively. He looked more somber than at any time during his dissection of her actions last night. Her heart pounded and she had to fight back tears. *This is the part where he says that I'm fired...*

The Glacier Gal was almost motionless now, rocking gently in its own wake, but Sven seemed oblivious to that. He was looking outside, but without really seeing a thing. Finally, he turned his head back to her.

"I've gone into great detail telling you what you did wrong. But you're young and you'll learn with time. But what about your old captain?"

Gerri instinctively started to protest his use of 'old,' but she clamped her jaws shut. He was in no mood for an interruption.

"Let's talk about *my* mistakes. They were doozies, and I have no excuse for them." He ticked off on his fingers. "My first mistake was being in such a hurry to fix the stove. It could have waited until we were anchored. We certainly didn't need it while we were underway.

"My second mistake—my big one—was leaving you alone to handle the storm. You're a good student, but that storm was just too much for you to handle so soon. It's..." He looked at her with a ghost of a smile. "You're the teacher. I'm sure you can imagine. It's as if I was a driving instructor who, after three lessons, turned you loose on a crowded freeway while I worked on something in the back seat."

Sven looked haunted and Gerri's heart went out to him. This wasn't the direction that she had expected in his comments. She squeezed his arm. "You've been good to me, Sven. I could have asked for help."

"I could have lost you, Gerri. I would never have forgiven myself—never."

She leaned into him and put her arms around him. "But you didn't." She looked for something to put a smile back on his face. "And I'm glad," she added with a grin.

That earned her a quick smile and a return hug. They stood there silently for a moment. Then Gerri couldn't resist asking, "Why were you so anxious to fix the stove anyway?"

Sven considered his answer. Here was a woman who had, in a short time, become very important to him. If he was to be honest with himself, he hoped very much that this morning's love making would be repeated. At the very least, he hoped that the chemistry between them would stay intact. Yet, for all of her affectionate nature, this was just a summer adventure for her. Confessing that his judgment had been impaired by a surpassing desire to spend time relaxing with her might well make her nervous. He opted for the safe lie.

"I don't know. Just stubborn, I guess." He looked around. "It's time for us to get to work."

CHAPTER 22

Sven took one last look around the deck before he was ready to declare his working day done. There would be no containers left unsecured to roll around during a storm. Ever. Finally satisfied, he turned toward the cabin where Gerri was finishing the evening meal.

As he approached the door, he paused as he heard Gerri singing. He stood and listened for a moment. He never tired of listening to her. She created a mood of beauty in sound—much as Sven tried to create visually in his paintings.

As a bonus, she was dancing in place—undulating in an innocent but most enticing way. He smiled as he stared. Their love making this morning had heightened his sensitivity to her. He had to remind himself not to scare her by being too aggressive.

She must have sensed him in spite of his effort to be unobtrusive. She turned her head. "Oh, there you are. You took longer than I expected."

He came up behind her and put his hands on her arms—resisting the impulse to kiss her on the nape of the neck. *Will I ever have a chance to do that?* "Just making sure that everything is shipshape. Anything I can do?"

"No, everything's done. You timed it just right." She grinned slyly and nudged him out of the way with her hip. "Just fill your bowl."

Stew: it sounded prosaic, but in Gerri's inspired hands, it was a welcome treat. He glanced at the shelf where she kept the spices. There had to be at least a dozen, and Gerri had informed him that they were a bare minimum. During his time as cook, there had been exactly two:

salt and pepper. Sven reflected—and not for the first time—that Gerri was worth her wages for her cooking alone.

He deposited his bowl on the table and sat down to eat. As he swallowed his first bite, Sven rolled his shoulders and thought about how many salmon he'd hauled aboard today. "Today was a good day."

Gerri looked up, startled, and quickly dropped her eyes. Sven realized that he'd been misunderstood and quickly added, "This might be our biggest payday of the summer." The last thing he wanted to do was to rub her nose in what she obviously wanted to be a casual interlude.

She nodded with relief. "Good." She had feared that Sven knew she was thinking about their lovemaking. If he was commitment-phobic, she mustn't seem to be obsessing about it. Remembering his rolling of his shoulders, she added, "Never have sore muscles felt so good."

As soon as the words were out of her mouth, she realized the double entendre. *Can't I stop thinking about this morning for one minute?* She frantically sought a change of subject. "And I want to thank you for that extra tutorial you gave me on the way here."

The storm was gone, but a heavy swell had remained. After they quit fishing for the day, Sven had used that swell as an opportunity to drill Gerri some more in piloting the boat in heavy weather. He had been more systematic in his instruction—having her successively maintain different headings relative to the waves, even at the expense of delaying their arrival at their anchorage. "You did well. I didn't want you to think, after last night, that you can't handle it. Even though I should have been there to oversee you, you were OK last night until you left the wheel."

"Yes, I get that now. The worse the weather, the less I can let my attention wander."

Sven nodded and eyed her covertly as he ate. Her eyes still looked everywhere but at him. He put on what he hoped was a casual, unthreatening expression. "While we're analyzing the day, this morning was pretty wonderful, too."

Gerri's eyes flicked up and met his. "I'm glad you thought so; so did I."

Sven surreptitiously exhaled in relief. She hadn't seemed offended. 'Wonderful' was an understatement, he thought. He ached to have another taste of her loveliness and her eager enthusiasm. How might that happen? He had to remember not to go beyond the limits: he was an instrument of her adventure—no more. "Are you going to be able to sleep OK tonight?"

"I slept well last night."

That didn't give him much of an opening.

"Of course, that was when I was cuddled against you," Gerri added, "You made me feel safe and warm." She looked at him shyly, trying to gauge his reaction.

"I slept well, too." *At least, once I stopped worrying about you and finally got to sleep...* "We can do the same thing tonight, if you'd like." *Too bold, perhaps?* "And I'll keep my hands off of you if that part of your adventure is finished."

Gerri stirred the dregs of her stew as she considered her response. She had loved the experience of being in Sven's arms and she wanted more—much more. But this was a big step. She could convince herself that this morning was an emotional response to a life threatening crisis—for both of them. But she couldn't deceive herself from here on in. To repeat their 'adventure' (no matter how she termed it) was to embark on an affair. And that was daunting. It was also, heaven help her, exactly what she wanted.

Of course, the people in South Carolina would view it very differently: it would be an affair with a white man, and one who didn't want commitment at that. All of the stereotypes about white men toying with black women would come into play. But that was only if she told her friends.

Her mother would be disappointed—but Gerri was a grown woman now and her promise to her mother had been kept. She didn't have to tell her mother either. And she could have a clear conscience about that.

Thurman and others at Peedee State would be fulminating with outrage if they knew. She almost smiled at the thought. But it was absolutely none of their business, and she certainly had no intentions, unlike some of those oh-so-sophisticated big city girls, of sharing this part of her summer experience with any of them.

Last, but not least, was the matter of Sven. Gerri had plenty of birth control pills left, so she wouldn't be giving him any unwelcome surprises that way. And they appeared to have an understanding—partly unstated, to be sure—that this would be a fling which would not outlast the summer. That last did not please her—in spite of the talk about sexual freedom, Gerri hadn't really comfortably adapted to the new rules.

But she'd take what she could get. And she had to admit that ending the affair at the end of the summer was doing them both a favor. There was no way that a romance could blossom in the hostile racial environment of South Carolina.

With that, she made her decision and grasped the courage to look up at Sven. "The adventure doesn't have to be over."

Sven's heart wanted to soar with excitement, but he wasn't quite sure. He cocked his head in puzzlement. "Doesn't have to?"

Gerri played back her words. "Oh. That's Southern talk, I guess." She took a breath, reached out, and squeezed his hand. "I don't want that part of the adventure to be over."

Sven felt that he must be grinning like an idiot. "Good. I don't want it to be over either."

Gerri wasn't quite ready to confess that she'd been thinking about their love making off and on all day, but she did feel emboldened. With studied casualness, she got up to clean her bowl. As she stood at the sink, she remarked, "You know, it really wasn't what I expected. It was more fun than I thought it would be."

Sven, who had gotten up with her, reached for her bowl. "I'll clean up—you cooked." Then he smiled with barely repressed laughter as he realized what she had said. "What? You thought it wouldn't be fun?"

Gerri glared at him, suppressing a smile of her own. "If you laugh at me, I'm going to hit you."

"I wouldn't dream of it," Sven said, his smile getter broader.

"I'm serious. I imagined that there would be passion, exertion, and sweat—and eventually…" She paused and gulped. This was not the kind of conversation that she was used to having with a man. "Eventually an orgasm. But I guess I didn't envision laughter and joking as part of it. I liked that part."

Sven thought about that. Gerri was right on the mark. Sex with Laura had always had a serious air. In a way, Laura was a prisoner of her own reputation. She was expected to be a femme fatale and she couldn't relax, lest she fall short of that mark. She was the girl who had it all, or so everyone told her—all except the freedom to simply discard her reputation. As he had been many times before, Sven was struck with a momentary wave of sadness. Nobody, including Sven, had simply loved Laura for herself. And her life was cut short before she could hope to change that.

With Gerri, it was different. There had been no expectations, no pressure. And Sven truly enjoyed everything about her, so the sex was a natural extension. Yes, it had been fun as well as passionate, and it was a first for him as well.

Gerri nudged him. "First, you laugh, and then you get all quiet. Say something."

Sven looked at her and put down the bowl he was cleaning. He slowly tilted her face up for a kiss. As she returned it, his arms slowly embraced her. He held the kiss until they were both out of breath. Still embracing her loosely, he said: "I was thinking about what you said. It had never occurred to me, but it's true. And I liked that." His smile became mischievous. "You know what they say: From the mouths of babes…"

Gerri was immensely pleased at his approval, but didn't want to admit it. She scowled and thumped his back. "Babes? You think I'm that young?"

Sven laughed. "I've always thought you were a babe. A real babe."

"Good recovery, mister."

"Except of course when I thought you were a guy."

———

Gerri took longer than usual getting ready for bed that night. She had to dig through her bag to find the nightgown that she had packed but never used. She also took extra time making sure that she was especially fresh and clean. The more she prepared, the more she thought about the course she was embarking on. The more she thought about that, the more she got nervous. By the time she left the fo'c's'le and got to Sven's bed, she had worked up a real case of nerves.

Sven was lounging in his bed, calmly reading a book. He wasn't wearing anything above the waist. He had a cover loosely thrown over him, so Gerri couldn't see anything else. Her mouth went dry thinking about it.

"I'm sorry I took so long. It took me a while to find this." She grasped the nightgown in each hand and stretched it in front of her, as if inspecting it. Her mother had purchased it for her so, needless to say, it was modest. It was full length with some ruffles around the collar, but no lace or revealing décolletage. It's white color connoted innocence, although Gerri didn't feel very innocent at the moment.

Sven had been staring at her covertly since she walked through the door. "I like it. It looks very feminine; very demure."

Is 'demure' what I want at a moment like this? Wouldn't 'sexy' be better? Like I have a choice! "Umm...thank you."

Sven looked at her more closely. She was obviously uneasy. *Is she having doubts? She's adventurous, but this must go against the grain—after all, 24 hours ago she was a virgin.* He didn't want to rub her nose in what they were about to do, so he decided to omit 'alluring' and 'enticing' from his description of her nightgown. "Come join me," he said, "It's been a long day."

She scrambled into the bed and, pulling the covers up, leaned against him. He pulled her into a long kiss. Between her lips moving against his and her body wriggling against his, he groaned. He was determined to take it slow, but she was testing him. More to remind himself than anything else, he whispered, "Let me know if I'm going too fast. I don't want to push this."

Gerri barely heard him. She loved the feeling of his solid body against hers. In fact, she could feel his erection and couldn't resist grinding her hips against him. *I guess I don't need to worry about him not saying 'sexy.'* The covers that she had pulled up a moment ago now seemed too warm and too restricting. Her case of nerves had evaporated at his first touch. She wanted to touch him, skin to skin. The nightgown with which she had wanted to impress him just seconds ago was now an impediment. *Would I seem too, umm, brazen if I asked him to take it off?*

She was spared that decision, however, as Sven spoke. "Do you mind if I take your gown off?"

She found the tentativeness in his voice oddly reassuring, but she couldn't resist teasing him anyway. "Are you afraid of ripping another garment? You could get a reputation here."

Sven laughed. "We couldn't have that, could we? Anyway, your gown is too pretty to rip."

Gerri sat up and shifted her weight to help him remove her gown. As he did so, she watched his eyes, and glowed from the appreciation that she saw there. When he finished, she lay back down, splaying her arms as she smiled at him. She couldn't believe how deliciously wanton she felt. Her old insecurities seemed meaningless now—there was no doubt that Sven appreciated her body.

Sven feasted his eyes as Gerri lay back gracefully. He had to remind himself not to pounce on her and, as so frequently happened to him in gazing on some scene of beauty, he imagined how he might paint her as she was now. The brown of her torso merging to the darker color of her pelvis, the shadows of her face, and the curve of her breasts as they lay back against her chest—with the whole tableau set off vividly by the white bedding. Last, but not least, she had the slightly smug, slightly challenging, and totally arousing expression of a woman who knows that she's appreciated. He sighed.

"Getting an eyeful?"

Sven tucked his fantasies about painting her into the back of his mind. He would never do it without her permission, and he was willing to bet that her permission would never be granted. On the contrary, the idea would horrify her. But that expression of hers… Maybe he'd find a way to work it into a more modest portrait. Someday. Of course, he had more important things to think about now. "Yes, and a beautiful one at that."

Gerri tugged at the cover. "My turn."

Sven quickly slipped his underwear off. "I don't want you to be labeled as a ripper of clothing, either."

Gerri giggled at the thought. "I'm not worried. Nobody would believe you."

He lowered himself to lie beside her, his face only inches from hers. One arm supported his head while his other hand caressed her belly. "Your skin is so soft. How do you do that?"

Gerri took a breath. His hand was so hot. But rough—definitely no soft skin there. She considered his question, but she wasn't ready to spill her secrets just yet. She remembered from those same sophisticated girls that 'guys like what we do,' meaning makeup and lotion, 'but they get annoyed when they see it being done.' Gerri didn't use makeup, but she had to plead guilty on the lotions. She parried his question. "Do you like it?"

"Oh, yes." He continued his exploration, turning to her hands. "But even your hands are soft. With all of the work we do, they should be like mine."

Gerri found it harder and harder to concentrate as Sven moved back to her torso and started caressing her breast. "I…" She caught her breath. It was too much work to evade his question while his hand was driving her crazy. "OK," she finally gasped, "Remember when you gave me a hard time about how heavy my bags were? I have lotions and skin creams in there."

"Well, I guess I can't tease you about that any more. I like the result." With that, he lowered his head to her other breast and teased the nipple with his lips.

Gerri was already impatient. She realized that Sven was controlling her motion—and their pace—with the weight of his arms and legs. On impulse, she squirmed out from under him and sat astride him. *Oh, this is good.* She felt in complete control. She grasped his organ, held it against her pelvis, and stroked his rigid length up and down. She watched his face as she did so.

Sven's jaw dropped. "Gerri…umm…slow down. You're going to finish me off too soon if you keep doing that."

Gerri considered, ever so briefly, making some joke—perhaps an outrageous demand for her compliance—but she knew that the time for that had passed. She gave Sven one long stroke with her hand, then raised up on her knees to guide him into her body.

Sven sighed as Gerri sat back down on him, pushing him into her—a deep sigh, replete with satisfaction and yearning for more. He extended his arms and pulled her down onto his chest. Then there were no words as they stroked together—occasional grunts and mutterings communicated their pleasure as they moved.

Finally, Gerri's movements grew more frantic and she started a corkscrew-like motion. Sven grabbed her hips and drove into her until he heard her cry of triumph. That sent him over the edge and he cried out hoarsely and he lost himself in her.

Gerri collapsed against him and panted as she listened to his breathing and felt his heartbeat. "Mmm, nice," was all she could manage.

Sometime later, Sven woke from a doze, and arranged Gerri, now fast asleep, more comfortably beside him. *And why shouldn't she be? She just got through with one of the most eventful days of her life.* Within thirty seconds, he was unconscious as well.

CHAPTER 23

Gerri woke up early the next morning and lay there listening. She smiled at how she had internalized Sven's nautical habits. She listened for the sound of rain (none, although she could see through the window that it was cloudy); wind (just a little—not enough to cause them problems or discomfort while fishing); any errant noises that might indicate problems with the boat or with the anchorage (thankfully, none).

She turned over to face Sven and involuntarily emitted a loud groan.

His eyes flew open and he gave her a worried look. "Are you OK?"

"Sore muscles," she said with a wince. She then bit her tongue, deciding that it would be unseemly to remind him that she had exercised some muscles vigorously in the last twenty four hours which had never before been exercised. Unfortunately, from the look on his face, she didn't have to. It was the smug look of a well satisfied man—one whose major concern in life at the moment was trying not to laugh.

Gerri laughed for both of them, but she also shoved him. "It's all your fault, you brute."

As if he had been given permission, Sven started chuckling. "My fault? I seem to remember some little cowgirl who wanted to ride bareback—or should I say, bare bottom."

"It's not my fault that you're built like a horse." With that, she buried her face in his chest. *What's got into me? I can't believe that I said that!*

Sven put his arms around her and held her for a minute. Then he said, "I guess then that I should say 'My fault? Neighhh…'"

"That was so bad," she laughed, "You have no shame."

"None." He paused. "Wally claims that I start punning only when I'm happy. I'm certainly happy now."

"Good," Gerri wriggled, "me, too."

Her movements reminded her again of her sore muscles. On the farm, they treated sore muscles by going out the next day and working some more. They didn't really have much choice, but it was effective. Gerri didn't want to suggest sex again, though, from what she could feel of Sven's body, he would be more than willing. She supposed that they could get an early start on the fishing day, but...

"Sven, I'd like to take a short walk. I need to stretch my legs."

"OK, let me get ready." As Sven started to get up, he, too, groaned. Gerri wasn't the only one with unused muscles, he realized.

"I can go by myself if you want. I can handle the rowboat."

Sven sat on the edge of the bed and took a breath. "No, I'll come with you."

"Don't you trust me?" Gerri sat up with a frown.

He turned and looked at her with a wry smile. "No, I don't trust you." Gerri looked surprised and hurt. He continued. "I don't trust you not to tease me forever and ever about how you wore me out last night." With that, he reached over and grabbed her, pulling both of them down to the bed.

After a torrid kiss that had Gerri rethinking the possibility of sex as a restorative, she forced her thoughts back to the walk. She grinned and said, "I hadn't thought of that, but it would be tempting, wouldn't it?"

When they reached shore, Sven directed her to a creek. "The beach is muddy. I'll get out here with the bow line and pull the skiff up to the tree line."

Gerri looked at the creek calculatingly. "I could row up there. The current doesn't look that fast."

"Maybe you could. I grant that you're strong. But it's harder than it looks. If you row at six feet per second—which is a lot of effort in this skiff—and the creek flows at five, then you're only making one foot per second. Then, if you hit a sandbar..."

Gerri was delighted by his acknowledgment of her strength, but distracted by his arithmetic. Maybe that would be an entry for her teaching journal. She didn't have that many algebra entries. She filed it away to think about later.

Sven mistook her silence for resentment and tried to mollify her. "Look at the bright side. When we come back, you'll be rowing *with* the current. You'll be really rolling." Gerri didn't say anything. He tried again, breaking briefly into song. "Rolling on the river…"

That grabbed her attention away from her journal. "Sven! You've been holding out on me. You have a nice voice. Did you ever sing in a choir?"

"Oh, no. I'd be afraid to sing in public."

"You'd be great. At least you stayed on key." She entertained a brief fantasy of Sven being at Pee Dee State and in the choir, and then sighed. *So far away—both in miles and in circumstance—and so hopeless to think about.*

After Sven had the boat far enough up the creek, he tied the bow line to a tree and pointed. "Right there is a trail that we can take to go up the hill. At the top is a ridge with a nice view."

"A trail? I thought that we were in the wilderness."

"We are. It's an animal trail."

Gerri stopped in her tracks. "An animal trail? What kind of animals? Not big, hungry ones, I hope."

Sven grinned at her. "Probably not. And we'll scare them away if we're noisy. If necessary, I'll sing some more. That'll scare them for sure."

They compromised—they both sang as they climbed the trail. Sven's repertoire was limited, so he stumbled through snatches of several, including as much as he could remember of 'Proud Mary.'

Gerri didn't want to try that one, however. "It's not my type of song—too country and western."

Sven thought about that for a minute. "I think you'd make it sound good, but you may be right. You're more the Dinah Washington type. Ballads, you know?"

"Thank you. I wish I could be that good."

"On second thought, your voice is kind of low pitched. Maybe Nina Simone?"

Gerri laughed. "That's funny. My mother heard me trying one of her songs once and told me I wasn't doing a good job."

"What? That's hard to believe."

"It was a sad song. 'Rags and Old Iron.' She said I got the melody OK, but that I wasn't convincing—I didn't get across the sadness."

They were approaching the top of the ridge. "I don't know that one. Will you sing it for me?"

Gerri didn't answer right away. "Maybe on the way down. This climbing uphill is a lot harder than I'm used to—it takes all of my breath." They came out of the trees and she twirled around. A vista beckoned. There were steep, forested hills in abundance. Further away, there loomed craggy mountains—many of them covered with snow even in the summer. Below them were waterways, snaking through the terrain. She could see the Glacier Gal directly beneath them, looking oddly small and insignificant from their vantage point. "Oh, Sven. This is beautiful. They don't have any views like this at home."

"Don't you have any hills in South Carolina?"

"Not in my part. Not even little hills—it's totally flat."

"Huh! I'm afraid I'd go crazy there."

Gerri felt obliged to defend her home. "It has its own type of beauty. It's very lush. But it's not spectacular the way Alaska is."

On the way down, Gerri sang the song for him. When she finished, she waited anxiously for his reaction. "Well, I think it sounds pretty. But I guess I understand your mother a little bit. You didn't really sound very sad."

Gerri made a face at him—which he couldn't see anyway walking in front of her. She could take criticism, she reminded herself. Her choir director had been a hard taskmaster. Somehow, though, coming from Sven it seemed to get under her skin more. She was still deciding upon her response when he spoke again.

"Sometimes when I'm painting, I find the mood difficult. I try extra hard to put myself into the painting. If I'm painting something sad, I try to think of the saddest things I can. It sounds silly, but it works for me."

"Hmm. I'll think about that. Sometime." She couldn't help but wonder what sad thoughts Sven evoked at those moments. Laura's death? His teenage estrangement from his parents? The hostility he encountered from Mindy and others? Perhaps, if Wally was correct, even the circumstances of his marriage to Laura? Surely he had many sad thoughts to choose from. Gerri believed that he deserved better. She wished that she could chase all of his sadness away.

Sven thought about Gerri's testy reaction. What would he do if someone criticized his painting? He was spared any direct criticism because of his anonymity. Maybe that was just a form of cowardice. No, he couldn't really blame her. "Don't take what I said too seriously. It was just an observation from someone who's not knowledgeable anyway."

Gerri changed the subject as they neared the beach. "This was a great walk. Let's do it more often."

"OK." Sven smiled wryly. *If she had any idea... Her wish is practically my command.*

———

The morning walks became a routine. Some days they walked along a beach; some days they ventured into the woods and up a hill. That made for harder walking, but in a perverse way Gerri liked it more. Certainly they could cram more exercise into less time. And the views that they garnered from the hilltops were worth the effort.

They never did meet any 'big hungry animals,' but the possibility lent an air of adventure—and a whiff of danger—to their outings. Once they heard a crashing in the brush and Gerri froze, her heart beating a mile a minute. Sven pointed at something, but it was gone before she could turn her head.

There was plenty to see, however, and Sven was an enthusiastic guide. The unfamiliar sights ranged from awesome (the largest trees Gerri had ever seen) to awful (a plant with vicious thorns that Sven called a devil's club—an especially apt name she thought as she gingerly examined one) and from delightful (pretty stalks of flowers called fireweed) to delicious (some tiny button mushrooms that Sven pounced on and gathered into a small sack).

She was surprised that the mushrooms were edible, but more surprised that Sven cooked them expertly after their fishing was done for the day, and they had anchored for the night.

"I thought you couldn't cook," Gerri said half-accusingly.

"I never said that. You said that," Sven said with a smug grin.

"And I still say that." Gerri cast him a sideways glance and a small smile. "But these are very good."

"Thank you. I have a small number of things that I cook well," Sven admitted, "But those are treats. A few wild things, a few desserts, and smoked salmon. Although I'm not sure that I'd call that last cooking."

Gerri's interest was piqued, and she was already looking for ways to know Sven better. "I'd like to taste some of your recipes some time."

Sven thought about that for a moment. He'd been searching for a way to see more of Gerri in different circumstances, and he was painfully aware that she would be leaving soon—in fact, she'd already made reservations for her flights home. It pained him that it was happening so soon, but true to his vow, he kept things casual. This, though, was too good an opportunity to pass up.

"Why don't you come to my house on your last night in Alaska? I'll cook you one of my favorite desserts."

Gerri beamed. "I'd love to. Do you have any smoked salmon?" Mindy had extolled its virtues, but unfortunately didn't have any available.

"I tend to smoke it in the fall and eat it over the winter, but I do have some left at home."

The next morning, Sven picked up where he had left off. They had barely started their walk when he veered off the trail. "Salmonberries," he announced when Gerri caught up to him.

She took the one that he offered and looked at it. It was almost like a raspberry, but yellow-orange in color. She tried it. "Pretty good," she agreed as they continued walking. She smiled at his penchant for pointing out things and decided to tease him about it. "You must have taken a course in botany to be able to name all of these plants."

"No, 'fraid not."

"Well maybe they're all secretly marked with signs that only you can see."

He didn't answer right away. By the time he did, Gerri had already decided that he was ignoring her lame joke.

"Actually, it would be nice to have a trail with the names of all of the plants marked on signs."

Gerri had heard of this. "There are such things…"

"I'd call it the appellation trail," he continued.

Gerri cocked her head as she gazed at his back. "That name is already taken." She had started to tell him about the Appalachian Trail, when he turned and grinned at her.

"No. *Appellation Trail.* An appellation is when you give something a name."

"Oh, good grief," she laughed. "You snuck that one right by me. If Wally's right, then you must be especially happy."

"Why especially?"

"I figure the more obscure the pun, the happier you are."

"I *am* happy." He turned and recommenced walking. "But that was only semi-obscure. I don't tell anybody my really obscure ones. The only thing that people hate more than a pun is a pun that they can't understand."

Gerri thought about that. "OK," she challenged him. "Tell me one of your really obscure ones."

He was silent for a minute as they walked through the woods. Finally, he seemed to come to a decision. "OK, I'll tell you a little story.

"A man and a woman were relaxing on a deserted ocean beach, watching the surf. The woman spoke dreamily. 'Sometimes, I think that I'd like for us to make love.' The man looked at her with surprise and delight. He reached for her and started to pull down the strap of her bathing suit. She squirmed away. 'No,' she said, 'I didn't mean littorally.'"

Gerri was determined to get this, but she couldn't make any sense of it. "Don't tell me—let me think a little bit."

Finally, she was ready to give up, but she thought she'd try for 'partial credit' rather than drawing a total blank. "OK," she grumbled, "I don't get it, but there was something a bit off about the way you said the word 'literally,' so I think it has something to do with that."

"You're on the right track. 'Littoral' refers to the seashore and the waters next to it—anything below the high tide line."

"I've never heard of that."

"Actually, it's even worse. I'm not sure that the adverb form—littorally—is even a word. So I'm really cheating. Definitely not a pun to share with people."

Gerri decided that it made a weird sort of sense. "Well, I asked for it. Where did you ever hear of that word?"

"I was in the Navy. They used it. Littoral operations are completely different than deep water operations."

Gerri was struck anew—there was so much that she had yet to learn about Sven. "I'd love to hear about that some day." *And still,* she added silently, *I think you're right not to share that pun.*

————

Later, after she was back home in South Carolina, Gerri would look back at this period as the happiest time of her life. That's not to say that it was an easy time. They worked hard. The early morning walks, though cherished, made their days longer. Her relationship with Sven made Gerri want to work harder—when she was gone she wanted him to remember her fondly, but also as an exceptional first mate.

Best of all, since they had abandoned any pretense of sleeping separately, they had the comfort of knowing that each day would start and end in each other's arms.

CHAPTER 24

Her adventure had to end sometime. At the beginning of the summer, that had been a matter-of-fact acknowledgment for Gerri—tinged with an eagerness to be home again and to relate her experiences triumphantly to her family. Later, contemplating it was bittersweet. Her eagerness to be home was balanced against the knowledge that she would be leaving dear friends—Sven, Mindy, and even Mrs. Kallek—whom she would likely never see again.

Since she and Sven had become lovers though, the knowledge was downright painful, and she tried her best to avoid thinking about it. Today, however, she could not avoid these thoughts. This was her last full day in Alaska; her last day on the Glacier Gal; and, worst of all, her last day with Sven. She had vowed not to dwell upon it, or at least not to talk about it. Sven seemed to have reached the same conclusion. He didn't talk about the future beyond today. But, as she stole sidelong looks at him in the pilot house, he seemed unusually pensive.

At least this day would be wonderful. They had planned it meticulously. Sven had sold their last catch to a fish buyer last night. Now they had about a six hour run to get to Juneau. Once there, Gerri would visit Mrs. Kallek one last time to say goodbye and thank her for her advice and friendship. While she was doing this, Sven would be baking a blueberry pie—this morning's walk had been devoted to berry picking. Sven knew where there were plentiful wild blueberries and they had more than enough.

After she had seen Mrs. Kallek, Sven would take her to his house and they would eat some fresh blueberry pie. After that, and before Gerri went back to Mindy's, they would make love one last time. Gerri was well aware of Sven's aversion to commitment. How could she forget it? And she respected it. She would not say one word about commitment. But she would use whatever powers she had as a woman to make tonight an experience that he would never forget. Every time he went to sleep in his own bed, Gerri wanted him to remember her and remember their last night.

Then, early in the morning, a doubtlessly groggy Mindy would drive a doubtlessly groggy Gerri to the airport to catch her flight. She would leave with a fat bankbook, gifts for her family, and memories that would last her a lifetime. She would also leave with a gaping hole in her heart.

The weather, fittingly, was stormy. A southeaster had blown up and the seas were rough. Sven was using the weather to give Gerri a final exam, of sorts, in handling the boat. Even though it was fatiguing steering the boat in this weather, she was doing well. She glanced at Sven again. He was grumbling and rubbing his stomach.

"My stomach's acting up. I think those sausages are bothering me."

"I'm sorry. But you certainly ate enough of them."

"Only because you didn't want any. I don't want to leave any food on the boat. I've had them for a while—maybe I should have thrown them out."

"I checked them before I cooked them. They seemed OK." Actually, Gerri was pretty sure that they were OK. They hadn't always had reliable refrigeration on the farm and Gerri's mother had taught her well. Nowadays Gerri could trust her nose to tell her whether something was edible. Still, it was possible that they were bad. Something had clearly not agreed with him. She hoped that he was able to purge them from his system before they reached Juneau.

Sven cursed his luck. Normally, he had a cast iron stomach but today, of all days, he had overeaten. He wasn't really that hungry—he just hadn't wanted breakfast to be over. As long as they were sitting, eating, and talking it was like any other morning. When they finished, however, he would have to face it. Instead of motoring out to some fishing grounds, they would run straight to Juneau. There would be no more Gerri on the Glacier Gal. He didn't want to think about it. So he sat there eating and talking about inconsequentialities.

He didn't know what was bothering him, but he knew that he had to get rid of it in a hurry. He had big plans for the evening. He didn't know how he would find the exact words but, somehow, he was going to tell Gerri how precious she was to him. Dare he use the word 'love?' She had made it abundantly clear that this was a summer thing, and he didn't want her going home with regrets or guilty feelings. He hoped that somehow the words would come to him.

As time went on, Sven was feeling worse instead of better. The pain in his gut was sharper than ever. He actually considered sticking his finger down his throat to try to get rid of those infamous sausages. No, he would try to lie down for a while.

The weather was rough and the Glacier Gal was fighting her way against the wind and sea as they headed through Icy Straight. Gerri was doing most of the steering and was handling the conditions well. Sven was glad to see that she had her confidence back and he had no qualms about leaving her alone at the helm for a while. He only hated that he was so weak.

"I'm going to go back and lie down for a while. Are you OK here?"

Gerri cast him an anxious look. "I'm OK, but I'm worried about you. I think those sausages might not be the problem."

"You might be right. I might have caught some 24 hour bug."

She looked dubious. "I don't know how. We haven't been around people except briefly last night when we were on the fish buyer scow."

Sven paused as a stab of pain hit him. "I don't know either, but I think a little rest will set me right." He squeezed her shoulder and turned to go.

Gerri was starting to get seriously worried. She didn't find the 'bug' idea any more plausible than the 'bad sausages' idea. "Sven, wait." He turned back to face her. She kept her eyes on the water ahead so that he wouldn't see her fear. "Suppose... Just suppose this were something truly serious. What would you do then?"

"Don't worry," he scoffed, "I'll be fine." He thought he sounded convincing. He would have been even more convincing if he hadn't doubled over slightly while he was turning.

"No, wait. Just as a hypothetical question, what would you do... Scratch that. What would any fisherman do if he had a heart attack or something?"

Sven forced a chuckle. "Hypothetically? If you had a medical emergency, you would call the Coast Guard. They can pick a person up and fly him or her into Juneau, if necessary. But this is just a stomachache. I'll be fine after I rest."

"OK. I'll come and check on you." She turned from the wheel and gave him a brief hug.

After he left, she checked their position on the chart. The weather was slowing them down. They were still hours from Juneau. She wasn't convinced by Sven's reassurances. He had flinched noticeably when she hugged him.

As part of her general education in seamanship, Sven had shown her how to make a distress call. Her lips drew tight. *I might just be doing that...*

Gerri kept one eye on his cabin and, an hour later, she quickly darted back there to check on him. "How do you feel?"

"About the same—maybe worse. I threw up a while ago. Maybe that will help. But it hasn't yet."

Gerri wanted to try out an idea. "Let me see where it hurts." She quickly pulled his shirt up and started probing gently. When she got to the lower right of his abdomen, he groaned and rolled away from her. *Appendix,* she muttered.

Just then the boat lurched. Gerri raced back to the pilot house and adjusted the heading. She knew now that she wanted to call the Coast Guard. *Maybe I should wait a bit longer.* She knew she would feel stupid if this was a false alarm. But no—she was willing to feel stupid, but she wasn't willing to take chances with Sven's life.

She felt better for having made the decision. She would tell Sven later, when it was too late for him to argue. After checking their position carefully—she didn't want to be branded as a novice who didn't even know where she was—she made the call.

"This is the Glacier Gal. We have a medical emergency." She gave Sven's symptoms and the boat's position.

"Stand by one." While she waited, she realized that her hands were shaking. Actually talking to the Coast Guard underlined the urgency of the situation. After what seemed forever, but was actually only a minute, the radio crackled again.

"Sounds like your guess might be right. The cutter is about thirty minutes away from you and we're starting in your direction now. Do you see an island on your port side?"

"Yes, I do." Of course she did. They sounded patronizing, but she was too worried to be offended.

"Proceed to the cove on the west side. We'll meet you there. The transfer and the helicopter takeoff will be easier if we're protected from the worst of the waves."

Gerri quickly agreed and turned the boat to the indicated direction. Her heart was still pounding, but she was relieved. They were taking her seriously. And the helicopter would get Sven to the hospital in Juneau much faster than even the Coast Guard cutter could.

She idled the engines when she got to the cove and went to talk to Sven. She had to hurry because she could see the cutter already and she didn't want Sven to make a macho scene.

"Sven, I called the Coast Guard. I'm worried about you. They're almost here and they're going to fly you to the hospital."

But Sven didn't have the energy to mount a serious protest. He looked at her rather foggily and muttered, "A mutiny. A mutiny on my own boat." Then he flopped back down.

Does he really resent me? Gerri wasn't sure. Had she seen a small, strained smile playing over his face? Or was that scary looking scowl of his directed at her?

If Gerri hadn't been so worried about Sven, she would have found the performance of the Coast Guard cutter's crew fascinating. The cutter approached quickly, slowing down at the last moment. They already had bumpers in place to protect the two hulls from scraping. Then, while the Glacier Gal was still tossing in their wake, several crew members swarmed down a ladder and tied the two boats together. They were impressively efficient.

One, carrying a medical supply kit, looked at Gerri questioningly. She led him to Sven's bunk and stepped back to watch anxiously. After a few moments of examination, he muttered something to another Coast Guardsman who went back out on deck. Gerri wondered about that, but decided to stay close to Sven. Her decision was rewarded when the medical officer turned to her.

"You were right. It looks like his appendix. As bad as his pain is, it may have burst. We'll fly him in to Juneau."

Gerri remembered the small helicopter tied onto the deck of the cutter. "How long will it take?" She realized that her voice was shaking.

"No more than twenty minutes. We'll call ahead for an ambulance." He seemed to consider her situation for the first time. "Are you alone?"

She looked at Sven. "There's just the two of us."

The other man returned with a companion and a stretcher. Within seconds Sven had been carried out on deck and they placed his stretcher on a platform which been winched down while they were in the cabin. As much as she appreciated their speed, part of her was dismayed to realize that Sven was leaving her. She moved up to the stretcher and bent over him. His face was covered in sweat. She squeezed his hand and kissed his forehead. *I love you,* she wanted to say, but they were already winching him up to the cutter's deck and she had to move quickly out of the way.

The helicopter perched on a platform, raised above the rear deck of the cutter. Its rotors were already moving as they loaded Sven aboard. Gerri stood in the blast of the downdraft and watched the helicopter take off. She felt desolated and depressed. Sven was flying off to an unknown fate, and when the cutter had left, she would be truly alone. And she would bear the responsibility of getting the boat to Juneau through this nasty weather.

Several crew members stood by the lines, waiting for instructions, while another man—an older man—climbed down the ladder. He looked around the deck and then extended his hand. "Miss Barton?"

"Yes." Gerri shook his hand.

"I'm Captain Counselman. We talked on the radio. I understand that you're alone on the boat." At her nod, he gestured up to the deck of his vessel. "You're going to need help. Crewman Knox has volunteered to ride into town with you—just to make sure that everything's all right."

Gerri followed his gesture and stared with horror. Standing there looking down at her was Ferret-face. He tried, under the gaze of his captain, to project a benign smile, but Gerri could see a nasty edge of anticipation that he hadn't quite concealed. "No," she said vigorously, shaking her head. Was she even allowed to refuse? Bringing the boat in alone was a scary thought, but sharing it with Ferret-face—Knox or whatever his name was—was infinitely worse.

"Are you sure? He said that you're a waitress who is just riding with Mr. Halvorsen."

She bluffed more confidence than she felt. "No," she repeated, "He is not welcome on this boat. I'm the first mate of the Glacier Gal. So, now I'm the acting captain. I can bring the boat in myself and I don't want him on board."

Counselman frowned at her for a moment and then turned and stared up at Knox. "OK," He finally said. "I hope you know what you're doing."

With that, he swung back up the ladder, and the cutter was soon gone.

Gerri contemplated her situation. Sven was in good hands—that was the most important thing. And she had dodged a nasty bullet. If she hadn't seen who Seaman Knox actually was, she might have accepted the offer of assistance. She shuddered.

But here she was. There was nobody to help. She had to navigate the Glacier Gal into the Juneau harbor in rough weather and approaching darkness. *Darkness!* Due to the long summer days, she hadn't had any practice in navigating after dark. She raced to the pilot house. There was still a chance that she could get to Juneau before dark, but the days were getting shorter, and the rendezvous with the cutter had taken some time.

The next few hours were among the most stressful of her life. As she piloted the boat, she tried to look everywhere at once. She consulted the charts frequently and memorized what to do if darkness fell. This was still wilderness. There were lighthouses that served as navigation aids, but they were few and far between. Then there was the problem of telling which light was which in the dark.

Finally, she reached Point Retreat. She had passed here before—with Sven and in nicer weather, but now the name seemed daunting and a bit scary. But retreat was not an option for her tonight.

Still clear in her mind was the advice that Sven had given her on the night she went overboard: She went well beyond Point Retreat and then turned quickly. This took her from a following sea to a headwind, but prevented the boat from being broadside to the waves for more than a minute.

Now, she breathed a sigh of relief. The worst was over. The rest of the trip would be in more protected waters. And although she wouldn't make Juneau before dark, she would be in sight of the town at sunset, and the city lights should make that final stretch easy. Now that she could relax a little, she could feel the soreness in her shoulders from holding the wheel for so many hours. She waved her arms around to loosen up.

Once again, as she had every few minutes, she wondered how Sven was doing. She considered asking for information on the radio, but she didn't know whom to ask. The Coast Guard wouldn't know—after they had delivered him to the ambulance, they wouldn't be involved any further. No, she would do the best job she knew how of getting the boat into the harbor. Then she would race to the hospital to see him.

Finally, it was over. She reached Juneau and, remembering the speed limit, eased into the boat harbor. Since she had to moor the boat without help, she used a trick that Sven had taught her. After the boat was in Sven's slip, she kept it idling in forward gear so that it pushed gently against the dock and kept the rudder turned hard over to keep it pushing against the side float. All this so that she could jump out and tie it up without it floating away. She allowed herself a moment of pride as she completed the mooring—she would definitely brag to Sven about this.

After she shut off the engine, she took a moment to lean against the wheel and let the tiredness seep through her body. She took a last look around. Time to get to the hospital.

As she was leaving the pilot house, she felt a slight rocking of the boat. Somebody was coming aboard. *Maybe there's news about Sven.* She hurried out to the back deck.

"Wally, is that you?"

But the figure trying to climb over the gunwale was far less welcome than Wally. She registered the smell of alcohol as he spoke. "You bitch. You got me in trouble with my captain. You owe me. And now I'm going to collect."

CHAPTER 25

It was Ferret-face! The Coast Guard cutter was much faster than the Glacier Gal, so they'd probably been in port for hours—enough time for Ferret-face to find some liquor and nurse his twisted grudge. Adrenaline flooded her system as she watched him. He was clearly unsteady on his feet, but still very capable of doing considerable harm.

"Sven will kill you if you do anything to me." Why she said that, she didn't know. She had had some notion that she could talk her way out of this. That instantly proved futile.

His advance was slowed as he caught his foot in a coil of line on the deck. He spoke scornfully as he tried to shake it loose. "Halvorsen isn't going to kill anybody. He died on the flight in to town."

Gerri's knees buckled. She couldn't imagine a world without Sven. She couldn't abide a world without him. *Why didn't I call the Coast Guard sooner?* Sven had rescued her. Twice. And she had failed him. She tried to scream—in anguish more than outrage—but only a moan came out.

Gerri desperately scanned the dock. No one was in sight. There would be no bystander to rescue her. And no Sven. Oh God, why hadn't she told Sven how she felt? Even if he were commitment-shy, she would have wanted him to know how she felt about him before he died. If she could let herself believe in romance, she might imagine that that knowledge would have made him fight harder to live. *Silly girl!*

She forced her attention back to Ferret-face. He had freed his foot, but clung to a guy line for balance. She would mourn Sven later; for now, it would take all of her strength and concentration to stay away from this beast. She moved to the opposite side of the open hatch. He would have to come around it to reach her. But he was between her and the float, so there was no escape that way. If she wanted to get off the boat, she would have to jump overboard into the frigid water. *Not yet,* she told herself. That was a last resort.

As she moved, she looked around for a weapon. Her eyes latched onto one of those fifty pound, spherical lead sinkers resting on the deck at her feet. Briefly, she flashed back to her first encounter with Sven—wouldn't that be a nice irony if she could use it… If she were Sven, she could throw it at Ferret-face and drop him in his tracks. But, though she could lift it, she couldn't throw it with force. Then she saw a gaff hook clipped to the gunwale near her. She bent over to grab it. When she looked up, Ferret-face had darted around the hatch and was only a few feet away. Without thinking, she pushed the sinker with her foot as hard as she could, rolling it toward him across the deck. He wasn't expecting that and, with his diminished coordination, couldn't get out of the way. He yelled in pain as it hit his ankle and his arms started wind-milling for balance. She had only a second to react. Reaching forward with the gaff hook, she pushed him in the chest. If she could get him to fall down, she would have time to escape.

He stepped back instinctively, but his foot hit another sinker. He fell backward and, as Gerri watched, hit his calves on the gunwale. His legs buckled as he toppled over the side into the frigid water. Only then did she allow herself a smile of relief as she leaned, exhausted, against the one of the trolling poles.

Wally Trager put down his binoculars and blew on his hands. The weather was lousy. A raw wind was blowing straight down the channel toward him. And as he stood on the bridge between Juneau and Douglas Island, he had no protection from it.

He had heard about Sven from another fisherman, Jimmy Cavanaugh, who was monitoring the short wave distress channel. He had rushed to the boat harbor, but there was nothing that he could do for

Sven now. The next thing was to worry about the Glacier Gal and—yes—Gerri. The rumor mill had said that she had refused help and was bringing the boat in by herself.

There was nothing that Wally could do to help. He'd tried contacting her on the radio, but she wasn't answering. Probably because she'd turned the radio off to avoid the distraction. At least he hoped that was why.

But he could try to allay his fears by watching for the boat. It should be coming down the channel any minute and the bridge was high enough to give him a good vantage point and close enough to the boat harbor so that he could get there when—he didn't want to say 'if'—the boat arrived.

He could see one set of running lights a few miles down the channel, coming toward town. It was too far in the rain and the gathering dusk to make out the identity of the boat. In a few minutes—and when his hands were warmer—he would look again.

Finally, he saw it—the Glacier Gal. He took a deep breath of satisfaction and let it out slowly. He knew that Sven had been giving Gerri some training, but he didn't know how much. Sven had bragged that she was a sponge for knowledge, but there were any number of ways that things could have gone badly for her on the way in.

As the boat passed under the bridge, he got ready to walk to the harbor. He paused though. He couldn't resist the temptation to see how she would handle the docking by herself. He hoped, for the sake of the boat, that she didn't mess it up too badly. Besides, he told himself, he wouldn't get there in time to help anyway and he could see her attempt better from here.

A few minutes later, he was walking briskly toward the harbor, chuckling to himself. He had had his reservations about her at first—well, actually he had had his reservations all summer, but her docking was smooth as silk. If he didn't know otherwise, he would have thought it was Sven himself piloting the boat. And at such a stressful time. He owed her an apology for doubting her, and he meant to give it.

On the way down the ramp to the boat harbor floats, he saw Cavanaugh again and called him over. "The Glacier Gal just got in. Walk with me. We'll fill Gerri in about Sven."

Cavanaugh fell in step beside Wally, who continued talking. "She docked it pretty as you please. It's hard to believe that she didn't know anything about boats at the beginning of the summer."

"Hmmm," Cavanaugh said. He acknowledged Wally distractedly, but he wanted to share what he felt was more interesting gossip. "You'll never guess what I saw. Remember that Coastie, Knox? The bad news one? Well, I think he's finally got in more trouble than he can handle."

Wally made an encouraging grunt, though he knew it wasn't necessary—Cavanaugh was going to share his gossip regardless.

"I was standing at the foot of the ramp and I heard yelling from the Coast Guard cutter. Knox was on the float screaming and cussing. I don't know what it was about, but he was ordered to come back aboard and he flat refused. Then he came storming down here past me."

Now Wally was interested in spite of himself. "How long ago was this? I just came down the ramp and I didn't see him."

"Just a few minutes ago. He didn't go up the ramp. He headed down toward the other end of the floats. I don't know where he thought he was going, come to think of it."

Wally suddenly had a very bad feeling. *The other end of the floats— where the Glacier Gal just docked!* Cavanaugh had heard about Sven decking Knox—Hell, everyone had. But nobody but Wally had been told about the connection to Gerri. He broke into a run.

"Hey, what's your hurry? She's not going anywhere."

Leaving Cavanaugh without an explanation, Wally turned the corner to the Glacier Gal's berth. The float was slippery from rain and he almost fell, so he slowed slightly. Then he heard a scream and a big splash and sped up again.

When he came into sight of the boat, he slowed to a walk. Gerri was leaning on one of the trolling poles, looking exhausted, but otherwise unharmed. He didn't see Knox at first. He followed the sound of further splashing and cursing and saw Knox treading water beside the boat.

Maybe it was the relief that Gerri seemed unhurt, he didn't know, but he started laughing. Gerri saw him and frowned. "He attacked me. He was going to…" She shook her head and waved vaguely at the cabin.

"I'm sorry, Gerri. It's not funny. He just looks like such a fool. Are you all right?"

Gerri summarized briefly as Wally climbed aboard. Cavanaugh arrived, puffing. He was a powerful man, but overweight—this was probably the first time he had run in years.

Wally tossed him the gaff hook. Knox was trying to climb up onto the dock. "Kick him back in the water, Jimmy, but don't let him swim away. He tried to attack Gerri."

He then put an arm around Gerri. "Don't worry about Knox. We'll take care of him. You've had a rough enough day already."

Gerri, reminded of the larger disaster, came into Wally's arms. Her tears started to flow. "Oh, Wally, I feel terrible about Sven. If only I'd called the Coast Guard sooner, it might have made a difference."

Wally didn't process her words right away; he was too distracted. It had been a long time since he had had his arms full of friendly girl-flesh. He allowed himself the fleeting thought: Gerri—color-be-damned—felt every bit as good as any white woman he knew. But he dragged his mind back to the matter at hand and tried to comfort her. "Gerri, you did fine. I'm proud of you. Sven's going to be OK. And it's because of you. I know that stubborn fool would have waited until it was too late if he had been alone."

Gerri drew her head back and looked at him. "He's not dead?"

"Hell, no, he's not dead. Did this asshole…?" He turned to look again at Knox. Cavanaugh had hooked the gaff through Knox's shirt so he couldn't swim away. *Jimmy and I will make sure that this guy has the worst day of his life.* He turned back to Gerri. "You know where the Coast Guard cutter is? We'll take Knox back there. Why don't you come over when you're ready? I expect that they'll want to hear your story."

Gerri was so happy to hear that Sven was alive that she almost danced. Wally, as the immediately available object of her gratitude, again had the thought: *Sven's a pretty smart guy after all…*

She quickly went to put her things together, while Wally joined Jimmy Cavanaugh in securing Knox for delivery back to the Coast Guard cutter. As she was about to disappear into the Glacier Gal's cabin, Wally called out to her. "Gerri. You did a hell of a job today, including the landing. I watched you dock the boat. Very nicely done."

Gerri flushed at the unexpected words of praise. *From Wally, no less.* "Thank you, Wally. For everything. I'm leaving tomorrow morning, so…well…just thanks."

Wally tipped an imaginary hat. "No thanks necessary. We fishermen have to stick together." Gerri started her final cleanup of the Glacier Gal, feeling better than she had thought imaginable five minutes ago.

Wally wore an appropriately grave expression, but inwardly he wanted to shout with satisfaction and relief. He had gone to Captain Counselman to complain about Knox after Sven's encounter with him in the Arctic Saloon. Knox was a disaster waiting to happen. It wasn't that Wally was worried about Gerri—frankly, she wasn't on his radar back then. And it wasn't that he was worried about Sven—Sven could take care of himself. But suppose it had been someone else who had the run-in with Knox?

But Counselman had not been sympathetic. He had talked to Knox and the crewmate that shared Sven's swift chastisement in the bar. Both had denied that Knox had had a knife, and both insisted that Sven had started the fight.

Today was different. Wally told Counselman about Knox's attack on Gerri. He even claimed to be an eye-witness (Wally wasn't encumbered by legal niceties—and anyway, Gerri told him and he trusted her completely).

Counselman listened patiently to Wally's account and then responded wearily. "Yes, Mr. Trager, I remember our conversation earlier this summer. Believe me, I wish I'd pursued it more aggressively back then." He shifted uncomfortably and glanced at the two officers who were sitting silently with him.

"I can't discuss his record with you in detail, but Seaman Knox has been in trouble several times before. When he offered to help Miss… uhh…" He looked at his notes. "Miss Barton pilot the Glacier Gal back to Juneau, I thought that he was trying to redeem himself. The strength of her reaction disturbed me. I talked to him again on the way in to port.

"He became angry. He claimed that she was a militant who was trying to get him in trouble because he had a southern accent." He sighed. "That didn't make much sense to me. I don't even know what a militant is.

"What I saw didn't look like a militant. I saw a young girl—very young—who was stressed and very scared, yet who would rather take her chances alone with the weather than to be stuck on that boat with Knox.

"To make a long story short, I re-interviewed the crewmember who was with Knox at that bar, and he admitted that Knox had been bothering a waitress at the bar that night. And the waitress was a young Negro woman. Meanwhile, I was concerned about her progress and she wasn't monitoring her radio, so I had the crew keep an eye out for the boat. Shortly after they reported her arrival in the harbor, I was informed that Knox had left our vessel against orders. I sent a couple of men ashore after him, but they didn't see him. We didn't know that he'd stayed in the boat harbor."

———

Of course, Gerri knew where the cutter was—its berth was right by the entrance of the boat harbor and it loomed over the other, smaller boats. As she approached it, she saw two local policemen walking ahead of her. She slowed her pace nervously; she had grown up being wary of white policemen. Would they listen to her? Or to the crewman who tried to attack her?

They saw her and waited. "After you, Ma'am," said the younger one.

She had to smile at the salutation. The policeman who spoke—Officer Ryan, according to his nametag—frowned in puzzlement.

"Thank you," Gerri assured him. *Would I have gotten this courtesy from a policeman back home? I wonder.* Then she leaned her head close to him. "I'm 22 and I'm not used to being called Ma'am."

He glanced at the other officer, and then said quietly. "I'm only nineteen myself. Don't say anything, but I'm kind of new at this." Gerri couldn't be sure in the dusk, but it looked like he was actually blushing. *This was one policeman who was a breath of fresh air!*

The other officer interrupted rather officiously, "Is there a problem?"

"Not at all," assured Gerri with a small smile, "I'm just complimenting Officer Ryan on his courtesy."

The meeting on the cutter was anticlimactic. They had agreed how to handle Knox before she even came. They agreed that, although Knox would be charged with assault, he would be remanded to the Coast Guard for discipline. Captain Counselman was at pains to explain to Gerri that this did not constitute leniency. Rather, the Coast Guard had more leverage in punishing Knox for this and previous offenses. The city police would be constrained by due process and the fact that Knox had not done physical damage to her. Gerri and Wally each signed a statement stating what had happened. Captain Counselman terminated the meeting with an apology to Gerri.

As they were filing out of the wardroom, one of the other officers couldn't stand it anymore. He muttered, "Good old Knox. He gets beat up by a fisherman and he doesn't know when to quit. So then the fisherman's girlfriend throws him overboard." Wally allowed himself a small smile.

Back on the dock, Wally turned to Gerri. "I know you have plenty to do before you go. Feel free to use Sven's truck. I'm certain he won't mind. And Gerri?" He stuck out his hand. "Good luck. I know I haven't been the most friendly guy, but you've made a believer of me. I hope you can come back next year."

Gerri transformed the handshake into a hug. "Thank you. I'll try. It's been a wonderful summer." As she carried her bag up the ramp to shore, she played her last statement back in her mind. She had never been good at the socially correct lie. She'd love to be back, but in the real world, she doubted that she'd ever see this place again.

CHAPTER 26

Gerri sat slumped in a chair in a waiting room at the hospital, waiting for Sven's doctor who—it had been promised—would be out shortly. Her body, it seemed, was at war with itself. One faction wanted to get up and pace the room; perhaps even to go find someone to whom she could express her impatience and her worry about Sven— her exhilaration at finding out that Sven was still alive hadn't lasted long; he was still seriously ill.

The other faction wanted nothing more than to curl up on the chair and sleep. She had been operating on adrenaline overload and stress ever since Sven's symptoms started this morning. And in particular, she had been in constant activity since Wally and his friend dragged Ferret-face, secured with duct tape, down the float toward the Coast Guard cutter.

The activity had helped to keep her worries about Sven in check. Well, no, not exactly in check, but at least controllable. She was reminded of an incident years ago when she was in high school. One of her mother's cousins had died. They were not close—she had gone north before Gerri was born. Olivia Barton, however, had grown up with her. Olivia threw herself into a house cleaning project of uncommon vigor. When Gerri asked her about it, she had considered the question for a moment, and then said, "It's busyness therapy, Gerri. I can't think what else to do." Now, Gerri understood.

And busy she had been. As soon as Wally left, she tried to clean up the Glacier Gal. After all, she didn't know how long it would be before Sven was able to get back to it. She decided that the blueberries wouldn't keep, so she divided them into two portions. She would give half to Mrs. Kallek and half to Mindy. Hardly elaborate gifts, but they were from the heart.

She then drove Sven's truck to Mrs. Kallek's home. Walking was all well and good, but Gerri couldn't afford the time today. She had an interesting—though hurried—visit with Mrs. Kallek. They agreed to write each other after Gerri was back home. "Tell me about your experiences teaching," Mrs. Kallek requested. Gerri dutifully promised to do so, though she feared that there would be little to report—Mr. Harrison had again told Gerri's parents that she probably wouldn't get a classroom in the coming year.

As she was about to leave, Gerri mentioned Sven and his illness. "I remember Sven," Mrs. Kallek said. "He was a good boy. He never really applied himself, though. He was kind of a joker when he was young—he liked to construct some of the most elaborate puns. His last year, he seemed to have outgrown that. He was more serious, but he had so many distractions."

Gerri borrowed Mrs. Kallek's phone to tell Mindy that she'd be a little late and would explain when she got there. She didn't look forward to that. For all she knew, Mindy would rejoice at Sven's misfortune.

Then it was off to the hospital, where she waited. The 'go to sleep' faction of her body seemed to be gaining the advantage, as she sank into a light doze. She was awakened by a surprised voice.

"Well hello there."

She opened her eyes and then blinked. Standing in front of her was a black man—one of very few that she had seen in Alaska. He was a good-looking man, slender and about 5' 9", with a moderate 'fro and a short, carefully groomed beard. "Hello," Gerri said in surprise. Then she noticed that he was wearing a white coat. "Are *you* the doctor?"

He laughed. "Not you, too."

"I'm sorry," Gerri said, quickly gathering her wits. She could understand how people's prejudices or their well-meaning ignorance would cause him to hear similar questions all too often.

"Don't worry about it," he assured her. "You look tired. Who are you waiting for?"

"Sven Halvorsen."

"Ah, yes." He put his professional face on.

"I performed an emergency appendectomy. His appendix had burst, so I had to clean out the area. He's now on antibiotics and we're watching him closely, but he should be fine. It'll take a while to heal, of course."

Gerri nodded, somewhat relieved. "Can I see him tonight?"

"No, I'm sorry. He won't be awake until tomorrow sometime. And even then he'll be groggy for a while."

"I had hoped… I'm leaving tomorrow. Is there any possibility…?"

The doctor shook his head sympathetically. "These things take time. He's lucky to be alive, you know. According to the Coast Guard chopper pilot, he was out on his boat in the middle of nowhere. They got the call, lifted him right off the boat, and brought him straight here." He quirked a small smile, doubtless intended to put her at ease. "I don't know what happened to the poor guy's boat. Probably anchored out there somewhere."

Gerri didn't bother to return the smile. "The Glacier Gal's in the boat harbor," she said tiredly. "I was the one who made the call to the Coast Guard, and I brought the boat into town."

"*You* piloted it in? By yourself?"

Gerri just gave him an annoyed look.

"I'm sorry."

Grudgingly, she smiled. "Don't worry about it. I guess we're even."

He laughed. "I suppose so." He paused, sizing her up. "It's just that you look so young…like a college girl."

"A few months ago, I was. I graduated last spring from Pee Dee State College in South Carolina."

"And you ended up here running a fishing boat. That's an amazing story."

The 'I-want-to-go-to-sleep' faction of Gerri's mind was in the ascendency again. Mindy deserved better than a Gerri who collapsed upon arrival. She stood up with effort. "Unfortunately, I don't have time to talk about it. I still have a lot to do before I catch the plane in the morning." She extended her hand. "Thank you for everything, Dr.…"

"Wheeler. John Wheeler." He shook her hand enthusiastically. "And you are?"

"Gerri Barton." She knew better—she should have introduced herself without making him prompt her. Her tiredness was getting the better of her. She forced herself to think: *is there anything else that I've forgotten?*

"Is there any way that I could leave him a note?"

He thought about that for a second. "Give it to the nurse in front. She'll put it with his things."

As she left, he watched her for a moment. *Very interesting.* Sven Halvorsen had been brought in—in considerable pain—but all he was thinking about was 'Gerri. Is Gerri all right? Tell her...' At that point, his pain killers had kicked in and his voice trailed off. Dr. Wheeler started toward his next patient's room, reminding himself: *it's not nice to be nosy. And my love life is pretty much in shambles, so it's hypocritical to worry about someone else's.*

———

By the time Gerri finished describing her day, she almost wanted to laugh at the look of horror on Mindy's face.

"That sailor sounds evil. I hope he gets the punishment he deserves."

"I think he will. He had already been in trouble before. Wally Trager stopped me as I was leaving the boat harbor and relayed that the Coast Guard captain said they were shipping him south—I assume that's what 'stateside' means—and that he would end up in some sort of military prison. Wally gave an eye witness statement which should help." Gerri yawned. This couch was way too comfortable for someone as tired as she.

Mindy's civic loyalty bubbled up. "I hope this doesn't give you bad memories of Juneau. Serious crime isn't that common around here."

Gerri shook her head emphatically. "Not at all. I have wonderful memories of this summer. And of the two people I came to be so fond of—you and Sven. The two of you have been so good to me. I'll miss you both terribly."

Mindy paused, twisting her lips. Gerri had a hunch that she was discomfited by being lumped together with Sven. Gerri forged ahead. "I'm truly sorry about your history with him. And from what little he's said about the accident, I think he feels a tremendous guilt about it to this day. He's kind, gentle and funny. He's really a wonderful man. I'm not telling you what to think, but one day maybe you can find it in your heart to forgive him."

Mindy blinked. "I'll think about it," she finally said. Then, as if she couldn't let the issue rest, she asked, "What about his brawling? Did he ever do that around you?"

"He admitted to me that he'd done that in the past—during the period after Laura's death when he was drinking. But he hasn't done that for a long time. Except once—and then he was protecting me." She briefly described the encounter in the Arctic Saloon.

"Samantha told me about that," Mindy said. "But she didn't know the circumstances," she added grudgingly.

"It wasn't much of a fight," Gerri added cajolingly.

Mindy snorted with amusement. "It was never much of a fight for Sven. That's why Laura got so angry when he quit boxing."

Gerri wanted to change the subject, sensing that she had pushed Mindy as far as she could at one time. "Anyway, I have very fond memories, some terrific pictures, and even a nice nest egg in the bank from fishing.

"I have a few regrets. I never got a chance to take you to that spot under the glacier, And…" The thought that she would likely never see Sven again made her voice catch. She cleared her throat. "And I never got a chance to say goodbye to Sven."

Mindy looked at her speculatively. *This would explain a lot.* "You have feelings for him, don't you?"

Gerri nodded. The more she thought about their parting, the sadder she felt. She blinked rapidly. *I will* not *make a scene.* "We both knew it couldn't last. But I did want it to end better."

"Maybe you could see him tomorrow before you go."

"No," Gerri shook her head. "I'll be halfway to Seattle before visiting hours start. And Dr. Wheeler said that Sven won't be awake…"

"Dr. Wheeler? That's his doctor?" Mindy's voice sharpened.

"Yes," Gerri answered cautiously. "Do you know him? Is he a good doctor?" She regretted the second question instantly—Dr. Wheeler already thought that Gerri doubted him.

"I know him. I work with him at times. Yes, he's an excellent doctor." She pursed her lips. "What did you think of him?"

Gerri had the impression that her answer was important to Mindy, but she didn't know why. "He seemed very nice. He can be a bit annoying, but mostly very nice."

"Annoying how?"

"Well, he seemed to think that I was too young to bring the Glacier Gal in by myself."

Evidently, her answer passed muster, because Mindy leaned back with a wry smile. "I'm not surprised. He has a thing about age."

Gerri was hoping for elaboration, but none was forthcoming. She stretched and stood up. "I have two more things to do. Pack and write Sven a note."

"What about sleep?"

"Good question."

CHAPTER 27

Her family treated Gerri like a star. They met her at the Florence airport, and Gerri could hear the squeals from Marilyn and Joetta practically as soon as she got off the airplane. After they had gotten the first round of hugs out of the way and collected Gerri's baggage, they piled into the old family Chevy and drove home.

There was a steady stream of questions, especially from her sisters, but Gerri could see that her parents were hanging on her answers with equal avidity. When they got home, Gerri could see bright paper ribbon strung along the porch.

"Very nice," she said, pointing. "Who did that?"

"Joetta and I did it," Marilyn said proudly. "It was our idea."

Joetta chimed in. "Daddy helped hold the stepladder."

Once in the house, Gerri brought out her collection of pictures and gave them to her sisters. Each one elicited questions so Gerri finally gave up and went through them herself, passing them around and explaining each one. But even that didn't work, because Marilyn was always trying to look ahead.

"Who's this?"

Gerri looked at the picture Marilyn was holding. "That's Sven. He was my boss." That didn't quite sound right to Gerri. "And my friend," She added. That started her mind down that familiar path. *Was Sven OK? Was he out of the hospital? Will he write soon?*

"Is this your friend, Mindy? She's pretty."

"That's Mindy. And yes, she's very pretty." Gerri described again how they met and how much Mindy had helped her.

"Does she have a boyfriend?" Marilyn hadn't changed all that much, Gerri thought, as she exchanged glances with her mother.

"I don't think so. She never talked about one." Mindy had alluded to some unrequited attraction, but she hadn't identified the person. In any case, that was more detail than Marilyn needed.

But it was Joetta who ended up blindsiding Gerri. "Does Sven have a girlfriend?"

She paused. She had already decided not to tell her family about the full extent of her relationship with Sven. Then she realized that her mouth was hanging open and everyone was waiting for her answer. "No, I don't think he does." *But I wish...*

Later, her various relatives started drifting in, and she found herself telling her stories over again. Fortunately, she never ran out of things to say, and there were only two topics that she had decided were off limits: her affair with Sven and her being swept overboard. Either would have only served to alarm them.

It was evening and Gerri was talking to one of her young cousins when she heard her father at their front door. "Well! I didn't expect to see you tonight. How's your leg?"

"Good enough to get around," said a raspy voice. "Now where's my namesake, the world traveler?"

Sure enough, it was her great aunt Geraldine. She had a cane and was having a hard time getting around. Robert helped her into a chair, shooting a warning look at Gerri as he did so. His message was clear: *be nice.*

Gerri leaned over and kissed Geraldine on the cheek. "What happened to your leg?"

Her aunt made a dismissive noise. "Just an old person's aches and pains. Don't you worry yourself none about me. Now what's this about you up and running off to the ends of the Earth without telling anybody?"

Gerri was determined not to let her get her goat. "But I did tell Mom and Daddy. I wrote them a letter..."

"After you had done it."

"Well, the opportunity came up very suddenly. There wasn't much time."

"You mean you *took* the opportunity."

Was she really going to be this mean? But she was right, of course. Gerri looked at her pleadingly. "Yes, I did. I thought I'd never get another chance like that in my whole life."

Aunt Geraldine looked at her steadily. "Are you glad you did it?"

Gerri took a breath. *Be honest…* "Yes I am. I have memories that I'll treasure always and I made friends that I'll never forget. I'm very glad I did it."

Geraldine nodded; her eyes seemingly far away. When she finally spoke, Gerri had to lean forward to hear her. "Good for you, girl. Sometimes you have to follow your dreams." Then she smiled. "Remind me to tell you some day about my trip to Atlanta when I was about your age."

Gerri looked at her father. He shook his head; he hadn't heard this story either, but she was Olivia's aunt, not his. "I'll do that, Aunt Geraldine. I'll surely do that."

Later, when everyone had left and Gerri's sisters were finally in bed, Gerri and her parents talked in the kitchen.

"Ma, had you heard that Aunt Geraldine took off for Atlanta when she was young?" When she got a blank look, she filled Olivia in on what was said.

"No, I hadn't. But they wouldn't necessarily have told me. Geraldine was regarded as a bit wild in those days. She had some big dreams, but they didn't pan out. If she seems a bit…difficult, it might be bitterness. She loves you, though, in her own way."

Gerri nodded thoughtfully. When she was younger, her parents had told her repeatedly to be kinder to her aunt. Just yesterday, Gerri thought, she had had the nerve to ask Mindy to give Sven another chance. *Maybe I could use some of my own advice.*

Her father interrupted her musing. "We've held the money you sent."

"No. That's yours. I want to pay you back for everything you've done."

"But you'll have a job; you'll need clothes," her mother added.

"And, you splurged on an airplane fare—didn't even use the bus on the way back," her father chimed in.

Her mother shot him a look. "We don't mind that. And we don't want you to have to scrimp now because you're worried about us."

"Wait a minute." Gerri wanted to explain and this was as good a time as any with her sisters safely out of the way. She ran up to her room. When she came back, she handed her mother her checking account passbook.

Olivia held it out so Robert could see. "Juneau National Bank. So you saved out a little?"

"Open it."

Olivia opened it and her eyes grew wide. She slapped it against her thigh and looked at Gerri almost accusingly. "That's a lot of money. Is this for real?"

"It is real. Salmon get a good price, and Sven is one of the best fishermen around." She smiled in remembrance. "A highliner. That's what they call him. And we worked hard for that money." She paused while she gauged their reactions. "And remember, too: Sven's share has to last him all winter." She thought about his paintings, but didn't want to complicate the conversation any further.

Robert took the passbook from Olivia's hand and looked at it. He chuckled and shook his head. "We're in the wrong business, Olivia." He handed the book back to Gerri. "What are you going to do with this? You could buy yourself a car. Cash money; no note."

"Not now. I want to save it."

Olivia chuckled. "You always were a tight fisted child."

"Sven thinks I should wait. I'm sure I'll put it to good use someday." She had thought about this. Near the top of her list would be getting a place of her own. She loved her parents, but if she ever found someone who moved her like Sven, she wanted her privacy. It didn't seem politic to mention this now, however.

"So you and Sven talk about how to spend your money?"

Gerri grinned at her mother. "We talked about everything. Fishing with somebody is a good way to get to know them." Images of Sven came to her mind: him making some convoluted pun as they were setting hooks, the anguish in his voice as he talked about his past, and the warm look in his eyes as they lay in bed indulging in idle pillow talk after the day's work was done. "Yes, I'm very glad I got to know him." Belatedly, she realized that her mother would reach the very conclusion that Gerri wanted to hide, she hastily added, "And Mindy as well." She thought for a minute. "And Mrs. Kallek."

———

Next morning, Gerri was awakened by a knock on her bedroom door. "Gerri, wake up." It was her mother. "Mr. Harrison is here to see you."

Gerri forced her gummy eyes to look at her clock. She groaned—it was late. "I'll be there in a minute, Ma."

It was two minutes before she got to the living room, where Olivia was chatting with Mr. Harrison. Though that was a speed record, it didn't make up for her oversleeping. "Sorry, everybody. I guess I'm still on Pacific time."

Mr. Harrison turned with a smile. "That's quite all right." He stopped as he saw her and his jaw dropped. "Lord 'a mercy," he breathed.

He was looking at her hair. "I'm sorry. I didn't take the time to comb my hair."

He shook his head. "That's not what I meant. I'm sorry, Gerri, but they won't hire you if you come to the interview tomorrow in an afro."

"Really?" She asked, but with a sinking feeling of belief.

"I'm afraid so. Everyone is really touchy now that the high school is integrated. They have to let us in, but if you look like a militant… Well, they're afraid of anything that looks different—anything that they think might cause a disruption."

Gerri nodded, trying to keep the disgusted look off her face. Her adventure was truly over, she realized, and she was back to the realities of the South. "I'll get it pressed today, Mr. Harrison."

"Thank you, Gerri. I knew you'd understand." He shifted uncomfortably. "Something else you need to know. They're not going to offer you a teaching position. You can be a teacher's aide now, and some-day—possibly next year—you can get a classroom. That's the best I could do for you."

"Thank you for trying, Mr. Harrison." He had prepared her for this last spring, so she wasn't surprised, but she had still hoped…

The best face that Gerri could put on the situation, she decided in retrospect, was the pallid praise: 'It could have been worse.' She showed up for the interview dressed conservatively, with her hair freshly done, and tried her best to look eager and unthreatening. Mr. Harrison sat in on the interview, but he wasn't invited to participate. Gerri could appreciate even more, given his clear lack of influence, how much he had gone out on a limb for her.

They offered her the job—teacher's aide—and she did her best to look grateful as she accepted it. The pay wasn't much. Even living with her family, she would have to dip into her nest egg to make ends meet.

———

Sven was, in his own words, an impatient patient. He could muster an ironic smile at that phrase, but there was precious else to smile about. He was scheduled for release from the hospital tomorrow and he was more than ready. He had followed Dr. Wheeler's directives faithfully: after the initial rest, he had embarked on ever longer walks up and down the halls of the hospital. When he got out, he would continue that regimen through the streets of Juneau and through the woods behind his house. *Just as Gerri would have done.*

And therein lay the source of his discontent. He bitterly regretted the timing of his appendicitis. He had had a lot invested, emotionally, in their last night together. He had planned to give her the best night of her life. He had wanted to show her his home and give her a window on his life. And especially, he had wanted to tell her about his feelings for her.

Instead, he felt that he had failed her. Of course, the appendicitis wasn't his fault. He knew that. But still, through his frailty—he hated to use that word, but it fit—he had left her with an arduous—and arguably dangerous—solo trip back to Juneau.

And then there was that business with Knox. Wally had told him about it during one of his visits. Wally had been at such great pains to assure Sven that Knox hadn't even been able to touch her and that his captain had shipped him south for punishment. Wally, who usually spoke his mind and let the chips fall where they may, was obviously afraid that Sven would go looking for Knox with murder on his mind. Maybe he would have. He certainly would have been tempted.

There too, he knew rationally that it wasn't his fault, but he couldn't help being reminded of Laura's death. In both cases, he had failed as a protector. At least Gerri had survived her encounter with Knox unscathed. A reluctant smile curled his lips as he remembered Wally's description—Gerri had given a good account of herself and Sven was proud of her. But she shouldn't have had to.

He guessed that she wasn't angry with him. Dr. Wheeler had told him that she had visited the hospital. But even that was a source of frustration. When Sven had asked the doctor what she said, he had shrugged. "We only talked for a few minutes. I was busy and she was getting ready to leave town." He had probably read Sven's desolate expression, because he added, "She was thinking of leaving you a note. I don't know if she actually did. You can check with the nurses. I told her to leave it with them."

And he did check. Several times, until they were sick of hearing him. None of them remembered or could find a note. Gerri had evidently decided against it.

So all he had to do now was to wait. The doctor told Sven to stay in town for at least a week so he could watch him. Sven had nowhere to go anyway; the fishing season was just about over. Wally had reported to him that Gerri had left the boat looking shipshape. Another smile crept to his face. Wally had extolled Gerri's nautical skills in bringing the boat in and docking it solo. Who would have believed three months ago that Wally would turn into her biggest booster?

Sven mapped the next few weeks in his head. He had a standing arrangement with a hunting guide in Seattle to charter the Glacier Gal during the hunting season. That was a good source of extra money—not that he was hurting. He was frugal by nature, and he always tried to keep a generous reserve—major repairs on the Glacier Gal could come unexpectedly, after all.

But that wouldn't be for a month or more. In the meantime, Sven could at least look forward to his painting. In particular, he had several sketches of Gerri that he wanted to turn into paintings. These would not be sold in Taku Books. They were too private.

Eventually, he would go to the harbor and check on the boat. Not now. Everything on the boat would remind him of Gerri. Maybe it would be easier in a few weeks.

Chapter 28

Gerri sat in the school cafeteria eating her lunch, pondering it as she did so. It was clear that this white—no, make that integrated—school had a bigger food budget than her high school had had. But, oddly, the food didn't taste as good. Of course, Gerri's school cafeteria had been run by Miss Josephine, a treasure of a cook who seemed, day after day, to whip up tasty meals, even from ingredients of doubtful provenance.

Gerri wondered what had become of her. Miss Josephine clearly wasn't running *this* kitchen, and, though it seemed that she had been around forever, she was probably too young to draw Social Security. She sighed. Nobody—none of the blacks anyway—wanted to go back to segregated schools, but the transition wasn't always pleasant either.

Speaking of 'not pleasant,' her duties on this first day of school were mind numbing. To be sure, she would survive. She would do her best to be useful and cheerful; all of the time looking for an opportunity to teach math, even if it was only tutoring.

"May I join you?"

Gerri turned around and her head involuntarily jerked in surprise. "Thurman? What are you doing here?" Then she remembered her manners. Any lingering resentment she had felt for him was ancient history. "Be my guest." She gestured to the empty seat across from her.

He put his tray on the table and sat. "Same as you. I'm a teacher's aide."

"So you got your degree?"

"Yes. Summer school."

Gerri nodded. She wondered what had become of his plans to go to New York and what had become of Carlotta, but she wasn't supposed to know about them, so she couldn't ask. She didn't wonder *that* much, she realized in relief.

Thurman shifted uncomfortably in his chair. "Gerri, I want to apologize for the things I said last spring. I was upset."

A trifling apology was better than none. She nodded once, slowly. "Apology accepted. I did the right thing, but I didn't pick the best time to do it."

Thurman was happy to leave that topic. "I worked hard in that summer course, but it was worth it. Or," he looked around the cafeteria, "it will be worth it when they offer me a true teaching job."

Another sore subject for Gerri. She let her eyes slide over him looking for another line of conversation. "You cut your hair. I'm surprised."

Thurman gave her a half-smile-half-wince. "I was told quietly that they wouldn't hire me with the big 'fro."

"Mr. Harrison?"

"Yes." He looked Gerri over. "You haven't changed. Same hairdo and everything." He chuckled. "You'll always be the same, I guess."

Gerri wanted to glare at him. This sounded too much like the nonsense that she had overheard him spewing last Spring: Gerri is dull; Gerri has no sense of adventure; and so on. But she wouldn't give him the satisfaction of knowing that it hurt.

"So what did *you* do this summer? Help on your parent's farm? I didn't see you around school."

This is almost too easy... Gerri smiled sweetly. "I worked as a commercial fisherman in Southeast Alaska."

Thurman looked at her blankly for a few seconds and then burst into laughter. "That was good. Your delivery was perfect. You really had me going for a few seconds there."

Gerri just looked at him.

He frowned, uncomfortable that she was stringing the joke out. He tried again. "It's OK; I didn't go anywhere either."

Gerri had half a mind to leave him with his assumptions. She took another bite of her lunch. But she decided that she'd rather rub his nose in his mistake. She put her fork down and reached into her purse. She started to hand him her checkbook, but she didn't want him looking at her bank balance. Instead, she tore off a blank check and handed it to him.

He looked at it blankly. Then she could see it hit him as his eyes widened. "Is this real?"

She shot him a disgusted look. "Do you think that I'd spend money to get fake checks made?"

"It's just… I never thought…"

"I guess you didn't know me as well as you thought you did." Just then, the bell rang for the end of the lunch period. Gerri stood up. When Thurman made no move to hand her back her check, she reached out her hand. "I need that back. I'll be using it one of these days."

Thurman stood with her as he fumbled for something to say. "That's unbelievable. I'd like to hear all about it someday."

Gerri gave him a casual nod as she turned to go. She was in no hurry. She'd achieved her purpose. *My revenge?* She wondered if she had been tacky, but decided that she didn't care.

————

As the weeks wore on, Gerri gradually learned which teachers to avoid. By her rough measure, about 20% of the white teachers truly wanted integration to fail. Another 20% were sympathetic—albeit discretely—and wanted it to succeed. The remaining 60% were in the middle. They weren't necessarily happy about the new situation, but they were professional and worked hard to make it succeed in their classrooms.

She shared her estimates with Thurman at lunch one day, which was probably a mistake. He just laughed. "Trust you to reduce everything to numbers." Then he leaned forward and confided quietly, "I think they all want it to fail. Some are just better at hiding it than others."

Gerri just shrugged. Maybe he was right, but she would give them the benefit of the doubt. Thurman had a higher level of hostility than she—nothing new there. Idly, she wondered whether her summer in Alaska had made her more willing to trust. She wasn't naïve—she hadn't, and wouldn't, let her guard down. Even if they offered her a real teacher's job, she wouldn't lose her caution.

As the days stretched on, Thurman frequently joined her for lunch. He was constantly asking for more details about her summer. He appeared to have become fascinated by the 'new' Gerri, to the point that she half expected him to ask her out again. What would she say if he did? Probably 'no,' unless her life became unbearably boring.

She had examined her feelings carefully and concluded that Thurman didn't really attract her now. Could an attraction grow back? She didn't know, but she was not eager to work on that.

There were also some practical reasons to steer clear of him. His apology had been carefully limited. He hadn't mentioned Carlotta at all. Another reason was on Gerri's end—she hadn't been able to stop thinking of Sven. Even though she was angry with him.

He hadn't written her. Not even once. Not even some trifling little note to tell her that he was OK. She had exchanged several letters with Mindy—the first had arrived within a few days of her return home. She had even gotten a letter from Mrs. Kallek—confessing jokingly that she had used one of Gerri's examples in her trig class.

But nothing from Sven. Gerri had even swallowed her pride: in her last letter to Mindy, she asked about Sven and admitted that he had not seen fit to write.

———

Sven was lost in thought as he put the sacks of groceries in his truck. As she rang up his food, the woman at the checkout had given him a funny look. It was not his usual fare—his basket including fresh vegetables and even a couple of small jars of spices. He still ate at the Kash Café more often than not, but he had decided to experiment a little in his own kitchen.

He wouldn't admit this to anyone, but he missed Gerri's cooking. Of course, he missed everything about her, but with the cooking he had hoped that he could replicate at least some of her dishes. He had even bought a cookbook. As he had described it to Rosie Craig, "the most elementary one you have." Gerri had never used a cookbook on the boat, but Sven wasn't foolish enough to think that he would even know where to start without one.

Now, in the late October rain, he was starting to reconsider. Maybe this was a foolish idea, even if he *did* use a cookbook. He thought again of Gerri. She had not been afraid to learn new things. He could at least give the same effort. If he succeeded, he would feel a bit closer to her memory. If he failed, nobody would know about it but him.

As he placed the last of the groceries, he heard an angry voice behind him. "Why haven't you written Gerri a letter?"

He turned around and saw Mindy, looking irritated. He suppressed a groan. He hadn't seen her since Gerri left, and he certainly hadn't missed being the focus of her anger. "I don't have her address," he said, and added with forced casualness, "And I doubt that she is terribly anxious to hear from me."

Mindy glared at him. "Men are so stupid. She gave you her address in the note she left you."

For a moment, Sven's self-composure slipped and Mindy could see the raw need in his face. "Note? I never found a note. And I asked the nurses at the hospital. They couldn't find one either."

"She didn't leave it at the hospital. She left it on your boat. I know, because I took her to the airport, and she dropped it off on the way." She spoke less harshly though, because his pain was evident.

Sven slammed the door to his truck. He needed to get to the Glacier Gal right now. He would tear the boat apart, if necessary, to find this note. He wondered if he owed Mindy the courtesy of excusing himself. "I'll look again," he said gruffly as he circled to the driver's side.

His impatience was obvious—he was oozing anxiety from every pore. "Wait," Mindy implored. Then she gave up. She needed his help, but nothing would induce him to stay and talk right now. "I need to talk to you. Something else has come up."

Sven paused with his hand on the door handle. What was Mindy up to now? His curiosity outweighed his caution. "Can you come to the Kash Café?"

"Kash Café? I've never…" This was clearly out of Mindy's comfort zone. He watched as she pursed her lips. "Yes, I can come. What time?"

They agreed upon a time, and Sven set off for the boat harbor, trying not to look as if he was going to a fire.

As he drove, he puzzled over Mindy's behavior. She had been hostile—that was normal. But her hostility seemed focused. She was angry at him for not writing rather than being angry at him for his very existence. And this 'we need to talk' business. He had no idea what that could be about. Important enough to her to get her to come to the Kash Café. All of this set off his alarm bells, but he would listen to her. If it was anything concerning Gerri, he didn't dare ignore it. He was simply too hungry for any scrap of news about her.

After a brief search, Sven found the envelope. Gerri had left it under the pillow on his bed. There was an intimacy to that placement that excited him more than he wanted to admit. He stared at the envelope in his hand for a moment, savoring the anticipation and, frankly, a little bit apprehensive about what it might say.

Then he couldn't wait any longer. He tore it open. Sure enough, her address was prominently placed at the top. He eagerly read what followed.

Dear Sven,

I hope that you are well now. Dr. Wheeler assured me that if you were careful, you should be as good as new in a few weeks. And I hope you're being careful! If you are not, you'll have to answer to me (smile).

I cannot possibly find words to express my thanks to you. Thanks to your kindness and friendship, the summer was wonderful in <u>every</u> way. I'll never forget it (or you) for as long as I live.

You and Mindy both have been true friends. Someday, I hope the two of you will be on better terms—it couldn't happen to a pair of nicer people.

I'm putting this letter where you will find it, but no one else is likely to see it. I know that you leave your boat unlocked.

WRITE ME! My address is at the top (where you can't miss it).
No excuses!
Your favorite (I hope) mutineer,
Gerri

After he had read her letter, Sven just sat there—grinning like a fool, he realized—but he didn't care. Then his grin faded as he went through the letter again, trying to read between the lines. It was definitely an affectionate letter. That made him feel good. The underlining of the word 'every' seemed to be a subtle reference to their brief affair. Or was he reading in it what he wanted to see? There was no mention of love, but that would be asking too much.

More pessimistically, there was nothing there that suggested a change in her views—she probably still thought of him as part of her adventure. In fact, she had lumped Mindy and him together—and gave no hint that she expected to see either of them again.

Of course he would write her. He would start tonight. What to write was a harder problem. He would apologize for his delay in writing; that was the easy part. He would be affectionate, of course. But he wanted to say more. He sighed. Truth be told, he was afraid that he had fallen in love with her. And while he wouldn't use that word, he wanted her to know the depth of his feelings and, ideally, to respond in kind.

But he didn't know how to put that into a letter. More accurately, he didn't have the nerve to put that into a letter. Their agreement, after all, was that theirs was a casual, summer affair. He wanted to change that. But it was one thing to be talking to her—he could ease into the subject, abandoning it if he sensed that she was not receptive. Laying it all out in a letter was different. Once said, those things couldn't be unsaid, and he didn't want to scare her off.

What he *did* want was for Gerri to remain in his life. Any talk about love could come later. So how to achieve this minimal goal? It had seemed easier prior to his appendicitis. Have a memorable last night together, keep in contact through a correspondence… He had even imagined that he might wangle an invitation to visit her. Then, during this visit he would ask her to come up next summer and work for him on the Glacier Gal. No, make that work *with* him. She felt more like a partner than an employee.

But next summer was a long time from now. By then, she might be in another relationship. He remembered her saying something about settling down. With all of her good qualities, some guy was sure to snap her up.

There was an irony here. Back when he had dated Laura, his mind had never gotten beyond sex. When she had started acting available, he thought he was the luckiest guy in high school. Many of his classmates made their envy obvious. Other qualities—or a long term relationship—simply weren't on his radar. Then, she became pregnant. After that, it was pointless to think about her other qualities—he was simply determined to do the right thing.

Gerri, on the other hand, sort of snuck up on him. The sexual attraction was just as intense. In fact, it was more so. Gerri's affectionate enthusiasm in bed provided an important extra layer to the experience. For the first time, Sven understood the difference between having sex and making love.

But Gerri's other qualities cemented the deal for him. She was smart, always trying to be helpful without looking for credit, and she was even tempered. In fact, Sven had to think hard to come up with a time when she was genuinely angry with him—for more than a few minutes, anyway.

And there had been a few times when he deserved it. He remembered once when she was scribbling in that math journal of hers. The visibility that day was terrific, and he had pointed out a distant hill that was just visible over the horizon. That set her off. She had grabbed a piece of paper and started some calculations. Shortly, she had announced proudly that, knowing the earth's curvature, she could figure out the height of the hill if she knew its distance and vice versa. She tried to show him her calculations, but when she started talking about cosines, he had scoffed.

"It doesn't sound very useful if you have to use a trig table and a calculator," he had said. Why he had been so disagreeable, he didn't remember.

"No, no. The height is just proportional to the square of the distance," she had answered eagerly.

"If there's a cosine in there, I don't believe you." He had no idea why he had said that. Gerri had never lied to him—and why would she lie about something like that? He had only his hazy memories of high school math to go on, and maybe he was frustrated that he couldn't follow her better.

"It's a power series approximation—the angle at the center of the earth is so small. I can explain it to you if you like."

He had just laughed—she might as well have been talking in Greek. She looked hurt and stormed out of the pilot house, tossing back over her shoulder, "Go find some fish. I'll be back when I finish writing this up."

He didn't know about this angle she spoke of, but *he* certainly felt small. Fortunately, she had accepted his apology, delivered with much sincerity, when she returned to the pilot house. And when she had offered again to explain, he had had the sense to accept and try his best to understand.

He could wallow in his gloom for hours thinking of various 'Gerri stories,' but that wouldn't solve his problem. Somehow, he had to make up for not writing and get back into her good graces.

He glanced at the clock. Time to go meet Mindy. After he got back, maybe he would be able to come up with something to say.

On his way to Kash's, it dawned on Sven that he would have no patience for decoding a cookbook tonight. All he would be able to think about would be Gerri and his letter to her. His cooking experiment would have to wait for another day. So upon arrival, he gave his dinner order to Joe Kashiwara and settled into his customary booth to wait.

Ten minutes later, he glanced again at his watch. Mindy was late. His paranoia—developed over the years—kicked in. Was she unavoidably detained? Was she deliberately late to jerk his chain? Was she going to show up at all? And what was this all about, anyway?

Finally, just as his food arrived, he saw Mindy at the front door. She paused and looked around uncomfortably. Sven raised his hand

and waved at her. As she hurried over, he realized that it might appear rude to have started eating. He didn't know what was going on, but he wasn't going to be the first one to be impolite.

She slid into the booth opposite him. "Sorry I'm late. Something came up at work."

"That's no problem." He gestured at his plate. "Would you like to order something? I haven't eaten since this morning."

"No, no thank you." She took off her rain hat and shook it discretely on the floor. She took a breath. "Did you find her letter?"

"Yes. Thank you for that. I haven't had a chance to take the boat out since I got out of the hospital. I've been doing other things." He stopped. She wasn't interested in his recovery activities, and he *certainly* wasn't going to share his main reason for avoiding the boat—the melancholy of his memories of Gerri. He looked at Mindy expectantly. So far, their exchange had been polite, but a bit stilted. Sven shouldn't have been surprised, but he was anxious for her to get to the point.

Mindy was apparently as impatient as Sven, since she just nodded and started talking. "Do you remember Mrs. Kallek?"

"Yes, of course." Sven felt a stab of irritation. He had hoped that this was about Gerri. Evidently not. He remembered Mrs. Kallek with affection and hoped that it was returned—though he probably didn't deserve it, especially during his 'lost' senior year in high school. She just didn't happen to be the subject that he had hoped for.

"She's not well."

"I'm sorry to hear that." Sven was determined to make the best of this conversation—the first polite one that they'd had in years. "Isn't she about ready to retire? She's been teaching forever. In fact, my mother had her when she was in school."

"This is her 48th year of teaching. But she doesn't want to retire. Since her husband died, teaching is all that she has."

Sven tried to imagine teaching for that long. He shook his head. "So what does this have to do with me?" As soon as the words came out, he regretted the tone. He winced and tried again. "Sorry. I mean…"

Mindy waved him off, to his relief. Whatever was going on, she was too focused on it to think about arguing. "Gerri made friends with her last summer, and Mrs. Kallek remembered her. She wants Gerri to teach her classes—with her staying in the background. That way, she can stay involved, but she won't have the strain of the day-to-day load."

Sven blinked and took a breath. This had been worth waiting for after all. He forced himself to think rationally, tamping down the little voice in his mind which was excitedly chanting, *Gerri might be coming back! Gerri might be coming back!* As an antidote to his excitement, he tried to think of any catch to this. "Would this be a real teaching position?"

"Definitely. Mrs. Kallek sold the idea to the school system. Gerri would be the official teacher. Mrs. Kallek would come occasionally, and she would advise Gerri informally."

"A mentor."

"Exactly. She hopes that Gerri would accept that arrangement—they got along so well together. And that's how she got the school system to agree to hire someone whom they don't know at all."

"But suppose Gerri is happy where she is? She talked about settling down. Suppose she doesn't want to come back?"

"That's where we come in. We'll persuade her, and I think that there's a good chance that we can. Mrs. Kallek's classes are ones that Gerri is especially interested in, and she is only a teacher's aide now."

"Really? She couldn't find a teaching job?"

"You'd know that if you had written her." Mindy glared briefly, but then waved her hand placatingly. She was definitely too focused to fight—and now Sven could see why. She elaborated. "Politics. They're in the process of integrating the South Carolina schools and everything is in turmoil. Yuck! If I lived down there, I'd be angry all of the time."

Sven didn't doubt that for a moment. Mindy had always—even as a child—had a keen sense of injustice and a willingness—sometimes, it seemed, eagerness—to confront it. "OK. How do we persuade her?" He was sure that Mindy had a plan. Mindy always had a plan. "I don't know how much help I would be, but I'll do what I can."

Mindy did have a plan. "Mrs. Kallek gave me the school system's letter offering Gerri a contract. She also gave me a letter that she wrote personally, urging Gerri to come. I'm going to add a letter of my own and, if you're willing to write one..." She glanced at him and then continued. "We put all of this together and send it to her in a packet. Hopefully, with everyone urging her..."

"Sheer weight of numbers—wearing down her resistance," Sven supplied.

"Yes, and, if each of us is convincing enough, that might make a difference." Mindy secretly hoped that Sven, if he was willing to express some tender feelings, might be especially persuasive. She couldn't say that, of course, because she wasn't supposed to know about Gerri's crush on him.

Sven nodded thoughtfully. *That might work. I hope it works.* But it still left him with the problem of what to put in his letter—and the extra pressure on him to make it perfect.

Mindy watched the wheels turning in his head. It didn't take long for her to get impatient. "Well? What do you think? Will you write a letter?"

Sven had no intention of sharing his uncertainties with Mindy. "I'll help in any way that I can. Let me think about what to put in my letter. Can I give you my answer tomorrow?"

"That's fine. I have one more letter to get anyway."

"Here, then? Same time?"

"Well, no. I have a working dinner scheduled tomorrow." They worked out a compromise rendezvous at a fancier uptown restaurant.

As Mindy got up to leave, Sven asked, "Who's writing the other letter?"

"Dr. Wheeler. He met Gerri at the hospital."

"But he hardly knows her." Sven felt petty for saying that, but still he wasn't happy. *Did Gerri and the Doctor bond? Do I have a competitor? And could I compete with him—a handsome, professional black man?*

Mindy didn't seem to even consider the competition angle. "No, he doesn't know her well, but as a black man living in Juneau he might be able to tell her more of what it's like." Sven nodded again, and Mindy started to leave. Immediately, though, she turned back. "If you know of other people that she met who would be willing to write a letter, then by all means ask them."

By the next evening, Sven was thoroughly frustrated. He had spent every waking hour trying to come up with suitable wording for his letter. He even described the plan to Wally, in case he might provide some inspiration. He didn't, but to Sven's surprise, he offered to write a letter himself.

In characteristic Wally fashion, he managed to sound grumpy about it. "I'll jot something down. I think she's good people. A teacher—sheesh! She'll probably correct my grammar."

Mindy's dining partner turned out to be Dr. Wheeler. They were engrossed in conversation and didn't even see him coming. The doctor saw him first.

"Sven. You're looking as good as new." He glanced at Mindy with a mischievous smile. "I guess I must do good work."

"I guess you do. I feel fine."

Mindy gestured him to the third chair. "Have you got a letter for me?"

Sven heaved an involuntary sigh. He didn't have a letter—what he had was extreme writer's block. And even if he had been willing to confide in Mindy as to why, he certainly wasn't going to unburden his soul with Dr. Wheeler—a possible rival—listening. What he did have was a desperate, Hail Mary plan—together with a cover story which was barely plausible.

"I don't have a letter, but I have an alternate plan, if you're willing to consider it. I have a gift to send her, but I'm afraid to mail it."

"It's fragile?"

"Umm, yes." The gift was a painting of Gerri reacting to her first sight of a porpoise. Technically, he planned to give it to her parents, not Gerri—currying favor, perhaps? He probably could mail it if he packed it carefully enough, but it made a good excuse. "I could carry it down myself and carry the packet of letters as well."

Mindy's jaw dropped. "You would go all the way down there? Mr. cheapskate?"

When he and Laura were married, that label had been a standard one. Laura had actually meant it bitterly, but Mindy had just used it in fun. Without even thinking, Sven snapped back with his old epithet,

"Watch it, little snort." Then it was his turn to be shocked. "I'm sorry. That just popped out."

Wheeler laughed. "Little snort? I'll have to remember that."

To Sven's relief that distracted Mindy. "He used to call me that when I was a kid. He was married to my older sister." She turned back to Sven. "Do you really mean that? About going down there?"

Sven let out the breath that he had been holding. She actually seemed to be considering that. "I do. I don't have any commitments here for a couple of weeks. I'd like to see her again, and I thought that delivering this packet personally might be more convincing."

Mindy looked thoughtful. "What do you think, John?"

Wheeler looked at Sven speculatively. "I think that your going all that way would definitely make an impression."

Mindy looked interested. "How soon would you go?"

"In a couple of days."

"Fine. I'll get the packet to you tomorrow."

Sven nodded, but his mind was already 3,000 miles away.

CHAPTER 29

During his long trip, Sven had plenty of time to think. Way too much time, in fact. His thoughts cycled through the same things—wearing a path in his neurons if that was possible. He started by wondering what kind of reception he would get from her in South Carolina. Would Gerri be glad to see him? Shocked, certainly, but delighted? Or horrified? Even in his present worried and insecure state of mind, he was still willing to assume that she felt a basic fondness for him. If she was not pleased, it would be because of those around her. He couldn't do anything about her friends. All he could do was to be cautious and to try to avoid putting her on the spot.

Then his thoughts tended to wander toward reminiscences: Gerri working the fishing lines; Gerri rolling her eyes at one of his puns; Gerri's perpetual sunny demeanor and her ready, gorgeous smile; Gerri lying on his bed, looking at him seductively. Yes, she was fond of him—even if he was just part of her adventure.

But what would he say to her? He had this razor-thin excuse: the paintings. On impulse, he had included a second painting, one for Gerri herself in case she didn't come back. He had carefully packed them and persuaded the stewardess to store them in the airplane cabin. He had the packet of letters that Mindy had given him—including even a brief note from Wally. He could talk about the teaching job offer.

Eventually, of course, he would have to speak for himself. What then? He excoriated himself for his cowardice, but he thought he knew the cause: this was the first time in his life that he truly wanted to court a woman—the first time that it truly, intensely mattered to him.

Prior to Laura, he had had only the usual high school explorations. And Laura herself didn't count. She had basically fallen into his lap—no courtship involved. And she had gone so swiftly from a lust object to a responsibility that there was no time for genuine affection to grow—if it ever would have.

So he didn't consider himself to be a ladies' man. The few, casual relationships that he'd had since Laura weren't based on that sort of image. Nor were they deeply committed on either person's part. All he had now was his essential earnestness. That would have to suffice, somehow.

That was it, then. Thinking about it couldn't make it any better. He would give Gerri the packet and add that he, too, wanted her to come back. He would be cautious about saying too much—a declaration of love might scare her off completely. And that was unquestionably the worst possible outcome: if she declined to come back then, not only would he have lost, but Juneau would have lost. In that case, he would probably never see her again.

That decided, he reviewed the remainder of his itinerary. The plane was presently approaching Atlanta, where he would spend the night. In the morning he would fly to Florence, South Carolina, where he would rent a car. Gerri's house would then be less than an hour's drive away.

After he'd checked into a hotel, he set out to find a restaurant. He felt so stiff—he'd spent the whole day either sitting on a plane or in an airport—that he decided to take a page out of Gerri's book and just walk. He would dine in whatever restaurant caught his eye. In the meantime, this would be a good opportunity for people watching.

He was intensely curious about the South. He had read several books about the civil rights struggle in the time since Gerri had left. Some were saddening; some were enlightening. All of them were interesting. One of them was positively enraging—<u>Soul On Ice</u>. How could anybody talk coldly about raping women? Did the author's troubles, no matter how bad, justify hurting others just for his own satisfaction? And raping black women 'just for practice?' Just thinking about it made Sven curl his fists. Evil knew no color. If *anyone* decided to 'practice' on Gerri, Sven would, with great pleasure, beat him to a pulp. And yet, some seemed to think that Cleaver's book was profound. Sometimes Sven just didn't understand people.

As he walked, the neighborhood gradually transformed. There were fewer business suits and more light jackets and casual shirts over blue jeans. The jackets amused Sven since+ the temperature was in the low 60's—summer weather in Juneau. In fact, Sven in his light shirt got a few bemused glances from the other pedestrians.

He saw a restaurant which looked tolerable. 'Harry's, the Friendly Eatery' said the sign. He peered in the large window. *Nope, no business suits.* He went in and was directed to a table. He picked up the menu on the table and perused it. It didn't take him long—he had never been a picky eater until Gerri had spoiled him.

While he waited, he resumed his people watching. Most of the customers were white, which was interesting since the pedestrian traffic outside was about half and half, black and white. Since he was noticing, most of what he guessed to be the senior staff were white—the cook behind a long counter, the cashier, and some fellow who seemed to be the boss. *Harry, perhaps?* Several of the waitresses were black and, though Sven couldn't see the back, he was willing to bet the menial workers back there were black.

Soon, a waitress approached him. She was a very young, petite black woman with short hair. "Good evening, sir. Do you have any questions?"

Sven smiled back. She looked a little nervous and he wondered if this was her first job. He almost opened his mouth to ask, but thought the better of it. She might take that as implied criticism. He had chosen an entree, but he decided to make this a learning experience. "What's a hush puppy?"

Her eyebrows twitched as she tried to conceal a smile. She managed to describe a corn meal ball with spices, deep fried. "They're very good," she finally offered with a hopeful expression.

Sven gave her his order and added a side order of hush puppies.

She hesitated, and then asked, "Are you from up North?"

As she stepped outside her waitress persona to satisfy her curiosity *(was it my accent or my ignorance of hush puppies?)* she looked more than ever like a high school girl. Sven wondered what 'up north' even meant to her. Ohio? Maryland? Her frank interest was appealing. Maybe this was what was meant by the 'Friendly Eatery' sign.

"Yes. Way, way North. I'm from Alaska."

Her eyes got big. "I've never even met anyone from Alaska before. Is this your first time in the South?"

He nodded. *I guess the hush puppy question gave that away.* "I came down to surprise my girl friend with a gift. I'm hoping to convince her to move up there with me." Somehow talking to this friendly young lady—whom he would never see again—was unburdening. He could call Gerri his girl friend without worrying about whether she would approve.

"How did you meet her?"

"She came up last summer to be a fisherman. She had just finished college and she wanted to do something different. Now, I don't want to lose her."

Her look turned wistful. "Gosh, that sounds exciting. And romantic." Then she seemed to realize where she was. "I'll go put your order in. Back in a few minutes." She hastened off.

True to her word, she was back in less than five minutes. After she placed his order on his table, she hesitated. "Does she live in Atlanta?"

He shook his head. "South Carolina."

"Where did she go to college?"

"Pee Dee State."

She blinked in surprise. "That's a black college."

Another lesson about the South... Gerri had never mentioned it, but segregation was apparently rampant on all levels. He nodded slowly. "I didn't realize that, but I guess I should have."

"So, she's...black?"

Sven nodded again. Now, she couldn't conceal her grin. "That's really romantic."

After she left, he tackled his meal—as he continued his people watching. He noticed his waitress huddling with two others, both black. They were giggling and stealing glances at him. He idly wondered what had piqued their interest. There was no shortage of possibilities: his being an Alaskan, his ignorance of hush puppies, or maybe his having a black girl friend. Whichever it was, he didn't begrudge them their amusement.

Then the presumed boss, who had been standing nearby, approached the group and started berating them. Sven couldn't hear what he was saying, but the waitresses fled to their respective stations, looking distinctly unhappy. It certainly didn't seem like a 'friendly eatery' to Sven. They had been talking for only a few minutes and, prior to that, had seemed to be working hard.

It all came clear in the next minute as the boss approached Sven's table with an unfriendly look on his face. "I don't want you bothering my girls with a bunch of crazy stories."

The man was clearly spoiling for an unpleasant confrontation. That could only get his waitress in further trouble. Sven would not give him that satisfaction. He was willing to play dumb a bit if that would help to defuse the situation. He leaned back in his chair and looked at the man mildly. "I certainly didn't intend to bother the waitress. The 'Friendly Eatery' sign was what brought me in here, and I assumed that that included a bit of friendly conversation. I'll be glad to apologize to her if you like."

Sven knew damn well that the waitress wasn't offended; the boss was. It had to have been Sven's reference to a black girlfriend that got him upset. Sven's offer, as he had intended, took the man by surprise. "No, that won't be necessary." He handed Sven a slip of paper. "Here's your check. You can pay the cashier as you leave."

In other words, Sven thought, *don't talk to the waitress any more.* However, he thanked the man as if he were doing Sven a favor. As the man turned to leave, Sven called out to him. "By the way, the hush puppies were delicious. I appreciate the waitress's suggestion."

That man gave Sven a rather sour nod as he left. Sven had to conceal a smile—it had annoyed the man to have to acknowledge, even indirectly, his waitress's initiative.

As Sven examined the bill, he realized that the total had been filled in and a line drawn through the 'tip' item. Given the man's petty nastiness, Sven suspected that even if he added a tip, the waitress wouldn't get it. He sat there, toying with last bits of his food. After about five minutes, the man disappeared into the back of the restaurant. Sven quickly got up to leave, veering toward his waitress as he did so.

She looked nervous as he approached, so he hardly even slowed down. As he walked by, he handed her a $10 bill and flashed a quick smile. "Thanks for everything. I hope I didn't get you in trouble."

The bill quickly disappeared into her pocket. "It wasn't your fault."

After he got back to his hotel, Sven thought about this incident. It had to have been his mention of a black girlfriend which led to the waitresses' gossiping, which in turn mightily offended their boss. Another lesson in his education about the South—what a cauldron of hatred and paranoia seethed beneath the surface of many of the white folks here.

———

The next morning started badly for Sven. As his impatience to see Gerri grew, it seemed that the delays grew as well. The puddle jumper which was to take him to Florence was late. Further, he had to wait at the rental car desk because his car wasn't ready. When he finally got it, he couldn't find Gerri's address on the map that they provided, and the clerk had never heard of her street. He was at least able to give Sven directions to the high school where Gerri worked, so he decided to head there first.

Once he was finally in the car, he discovered that its A/C barely worked. And, while yesterday had been pleasantly warm in Atlanta, today was downright hot. A bank thermometer said 75°. *In November! How do they stand it?* In Juneau this temperature—even in the summer—would elicit comments about the heat.

As he drove, he reviewed his plans. After all of the delays, he should get to her school sometime around dismissal. The episode in the restaurant made him vow to be extra careful. Maybe he would tell them that he was delivering a package. He was afraid to leave the paintings in the car anyway—unless he could find a shady parking space, the inside of the car would be roasting practically as soon as he got into the building.

Finally, after an interminable drive, he was there. He sat in the car in the school parking lot and watched students pour out. Something was going right for once—it was evidently dismissal time. He got out of the car, grabbed the boxed paintings, and headed for the door.

CHAPTER 30

This had been a long day, and Gerri was ready for it to be over. It had started well. Gerri had awakened feeling snug under her covers in her cool room. She had taken to leaving her window wide open at night, even when it was cold outside. She compensated by having extra covers, and, if she closed her eyes and let her mind drift, she could pretend for a few minutes that she was lying in Sven's bed on the Glacier Gal. That never lasted long, and this morning had been no exception. She heard her mother's call and, groaning, threw the covers off and got up.

"Shut that window! You'll freeze to death." Olivia had stuck her head in Gerri's door.

Gerri obediently shut the window. She didn't bother to explain that in Alaska she had routinely gotten up on much colder mornings than this. And she certainly didn't share her sudden mental image of Sven—un-self-consciously naked and looking magnificent—walking around on those same mornings as they got dressed to start their day.

It was going to be a warm day, so Gerri didn't bother with a jacket as she set out on her walk to school. That earned her another remonstration from her mother. *It's really time for me to look for my own place. I've put it off too long.* She didn't blame Olivia, but as long as Gerri was living under her roof, it was instinctive for her to treat Gerri like a child—even though Gerri, at her own insistence, was helping with the expenses.

Her morning at school was uneventful. At lunch, she got a mild surprise—even though she had been half-expecting it for some time.

Thurman finally got around to asking her out. She didn't know what to think about that, so she promised him that she'd give him an answer tomorrow. Throughout the afternoon, it kept coming back to her mind. On the one hand, she didn't have any (what her mother would call) tender feelings for him anymore. And he had never come clean about Carlotta.

On the other hand, she deserved to have a little fun, and it wasn't like he was asking for her hand or anything. Maybe going out with Thurman would help her get her mind off Sven—Mr. can't-be-bothered-to-write Sven.

As she completed her work in Miss Carruthers' classroom, she continued thinking about what to tell Thurman. Since Miss. Carruthers invariably found her something mindless and demeaning to do, Gerri had no trouble letting her mind wander while she worked. Miss Carruthers was one of the more hostile teachers. She was barely older than Gerri, but she always acted as though Gerri was a child—and a slightly slow one, at that.

Today's task was to cut out Thanksgiving decorations from construction paper. Any student could have done this, but as Miss Carruthers had said in her grating voice, "I want my classroom to look special for Thanksgiving, so be especially careful."

Thurman had been tasked to work with her, and Gerri glanced at him as he sat in a student's chair concentrating on his cutting. He seemed to get along with Miss Carruthers fairly well. If Gerri were to be unkind, she would put that down to a hitherto unrevealed talent for obsequiousness. On the other hand, he had fewer illusions about this job—he didn't have a burning desire to teach and knew that the job was a temporary expediency made necessary by his delayed graduation. She sighed as she got up to get more construction paper. When had Thurman become a more accepting person than she?

As she walked past the window, she glanced outside. There was a man… She stopped and fought the urge to turn back and look again. *This is crazy!* The man, and his rolling, sailor's gait, reminded her intensely of Sven. Her heart briefly stabbed with longing—clearly it had not gotten the message that that man didn't even care enough to write.

As she returned to her seat, she sneaked another look out the window, but of course the man—if there had even been one—was gone.

When she got back to her seat, she just sat there. Her hands were shaking. This was intolerable. She had to do something to break this obsession with Sven. Miss Carruthers left the room on an errand, giving Gerri a strange look. Gerri ignored her; there was only one thing that she could think of to do. She turned to Thurman. "Thurman, I've decided. I will go out with you."

He looked up blankly, and then his face split in a smile. "Cool! I'll show you a good time. I guarantee that you'll enjoy it."

Gerri wondered about his phraseology, but she disregarded it. Finally, she was doing something! Her sudden good mood even survived the sound of Miss Carruthers in the hall. She was using what Gerri called her man-catching voice. Another of the many ways in which she annoyed Gerri was her frank insistence that she was only teaching until she found a man worthy of marrying. And sometimes, her search was offensively obvious.

Gerri idly wondered who her target was this time. She would give the woman her due—she was attractive in a stereotypical, southern belle sort of way, and her 'targets' seemed to be pleased with the attention. Anyway, that was the target's problem—Gerri was simply relieved that Miss Carruthers was out of the room.

She hurried to finish the last turkey and got up to put them on the teacher's desk. Before picking them up, she bent over the chair to count them. It would be like Miss Carruthers to yell at her for making one too few.

———

Gerri was not the first person to tell Sven about the astonishing difference between his fearsome scowl and his charming smile. She was just the first person who mattered. He was, however, willing to use that knowledge to his advantage. It took a couple of winsome smiles, but Sven got the lady at the central office to direct him to the classroom where Gerri was working.

He followed her directions with mounting impatience. He was forced to endure a brief delay when a rather strange woman accosted him in the hall. After he had broken free from her, he shook his head. What had happened to the world? In his memory, teachers were businesslike—even motherly. This woman was neither. As she talked to him, she fluttered her eyelashes and tried to stroke his arm. He had to take a step backwards to evade her.

Finally, he was outside the door to Gerri's room. The woman in the office had warned him that the teacher using this room didn't like outsiders barging in. He paused and looked in. There, to his fascination, was Gerri. She looked different, but she still looked trim and pretty, and Sven feasted his eyes for a moment.

She wore a suit with a skirt that stopped just above her knees. The skirt and the jacket were both black. He couldn't see her blouse because she was facing away from him. The major change was her hair—her afro was gone, replaced by short, straightened hair. He'd have to reserve judgment on that. As he watched, she stood up and bent over the seat next to her. As she did so, young black man sitting behind her bent over in his seat.

Sven saw red. The young man was trying to look up her skirt. She, oblivious, straightened up and walked to the back of the room. Sven gave the guy his most evil glare and cleared his throat loudly. It was the first time that he had consciously conjured up his fearsome scowl.

The man turned at the sound and looked shocked. His body jerked and a pencil dropped from his hands and rolled under a table. Sven watched as he stood and retreated a step. "Yes? Um, I mean, may I help you?"

"No." Sven kept glaring.

The man licked his lips and started to speak again. Sven stepped into the room and looked for Gerri. Out of the corner of his eye, Sven saw the man retreat another step, but Sven ignored him. Everything else went out of his head as Gerri turned and saw him.

Her jaw dropped and she froze for a second. Then she shook her head and spoke, almost in a whisper. "Sven? Is it really you? Or am I hallucinating?"

Sven forgot all of his vows to be cautious. He opened his arms and, in three large strides, was in front of her folding her in a hug. "If you're hallucinating, then so am I. Gerri, you have no idea how good it is to see you." She returned the hug with such vigor that he could feel the residual pain of his appendix scar.

He leaned back far enough to study her face. Different hairdo, but same Gerri. He focused his eyes on her lips. Just then there was a noise—the young man asked, "Gerri, do you know this… this…"

With his words, the spell was broken. Gerri stepped back and half turned, leaving one hand hooked around Sven's arm. "Yes, of course. I should have introduced you. Thurman, this is Sven Halvorsen."

Thurman pasted a fake smile on his face as she introduced them. He shook Sven's hand cautiously. He hated the man on sight. He looked as though he made his living attacking people in alleyways, not fishing in the wilderness. But most of all, Thurman hated the way Sven looked at Gerri.

By rights, Thurman believed, Gerri should be his. There was no one else that he would prefer in this hick town—until Carlotta came back, of course. And Gerri even owed him for that—Carlotta left when she found out that Thurman wasn't graduating in the spring, which was Gerri's fault.

Besides, he had an investment in Gerri. He had put up with her silly virginity promise for years, but since she had come back after this last summer she had seemed more sophisticated; more self-assured. And just now, she had accepted his offer of a date. He planned to take her to a club. A few drinks—assuming that she was also more sophisticated about that—and he liked his chances.

Gerri's gaze flicked nervously back and forth between the two men. She understood why Thurman was hostile to Sven—he didn't like white men, and Gerri had greeted Sven with obvious affection. In fact, Thurman's interruption was fortuitous in a perverse way. She had seen the look on Sven's face. In another moment, he would have kissed her and she would have reciprocated enthusiastically. Thurman could gossip about the hug, but he could *really* have made her life miserable around the school if she had kissed Sven.

But why was Sven glaring? He'd never even met Thurman before. Had she mentioned him by name last summer? Maybe. But Thurman was ancient history. *Well...* She *had* just accepted his offer of a date. She'd have to do something about that.

She noticed the muscles in Sven's forearm tighten and, simultaneously, heard Thurman grunt. That would be all that she needed—for Sven to 'accidently' break Thurman's hand. She quickly tightened her hand on Sven's arm and looked anxiously into his eyes, hoping that somehow he could read her mind.

Her mind wasn't that hard to read. Sven quirked a small smile at her and released Thurman's hand.

Thurman rubbed his hand unobtrusively and spoke to Gerri. "Gerri, may I speak to you alone for a minute?"

"I don't want to be rude to my guest. Can't it wait until Monday?"

"It's about our date. I have to make plans."

Gerri cringed. That was the last thing she wanted Sven to hear. And Thurman knew darn well that no specific day or time had even been discussed. "Monday will have to do. My guest has come a long way." Searching for a distraction, she saw the package that Sven had leaned against the door. "And I'm dying to know what's in that package. Is that for me?"

"Part of it is. And part of it is for your parents. I didn't want to leave it in the car because of the heat." He was not going to mention that the package was his ticket into the building.

Just then, Miss Carruthers returned. Her greeting for Sven was less effusive this time. He hadn't been receptive in the hallway and—she wasn't quite sure—had Gerri's hand been hastily removed from his arm as she walked through the door? "What's going on? I want those decorations done today."

"They're on your desk," Gerri assured her. "I was just leaving. He, uh, brought a package for me." She had no desire to introduce Sven to Miss Carruthers—and hoped she wouldn't be forced to.

"Wait a minute," Miss Carruthers sniffed. "I want to check them." Finally, when she found nothing to complain about, they were free to leave.

Their walk to Sven's car was largely silent. After Sven verified that Gerri had walked to work, his only response to Gerri's attempt at conversation was a muttered "Let's talk when we get to the car." Thurman's remark about a date with Gerri had hit him like a punch in the gut. Which is exactly what the bastard had intended, of course. Sven had looked at Gerri while she replied, but she didn't meet his eyes. Had she started dating this soon? And the same guy that had betrayed her so recently? There couldn't be that many guys with that name in this little town.

In fairness, he had to admit that the look she gave Thurman was an angry one—but was that simply because he wasn't supposed to reveal their dating? No, Sven didn't want to talk right now. He didn't want to say something that he would regret, possibly forever. And in case there was a scene, he didn't want it to be in the parking lot, visible to all.

Then there was the matter of his ostensible mission. His selfish purpose aside, they had entrusted him to make a convincing argument for Gerri's returning to Juneau. *His* hopes may have been dashed practically before he started, but the larger goal was still possible to achieve. He owed it to them. And, he thought ironically, he would not want to waste Mindy's politeness—her first toward him in almost a decade.

As they walked, Gerri was consumed by curiosity, but Sven was clearly in a bad mood. She didn't blame him—Thurman had behaved abominably. That sly, unwarranted reference to their projected date was uncalled for. She would have to clear that up with Sven. A voice in the back of her mind, though, asked why she should even feel guilty about that. He didn't want a commitment; he hadn't even written.

And Sven himself hadn't been polite. It was as if he had taken an instant dislike to Thurman. And it couldn't have been that he remembered the name, because he was glaring daggers at him before she introduced them. And the handshake—she shuddered. What a disaster that would have been if he had injured Thurman. Thank heavens he had ceased—with the barest hint of a sheepish look at her—when she had squeezed his arm.

When they were in his car, he finally spoke again. "How far is your house?"

"It's only about three miles. I can direct…" But he was shaking his head.

"Is there someplace that we can stop and talk privately?" He asked stiffly. "This will take a little while to explain."

Gerri was a bit nervous at his tone, but she felt a rush of pleasurable nostalgia, as she remembered that first night. The night he rescued her at the Arctic Saloon. She called it the first night because it was the start of their honest friendship—without her lying to him about her gender. She smiled impishly. "You mean like our Rock Dump?"

That earned her a return smile and the atmosphere in the car relaxed several notches. "Yes. I don't see any hollowed out mountains around here—but your equivalent."

She directed him to a deserted road leading to a local creek where they parked under a tree. Sven fished a large manila envelope out from under his seat and held it in his hands as he started talking.

By the time he had finished and handed her the envelope, her heart was pounding with excitement. "And it's all in here? Even the contract?"

"That's what Mindy said. And she's very organized, as you know."

"You haven't looked at it?"

He shook his head. "No, it's sealed and so are the letters inside. It's private between each writer and you."

"This sounds very attractive. I'm sorry that Mrs. Kallek is not feeling well. But I'm really flattered that she thought of me." She turned the envelope over in her hands, as if she could divine its secrets by touch. There was only one disappointment. "But you didn't write a letter."

"I wanted to see you. Especially since I let you down there at the end—I left you in a bad spot."

Gerri had to laugh out loud at that. "You didn't leave me in a bad spot. Your appendix did. And unless I miss my guess, it's buried in a landfill or washed down a drain. It's been duly punished. So stop being ridiculous!" Behind her levity was anxiousness, though. She wanted to be reassured that Sven, above all others, missed her and wanted her back. That reminded her… "Why didn't you write me? I wanted…" *To know that you missed me; that you thought of me constantly.* "I wanted to know that you were all right."

"I hadn't been back to the boat. I didn't know you had left your address there until Mindy told me a few days ago."

Gerri nodded. She loved the fact that the familiar, comfortable feeling with Sven had returned. She hated to spoil it, but the longer she waited, the worse it would be. "About today…"

With that, the floodgates opened. "I know it's none of my business, but how could you start dating him again? He betrayed you."

"I haven't dated him. He asked me and I told him I would think about it. There's no romantic interest anymore."

"So he was lying about that." Sven was sorry he had let the guy out of his grip.

Gerri sighed. "Not exactly. In a weak moment I said I would go out with him. There's not much to do in this town. It would have been just for the outing." She had no intention of explaining that the weak moment had been all about Sven.

Her answer seemed to mollify him. He sat there tapping his fingers on the steering wheel. "Did he at least apologize?"

"Sort of. He apologized for the way he spoke to me. But he didn't say anything about Carlotta."

Sven made a disgusted noise. "I wanted to pop him one."

"But you didn't even know who he was at first."

"The first moment I looked in the door, you were bending over a chair. And he, chivalrous prince that he was, was bent over trying to look up your skirt."

For some reason, Gerri erupted into peals of laughter. Sven looked at her reproachfully. "Well, it couldn't have done him much good. I was wearing dark pantyhose."

He made a sour face and muttered something about the principle of the thing. Gerri patted him on the cheek and grinned. "But thank you for caring."

In the ensuing silence, she looked again at the envelope. She was dying to see the letters. She wondered…

"Why don't you wait and read them when I'm not breathing down your neck," Sven said. "In fact, read them tonight when you're alone."

Gerri nodded. Sometimes Sven almost seemed to know what she was thinking. She remembered again that 'almost kiss' in the classroom. It would almost have been worth the abuse she would have gotten from Thurman. She took a breath. Now was not the time for dreaming; now was the time for being practical. "How long are you staying?"

"I have to take the boat out Monday, so I'll have to start back tomorrow afternoon. I wish I could stay longer, but…" He now regretted that he hadn't come earlier. Putting the finishing touches on the second painting had taken him longer than he had anticipated. He looked at her hopefully. "If you decide to come, I can hand deliver the signed contract to Mindy." He saw her frown. "If that's too soon, you can mail it."

"We'll see. I want to read this, and I may have questions. I'll want to talk to my parents." She thought for a moment. "And to Mr. Harrison, he's the one who got me this job."

"What about you? Do you have a place to stay tonight?" With a stab of regret, she wished that she'd gotten a place of her own. Her parent's house had no extra room, but with her own place, she could have invited him to stay with her—neighbors be damned.

"I'm staying in the Motel 6 down the road." He didn't want to presume too much: "Perhaps you can recommend a cheap place to eat."

"Don't be silly. You'll eat with us. I'm sure my family would love to meet you." *Until they realize that you're hoping to take me away…* "Are you ready and eager to meet them?"

Sven grinned as he reached for the ignition switch. "I don't know if I'm ready, but I'm eager."

Chapter 31

Olivia Barton gave the pot of greens an exploratory stir. Satisfied with their cooking progress, she glanced out the window and down the road. Gerri was not yet in sight.

However, she would be home soon, and Olivia knew that she would come in brimming with frustration about her job. Thank heavens it was Friday—Gerri would have two days of relief from her so-called work. It was ironic. In the bad old days before the integration of the schools, Gerri would easily have gotten a teaching job at the Negro school. She would still have had the usual teaching frustrations, but at least she would have been allowed to teach. And she would have been spared the daily contact with nasty white people—they would be very unlikely to be working at a Negro school.

Olivia would provide a sympathetic ear this afternoon, of course, but after Gerri had done some venting, Olivia wanted to have something to take her mind off those frustrations. Maybe she'd ask her some more about her summer. That was the one subject that seemed to cheer Gerri up.

Even now, Olivia found it hard to believe that Gerri had had such an adventure. And that she had done so well financially. More importantly, she had come back with more self-confidence and maturity. Olivia frowned. She didn't like that word, because it seemed to imply that Gerri was immature before she went. But whatever word Olivia used, the summer had been good for Gerri. She would have a lifetime of memories.

The only part of Gerri's adventure that gave Olivia pause was that man that she had worked for. Not that he didn't seem like a perfectly nice man, but at first it seemed that almost all of her anecdotes involved him—and in very flattering terms. It was as though she had a bit of a crush on him. Olivia was sorry that Gerri was face-to-face with the job inequities of the South, but that was nothing compared to the animus that she would face in an interracial romance.

Recently, however, Gerri had spoken of him less and less. Probably this was the normal waning of interest. Olivia reflected—not for the first time—on how thankful she was that that man was three thousand miles away.

She checked the window again. Gerri was overdue. She saw nothing except a car in the distance moving slowly up the road. Squinting, she tried to recognize it but couldn't. Theirs was a back road—not even paved. Through traffic was rare. In fact, the school buses dropped Joetta and Marilyn at the intersection about a quarter mile away, rather than come down this narrow, rutted lane.

As she watched, the car turned and pulled into their yard. That made her nervous. The sun reflecting off of the windshield made it impossible to see the passengers, but as the car turned, she caught a glimpse of a large, pale arm. The driver was a white man, and a husky one at that. She glanced at the clock, wishing that Robert was home. *Oh well, I should give the man the benefit of the doubt—perhaps he's just lost.* She walked toward the porch to see what he wanted.

As she stepped out, she was shocked to see Gerri climbing out of the car. A very ebullient Gerri, at that. "Ma, guess what. I have the nicest surprise." She turned back to the car, laughing. "Are you getting out? She won't bite."

Out climbed a very husky man with a somewhat shy grin on his face. "This is Sven. You remember my talking about him."

How could she forget? His sudden appearance made her nervous in spite of the fact he was a very attractive man and his grin was disarming. No, not nervous in *spite* of that—nervous *because* of that. The fact that this man had crossed the continent to see Gerri—and Gerri's excited reaction to him—spelled one thing to Olivia: trouble. In spite of her misgivings, however, she knew her manners. She advanced with her hand out and a smile on her face. "This is certainly a surprise. What brings you all of this way?" *Do I really want to hear the answer?*

Sven scanned Olivia's face with his artist's eye. Her resemblance to Gerri was unmistakable but, though she had an easy smile, there was wariness behind her gaze. *Can I really blame her?* If his crash course in southern race relations told him anything, it was that her trust wouldn't be given automatically. He decided to wait and let Gerri tell her about the job offer.

"I have a gift for your family; one that I didn't want to mail. And I brought some letters from Gerri's friends in Juneau." He glanced at Gerri, hoping to be rescued.

"It's a job offer, Ma. A real teaching job!"

Olivia's heart didn't know whether to soar or to sink. "Up there?"

Gerri nodded, practically bouncing with excitement. "I don't know all the details yet. I'm going to read the letters tonight." She gestured with a large manila envelope. "I invited Sven for dinner. I hope you don't mind."

"Of course not. We'd love to have you eat with us." Her instincts had been right, she reflected. This could be real trouble. But no more so for having him to dinner. "My husband will be home in an hour or so. Please make yourself at home."

———

The dinner was half over before Gerri started to relax. She'd never been in this position before. She had two sets of people, each very dear to her, who didn't know each other at all. She desperately wanted them to like each other. From there, she somehow got the notion that it was her responsibility to make them like each other.

She gradually realized that she did not have to force the conversation—Sven's and her family's interest in each other was obvious. In fact, her sisters were peppering Sven with questions until Gerri was afraid that he wouldn't have a chance to finish his meal.

Joetta hung onto his every word. Marilyn did as well, but with a big-eyed flirtatiousness that made Gerri want to slap her. The only saving grace in that was that Sven glanced at Gerri with shared amusement.

Her father was not saying much, but that was his nature—he wasn't inclined to compete with the girls in conversation. He was smiling and interested—and once he gave Gerri a wink.

Her mother was the only person who made her uneasy. She smiled at the right moments, but Gerri could see through her façade of manners. She was not happy about this. Gerri didn't know why; Sven had been on his best behavior. Perhaps she was worried about the prospect of Gerri's leaving again. One thing was certain—Gerri would find out eventually; Olivia would see to that.

When the meal was finished, Joetta and Marilyn were dispatched to the kitchen to wash the dishes. Marilyn made a token protest, "What about Gerri? Why are we doing all of the work?"

"Gerri has a guest. Now hurry up so that you can see Sven's present when we unwrap it." That got rid of them in a hurry.

Sven turned to Olivia. "Mrs. Barton, that meal was delicious. I can see where Gerri got her cooking skills."

"Thank you. Did Gerri cook for you?"

"Yes. And by her own request, I must say." He gave Gerri a sly grin.

Gerri smiled in spite of herself. He had asked her as they approached her house whether there were any topics which should not be mentioned. She gave him four: her masquerade as a male, her fall overboard, the attack by Knox, and (of course) the fact that they had become lovers. His grin was a private ribbing about the first—how neatly she was hoist on her own petard when she first offered to cook. She remembered it still: "I'll bet that in your family, the females did all of the cooking."

"Tell me, Sven," (Gerri wanted to change the subject, and maybe to put him on the spot just a bit.) "What has made the biggest impression on you so far in South Carolina?"

Sven toyed with his napkin as he thought that over. Of course, seeing Gerri again had impressed him the most—it was the primary, albeit secret, reason that he had come. He couldn't be sure how her parents would react to that—better to leave it unsaid. The fraught racial relations certainly had made a big impression, but that didn't make for light dinner table conversation with people he hardly knew. He went for the safe topic.

"The weather. I knew it would be warmer, but I never thought that it would be this warm. This is warmer than most summer days in Juneau. November! Does it ever get cold here?"

"Oh, yes," her father replied, "It was down below 50° last week."

Sven shook his head, as he looked to Gerri for support. "But still—even that could be a summer day in Juneau. Does it ever freeze in the South?"

"It froze a couple of times last year," Gerri offered. "Even in Florida it freezes once in a while."

"Cost the farmers millions of dollars when it froze the oranges," her father added.

"I guess there's a lot I don't know about the South. Can't they do something about that?"

"Not much. It's not like they can move the trees inside."

Sven thought about that for a moment. Gerri, watching his expression, would have been willing to bet that he was coming up with one of his puns, but they were interrupted by the reappearance of the two girls.

As Sven unpacked the box he had brought, Gerri was as anxious as anyone. When he got the first picture out and displayed it, she smiled happily. He had turned the sketch of her seeing the porpoise into a painting—and it was gorgeous. She wasn't the only one who noticed.

"That's beautiful," said Olivia. "Gerri, you look so happy." She gave Gerri a calculating look.

After Sven had explained the circumstances of the picture, he reached for the remaining one. As he was about to produce it, he paused and looked at Gerri. Yes, he knew that Gerri looked beautiful in the first picture. After all, he had painted what he had seen.

Yet, in a flash of insight, he realized that he had made a terrible mistake. The second picture was a private picture. It was more intimate and really should have been shown to Gerri alone. Better yet, he should have kept it in Juneau and given it to her when, or if, she came up there. There was nothing improper about it, but Gerri's mom had been watching him with too much speculation in her eyes. In this moment he knew: it was not that Olivia distrusted him in any generic way, but rather that she distrusted him with Gerri; that she didn't consider him to be an appropriate suitor. And he, with this picture, was rubbing her nose in the fact that this was his intention.

He had but a moment for regret. There was so much that he didn't know about the South—that some innocent banter with a waitress about his girlfriend would offend her boss, that some young teacher would behave totally unprofessionally when he passed her in the hallway, and even that crops could freeze in Florida. And now, most hurtfully, that it wasn't only whites who could object to a relationship between Gerri and him.

But it was too late now. He pulled the second picture out of the box and displayed it hopefully.

Gerri gasped when she saw it. "The ice cave under the glacier," she murmured. She felt herself flushing, as the others exclaimed over it.

Joetta was too young to completely parse it. "Ooh, it's even prettier," she said excitedly.

Marilyn added, "Wow! It makes you look…" 'sexy' was what she had been about to say, but she stopped, uncertain of what her parents would say.

Robert added, "Gerri, you certainly look grown."

Olivia didn't say anything. She just raised her eyebrows. Unfortunately, that was all too clear to Gerri.

The picture showed Gerri standing in the ice cave, one hand on her hip, looking at Sven. Gerri had to admit that this picture also made her look beautiful. But where the other picture showed the innocent beauty of a joyful young girl, this picture showed the confident beauty of a woman, looking boldly and slightly challengingly at the artist. It was an altogether seductive effect, and if they had been alone, Gerri would have expressed her gratitude appropriately. But they weren't alone. She didn't relish the conversation that she knew her mother was planning.

Sure enough, as soon as Sven had left with promise to return tomorrow, Olivia cornered Gerri. "We need to talk."

Gerri shook her head. "Ma, I can't talk tonight. I haven't even looked at the packet yet." She knew that this was as much about Sven and the second picture as it was about the packet, but she wouldn't admit that. "And today was an awful day at work." That was only a slight exaggeration. "As exciting as this is," she waved the envelope, "I'll probably fall asleep reading it." *OK, that's a lie...* "Let's talk later tomorrow after I know better what's going on."

Olivia started to open her mouth to insist, but Gerri spoke quickly. "And while I'm reading and sleeping, you should think about where to hang *your* picture." *Did that remind her that the second one is mine? Even if this doesn't pan out, I need to get my own place.* With that—and with intense relief—Gerri made her escape.

CHAPTER 32

Alone in her room, Gerri raised her window, snuggled under her covers, and opened the envelope. On top was a letter from Mindy.

Dear Gerri,

It's exciting to be able to write this, even though I'm so sorry that Mrs. Kallek is not well. OK: business first. The contract enclosed is legit—I checked with someone I know on the School Board. You'll notice that if you accept this, you'll be making substantially more than you are now—more than enough to make up for the cost of your travel up here.

Gerri glanced at the contract page and chuckled. *Way more...* She'd be making over double her current salary. Better yet, she'd be making at least 50% more than Miss Carruthers. Of course, the cost of living was higher...but not that much higher. If she accepted this, she would make sure that the salary got out. *Thurman—he can be counted on to blab!* She turned back to the letter.

You can stay with me again (I insist!). I've already cleaned out that extra room so you won't have to sleep on the couch. There's plenty of closet space in there, plus there's a storage area in the basement, if necessary (I know that teachers have bigger wardrobes than fishermen!).

There is a letter enclosed from Mrs. Kallek in which she explains what kind of arrangement she's hoping for. I had a chance to talk to her and she really likes you.

There are a couple of other letters enclosed. I asked John Wheeler to write one to give you the 'black perspective' (I hope that doesn't sound racist!). I know I said he can be annoying, but he's really very nice and I trust his judgment.

The last letter is from a friend of Sven's, Wally Trager. I don't know him, but Sven wanted to include it.

Sven didn't want to write a letter. But I can tell you that he didn't forget about you. As soon as I told him that you had left a note on his boat, he jumped in his truck and raced down to the harbor. I'm trying to be nice to him as you said I should. It takes some getting used to, but so far he doesn't bite.

He wouldn't say anything, but I think he does care for you. Sigh! Remind me, if you come, to tell you about my crappy love life.

Love, and hope to see you soon,
Mindy

Next, she turned next to the letter from Mrs. Kallek.

Dear Gerri,
Perhaps I should say 'Dear Miss Barton' but I think of you as Gerri and people seem less formal now than they were in my day.

Mindy Shumacher said that she would explain the broad outline of the offer. I do hope that you are not offended by the restriction in the contract.

With a frown, Gerri went back to the contract. There, at the end where she hadn't noticed it: "Mrs. Kallek will serve as the liaison between you and the school administration as needed for the purpose of orientation." She thought about that. It could mean a variety of things—some of them bad. But she had an instinctive trust in Mrs. Kallek, so she would certainly hear her out. She continued with the letter.

… From the school system's point of view, hiring you is a leap of faith. The administration has had no contact with you at all. I argued vigorously and, ultimately persuasively, that my several conversations with you over the summer were more than the equivalent of a job interview. Their solution was, in a sense, to make you my responsibility.

But I must make a confession. This is the way I want it as well, for the most selfish of reasons. My health is not good. I just don't have the strength to continue my teaching duties. Yet, I don't want to retire and spend my remaining days staring at the wall—or worse, at a television set.

My hope is that we can be a team. You will be the teacher— make no mistake about that. I will attend some of your classes and, now and then, share some advice. I think I still have something to offer. My body is rebelling, but my mind is still there.

Even though there are things that I can teach you, I value your ideas as well. I see you as a kindred spirit—you have the same enthusiasm that I like to think that I still retain.

So please consider this offer. I look forward to hearing from you soon.

Sincerely,
Helen Kallek

By the time Gerri finished this letter, her eyes were blinking with tears. How sad it was to have your body give out when your mind was still motivated. She felt honored that Mrs. Kallek had such faith in her, and she was determined to justify that faith.

Paradoxically, the restriction in the contract comforted her. As she had scanned through her initial pass of the contract, a corner of her mind had kept saying 'this is too good to be true—what's the catch?' It was still good, but no longer stretched her credulity. She realized that, even without reading the other letters, and even without knowing where she stood with Sven, she wanted to accept this offer.

She picked up the letter from Dr. Wheeler.

Dear Gerri,

Mindy asked me to write about my impressions of Juneau as a place for a black person to live. I understand that this will be one of several letters intended collectively to convince you to come. She is, as you know, very well organized—truly a force of nature and, though she can be exasperating, she's very hard to resist when she wants something.

Not that I tried to resist in this instance. Juneau has been a nice place to live. The people are generally open-minded. The few racial problems that I've encountered usually stem from obliviousness—rarely malice.

I came here to satisfy a 'work off my med school expenses' agreement. Now, having satisfied the terms of that agreement, I find myself still here. Some of the friendships I have formed (particularly with Mindy) and the satisfaction I get from serving the outlying villages have kept me from moving away.

It's true that there are not many black people here. There are some. I've been told by those who knew me previously that I should live where there are more. But I think of myself as a colonist in this respect. Shouldn't black people spread throughout the country, rather than ceding some areas solely to others?

I'm sure I'll see you if you do decide to come, since Mindy is our connection. I heard more from Sven about your seamanship talents, and I'm impressed. Sorry for disbelieving you!

Sincerely,
John Wheeler

Gerri laid John Wheeler's letter down with a smile. He hadn't said anything to dissuade her from accepting this job. But even more interesting was the dynamic between John and Mindy. Gerri knew that they interacted professionally—some of Wheeler's medical visits to the outlying villages were coordinated and subsidized by Mindy's office.

But what intrigued Gerri about their letters was what they said about their personal interactions. Each had described the other in glowing terms, while still expressing annoyance/exasperation with the other. From the moment they had met, Gerri had been aware that Mindy had a fiery personality. And John had shown in their brief contact at the hospital that he was more than capable of making an inartful remark. She could only imagine the sparks that could fly when those two disagreed. With a smile on her face from that image, she turned to the final letter.

Hello Gerri,
I figure I'm the last person who you expected to write. Sven told me about your job opportunity. Mrs. Kallek is a good teacher, though you'd never know it to see my grades. You could do a lot worse than work with her.

This is the Last Frontier (yeah, I know you've probably heard that a lot already). It takes a person with grit and guts to ~~survive~~ thrive here. (I knew I shouldn't of wrote this in ink). You've shown me that you have them ~~in spades~~. No offense, that's just an expression.

Another reason I'd like to see you come back. Sven is a very self-contained person. That's the only reason he was able to shake off all of the B.S. that he got from the Schumachers and their friends over the last few years. But he can go too far with that. You seem to bring him out of his shell. I think that's a good thing for him.

So come on. You know what they say. You're not a sourdough until you've made it through a winter here. You don't want to be a cheechako all of your life, do you?

Sincerely,
Wally Trager

With all of the reading done, Gerri turned out her light and lay back. Each letter was interesting, and each told her something more about the writer than she had known. Wally, for all of his rough edges, was really imbued with the spirit of the frontier. Or maybe his rough edges went along with that. Either way, Gerri didn't need his challenge to motivate her. She had already decided to accept this offer.

Unfortunately, this decision came with a lot of complications. She would have to see Mr. Harrison and explain the situation to him. He had stuck his neck out for her, and she owed him that. She would have to go shopping—she didn't have any clothes that would stand up to what she imagined a Juneau winter would be like. That was problematic, since no store around here would carry such things. She would ask Sven's advice on that.

Sven: now there was another issue. She still didn't know where she stood with him. He had greeted her warmly at the high school and, after the initial misunderstanding about Thurman had been resolved, had been very affectionate on the way home. He was on good 'guest behavior' through the evening at her parents' house, so she couldn't glean anything from that. On the other hand, he took his leave right after the pictures had been presented and didn't make any attempt to get her alone for a special 'good night.'

She wasn't going to let this uncertainty influence her decision, however. This was an exciting opportunity, and she wasn't going to derail it by playing a flighty, lovesick female. She smiled wryly in the dark. No, she wouldn't be flighty. The lovesickness she couldn't help, but she could keep that to herself.

The last complication was telling her family. And judging by the body language at the kitchen table, Olivia would be the biggest objector. She'd save that confrontation for last, when she had gathered as much information as she could.

———

Dressing Saturday morning was easy for Gerri. One dress practically leaped out of the closet at her. It was her favorite dress, even though she had only had a chance to wear it once. It was a bright orange sun dress which fit her perfectly. It was not a dress that she dared to wear to school. It was completely decent, with a very slightly scooped neckline, but it was cut very low in the back. Even Miss Carruthers, who sometimes seemed to dress for the hunt rather than for teaching, wouldn't wear a dress like this to school.

As for wearing it on social occasions…well, she hadn't had much of a social life since coming back to South Carolina. *And why was that?* Well, she decided, most of the friends that had graduated with her had moved to more populous areas to get jobs. The few males that remained didn't particularly interest her. In fairness, though, they hadn't exactly been beating down her door. They seemed to think that she was Thurman's and that their breakup last spring was just a spat. She had no solid evidence for this, but she suspected that Thurman encouraged that view.

As she came out of her reverie, she held up the dress for a final inspection. It was going to be warm again today, so she could get away with wearing it, but her real reason was Sven. Only once had he seen her in a dress and that was at the dance in Pelican. Yesterday didn't count, since that dress was one of her severe, conservative school dresses. Whatever happened or didn't happen between them, Gerri wanted him to see her—just once—looking utterly feminine.

Of course, this dress would be to her mother as a red flag is to a bull. But Gerri had her cover story ready.

Her parents were eating in the kitchen. "Daddy, can I borrow the car this morning? I have to go talk to Mr. Harrison."

Her mother jumped in first. "Are you sure that dress is appropriate? It's November, after all."

Gerri looked down, spreading the skirt. "I'm not going to school. And I like this dress. This may be my last chance to wear it until next summer."

"Does that mean that you've decided to go?"

"I think so. The offer is very attractive. The salary is twice what I make now, and it will give me some actual teaching experience. That will make my application for next year more compelling."

"But how do you know that you'll like it? It's a mistake to go flying off just because this S'ven shows up at our door."

She pronounced Sven as if it had two syllables. Gerri wondered whether she had done that on purpose. She decided to give her the benefit of the doubt. "It's 'Sven.' One syllable. It takes a little getting used to."

"I don't care. You said that we'd talk about this."

Talk, yes, but let you decide? No. "I haven't forgotten that. But I'm still getting information. There'll be time later, after Sven is gone."

Her father jumped into the fray. "You may take the car. I wouldn't want the road dust to get all over that nice dress." That earned him a dirty look from Olivia, but Gerri fled before she could reopen the argument.

Her talk with Mr. Harrison stretched to an hour, but nothing happened to make her change her mind. He expressed his regrets that she was leaving, but once he saw the contract—and the salary—he didn't try to make her reconsider. The only request he made was that she give two weeks' notice. "I hope that you'll be applying here again next year, and I want them to remember that you behaved completely professionally."

She readily agreed. As she reflected on her way back home, packing and clothes shopping would take much of the two weeks anyway. As she pulled into the yard, her heart started beating faster. Sven's rental car was parked there, under the trees.

———

When Sven arrived at Gerri's house Saturday morning, she wasn't there. Olivia met him at the door.

"I'm sorry; she's not here, and I don't know when she'll be back."

Sven got the impression that Olivia would be just as happy if he turned tail and left. But he knew (or hoped?) that Gerri wouldn't be too long. After all, she knew he had to leave today. "Do you mind if I look around while I wait? I haven't seen too many farms."

"Of course not." She gestured vaguely toward the barn near the house. Remembering her manners—it wasn't his fault that he was trouble—she added, "Thank you so much for that picture. Robert is going to hang it in our front room."

He nodded. "My pleasure."

As he walked, he tried to memorize some of the scenes for possible paintings, but his heart wasn't in it. He was too busy thinking about Gerri and his missions. Paramount was his ostensibly primary one—to convince her to accept the job and to facilitate her coming to Juneau. If he couldn't do that, then his private mission would perforce have failed.

In a sense, it had already failed. Bringing the second picture had been a mistake. And finishing it had delayed him, squeezing his visit to barely a day. On the other hand, there wasn't much that he could have done under the watchful eye of Gerri's mother, so maybe his short stay would be for the best. There was no way to reassure Mrs. Barton that his intentions were honorable—the old-fashioned courtship that he desired would have to wait for Juneau.

As he walked past the barn, he heard noises inside. He poked his head in. "Hello?"

Robert Barton came out through an inner door carrying a box. "Good morning."

"I'm just looking around while I wait for Gerri. Can I help you with that as long as I'm not doing anything?"

It turned out that Mr. Barton was cleaning out a storage room. As they worked, Sven ventured to ask, "Do you know whether she's decided to accept the offer?"

"Not for sure, but I suspect so. She's talking to Mr. Harrison now. He's the one who helped her get her job here."

Sven was relieved that Mr. Barton seemed less hostile than his wife, but didn't want to press his luck. He was trying to formulate another question when Mr. Barton continued.

"She promised to talk about it, and I know that Olivia will try to talk her out of it. But Gerri's a grown woman, much as it bothers Olivia to see that."

Sven searched for words to reassure him. He'd learned his lesson from watching Mrs. Barton—there would be no mention of any courtship. "I think she will like it. There are several people, including me, who count themselves her friends and who will look out for her."

"Hmmph." As he digested that, Mr. Barton worked in silence. "What about the weather?"

"She'll definitely need some winter gear. I've arranged for some friends in Seattle to help her shop there as she passes through."

"Seattle? Not Juneau?"

"Seattle's a big city with a wide selection of clothes. I'd stay and help her myself, but I have to be back in Juneau. I have a hunting party chartering my boat and I have to get it ready."

They were working as they talked, and when they finished, Sven paused to see if Mr. Barton had any other questions. Instead, he had moved to the doorway and was looking out. "That sounds like Gerri coming down the road now. Yep, that's her."

Sven eagerly grabbed his shirt. Working in this heat had quickly bathed him in sweat, so he had shed it in a futile attempt to stay cool. He wasn't used to working hard in this kind of heat. It reminded him, rather unpleasantly, of the boxing gym in Seattle where the temperature was always cranked up high. *No hugs today, at least until I can clean up somehow.*

As she stepped out of the car, he had to catch his breath. Gerri was a vision in bright orange, her dress dancing around her knees as she walked toward him. Mrs. Barton appeared on the porch behind her and called out to her. As Gerri turned around to answer her, he could see what would have been the back of the dress, if it had had a back. He groaned softly. No back meant no bra. *So sue me for noticing—I'm a male!* He found himself hoping that this Mr. Harrison was at least 80 years old.

As she got closer, he could see that the dress fit well—it was really quite decent. Unless you considered a woman's back erotic—and from this moment forward, Sven knew that he would.

"That dress looks lovely on you. I've never seen one quite like it." He was already starting to memorize the scene for some future painting.

Gerri was delighted with his reaction. "Thank you. It's called a sun dress."

"That's apt." *It makes me want to give her a son.*

Gerri repeated her kitchen gesture of spreading the skirt out. "You mean because of its color?" She felt the heat rise in her cheeks. *Maybe he meant because it lets so much sun touch me...*

Sven thought fast. He could see over her shoulder that Mrs. Barton was bearing down on them. He didn't dare tell Gerri truly why he had said that. That would be coming on way too strong. But he couldn't resist the pun, so he depersonalized it. He grinned roguishly. "Because every man that sees you in it will want to give you a son."

If Gerri thought that her cheeks were warm before, they were hot now. It was bad enough that Sven was bare chested—he ought to come with a product warning label. But maybe, she thought, this was an excuse to find out where they stood. "Sven, tell me. Do you want us to go back to being like we were before?"

No! I want a courtship, not just a shack-up. Mrs. Barton was almost within earshot. "No," he said softly. "Not like we were before."

Before he could elaborate, he heard Mrs. Barton's voice. "Gerri, what did Mr. Harrison say? I've been worrying all morning."

Gerri was spared the embarrassment of having to react intelligently to his rejection. She blinked back her disappointment and turned. "Sure, Ma. I'll go get Daddy. I'm sure he'll be interested. And Sven, would you mind sitting down with us? I have some questions for you, and my parents may as well."

Olivia was not eager to have a group meeting. Some of the things she wanted to say couldn't politely be said in front of Sven. But she couldn't see a way to gracefully refuse.

———

Eventually the talking was done. Sven ran out of time and had to go. He had not mollified her mother, Gerri thought, but he had done his best. The only moment with 'secret meaning' was when he assured them—while looking at Gerri—that he would "Do everything in his power to protect her." She had responded, with a smile meant just for him, "And I'll do the same for you, even if I have to be a mutineer."

He had been gone now for only an hour, but she already missed him. His disinterest in an affair had hurt, but she reminded herself that he was a good and true friend. And that he had already protected her from harm on two occasions. She would just have to settle for that.

CHAPTER 33

Gerri sat in her family's kitchen Sunday evening, listening to her sisters. They had been hanging around her all weekend. The only time she had been this popular before was for about a week after she got back from her summer adventure. She would not complain, however—she would surely miss them when she was gone.

"I'm going to get your room," Marilyn said smugly. Then she had second thoughts. "Does that mean that you won't come back?"

"I'll be back. And you *should* get my room. It's time. Even if I wasn't leaving now, I would have gotten a place of my own soon."

Joetta asked anxiously, "Will you be back for Christmas?"

Gerri paused to consider her answer. "I doubt that I'll be able to come back. It's a very long trip."

"Will you send us Christmas presents?"

"Yes, I will." She considered the complications. Christmas was only about six weeks away, and she expected to be super-busy once she got to Juneau. "If I can't send you anything else, I'll send you each a check."

"I guess that's OK." Joetta sounded vaguely disappointed.

"Sure. And it'll be a check on a Juneau bank. Won't that be an interesting souvenir?"

"You mean I can keep it?"

"She's teasing you," Marilyn chimed in. "If you keep the check, then you can't get any money for it."

"Don't worry, Joetta. I'll send you each two checks. One for you to keep and one to cash and get the money."

"See," Joetta accused Marilyn. "She wasn't teasing me."

"I'll give you one present right now. I'll clean up the kitchen for you. You can go play. Or, better yet, get ready for school tomorrow."

It took them no time to accept that offer and Gerri found herself alone in the kitchen. She felt a sense of relief—she loved her sisters, but she needed time to think as well.

As she worked, she let her thoughts wander. And they wandered straight to Sven. She had hoped for more from him, but Wally was right—he was self-contained. Aside from his friendship with Wally, he had never mentioned any other friends.

Maybe the people in Seattle who he had arranged to meet Gerri at SEATAC were his friends, but he had never mentioned them before. Still, they must be close to him if they were willing to spend a day shopping with her at his request.

The fact that he hadn't mentioned anyone to her might not mean anything. He hadn't mentioned the chartering of his boat for hunting parties either. But an explanation was staring her in the face—she wasn't as close to him as she had thought.

She wondered what he did in the winter. Work around his house? She felt a stab of disappointment, remembering their plans for that last night. Maybe he painted. That took her down another sidetrack. His sketching, the few times that she had been privileged to watch him, had seemed effortless. But there must have been times when he struggled to get inspiration. She recalled his advice about singing that sad song—to immerse yourself in feelings of sadness and create a mood.

She looked around. There was no one in the kitchen. Maybe she would try that right now, while she was finishing up the dishes. What to use as her motivation for sadness? Maybe the fact that she wouldn't see her family for months at least? She tried to think about that, but it wasn't convincing—she would be busy in her new life and she would write frequently. Maybe she would even splurge on a few long distance phone calls. Those thoughts couldn't generate the mood that she sought.

Sven! She thought about their affair, about how happy she had been, and about how fleeting that time had been. Yes, she realized, that could certainly weave a skein of melancholy around her. With those thoughts running through her head, she started singing the song.

Olivia walked by the kitchen on her way to put some clothes away. She heard Gerri singing 'Rags and Old Iron' and smiled. Gerri shared her love of Nina Simone, and, even though she couldn't give this song its due, Olivia was glad that she was singing again. It took only a few bars for Olivia to stop in her tracks. The haunting sadness that Gerri was evoking from the song tugged at Olivia's heart. Nina herself didn't do it any better.

Olivia stood out of sight in the hallway as she listened. She felt almost as though she was intruding on some very private grief. *I surely have a talented daughter!* Then she got suspicious—how did Gerri grasp this song so completely? What personal grief inspired this empathy? She knew that it was probably unfair, but she wondered whether something had happened with this Sven person. She worried about Gerri, even though Gerri had laid out in detail her reasons for accepting the job—repeatedly, in fact, in several discussions since Sven had arrived.

When the final notes faded, Olivia moved into the kitchen. "Gerri, that was absolutely beautiful. How were you able to capture it so well?"

Gerri turned and smiled. "Thank you. I sang it much better, didn't I?"

"Much better. It made me want to cry. How did you…" She stopped. She wanted to say, 'What happened to you?' but that sounded accusatory.

"Sven helped me." She saw her mother frown and hurried on. "He told me how he tries to set a mood within his mind when he's having trouble portraying it in a painting."

Olivia thought about that. The obvious follow-up question that popped into her mind was 'And what were you thinking about for this inspiration?' but that seemed too nosy so she reluctantly refrained from asking. But with the thought in her mind, she couldn't resist one final entreaty. "Gerri, I'm sure you like Sven, and he seems to like you, but don't let yourself get involved romantically. There's only heartache there. Think about the implications. If you were involved with a white man—married even—you would be cutting yourself off from South Carolina completely.

"Remember Juanita; that classmate of Rich's? She thought she was in love with a white boy, but she got only sorrow. So did the boy, for that matter. This town is not the worst place in the South, but you would still not have a comfortable time."

Gerri listened with ironic amusement. Her mother was imagining something that was unattainable. Gerri didn't want to air her business, but it would cost her nothing to give some reassurance. "Ma, you have nothing to worry about. I promise that there is no romantic relationship, and there will be none. In fact, that's the easiest promise that I've ever made to you."

Gerri wasn't going to say any more, but a random thought crossed her mind. *Sven and his puns—it must be rubbing off on me.* "Remember, Ma. I was trolling for salmon, not trolling for love." *Even though I thought for a while that I'd found it anyway.*

Olivia still wished that she knew more about Gerri's relationship with Sven, but, as Robert had had to remind her more than once this weekend, Gerri was an adult now. Gerri had always kept her promises before, and the emphatic way that she made this one was comforting.

She hugged Gerri, saying as she did so, "Thank you Gerri. You've been a good girl and I don't mean to doubt you."

———

Gerri sat in the school cafeteria, going over her mental list of things to do in the next two weeks. At the same time, she kept an eye out for Thurman. If the school rumor mill was functioning at its usual efficiency, he would show up at any minute—probably offering reasons why she shouldn't go.

He didn't disappoint. "Is it true? I can't believe it."

She wasn't going to make it easy for him. "I can't answer that until I know what 'it' is," she said dryly.

"You know what I'm talking about. Stop playing those logic games. I know you only do that to annoy me."

Gerri thought about that. He had a point. When they were dating, that had been one of her defenses against his verbal aggressiveness. One of her psych major friends had a name for it, which Gerri didn't remember. Gerri had called it defensive bobbing and weaving. *I really should put that tactic aside...I don't need it anymore.* "I'm sorry, Thurman. Yes, it's true. I gave my notice this morning, and I'll be leaving as soon as my two weeks are up."

He spluttered, "There are so many reasons why this is a bad idea."

Gerri held up a hand. She didn't want a reprise of her mother's objections. "Let me give you one big reason why it's a *good* idea." She pulled out of her purse a copy of the contract that she had signed and sent back with Sven. She turned it to the second page and handed it to Thurman. Not only would this spike his rhetorical guns, but it would serve her petty purpose of adding her new salary to the rumors.

He was silent as he skimmed it. When his scowl deepened, she knew that he had come to the salary figure. Grudgingly, he spoke. "That's a lot of money. Are you sure that this is on the level?"

"Yes, I ran it by Mr. Harrison. And the teacher that recruited me is someone I like and trust. And last, but not least, it's a real teaching position."

"You still shouldn't do this. It's a big mistake." She watched his expression as he spoke. He was getting that all too familiar stubborn look, where he would tolerate no dissent.

Gerri didn't want to part on hostile terms. She tried a different tack. "Consider this, Thurman. How do you see your future in the next few years?"

He looked at her with a sly half smile. "You want me to come with you?"

Gerri closed her eyes and shook her head in amazement. *The male ego is such a wondrous instrument of creativity!* "No, I don't want you to come with me. Do you see what you're doing now as a permanent job?"

He snickered. "You must be kidding."

"Well, I feel the same way. If you got an offer of a better job, with twice your pay, wouldn't you take it?"

"If I had to go to the Arctic?" He mocked a shiver.

"It doesn't have to be the Arctic." She recalled once, years ago, when he had rhapsodized about Jamaica. "Suppose it was somewhere in the Caribbean."

He looked at her speculatively. Then he dropped his eyes. "I see your point. I just hope you know what you're doing."

Since the argumentativeness seemed to have leached out of him, Gerri took another bite of her now-almost-cold lunch. She cast about for a change of subject, but the school bell rescued her.

After the rumor mill publicized her departure and Thurman, apparently, filled in the details on her new salary, she seemed to have acquired a sort of grudging respect from the other staff. To a trusted friend, Gerri would have added a disclaimer about the cost of living, but there was no one at the school in that category.

Miss Carruthers greeted her the next morning almost cheerfully. "Good morning. My heavens! I heard that you're leaving us. What a surprise."

"Good morning. Yes, I'm looking forward to it. It should be quite an adventure." It seemed harmless to recycle her description of last summer's trip.

"Alaska! Gracious!" Miss Carruthers got a faraway look on her face. "Is that where that big husky guy was from?"

Dream on, girl! "Yes. He was delivering their offer."

Students were starting to stream into Miss Carruthers' classroom and she gave a ladylike double take. "Let me tell you what I need done this morning…"

The attitude was better, but the work was still mind numbing. By lunch time, Gerri desperately wanted the day to be over. She half-heartedly looked for an empty table, but Thurman was gesturing to her. She dreaded a continuation of his haranguing about her departure, but she couldn't politely ignore him.

To her relief, he seemed to have no interest in that argument. "Everybody's buzzing about you," he said with a smile, "How are your preparations for your trip coming?"

She was glad to have a sympathetic ear. "They're coming. I'm going to have too much for airline baggage limits, so I'm boxing stuff up and mailing it."

"Do you have a place to stay?"

She nodded, mouth full of food.

He nodded as well, as if she'd said something profound. "I've been thinking about the date you promised me. I want to make it something special."

Gerri almost choked. She was hoping that he'd forgotten about that. "I don't think I'll have the time. Packing, shopping, you know..." She waved her hand vaguely.

"Oh, come on. You can find a free evening or two. All work and no play, you know. Besides, think of how much time we had together until our spat. We should really go out again, just to say a proper goodbye."

She was shaking her head, trying to figure out how to be diplomatic, yet not give in. Her notion of a proper goodbye seemed to be at odds with his.

Thurman watched her speculatively. Then he spoke again, reaching out and rubbing her hand with his thumb. "We have unfinished business, you and I. Don't forget that."

"What unfinished business?" She wasn't sure what he was talking about. She wasn't sure she even wanted to know.

"That promise that you had to make to your mother. You kept it, and I helped you wait. Now that you're more mature and more sophisticated, well... we owe it to each other to share that experience. Something to remember and treasure."

She jerked her hand away from his. Diplomacy no longer concerned her. *What a fancy, flowery, disgusting way to say 'Give me sex.'* "There is no unfinished business. I made that promise to my mother willingly and I kept it willingly. As far as going out with you, I thought that maybe we both could use an outing. I don't consider it to have been a promise—certainly not in the same vein as what I agreed upon with my mother."

He started to make a sharp retort, but noticed that the occupants of the adjacent table were following their exchange with interest. "OK," he shrugged. "You can't blame a guy for trying."

———

Somehow Gerri made it through the next two weeks. How the time could have dragged and raced at the same time, she couldn't imagine, but it did. It dragged as she anticipated her trip and raced as she scurried around shopping, packing and mailing.

Thurman, to her relief, never again brought up her alleged 'debt' of a date with him. The others at the high school, blacks and whites alike, were constantly showing their curiosity about her trip, and a few of them expressed genuine wishes of good luck.

Her family wished her a tearful goodbye at the Florence airport. She included a note for Rich in her mother's latest letter to him, along with a promise to write a longer letter when she settled in.

She endured a long trip across the country in the coach section in the rear of the jet on a red eye flight. She smilingly considered the analogy to the 'rear of the bus,' but not seriously—she knew that she was lucky to get a seat at all considering how late she had made her reservation. Being one of the last people off the plane was a small price to pay for getting there at all.

So here she was, walking down the endless concourse at SEATAC airport, looking for someone named Elaine White. Gerri had kicked herself for not asking Sven for a description, but he had been so confident that a sign with Gerri's name on it would suffice.

As she walked, she was struck anew at the differences between here and South Carolina. There were relatively few black people, more Orientals than she was used to and, of course, mostly white people.

As she looked for her sign, she started people-watching, trying to imagine where the few black people that she saw were coming from and where they were going. There were two soldiers in uniform—going home? She hoped so, but more likely traveling to some duty station. They saw her and she could see them eyeing her hair. She had decided to put it back into an afro, swayed by the ease of care and possible difficulty in getting hair products in Juneau. And, OK, swayed a little bit by the fact the Sven seemed to prefer it that way. Her getting over him was still a work in progress.

The soldiers' verdict to her hair was mixed. One of them frowned, but the other one smiled at her and murmured "Right on, Sister" as they passed.

There was a little girl—well, Joetta's age, and Joetta would object to being called a little girl. Her hair was freshly pressed and she was wearing what were probably her nicest clothes. Gerri remembered her from her flight. She had been unaccompanied. Fortunately, she now had a flight attendant walking with her, so she was being taken care of. Coming home to a family, perhaps?

The only other blacks she saw as she walked were a man and a woman standing by the side on the concourse and looking anxiously back in the direction from which Gerri had come. They seemed to be in their late thirties and they were both big. The man was every bit as burly as Sven, but with a little gut. The woman was tall and buxom, but carried her weight well. As she passed them, she could hear them arguing in low voices.

"I told you we should have gotten here earlier," the woman said.

The man muttered something indistinct. They apparently fell in behind Gerri, because she could hear the woman's next words clearly.

"You should have asked him what she looked like." Now Gerri pricked up her ears, wondering if possibly…

"He was in a hurry. He was about to miss his plane."

"How long does it take to say, 'Sven, what does Gerri look like?'"

Oops. Why did I just assume… Quickly, she turned around. "Excuse me. I'm Gerri." She wanted to say 'you were supposed to have a sign' but that seemed churlish.

The man grinned. The woman stared at Gerri with astonished eyes. "*You're* Gerri?" Only then did she belatedly display the sign that she had held at her side. "I'm so sorry; I got tired of holding this up. I'm Elaine White and this is my husband, Ronaldo."

They shook hands all around with Elaine, in particular, grinning from ear to ear. Finally, she couldn't contain herself. She turned to Ronaldo and jiggled his arm. "Sven found himself a sweet little soul sister. Isn't that nice?"

Gerri started to correct her, but decided against it. *After all, how often is it that I get called 'little?'* She could always set her straight later.

Elaine was a talker. For most of the drive downtown, she alternated between pointing out landmarks on their route and describing the elaborate plans she had for shopping. Sven had apparently supplied Elaine with a list of items to be purchased. Most of them concerned Gerri's comfort—coats, boots, and mittens to keep her warm and dry. "He wants you to be comfortable, honey. He wants you to like it there." Elaine grinned at her obvious implication. Gerri debated whether to explain Elaine's misunderstanding, but she just didn't want to go down that path of conversation.

Instead, looking for a change of subject, she asked, "How did you two meet Sven?"

There was a pause. Ronaldo chuckled.

Elaine looked at him warningly. "Ronnie..."

He ignored her. "He beat the shit out of me. That's how we met."

"Sven did *what*?"

Elaine turned in her seat to explain, but Ronaldo cut her off. "Let me tell this part, dear. You weren't even there." He paused, gathering his words, as Elaine cast Gerri a worried look.

"I used to be a boxer—a pretty good one, if I do say so myself. This kid came into my gym—Sven, but I didn't know his name then. He was doing real well against the tomato cans and everyone was raving about him. They told me to go a few rounds against him. Well, that pissed me off. I had a good record—never hit the top ten rankings, but good. I figured I was too good to be warming up some asshole white kid."

"Ronnie. We don't know if Gerri's comfortable with that kind of language." She turned to Gerri. "Ronnie only starts talking like that when he remembers his boxing days. He knows better. He's an accountant now, and he's one of the smartest men I know."

Ronaldo smiled slyly as he glanced at Gerri in the rear view mirror. "Funny, but she started saying that right after I proposed to her."

Elaine laughed and swatted him on the arm. "Be quiet! That's not true and you know it. Now you wanted to tell the story, so tell it. And you don't have to give all of the gory details. That'll just get me upset."

"Anyway, they put us in the ring. Right from the beginning, I had an attitude. I was talking some cash shit—sorry, dear—talking trash. Sven was raw, all right, but he was fast. And his punch—my God! I sparred against Ingemar Johansson once, you know who that is?" He glanced at Gerri in the mirror again.

"Toonder and Lightning?"

"Oh, you follow boxing?"

"No. I just…it's not important. Please continue."

"Well, if Johansson was thunder and lightning, then Sven had a couple of atom bombs hanging off the ends of his arms. I've never been hit so hard in my life. Within a minute, I was out on my feet. I could take a punch; I'd never been knocked down. But I was that day." He glanced at Elaine. "OK, your turn. I don't remember much after that."

"They got him to the dressing room all right, but he collapsed again. Then they took him to the hospital. For a while, the doctors thought he might have permanent damage. A few days later, after he had stabilized, I went to the gym. We were going to be facing some large medical bills, and I wanted their help. I figured that there must be some insurance or something.

"Well, they didn't give a shit—sorry, Ronnie; you've got me doing it. I was scared and desperate and I pitched a fit—a very loud one— right there.

"Turns out Sven was there and he heard me. They hadn't told him about any of this. He was horrified. I wanted to hate him, but he was really a sweet, gentle boy. He got dressed and came to the hospital with me. I don't think he ever went back to that gym.

"He stayed in touch, even after Ronnie was out of the hospital; even after he was out of rehab. He apologized over and over for not being able to help us, but he was just a kid—he didn't have any money.

"Months later, when his wife died… You know about that?"

Gerri nodded.

"He sent us a big chunk of the insurance money. We wanted to refuse, but he wouldn't let us. Said that Ronnie's injury was his doing, and he wouldn't have any peace if he didn't help."

"And that's why he quit boxing?"

"Yes, but I don't think he told anybody. He felt ashamed for what had happened."

"I felt sorry for him," Ronaldo interjected, "Giving up his dreams."

The car was silent for a moment. "I don't think he even knew what his dreams were," Elaine said thoughtfully, "When he came face to face with some of the possible consequences, it was more like a nightmare."

CHAPTER 34

Once they got into the downtown area, Elaine was all business. "If you're going to catch a flight tomorrow morning and still get some sleep tonight, we don't have any time to waste, so we're going to try to get everything in one store. It's a big store, so I think it'll work out."

Big store... "Is it Frederick & Nelson?" Gerri asked hopefully.

"No, it's called R.E.I., for Recreational Equipment, Inc. It's an outdoor type store. Camping and hiking stuff. Sven wants you to be nice and warm." She cast Gerri a sly glance, but Gerri didn't take the bait.

Ronaldo had to go to work, so they made arrangements to meet him later. It was indeed a big store. Gerri would have loved to have had the time to simply explore. There was everything from tiny stoves to specialized hardware apparently to allow a person to hang from a cliff. She shuddered at that idea. But she was still fascinated, even though she would never use some of these things.

They hustled through the shopping. The few times that Gerri objected about the price of an item, Elaine reminded her, patiently but insistently, that Sven wanted her to be comfortable and assured her that he knew what he was talking about. Thus, she ended up paying more for a coat—a down jacket—than she could ever have imagined. It certainly was warm—trying it on in the store convinced her that this coat would probably be uncomfortably warm even on the coldest day South Carolina had to offer. This made her wonder briefly if she knew what she was doing, but she squashed her misgivings. *Sven knows best and he's a friend even if he doesn't have any romantic feelings toward me...*

When they finished, they relaxed in a small café where Ronaldo and Elaine had arranged to meet.

"You heard our horrible story," Elaine said, "So tell me about how *you* met Sven."

Gerri gave her the thumbnail version of their initial meeting. When she finished, Elaine was laughing. "And he really believed that you were a boy? Oh, am I going to tease him about that."

Gerri, for some reason, felt obligated to defend him. "I let my hair look nappy; I wore shapeless clothes; and I tried to keep my voice pitched low." Elaine shrugged, unconvinced. "And Mindy—the woman that I was staying with—warned me not to smile. She said that my smile would give me away. That was hard, 'cause every now and then Sven would start making these awful puns."

"Yeah, he will do that," Elaine said distractedly. "That name sounds familiar. What's this Mindy's last name?"

"Schumacher. She's his ex-sister-in-law."

Elaine looked askance. "I thought so. That sounds like trouble. You know she hates him, don't you?"

Gerri stared at her plate. "I know. And it bothers me, 'cause they're my two favorite people in Juneau. When I left I asked her to reconsider her feelings. I think she's trying to. I don't know how that'll turn out."

Elaine consulted her watch. "We've got time. So tell me how he discovered that you weren't a guy."

Gerri grimaced and stared at her food as she talked. That was not a time that she felt proud of. But she bravely waded through it. Again, she found herself defending Sven. "I don't blame him for firing me. I made him feel like a fool. And he found out in the worst possible way."

Elaine didn't answer immediately. When Gerri looked up, she was shaking with silent laughter. "I can't believe that you hid your face while Sven was undressing. That's a lot of man there."

Gerri's face felt like it was on fire. Only her dark complexion saved her from being beet red—which would have made Elaine laugh even harder. "It wouldn't have been right." She wanted to say that Elaine was absolutely correct about Sven, but that would have required divulging their affair. She wasn't ashamed, but she wasn't so sure about

Sven—especially since he hadn't wanted to continue said affair. He deserved her discretion. And discretion came naturally to her. She was reminded again of those girls at school who bragged about conquests— no, that wasn't her.

Elaine's curiosity continued unabated and the conversation moved to the night of their 'reunion' at the Arctic Saloon. After she had related that, she defended Sven yet again. "It scared me at the time. I didn't actually see the fight, but it seemed so easy for him. He was so matter-of-fact and businesslike about it. But he wasn't enjoying it, and, anyway, they left him no choice."

Elaine looked thoughtful. "No, I'm sure he wasn't. He's a sensitive guy at heart. Sometimes I think he should have been a poet or something."

Gerri grinned. Elaine was close, though Gerri couldn't tell her that. A poet and an artist were probably kindred spirits—just a different way of expressing themselves.

"I would have loved to have seen that," Elaine said. She saw Gerri make a face. "Not the fight—you wading out there with a bottle of champagne." She looked at Gerri assessingly. "You're good for him."

Gerri sighed. Elaine was back on her hobby horse, and Gerri didn't know how to respond. She was rescued by Ronaldo, who suddenly appeared at their table.

"Are you ladies ready?" He eyed their collection of bags. "I hope so. The car will barely hold all of this anyway."

———

This was the second time that Gerri had flown into Juneau, and it had a very different feel from the first. The weather this time was clear, brilliantly clear. She appreciated the scenery just as much as she had the first time. But rather than gazing in uncomprehending wonderment, she was also trying to match the shorelines below to her memory of the charts on the Glacier Gal. She actually had some success with that, especially as they got closer to Juneau. That was exciting and sparked some wonderful memories. And some not-so-wonderful ones—she thought she could see the location from which the Coast Guard boat had flown Sven off to the hospital.

There was a second way in which the trip was different, and this one was more ominous. As they started their descent for Juneau, Gerri could see big whitecaps—it was evidently very stormy and the water was roiled up. As she was noticing this, the plane started bucking in the air. As they got down to a few thousand feet in altitude, the turbulence got more violent. She covertly scanned the faces of the other passengers, hoping that they would all look blasé. A few did, but more of them looked as worried as Gerri felt.

It did not help when the Captain came on the loudspeaker and said, with unconvincing calm, "Notice the seatbelt sign. There's a Taku blowing and we're going to have some pretty rough air for the rest of the way. We should be landing in about twelve minutes. If it gets too rough, we'll abort the landing and divert to an alternate location."

Gerri remembered that the Taku was the local name given to the Northerly winds—frequently violent—that blew off the icecap behind Juneau. That was bad enough, but the 'divert to an alternate location' sounded even worse. On the other hand, the last thing she wanted was a pilot who stubbornly pushed through severe weather. She turned to her seatmate.

"Where would this alternate location be?" Mindy was supposed to meet her. She was probably waiting right now.

"I'm not sure. It depends on the weather in the other places. Let's hope that it doesn't happen; I've got a meeting tomorrow."

"But…" Then she remembered: there would be no 'drive the rest of the way;' you couldn't drive into Juneau. And Gerri, too, had a meeting tomorrow—the all important introductory meeting with Mrs. Kallek and the High School Principal. All she could manage was a weak nod of agreement.

On the final approach, the turbulence, if possible, was even worse. Unlike the previous trip when she worried about seeing a runway, this time she worried about hitting the runway. Finally, she felt the wheels touch down—hard—and she let out the breath that she didn't even realize she had been holding.

Gerri's stress was swept away when she got into the terminal. Mindy was waiting with a huge smile on her face. They squealed and hugged. Mindy looked her over quickly. "I thought you decided to get rid of your 'fro."

Gerri made a face. "It wasn't so much that *I* decided. I was quietly told that the school back home wouldn't hire me if I wore one. Do you think it'll be a problem here?"

Mindy hesitated. "I hope not, but we'll see. You've got a secret weapon. I've been invited to attend the meeting with you, Mrs. Kallek, and Mr. Cunningham."

Mr. Cunningham was the high school principal, Gerri knew. "How'd you swing that?"

Mindy grinned mischievously. "I've gotten more subtle in my political work. I wangled—mostly on my willingness to spend the time—a position of outside advisor to the Future Office Workers club at the school. It's mostly girls. They come in assuming that it's about preparing to be a secretary, but I try to show them that they can be bosses as well. Women's Lib on the sly."

As they went outside to Mindy's car, Gerri gasped as the wind hit her face. Though it was bitterly cold, her coat kept her body comfortable—but next time she would be sure to wear a scarf around her neck and lower face. Mindy saw Gerri's startled look as the wind hit. "Sorry it couldn't be a warmer day, but it's supposed to get better tomorrow. I see you're prepared, though. Sven said that he was going to make sure you got proper clothes." She cast Gerri a sidelong glance and resurrected the slang game. "I guess he wasn't just shuckin' and jivin'. That coat looks real warm."

"It is. In fact, it's pretty bitchin'." Gerri was actually a bit uncomfortable with that word—it seemed vulgar to her—but she wasn't about to lose another round of the slang game.

Mindy laughed. "By the way, he asked me to tell you that he's out with a hunting party. He'll call you Wednesday when he gets back."

The howl of the wind took on an ominous tone. Gerri stopped in her tracks. "He's out in this weather?"

Mindy shrugged. "He didn't seem worried."

Gerri shivered. The infamous storm of last summer—the one during which she fell overboard—didn't have winds nearly as bad as this. She *really* didn't want to think about Sven out in this weather. She struggled for a change of subject. "Are you two getting along?"

They had reached the car and loaded Gerri's baggage. Mindy delayed answering until they were both inside. "I guess. We haven't had any sharp words. I haven't completely gotten used to the idea of just chatting with him, but I'm working on it."

She seemed uncomfortable, so Gerri searched for a change of subject. "You've had me dying of curiosity. Remember, you were going to tell me about your crappy love life."

Mindy winced and concentrated on the road. Gerri could feel the Taku wind trying to push the car around. "You're going to think I'm an idiot—or worse. I'll tell you when we get back to the house."

After Gerri had unpacked and eaten, they sat down in Mindy's living room. "OK, spill. Why am I going to think that you're an idiot?"

"Because I'm interested in someone who's not capable of being interested in me. And because I should have known it before I ever got interested."

Gerri looked at her, puzzled. Before she could speak, Mindy asked, "OK. Who do you think is the best catch around here?"

"I haven't really met that many people…"

"You've met him." As Gerri started to answer, she added, "And, no, I don't mean Sven."

Gerri's face got hot. *Am I that transparent?* Then the answer became obvious, even though it was unexpected. "Dr. Wheeler?"

Mindy nodded, and then looked at Gerri almost challengingly. "It's not because I want to experiment or because black men are supposed to be exotic. And it certainly isn't some notion about their alleged sexual prowess." She rolled her eyes. "He's just a smart, dedicated man. And when we're not fighting, I really enjoy talking to him." She flashed a brief grin. "Actually, I enjoy talking to him even when we are fighting. We've each got a mouth, but neither of us holds a grudge." Having spoken her piece, she leaned back and watched Gerri think.

"And he's not interested in you?" That sounded uncomfortably like Sven's feelings for Gerri—friendly, when friendly wasn't enough.

Mindy considered the question. "I don't know. Sometimes I think he is interested, but that may just be wishful thinking." Gerri cocked her head in inquiry, and Mindy was all too interested in elaborating. "He's very kind, very solicitous. And sometimes—I don't know—he'll be looking at me. But other times he can be distant." She laughed apologetically. "I'm a mess, aren't I?"

"No, you aren't. It's hard to tell sometimes. I know the feeling." Again, Gerri was reminded of her uncertainties about Sven—at least before he told her he wasn't interested. But she moved on quickly, lest the conversation veer toward her own lovesickness—if one more person told her that Sven really did care for her romantically, she would scream.

Gerri flashed a grin. "So we need to figure out what's in his head."

"Always a challenge with a man," Mindy said sardonically.

Gerri stared at her thoughtfully. "And you can't be the one to ask him. That's tacky—too forward." Mindy nodded vigorously. "So it's up to me as your friend to ask him."

Mindy grimaced. "He'll still know that you're asking on my behalf."

"Not if we're sneaky. Let me think." Gerri smiled in reminiscence. This took her back. Not to college. Those girls didn't need artifice—they were perfectly comfortable offering themselves up. If the particular target wasn't interested in some free sex—most were, of course—the girl would move on to the next. No, this took her back to high school.

"How does this sound?" Gerri asked after a moment's thought. "Invite him to dinner one night soon. Tell him it's to welcome me back. He wrote one of the letters to me, after all, so that's plausible."

"I can do that, and I think he'll accept. But…"

Gerri held up her finger for attention. "After the dinner, I want you to do two things…"

CHAPTER 35

Monday morning was much warmer and less windy, as promised. *It's actually above freezing,* Gerri thought. That made her laugh: how ridiculous that would sound in South Carolina. She made a mental note to mention it in a letter to home. The meeting with the principal was early in the morning so that it would be finished before classes started. Between thinking about the meeting and the classes which would follow, Gerri was a nervous wreck.

The meeting turned out to be one of the strangest that she had experienced. Initially, it was routine: an introduction and a few more papers to sign. Then it veered off. Mr. Cunningham cleared his throat nervously.

"That's a very, umm, unusual hairdo you have, Miss Barton. Aren't those used to signify some sort of, umm, radical politics?"

Gerri cringed inside. Was this to be a repeat of her experience in South Carolina, albeit more subtle? She answered cautiously. "That's a complicated question. They can be. But not in my case. I've worn my hair straightened for most of my life, but here, in this wet climate, this hairdo is simply much easier to care for."

Mr. Cunningham shifted uncomfortably. "Well, proper hair care certainly takes effort…"

Mrs. Kallek interrupted with an apparent non sequitur. "Herbert, as you know, I'm Jewish, so…"

"Yes, and that's perfectly…"

"I wasn't asking for permission." She flashed a brief smile to take the bite out of her statement. "I think I have some insight as to what

Gerri goes through. Many of us, including me, have kinky, curly, frizzy hair. And many of us go to a lot of trouble to straighten and generally manage it.

"Years ago, I spent a significant amount of time doing this. You probably don't remember, Herbert—you would have no reason to pay attention to such things—but when you were in my classes, my hair conformed much more to the prevailing fashions. One day my late husband, bless his soul, asked me why I went to all of that trouble. Knowing that he supported me gave me the courage to stop trying to meet some arbitrary fashion standard.

"I'm certainly not an expert on black people," She cast an apologetic glance at Gerri. "But I would bet that Gerri would have to go to even more trouble than I did to keep a straight, so-called stylish hairdo."

Gerri nodded emphatically and murmured, "That's true. It's a lot of trouble. Especially in wet weather" Gerri didn't know whether to be more surprised that Mrs. Kallek butted in on her behalf or the fact that she used to teach Mr. Cunningham. It made sense, though, and probably explained the interesting dynamic: she called her boss Herbert and he called her Mrs. Kallek.

"If I may add two cents worth," Mindy said diffidently, "I definitely agree with Mrs. Kallek. My hair—long and straight—happens to coincide with the styles of the 1960's, but if I had grown up in the 50's as my sister did, I would have been spending a lot of time wearing curlers. So I applaud Gerri for having the independence to choose a practical style for her. And," She looked at Gerri and smiled impishly, "I'll bet she's found that a lot of guys think it's exotic and cute."

Gerri lowered her head and shrugged, thankful once again that her blushes weren't visible. *Sven likes it...or he did like it,* she thought.

———

As Gerri and Mrs. Kallek walked to her—and now Gerri's—classroom, Gerri tried to put her bemusement into words. "I certainly didn't expect the meeting to be like that."

Mrs. Kallek made a dismissive noise. "Hair styling as a prerequisite for a teaching job! It's almost enough to make me a Women's Libber."

"Almost?" Gerri grinned.

"Well…" Mrs. Kallek walked in silence for a few seconds. "Parts of it. I don't quite understand why everybody wants to be called 'Ms.;' I'm happy to be called Mrs. myself. Of course, the people who worry about a woman's marital status don't seem to think it's significant to know a man's marital status." She shrugged. Then, she gestured Gerri into a room.

Gerri scanned the room eagerly. This was to be her professional home. She decided that she liked it. It wasn't fancy, but it was laid out neatly. The large windows showed promise of a nice view when the sun came up. That was one thing she'd have to get used to—now, during the short days of winter, she'd be starting her first class of the day while it was still dark.

After Mrs. Kallek had shown her where the supplies were stored, she had one final caution to impart. "After I introduce you, I'll sit quietly in the back. I don't want them deferring to me. The only time I'll speak up is if somebody is disrespectful because you're black. I don't expect that—I think these kids are too polite for that. But if it does happen, we should take them straightaway to Mr. Cunningham." She must have seen Gerri's apprehensive look, because she quickly added. "He won't stand for that either—in spite of that nonsense about your hair. He assured me of that before we sent the letter."

To Gerri's relief, no visits to Mr. Cunningham were necessary. The students were generally polite. In fact, they seemed to have a fascination with her. She didn't like the idea of being considered exotic, but as long as they worked with her in class, she could live with it.

Time was a blur. She was concentrating on learning her students' names, what they knew, and how they learned. After the first day, Mrs. Kallek came for only some of the classes. She sat in back and watched. Afterwards she and Gerri talked about what had worked and what hadn't. Gerri loved this—it was like a combination of a graduate seminar in teaching and a really fruitful collaboration. Of course, Gerri was also putting in long hours on preparation every evening—that was her responsibility and hers alone.

Wednesday evening, true to his promise, Sven called her. "I'm back in town for a couple of days. I was hoping that we could get together."

Gerri hesitated. She wanted to see him, too, but she wondered whether that was a good idea. He would be a profound distraction to her—doubtless much more than he could imagine. "I don't really have time tonight. I'm spending all of my evenings preparing for my next day's classes."

Sven felt the distance in her voice. He tried again. "Remember, I have that picture of you under the glacier that you asked me to carry back with me. I'd like to give that to you."

"I remember." She loved the picture, but her expression in it was too revealing. "It might be better for you to hang on to it for a while. What would Mindy think if I suddenly acquired a Hush picture?"

Sven made a face. He couldn't argue with that—just one more way in which he hadn't thought it through when he decided to give Gerri that picture. Still, her objection sounded more like an excuse for not seeing him. Already, she was slipping away from him. He suppressed a sigh. "All right. How about Friday? You won't have classes the next day. And I'm going out again early Saturday morning with another hunting party."

Gerri was tempted. Could Sven join them for dinner? *No. I wouldn't be able to concentrate on getting information from Dr. Wheeler if Sven was there. And who knows how he would get along with Mindy?* After a hesitation, she declined. "Friday won't work. We're having Dr. Wheeler over for dinner."

That made Sven uneasy, reminding him about his fears that Gerri would be more interested in the doctor than in him. Cautiously, with forced casualness, he asked, "What's the occasion?"

Gerri parroted their cover story—she wasn't about to betray Mindy's confidence. "I guess it's sort of a welcoming dinner for me," she said vaguely.

Sven winced. That really hurt. He told himself that he had no right to be upset, but it still hurt. He beat a strategic retreat. "OK. I should be back next Tuesday. I'll try to call you then."

Gerri hung up, feeling depressed. She missed Sven. But this was for the best—maybe if she stayed away from him for a while, she'd get used to it. She didn't want to do something stupid and throw herself at him. And then there was the promise to her mother. Gerri had always kept her promises in the past, and she had no intention of breaking this one.

———

Gerri enjoyed the dinner Friday night, on several levels. She and Mindy had outdone themselves in the kitchen and it showed. The conversation flowed easily. After exchanging 'how did I end up here' testimonials with Dr. Wheeler (John, as he insisted that she call him), Gerri fell silent while the other two talked. And argued. And laughed.

Their verbal chemistry was obvious. But she watched him surreptitiously as the dinner wore on. His eyes followed Mindy constantly—he always seemed to be aware of where she was. Gerri hid a smile—it looked to her like there was hope for the two of them.

After dinner, as Gerri had planned, Mindy brought out a picture of her sister, Laura. Gerri had seen it before and knew that Laura was glamorous. In fact, she had to concentrate on the business at hand, lest she start dwelling on how hopeless it was for her to think of competing for Sven with Laura's memory.

Their plan was for Gerri to act as though she was seeing it for the first time. She gushed to Mindy and John about Laura's beauty. John seemed more reserved. As per the second part of their plan, Mindy left the picture with the two of them and excused herself to the kitchen.

When they were alone, Gerri turned to John. This was the moment that would make or break her plan. She began baiting him. "What do you think, John? Don't you think her sister is beautiful?"

John shrugged with an annoyed look on his face. "Yeah, she's good looking, I guess."

"I know it's tough for Mindy. Having a sister like that, she always feels like she's in her shadow."

John made a disgusted noise. "That's silly." Gerri gave him a calculatedly blank look. He looked at her exasperatedly and elaborated. "It's all fine and good for a girl to be modest…"

312 | L. LANGDON

"Girl?" Gerri wondered if she was going too far, but Mindy had mentioned that John had an age hang-up.

Again, he looked annoyed. "Woman. You know what I mean. He took a breath and Gerri could see him deciding whether to shut up. Fortunately for her, he was too irritated to exercise discretion. "OK. Put it in terms of movie actresses. This," he gestured at the picture, "This is Jayne Mansfield. Fine. A lot of people like her." He shrugged to suggest that he was not among them. He then lowered his voice and waved his hand toward the kitchen. "But out there...out there is goddamn Grace Kelly. How on *earth* could Grace Kelly feel eclipsed by Jayne Mansfield?"

"I think Mindy's very attractive, too," Gerri murmured. She'd gotten most of what she wanted, but not everything. Still, she didn't want to overplay her hand. She leaned back in her chair casually. "You know, you two have a lot in common. Why don't you ask her out?"

John looked startled—and then he hesitated. "She's a lot younger than I am," he finally said.

Gerri shrugged with exaggerated casualness. "Seeing the two of you talking, it doesn't seem as though age is a problem. Besides, time tends to blur that sort of distinction."

Now he looked suspicious. "You know what they say about black men chasing white women. In fact, I'm surprised that you didn't think of that yourself."

"I admit that I don't know you well, but I didn't think of it that way. I just see two people who really seem to enjoy each other."

"You may not see it that way, but other people will." His fist clenched in his lap. "I refuse to be a stereotype."

"Hmmm." Gerri let the silence grow. "You might consider that when you try so hard *not* to be a stereotype, you're still letting other people control what you do." She had gone as far as she dared, Gerri decided, and was about to change the subject when she saw that he was lost in thought.

He affected a casual smile and a shrug. "It's all moot. She probably wouldn't be interested in an old guy like me."

Gerri wanted to shake him and say, *Yes she would! Yes she would!* But of course she couldn't. She shrugged—John wasn't the only one who could fake casualness—and said, "There are no guarantees, but I didn't get the impression that the chemistry went in only one direction." Then she made a great show of looking toward the kitchen. "Maybe we should see what she's up to. I don't want her to think that I deserted her."

———

John was barely out the door when Mindy turned to Gerri expectantly. "Well?"

"He definitely likes you. And he definitely finds you attractive. Very attractive. In fact, he compared you to Grace Kelly."

Mindy blushed to the roots of her hair. "Oooh…" But she abruptly returned to the practical. "So why doesn't he say anything?"

"I think he's concerned about how other people would react."

Now Mindy flashed to instant anger. "The race thing? Who cares what the racists say?"

"Well, it's a little more complicated than that." Gerri paused. She really didn't want to have this conversation. She realized at that moment that she had never previously in her life had the occasion to try to explain black people's foibles to a white person. But if Mindy was her friend, it would be cowardly to avoid doing it. To buy some time, she sat down and clasped her hands in her lap. Mindy sat opposite her with a worried look on her face. Gerri found Mindy's anxiety distracting, so she stared at her hands as she spoke.

"There is a large—embarrassingly large—amount of color prejudice in the black community. There's an old saying: 'If you're black, get back. If you're brown, stick around. If you're white, all right.'"

Mindy couldn't contain herself. "Black people think that way? Why? They ought to know better."

"I agree. But I suppose when you've had it drummed into you for generations that white skin is more valuable, you tend to internalize those values. And it's especially prevalent in judging women. The stereotype is that black men want to chase white women. Those fears caused many lynchings, even though they're greatly exaggerated.

"There is a residue to this attitude, however. It teaches black men to value women who *look* white—who have light skin and more, umm, European features. Dark skinned women are frequently undervalued by the men of their own race.

"I think what bothers John the most is not the reaction of the whites—although that can be unpleasant and downright dangerous—but the reaction of the black people, particularly women, who would see him as betraying them."

There was a brief silence. Suddenly, Mindy put her hand on top of Gerri's. Gerri looked up to see an expression of pity on her face. "I'm so sorry," Mindy said. "I didn't mean to cause you any distress."

Gerri shook her head violently. "No, no, no. I've never been in that situation myself. And I have no romantic interest in John."

Mindy frowned thoughtfully. "What about that ex-boyfriend of yours? Did he...?"

Gerri gave a brief snort. "I don't even know. I never saw the girl. And I didn't care in the least what she looked like." *That was mostly true,* she told herself. "The issue for me was the fact that he lied. And I wasn't really sorry to have that relationship end. I've realized since then that it's possible to have much stronger feelings for somebody."

Gerri could see a light go on over Mindy's head. *Why the heck did I have to say that? I don't want to talk about Sven.* "Anyway," she added hastily, "We're trying to fix *your* crappy love life, not mine."

Fortunately, Mindy was more than willing to return to the subject of John. "Do you think he'll say anything?"

"I don't know. The only advice I can give you is to be receptive, and be understanding if he wants to be, umm, circumspect at first."

Later, as she slipped into bed, she thought about Mindy and John. She hoped that they could find happiness. And she couldn't help the ironic thought: *Would that my 'crappy love life' could be resolved so easily...*

She fell asleep vowing to call Sven the next day. It had simply been too long since she had seen him. Surely, she could talk to him without making a fool of herself. Couldn't she?

She slept well, dreaming about Sven and the time they had shared on the Glacier Gal last summer, when life had seemed so simple.

When she awoke, she called his home right away. But there was no answer.

———

Sven had left Juneau about two hours ago. The weather was placid, and they were making good time. He glanced back toward the galley. His two clients seemed energetic, even with their early start. The big boss, as Sven was already privately calling him, was sitting and the other guy was fixing breakfast—they had been told that cooking was not part of the service. Sven was bored with this trip already. He would rather watch or paint wild animals than shoot them. These hunting charters were uncommon for him—this was the first time he had consented to two in one year. But the trip to South Carolina had eaten up quite a chunk of his savings. And—as if he could forget—he wanted to be able to buy a ring for Gerri.

Thinking of her turned his mind to his dilemma. He had been tempted to call her before leaving to say goodbye, but he couldn't. He had no idea how late that dinner party had lasted, and he might have awakened her out of a sound sleep. And awakened Mindy too, spoiling any good will that was developing. And that was assuming that Gerri stayed at Mindy's last night. No! He wouldn't even let himself consider the alternative.

He looked around. Ahead, down Stephens Passage, the winter sun was making its slow way over the mountains, announcing its approach with gorgeous magenta streaks on the undersides of the clouds. Lost in his reverie, Sven almost called to Gerri to share the view. When he realized his mistake, he shook his head. *This is going to be a long trip…*

CHAPTER 36

By the start of her second week, Gerri had fallen into a comfortable, albeit hectic, routine. Mindy would give her a ride to school in the morning. After school, Gerri would talk with Mrs.Kallek—if she had come to school that day—and then walk home. She knew that walking home wouldn't always be possible. Even dressed warmly, she could feel the cold, and her co-workers were fond of telling her 'wait until we get this year's first two-foot snowstorm.'

She had not heard from Sven since that phone call when she had rebuffed his attempt to see her. She had tried calling him twice more, but he didn't answer. Surely he would be back by now. She was evidently not a priority for him just now—and she knew that it was her own fault. She told herself that it was for the best—that she would heal faster if she didn't see him. But she missed him terribly.

At first, she brought a bagged lunch so that she could work on her lessons as she ate, but on her second day a woman poked her head into Gerri's classroom with an invitation. "Hey, come and join us for lunch. You'll go crazy if you stay in this room all day."

Gerri considered that briefly. "You're right. I need a break." As she stood up, the woman extended her hand.

"I'm Sharon Ingram. I teach English."

As they walked to the cafeteria, Gerri made conversation. "So, do you teach English literature? American literature?"

Sharon laughed. "Yes, both. But I'm even worse: I have a fondness for grammar. One which my students generally don't share, I might add."

"I can empathize."

Sharon cast her a sidelong look and asked with a half smile, "With me or with my students?"

Gerri decided to go with honesty. "With both, actually. I appreciate its importance now, but I remember suffering through some of the subtleties at times. My high school teachers always seemed to find the weird examples."

"I try to. And there are plenty of them around. You were probably one of those logical math whizzes who hated the inconsistencies."

"Guilty—on the hating of inconsistencies, not on the whiz part."

Once in the cafeteria, Sharon led Gerri to a table. There was a man already eating there. He seemed to be in his thirties. When he saw them, he raised his hand in greeting and worked to swallow the large bite he had just taken. "Hi, I'm Jake Devlin. I teach science." He cast a look at Sharon. "And my other job is to make Sharon's lunch periods miserable."

"Watch yourself or I'll tell my students to start correcting your grammar in class."

Gerri soon came to look forward to those lunches, not only as a break in her workload, but as a source of news and gossip. She found herself an amused spectator to the good-natured bickering between the other two. On Friday of her second week, she decided to jump into the fray. "It's a good thing I'm here, or y'all would be having a real food fight."

Jake laughed, but Sharon looked thoughtful. "You know," she said, "I'm starting to hear students saying that in the hallways."

Jake managed to look both skeptical and puzzled. "What? Food fight?"

Sharon shook her head. "No. 'Y'all.'"

"And that's bad?" Now he looked genuinely amused.

"No." She looked at Gerri reassuringly. "I know there are regional dialects. It would be bad only if I thought that they were making fun of Gerri."

Jake leaned back with a smug expression. "You're my witness," he said to Gerri. Then he turned to Sharon. "Leaving aside the issue of possibly mocking Gerri, on which I totally agree with you, this may be the only time I ever get to teach you something about grammar."

Sharon had a dubious expression, but he ignored that and continued. "You can do better in defending that usage than by appealing to a dialect. It actually tries to solve a defect in the English language." He paused and took a drink, obviously trying to milk the moment.

"Go on," said Sharon impatiently.

"There's no distinction in standard English between the second person singular and plural pronouns. It's just 'you' and the listener has to figure out what's meant."

"But the context…"

"Not always. And not always easily. If I'm telling my class about a test they took, and I say: 'You did badly on this test,' then they can't tell what I mean without watching my eyes. Are my eyes locked on one kid? Or are they moving around the room? Using 'y'all' for the plural is just a way to disambiguate that pronoun." He grinned with mischief. "See? And you didn't think I knew any big words."

Sharon cocked her head and looked at Gerri. "Is that how you use it?"

Gerri shrugged and nodded. She didn't want to say *of course*, since that seemed impolite.

Now Sharon looked thoughtful. "Hmmm, I never thought of it that way."

"Furthermore," Jake was more than willing to press his advantage. "Some people in New Jersey use 'youse' to solve the same language problem. It's considered bad grammar by the purists, but it does serve a purpose."

"It's considered bad grammar by *everybody*," Sharon interrupted testily. "So… How did you come up with this?"

Jake turned to Gerri for sympathy. "Notice the emphasis on the 'you.' I tell you, I get no respect."

"Yes, Rodney Dangerfield," Sharon said with a smile. "But seriously, I'm interested."

"As Sharon knows," he said to Gerri, "English is not my first language. My family moved from Ireland to New Jersey when I was five. I picked up 'youse' from the other kids—we weren't in the best of neigh-borhoods—and found out in school that it wasn't considered proper. To me it always seemed reasonable, so later, when I heard 'y'all' the similarity was obvious."

Sharon nodded thoughtfully. Gerri chimed in, "I'm surprised that you don't have an accent."

Jake made a sour face. "I worked hard to get rid of it. My neighbor-hood was predominately Italian. Too much of an Irish accent would get a kid teased or even beaten up. Later on," he paused and flashed a roguish smile, "a bit of a brogue could be very useful with the girls, but now that I'm married…" He shrugged and heaved a fake sigh of regret.

Gerri laughed. She thought briefly of correcting 'girls' to 'women' out of loyalty to Mindy, but held her tongue. Thinking of Mindy did remind her… "My roommate argues for another defect in the lan-guage. There's no gender-neutral third person singular pronoun corre-sponding to the plural 'they.' So you have to specify a person's sex even when it's not known or not appropriate."

Jake made a face. "Who cares?"

Gerri was considering whether to start an argument by defending Mindy when Sharon jumped in. "You should care. When you have to specify a person's sex but you don't know it, the tendency is to use the male—he or him—and that tends to make women more invisible."

Jake threw up his hands in surrender. "If I dispute that, Sharon will tell my wife, and then I'll hear about it forever. Let's change the subject."

In the ensuing silence, they heard the howl of a particularly strong gust of wind. Jake was relieved at the distraction. "It's bitter out there today. You walk home, don't you, Gerri?"

"Yes, but I dress warmly."

Jake gave an exaggerated shudder. "Still, nobody should be out in this kind of weather if he doesn't have to."

"Aha!" Sharon said triumphantly. "You just illustrated Gerri's point. You don't mean that only men should stay inside, so technically you should have said 'he or she,' and that sounds awkward."

But Gerri wasn't listening anymore. '*Nobody should be out in this kind of weather...*' *Sven!* What if he didn't get back from that hunting trip? What if something had happened to him in this awful weather? That would mean that he hadn't failed to call out of indifference. She found herself irrationally relieved by that prospect—for about a second, until she realized what that would mean. Then she felt terrible for her self-centered, selfish thoughts.

She had to know—but how? *I can see if the Glacier Gal is in the harbor...* She was over her moment of selfishness—she desperately hoped that the boat was there.

"Earth to Gerri. Are you still with us? Do you want that ride?"

"I'm sorry, Jake. I just remembered an errand I have to run before I go home. Thank you anyway, but I'll pass on that ride."

"Are you sure? Can't it be put off until a nicer day?"

She shook her head. "I can't put it off. It's very important." *Life or death, in fact.*

————

Gerri trudged toward the boat harbor, thankful once again that Sven had been so insistent about her clothing purchases. The wind was behind her, which helped, but the down parka was, once again, proving to be her favorite article of apparel. Not that the coat would save her if she was wearing the skirt and blouse that she had taught in. She stopped by the teachers' bathroom at the end of each day and changed into insulated pants—also specified by Sven. The outfit was so toasty that she had to get outside as soon as she had changed, lest she start sweating.

Even so, she wasn't eager to have Sven see her like this. The protective clothing made her—in her opinion—look like the Michelin Man. She smiled as she thought about the gender/grammar arguments at lunch. *Was there a Michelin Woman?*

As she turned onto the boat harbor dock, the wind hit her in the face. She gasped and paused for a moment. The wind was bringing tears to her eyes and she could hardly see. To make matters worse, its strength was almost enough to blow her over. She crept down the ramp to the floats, holding on the railing for dear life.

She walked toward Sven's slip. To add insult to injury, there were a few icy spots, even though it hadn't snowed for days. *Not long, now...* She vowed that once she saw the Glacier Gal, she would turn around immediately and go home. It was Sven's own business if he chose not to call her. After all, he had made his disinterest clear. She refused to look clingy. *A clingy Michelin Woman? No thank you!*

———

She stood, unmoving and shocked. His slip was empty—the Glacier Gal was not there. Turning, she scanned the other slips, heedless of the sting of the wind. Somehow, without conscious effort, she had convinced herself that the Glacier Gal would be safely sitting there—that everything would be all right. Then she could slink away quietly, knowing that she'd been foolish but comforted that Sven was OK.

After her initial shock wore off, she considered her next steps. Call the Coast Guard? That would make her a laughing-stock. She had no idea of Sven's route or schedule. Maybe that was it: maybe she had misunderstood his time of return. But that didn't comfort her. She had the awful feeling that something was dreadfully wrong.

What could she do? Nothing. But if she simply went home, she would be worthless until there was a resolution. *Wally! Maybe he would know something.* Sven had remarked once that Wally lived on his boat year-round. Gerri set off towards his slip, walking faster and faster in her impatience until she almost lost her traction and forced herself to slow down. She could tolerate looking a bit foolish in front of Wally, but falling flat on her back in her haste—that would be just too much.

After she stepped onto the deck of Wally's boat, she paused to compose herself. She wanted to project a friendly concern—but in a calm way. He would, she hoped, have some reasonable, reassuring explanation. Then she could nod sagely and move on.

She was startled when the cabin door opened suddenly and Wally said gruffly, "Come on in before we both freeze."

"How did you know…" She hadn't even knocked.

He looked amused. "I felt the boat move."

As she entered his cabin, Gerri shook her head to clear the cobwebs. "Oh. Of course." Even the Glacier Gal—a larger boat—rocked very slightly when someone stepped aboard. She tried to regroup after that inauspicious start, but Wally spoke first.

"Welcome back. I expect you're giving the high school kids all they can handle, aren't you?"

She had to force herself to concentrate. *Have I forgotten all of my manners?* "I, I hope so. Teaching is hard work."

Wally could see that she was flustered and he took pity on her. "You're here to see about Sven?"

"Yes." She tried to be casual, but her words came out in a rush. "His boat isn't there. I suppose that there's some reasonable…" She stopped upon seeing Wally shake his head.

He waved her to a bench in his tiny galley and watched her assessingly as she took off her heavy parka. It was sorely tempting to give her a facile, sugar-coated explanation. If he got her all upset, then he'd have to comfort her—and he wasn't good at that sort of thing.

On the other hand, this was the girl who started out knowing nothing and ended up capable of navigating the Glacier Gal by herself when Sven got appendicitis. She deserved to be treated like a professional, even if that was more uncomfortable for both of them in the current situation.

"You know he's out with a hunting party, right?" Gerri nodded. "He radioed in a few days ago that he was going to wait out the weather in Gambier Bay." He looked at Gerri inquiringly.

She frowned as she frantically tried to visualize the charts that she had spent so much time poring over last summer.

"It's south of here," Wally prompted. "You did most of your fishing further west; towards Pelican and the ocean."

"Yes, but I…" After a few seconds, that area snapped into focus. "I remember it. We never went down there, but it's about…seven or eight hours out, I think."

Wally couldn't hide a small smile. "That's about right—in decent weather, anyway."

Gerri was irrationally pleased at his obvious approval. *I guess I redeemed myself...* Then she shook her head imperceptibly. *Stay on topic.* "And he's still there?"

Wally looked uncomfortable. "Well, no. I got another call from... well, you don't know the guy, but Sven asked him to deliver a message. It seems that one of these hunters was really desperate to get back—something about a vital business meeting in San Francisco tomorrow. So Sven started out this morning for home."

As he spoke, Gerri became aware of radio static in the background. Wally had probably been monitoring the short wave marine band all day. "What time did he start?"

Wally was hoping to avoid this part. "About six in the morning."

Gerri's heart sank. "So he's overdue."

"Yes, he should have been here three or four hours ago."

She thought about that, trying to find a reassuring explanation. "But he would have called, wouldn't he, if he had gotten in trouble?"

Wally shook his head, and Gerri realized that he, too, was very worried—and angry. "No, he can't. It seems that they had a very successful trip. They lashed the carcasses of the animals to the boat for the trip back. One of those idiot hunters tried to hang a big buck from the mount for Sven's radio antenna. It ripped the antenna off in the heavy weather. So Sven has no radio capability."

Gerri's heart sank even lower. "So that's why he had this other guy relay the message for him."

Wally nodded and stared at her, watching her reaction.

Gerri started to get angry. "So why the hell did he leave Gambier Bay? Just tell his customer that he'll just have to wait."

Wally couldn't have agreed with her more. In fact, he would have expressed himself in even stronger terms. Though, now that he thought about it, this was the strongest language that he'd ever heard Gerri use. His situation was made more delicate by the fact that he had a pretty good idea why Sven took this chance. The customer had offered Sven a very sizeable bonus to get him back on time and, Wally was pretty sure, Sven wanted to build a nest egg to woo Gerri. But he couldn't tell her that.

He tried to concentrate on how he could reassure her without actually lying. "He might be perfectly OK. Sure, there are things that could have happened, but he could just be delayed."

That would be a big delay, Gerri thought, but addressed the other part of his remark. "Engine trouble, I suppose. But that's not very likely. Sven takes good care of his boat."

"I agree. If it *did* happen, the wind could drive him onto the rocks, but it's not very likely that it happened."

Gerri searched for other possibilities, slightly cheered that Wally didn't consider engine failure to be likely. "He could have hit something like a log. But that doesn't seem very probable either."

"True, and true."

She racked her brain. *Could he have made a navigation error and run aground?* But she couldn't believe that for a moment. Sven was an excellent seaman. She'd never seen him make an error like that.

Wally watched her, hoping that she would give up in her speculations. Then, he could remain silent with a clear conscience. When she showed no signs of doing so, he confessed his true fear. "What I worry about the most is ice."

She looked puzzled. "You mean hitting an iceberg?"

"No. That'd be like hitting a log—possible, but not likely." He paused. This was something totally outside her experience. He wished that he didn't have to explain it, but, he reminded himself, she deserved not to be patronized. "You wouldn't have seen this last summer. Remember how in a storm the waves come over the bow and spray everything?"

"Sure—too well." Gerri shuddered, thinking of the day she went overboard.

"Today's worse than anything you saw last summer. But, more importantly, the temperature is around zero. Most of the spray runs back off the boat, but some of it will freeze and stick." She seemed about to object, so he raised his finger to forestall it. "It may not seem like much—a few ounces with each wave—but it adds up. You're the math person," he couldn't resist adding, "add it up: a few ounces to a pound every five to ten seconds can build up fast."

Gerri's head spun. This was completely outside her experience. And he was right—this would be an interesting and exotic exercise for her notebook. If only she could use it someday when Sven was safely back home.

Wally continued. "Now, the first problem this causes is reduced visibility. As the pilot house windows build up a layer of ice, you can't see through them. You have to stick your head out the side doors to see.

"The second problem—the really devastating one—is the added weight. The ice won't usually build up in a balanced way. Eventually, the boat will list—tilt to one side. That will make it harder to control. It could even capsize."

He watched her for a minute as she digested his words. She looked utterly miserable. He wondered if he had been too frank. He couldn't un-say any of this, but it was probably time for him to shut up. He slapped his hands on his knees and leaned forward. "There's nothing we can do now but wait. If anyone can bring a boat through this, it's Sven."

Gerri caught his signal and suppressed a sigh. "Yes, I suppose so." She looked down at him as she rose to go. "Wally, please call me if you get any news—any news at all. And thank you."

She wrote down both Mindy's number and the number for the school and gave them to him. She paused one last time before she left. "I don't care what time it is. Call me at *any* time. Night or day."

Chapter 37

It was a long night for Gerri. Mindy was eating out with John, so the apartment was empty. Gerri moped through a dinner of leftovers, and then resolved to find something—anything—to do to keep her mind off Sven being out there in the storm.

That plan didn't work well. She started with her schoolwork, resolving to prepare for Monday's classes. After an hour, she conceded to herself that she wasn't getting anything done.

She then thought about the potential exercise for her math journal—the ice buildup—that Wally had alluded to. That was no good; it made her obsess even more about what might be happening to Sven. She was very careful about using the present tense—when it became past tense, that would mean either that he was home safely or that he had been wrecked. And Wally hadn't called, so it wasn't the former.

She had better luck in grading homework. It didn't require quite as much concentration as planning lessons, and some of the students engaged her attention by finding rather intriguing ways of getting things wrong. Eventually, though, she finished all of the homework.

As she was casting about mentally for something else to occupy her mind, she received a welcome distraction. Mindy breezed in, obviously in an ebullient mood. "We talked," she said, her eyes dancing.

Gerri smiled for the first time since she had left the boat harbor. "Tell me all about it." Mindy had told her about her dinner 'date' several days ago. At that time, Gerri had given her a teasing smile and said "Oooooh."

Mindy had quickly tried to lower her expectations. "It doesn't necessarily mean anything," she explained. "We share business dinners occasionally to talk about his work in the outlying villages and my department's support."

Still, Gerri had privately suspected whether there might be more to it, and now, it appeared as though she had been right.

Mindy talked over her shoulder, as she hung up her coat. "We're going to try to see more of each other, but not as stereotypical dates. No going to the movies for a while."

"So what *will* you do?"

"Well, dinners will work—people are used to seeing us eating together." She sat down opposite Gerri. "First, though, I'm going to teach him how to ice skate. That should look innocent enough."

"That sounds interesting. When will this happen?"

"We're going to start tomorrow. We're going to a lake out the road."

Gerri tuned out. A brief daydream flashed through her mind—Sven, back and healthy, teaching Gerri how to skate. That was quickly replaced by real life—Sven's unknown peril—and Gerri felt miserable again. She realized that Mindy was still talking. "I'm sorry," Gerri interrupted, "I'm not good company tonight."

"I'm sorry if you don't feel well. May I get you anything?"

"Physically, I'm just fine. I'm worried sick." Gerri hesitated. *Would I spoil the evening for Mindy if I mention Sven?* She settled for the practical. "Do you mind if I keep the phone in my room? I'm expecting an important call, and it may come late." *Or it may not come at all...*

"Sure," Mindy said, but she looked puzzled. She knew that Gerri didn't get many calls—early or late. She sat next to Gerri and put her hand on Gerri's. "What's going on?"

Gerri explained Sven's hunting trip and her worries. Mindy involuntarily looked at the window. "He's out on his boat in *this?*"

Gerri nodded sadly. "I wish he wasn't," and found herself giving more details.

Mindy glanced at the window again and shuddered. "I hope he's OK."

"If I get a call, I'll go down to the boat harbor and see for myself."

"Not a night to be out..." Then she had a brainstorm. "Take my car if you go. This isn't a good time for one of your famous walks."

"Are you sure you won't need it?"

"I'm sure. You know where the keys are." She pointed to the bookshelf. "Just don't forget to unplug the head bolt heater before you go."

"The what?"

Mindy briefly smiled at Gerri's look of mystification. "It's in the engine. It makes the car easier to start on really cold days. You just plug it into an electrical outlet when you park the car. You'll see the cord hanging out of the grill."

"Wonders never cease. I still have a lot to learn about this place."

Mindy disappeared into her bedroom, leaving Gerri alone with her depressing thoughts. Gerri was wondering whether she could possibly fall asleep herself when, a few minutes later, Mindy reappeared. She looked much more solemn and reflective than she had before.

"I really do hope he's OK." She paused. "I inherited my old clunker from Laura. Not directly, because she died before I started to drive. Sven bought and installed that head bolt heater for her as a birthday present. She complained about it—she wanted jewels or something like that—but I thought it was sweet. They didn't have much money then, but he wanted her to be safe."

She sighed. "He was kind of old-fashioned, I guess. They just wanted such different things out of life. I've tried to tell myself otherwise, but he really did try." With that, she disappeared into her bedroom again.

Gerri stared at her door for a long time—happy that Mindy was overcoming her bitterness about Sven, but miserable that Sven might not live to find out about it.

The shrill ringing of the phone disoriented Gerri. She blinked and looked around. She was still on the couch in the living room. Apparently, she had dozed off after all. A quick glance at the clock showed that it was after ten—she had slept for almost an hour.

When she picked up the phone, Wally spoke without preamble. "Someone radioed me just now. He thinks that he might have seen the Glacier Gal on its way in. He couldn't be sure in the dark."

"How far out?" Gerri, too, had no time to waste on amenities.

"Maybe ten minutes. I'll give you another call after I know whether it's him."

"Don't bother. I'm leaving now. I'll be there in ten minutes."

"Are you sure? It might not be him, you know."

"Wally, I'm going crazy sitting here waiting and worrying. For my sanity, I need to *do* something."

As Wally hung up the phone, he smiled. He wondered if Sven knew how lucky he was to have someone like Gerri. Then the smile faded. If this was a false alarm, then they would be running out of benign explanations for his delay.

She was there in six minutes—thankful that the streets were mostly dry and that the police weren't watching for speeders. She parked Mindy's car, slipped the key into her pocket, and stepped out into the bitter wind. She hurried down the ramp, dividing her attention between the dimly lit walkway and the harbor entrance. She hoped with all of her heart to see the Glacier Gal steaming in. There was one boat entering the harbor, but the running lights didn't look like those of Sven's boat. She was reduced to hoping for a miracle.

She tried to keep the moving boat in sight, but after she reached the bottom of the ramp, the other boats in the harbor blocked her view. All she could see was the mast light. She took some comfort from the fact that the unknown boat seemed to be heading to somewhere near Sven's slip.

As she got close, the scene popped into focus. It *was* the Glacier Gal! Gerri's knees felt weak with relief, and she had to pause and lean against a piling to steady herself. *Thank heavens!* She could also see why she didn't recognize it earlier. This was a beaten and distorted version of the Glacier Gal. Wally had been right about the ice. The Gal had thick, irregular layers of ice covering the front deck and the pilot house. The windows were almost invisible underneath the ice. And the boat listed to one side, presumably from the uneven weight of the ice.

The side doors of the pilot house were propped open, and she could see Sven stick his head out frequently—because of the ice blocking the front windows—to check his progress. She couldn't imagine how miserable it must have been to have piloted the boat that way. The cabin must be freezing cold. She shuddered involuntarily.

As she reached the slip, she saw Wally waiting to step aboard and get a line to tie up the boat. She also saw a stranger—looking utterly scared and helpless—watching from the door. One of the hunters, no doubt. And if she had to judge from him, Sven had had no help whatsoever on the return trip.

Wally saw her and threw her the stern line. No words were necessary. Gerri fastened it to the cleat on the dock—wrestling it with difficulty, since the line was frozen and stiff.

The stranger that she had seen, together with a companion, hastily climbed off the boat carrying duffel bags. They were totally oblivious to Gerri and Wally. As they passed, she heard a snatch of conversation.

"You and your damned meeting. I've never been more scared in my life."

"You had it easy. I was sick as a dog practically the whole trip back. And don't forget: That meeting is going to pay for this trip many times over."

Gerri looked back at the boat. There were several carcasses—large ones—still hanging from various supports. As the hunters left, they hadn't given them a second glance. Gerri gave Wally a puzzled look.

"Trophy hunters." He spat into the water in what she presumed to be a critical comment. "Sven will arrange for someone to come tomorrow and take care of them. The meat will be given away, and I imagine the heads will be mounted."

"So they'll just stay here overnight?"

Wally smiled for the first time since she'd arrived. "Nobody will take them. And you couldn't ask for a better freezer."

For some reason, that struck her funny. She chuckled, which set Wally off as well. Then she realized that Sven hadn't come out yet. Could he be hurt? Clearly, the hunters wouldn't have cared. She stopped laughing and looked toward the pilot house.

———

Sven shut down the engine and gathered his things. He had never felt so sore, cold, and exhausted. He had even passed the stage of shivering. He should never have accepted that bozo's bonus money—sizeable as the amount was. When the man pled with him to get them back, Sven had tried to tell them of the difficulties and dangers. The man had glibly assured Sven that they would help him with whatever needed to be done on the trip. He carried himself like a big shot—and his friend treated him like one—but Sven was convinced that he must have been a salesman in his regular life. *Say anything to close the deal...* They had both turned out to be worthless on the trip back. The salesman spent most of the trip being sick, and his friend sat rigidly, as if in shock, in the galley.

That was OK. He was done with them now, and he would make it home somehow. There was a bigger disaster looming outside the cabin. Gerri was here. His first reaction was unbridled joy. Joy at seeing her and joy that she would come out on a night like this to meet him.

But he quickly had doubts. She had obviously tried to put distance between them. And he was pretty sure that that was because of her interest in Dr. Wheeler. And how was Sven supposed to compete with that? What did he have going for himself, really? Sincerity and true devotion—yes. His physique--maybe, if she went for that. His looks—doubtful.

Gerri had seen him utterly helpless during his appendicitis attack. And now, when he stepped outside she would see him near collapse. He looked outside again. The hunters were gone, and Gerri and Wally were sharing a joke.

Maybe that was the key. If he could mask his weakness and be casual, she might at least remember his better side. If they were laughing, then so would he. Then later, somehow, he would try to figure out how to win her back. Somehow. He stepped out of the pilot house.

Gerri watched Sven approach; her eyes narrowed. He looked to be on his last legs. She was willing to bet that he had had to carry the whole load on this trip—those hunters surely hadn't been of any help. She watched him stumble as he tried to step over the gunwale. She remembered well her own hypothermia after her fall overboard. Was he even capable of getting home? Or should he go to the emergency room to be looked at?

Just as she was about to speak, he looked at them and said, with forced joviality, "Well, a welcoming committee. Just the thing after a nice trip."

Gerri was known for her equable nature. Indeed, it was part of her self-image. But this was too much. She had never been more scared in her life. Not even Sven's appendicitis attack had scared her this much. And it wasn't just 'foolish female fears.' Wally had been scared as well. And, from the looks of him, Sven wasn't home free just yet. And he thought all of this was funny?

She simply lost it. "You have a nerve. You think this is a big joke? But there are people who…" *Who love you…* "Who care for you and have been sick with worry about you."

Sven didn't have the energy to defend himself. And he knew that he didn't deserve defending. His attempt to appear confident and in control had been an utter flop. *How can I be so clumsy with someone I care for so much?* He gathered his remaining strength. "I'm sorry. No, I don't think it's a joke. Actually, it was a pretty rotten day all around."

Wally interjected accusingly, "Why did you let them talk you into coming back in this weather? You don't need the money."

Wally was sort of right, Sven had to admit—silently. Ordinarily, he would have resisted the hunter's entreaties with ease. He couldn't explain to Wally that he anticipated shopping for an engagement ring. Not in front of Gerri. Maybe not at all—Wally would probably disapprove. He finally settled for the weak retort, "Good question. It certainly turned out to be a mistake.

"He was desperate. And he and his friend said that they would do anything they could to help."

"Which was about nothing, I'll bet," Wally said disgustedly.

"Pretty much," Sven admitted.

"Why did it take you so long to get back?" Gerri tried to ask calmly. She already regretted her outburst—even though Sven had deserved it.

Sven looked at her warily. Could he redeem himself? Or did she just think it not worth her trouble to excoriate him? He decided to distract her with details. "I had to throttle way down to reduce the spray. The ice was building up too fast. And, of course, we were heading into the wind for much of the trip. I was probably averaging only a couple of knots." He broke into a spasm of shivering and leaned against the boat to steady himself.

Gerri was quick to notice. "We need to get you home. You need to warm up and to get some rest."

Sven knew that she was right—and he was warmed (figuratively at least) by the fact that she had noticed. But his pride wouldn't let him give in. "I'm fine." He gestured back to the boat. "I just need to take my pack up to the truck…"

Gerri grabbed his elbow. "Oh, no you don't. Forget the macho stuff. You can get the pack later. And you shouldn't be driving. I'll drive you. Mindy's car is warmer anyway." Her gruffness was an effective defense against emotion. It helped her fight off the urge to cling to him, seeking tactile reassurance that he was truly safe.

Any thought that Sven had of protesting further was squelched by his exhaustion. And even more by the fact that Gerri put her arm around his waist to help support him. He would enjoy her touch while he could—and try to forget that it was merely motivated by pity.

After Gerri assured him that she had the situation in hand, Wally bade them farewell and returned to his boat. He smiled after he was out of sight. He had been prepared to help Sven himself, but he was pleased at how it turned out. Gerri wasn't letting Sven get away with any of his nonsense. There was more to her than the mild little college girl of last summer. Sven was going to have a handful in her.

CHAPTER 38

Gerri got him home without too much trouble. He stayed awake enough in the car to give her directions and his house wasn't that far from the boat harbor. Getting him into the house was harder—he was clearly reaching the end of his endurance. With her aid, he got in and collapsed on his bed.

Gerri considered undressing him, but decided that that would be a bad idea. Holding him around the waist was bad enough. It reminded her all too vividly of the previous summer. No, she would not touch him unnecessarily. She just threw some covers over him and let him sleep.

While she tried to decide what to do next, she briefly looked around. She liked his house. It was obviously a bachelor's house, but it was roomy and had a marvelous view of the Juneau city lights and Mt. Juneau in the background. Of course, in the Alaskan winter night, only the silhouette of the mountain was visible. But that was still beautiful, since it was outlined by a brilliant blanket of stars.

She couldn't help but notice how neat he kept the house. Definitely not the stereotype of a bachelor. Maybe that stemmed from his experience on his boat, where everything had to be stowed away neatly.

She would have liked to have explored the house further, but she felt a bit like an intruder. Anything other than the living room, which they passed through upon entering, and his bedroom, which was upstairs, would have to wait for another time.

She looked in on him about thirty minutes later—still dead to the world. While she watched him, a shiver racked his body. She remembered her own bout with hypothermia. He had lain down with her and shared his warmth. She felt guilty for not returning the favor, but she knew very well how that would turn out. She settled for searching his closets for another blanket which she put over him as well.

Even though she didn't trust herself with him, she couldn't make herself simply leave. With a sigh, she went back to the closet with the blankets and made a bed for herself on his couch. Even though—or perhaps because—it had been such a stressful day, she fell asleep within minutes.

———

Sven awoke momentarily confused. He was in his own bed. The angle of the light coming through the shades told him that it was late morning. He tried moving. Every muscle ached. Then it all came back to him—the nightmare trip yesterday, the late night arrival, and Gerri's help in getting him home.

He darted a look to the side. No, she was not there with him—that would have been altogether too much to hope for. Then he realized that he was not so much *in* his own bed as *on* it. And fully clothed. A quick stab of disappointment shot through him. *What did I expect? Her affections have turned elsewhere. I should be grateful that she was loyal enough to be waiting for me when I got in last night.* He wondered idly if Dr. Wheeler would be upset at her for going out. *If I were a better man, I would hope he wasn't...*

A move to throw off the covers sparked a fresh wave of pain. Landlubbers assumed that being at the helm of a boat was easy—just standing (or sitting) and being alert. But in a storm like Sven had just been through, it was a far different matter. Sitting was impossible, and he had to flex his legs constantly to maintain his balance as the boat pitched. He was compelled to do this continuously for about sixteen hours. Add to that, the freezing cold from the open side doors of the pilot house—necessary for visibility with the ice blocking the windows.

Lying here won't make it any better. What he needed was a long, hot shower. But first, he would check to see if Gerri had left a note.

Groaning, he walked to the door of his room. When he opened the door to the hallway, he was struck by a blissful smell—bacon and something that might be pancakes. As welcome as the smell was, infinitely more welcome was the realization that Gerri was still here.

He stepped forward eagerly, but then stopped. *I'm filthy! I haven't had a shower in way too long and I still have on yesterday's clothes.* Regardless of the new, more distant relationship with Gerri, he didn't want her to see him smelling like a pigsty. Before he could creep back into his room, Gerri appeared at the foot of the stairs.

"How do you feel?" She looked up at him anxiously.

"Much better, thank you." He caught another whiff of her cooking, and it somehow destroyed his discretion. "Even if I didn't already want to marry you, the smell of this breakfast would make me want to."

Gerri clamped down firmly on her reaction. *He didn't mean to toy with me... that's just blarney. Or is it the Irish who use that?* "Breakfast will be ready in about ten minutes," She said briskly. "Is that too soon for you to clean up?"

He had a brief, horrified thought. *Can she smell me from downstairs?* Then he dismissed it. *She'd be right, after all.* "I'll try."

As he showered, he replayed his words to her. Had she been insulted? It was one thing to declare his interest, but an entirely different thing if she was committed to—or interested in—another. Saying the wrong thing seemed to be his norm lately. He would try to gauge her reaction—not that he was doing so well at that, either—and apologize if necessary.

Gerri watched Sven as he attacked his breakfast. *At least he still likes my cooking...* She wanted to hear more about his ordeal, but she didn't want to interrupt. By her analysis, he hadn't eaten anything in over 24 hours.

Finally, he paused and leaned back in his chair. Unbidden, he started telling her about his voyage home. As he spoke, she tried to reconstruct it in her mind. She felt a little sympathy for the hunters—even the summer storms that she had been in could have been terrifying for the uninitiated. She picked at the only detail that she could question. "But why couldn't you just steer by the compass? Then at least you could have had the door closed and let it get warmer in the pilot house."

Sven acknowledged her question with a nod and a ghost of a smile. Again, she felt that she had passed some sort of test. "Good question. In most places, we could. But there are magnetic deviations from iron deposits along the route. That screws up the compass."

Gerri couldn't suppress a smile and a rueful shake of her head.

Sven noticed. "What's the matter?"

"Nothing. It seems as though there are always more things to be learned about this place."

"Yes, but you're an apt pupil." Sven was on uncertain ground. He wanted to encourage her, but primarily he wanted to get the conversation to a more personal, intimate, level.

Gerri thought about his words. To her surprise, the subtle dangers of the wilderness didn't discourage her. She felt challenged by each new thing she learned. Then, she felt the cold splash of reality. All of her experiences and learning were tied to Sven. Her enthusiasm was a reflection of their relationship—their *previous* relationship. Now she had to guard against that enthusiasm leading her to make foolish decisions.

She made a show of checking her watch. "I probably should go. I'm glad that you're safe and I'm glad that you seem to be feeling better."

Sven felt the situation spiraling out of his control. *I'm not feeling better any more!* He had run out of clever ideas. A frontal approach was all he had left. "Is the doctor going to be upset that you stayed the night?"

That came out of left field! Gerri tried to imagine what he was talking about. Should she have taken him to the hospital? That didn't make any sense at all. "What doctor? What are you talking about?" She finally asked.

"Doctor Wheeler." Sven watched her expression carefully.

"What has he got to do with anything?"

Was this a good sign? Or was she merely surprised that he had deduced her relationship. Sven hated that he had to be the one to say it, but... "I thought that you and he..." He trailed to a stop at her astonished expression. "I mean that dinner…" *which I was conspicuously not invited to…* But Gerri was shaking her head vigorously.

"No, no. That was…" She stopped hastily. It was not her place to tell Mindy's secret. "No. That was just a dinner. He and I are not involved at all." Sven gave her a mildly skeptical look. "And we're not going to be. I don't know where you got that idea." *Maybe he feels guilty?*

Sven stared down at his empty plate. This was not the time for him to put his foot in his mouth. But he didn't know what to say. He abandoned any ideas of subtlety. Looking up at her, he asked, "Does that mean that there still might be hope for me?"

Gerri glared at him. He was surely toying with her now. "What are you talking about? You were very clear in South Carolina about not being interested."

Sven opened his mouth and then closed it again. She had to be talking about their aborted conversation in her yard. Desperately, he tried to figure out how to respond gracefully.

Seeing Sven hesitate, Gerri's irritation grew. She had to resist the impulse to slap the table in her anger and frustration. "You've forgotten already? I asked you—standing in our front yard—whether…" She trailed to a stop as he raised his hand wearily.

"That conversation was never finished. Your mother was bearing down on us like a freight train, so I stopped talking."

"Are you saying that my mother is big?" Somewhere in the back of her mind, Gerri knew that this was her anger talking—that she was being petty—but she was in no mood to apologize.

"No, no, no." Sven stopped for breath. He felt like he was in quicksand. Every step he tried to take sucked his other foot in deeper. He shot her a look that begged for understanding. "That was a figure of speech, ummm, a simile. I was talking about her approach speed and about the determination that I saw in her face. I like your mother, even though she doesn't like me."

"She…never mind." She took a breath to tamp down her anger. She didn't want to get sidetracked. She couldn't imagine what Sven claimed to have been about to say, but she knew that she'd better hear it or she would always wonder about it.

Sven tried to read her expression. He didn't see any encouragement. Was there at least a little curiosity? He plunged on. "If someone
looked at us from the outside last summer, they might have decided
that I was taking advantage of you."

"You weren't," she snapped. This reminded her of Sven's misgivings
after they first made love. She was tired of them. They struck her as
rather patronizing.

"Once before—with Laura—I was led by the front of my pants, so
to speak. I've always regretted that. If I had controlled myself, things
wouldn't have turned out so badly."

"You mean your relationship would have been stronger?" Gerri was
ashamed to have asked that—ashamed that she still wanted to know
the answer.

Sven hesitated. "May I speak in confidence? Will you promise not
to tell anybody? Especially not Mindy?"

Gerri nodded, aware that her heart was beating too fast.

"I think that Laura and I would have drifted apart, realizing how
different we were. There would have been no talk of marriage, but at
least we might have parted as friends."

Gerri played with her utensils. She felt a need to do something
with her hands—and her eyes. "So," she said tentatively, "You think
that we shouldn't have been intimate so soon? Are you worried about
spoiling our friendship?"

"No, that's not what I'm saying. Pardon my clumsiness; I've had
long enough to think about this, you'd think I could say it better." He
took a breath and gathered his courage. "I know better now the difference between love and lust. I lusted after Laura. I love you, Gerri. And
I want to court you the way you deserve to be courted."

Gerri slumped back in her chair, watching him. He didn't say
anything further. She was in shock. This was everything that she had
dreamed of hearing. She wanted nothing more than to jump into his
arms. And yet...

Was she ready for this? This was not a school girl crush. It was
not a casual summer love affair. This was a grown man who was talking about a serious, possibly permanent, relationship. Sure, her heart

wanted to say *yes, yes!* But she remembered her mother's words. She gasped. *Her mother!*

"Sven," she said haltingly. "I don't know what to say. You mean the world to me. But…"

This sounds like the start of a brush off. "I'm not trying to rush you. We can take our time."

"I'd like that. But…" She paused again. This time he waited. It wasn't a brush off, but whatever she *wasn't* saying wasn't going to be good. As he watched her, he more fully appreciated how young she was. Maybe she wasn't even capable of making a commitment.

"Sven," she studied his expression. Was he showing impatience? Disapproval? She feared that it was about to get worse. "I promised my mother that I wasn't going to get romantically involved with you."

His head jerked back. "Why the hell did you do that?"

Her hands were involuntarily making washing motions. "She was worried about me. It seemed like an easy way to reassure her, since I thought you weren't interested anyway."

He sat back in his chair. It was almost funny, in a way, but he didn't feel like laughing. "She disapproves of me."

"No," her eyes widened. "Not you personally. She's afraid that an interracial relationship will lead to heartbreak. We'd be hated by racist whites, and I'd be ostracized by many blacks."

"Why would you be ostracized?"

Gerri winced. She was having more than her share of uncomfortable conversations about racial relations lately. "Many people—especially those caught up in militancy—would consider me to be consorting with the enemy."

Sven sat and regarded her, trying to decide what to say next. He had this gift of saying the wrong thing. But right now, saying the wrong thing could be catastrophic. "So you want to be just friends. Platonic."

Gerri seemed even more uncomfortable, if possible. "I don't *want* that. It's just…I've never broken a promise—a serious one, anyway— to my mother."

He tried to put himself in her shoes. He certainly hadn't dealt well with *his* parents, and he was living with the consequences, even today.

He heaved a sigh. "OK, I understand that. But how long is this promise good for?"

"There wasn't a time limit."

"For the rest of your life?"

Gerri shrugged. "It shouldn't be. I don't know."

Sven wanted to backtrack. She *was* young. And he was just making her miserable. "I don't want you to break your promise if it means that much to you. I've certainly been no paragon of virtue in dealing with my parents. I don't want you to have regrets later. As I said before, I want to court you properly. And that implies not spoiling your relationship with your parents." And *that*, he reminded himself silently, meant not pressuring her. Even if he thought this promise of hers was a cockamamie idea.

Gerri squirmed under his gaze. Oh, how she wished that she hadn't made that promise. But she had. And she had always tried to be trustworthy—she was proud, maybe too much so, whenever her mother said 'you're our good child.'

Of course, she wasn't a child any more. But she still liked to think that she was 'good' (whatever that meant), even though she hadn't saved herself for marriage. And 'good' people didn't break promises willy-nilly.

She thought again about Sven's question. How long did her commitment last? Maybe that was a way out of this… "I'll write her and tell her that I made a mistake—that I can't keep that promise."

Sven's eyebrows rose and a smile creased his face. "Wonderful! Until then…" He said what he knew that he must. "Until then, I guess the promise will still be in force."

She smiled ruefully. "I suppose it must be."

He grinned. "We'll survive it." He felt like doing cartwheels even with the residual soreness from yesterday. Then he saw the loophole. "When do you propose to write this letter?"

Gerri considered that. Her impulse was to say 'today.' But she thought again. This would be a hard letter to write—and a hard letter for her mother to read. She scrunched up her face. "After Christmas. I don't want to spoil her holiday."

To her infinite relief, Sven nodded his approval. "OK." Then he stood and reached out his arms. "Can friends get hugs?"

His embrace practically took her breath away, but she didn't want it to end. She could feel his groan of satisfaction vibrating through her torso. But even as she basked in the comfort of Sven's arms, she couldn't stop thinking about her mother and her fears. Olivia was a wise woman, not given to frivolous concerns. And Gerri had to admit that those fears had some basis.

As much as she wanted to stop thinking and enjoy Sven's touch, she wanted even more to avoid leading him on.

"Sven?" She leaned her head back and gave him an imploring look. "One more thing: No talk about marriage—I'm not ready for that." *South Carolina's not ready for that and I don't want to be an exile!*

CHAPTER 39

Mindy looked up from the book she was reading and smiled as Gerri came through the door. "Well, well, look who's finally back. Is everything OK?"

"He's OK. He was pretty exhausted and pretty chilled. But he's OK."

"You stayed all night. Does that mean—as I believe the male chauvinist pigs say—that you got lucky?" Mindy wiggled her eyebrows.

Gerri had to laugh at the expression on Mindy's face. "No, not like that. But he's safe and that'll do for now." She summarized the events of the last twelve hours, omitting only her discussion with Sven about their relationship.

Mindy's eyes were wide by the time Gerri finished. "That's so scary. I can't imagine being out in a boat in this weather." She shook herself as if she felt a cold wind.

"So tell me about your morning. I've been dying to hear about it."

"It was wonderful." Seeing Gerri's eyebrows rise, Mindy grinned. "And no, I didn't get lucky either, in case you have a dirty mind."

"Nobody gave you a hard time?"

"Hardly anybody even saw us until we were almost done. One guy that I knew in high school came as we were leaving and he waved, but that was it."

"And the lessons went well?"

"They were great. Every time John lost his balance, he had to hold on to me." She paused with a smug look. "He lost his balance a lot. Even better, I think he was faking it—at least some of the time."

Gerri just rolled her eyes.

"I've got an idea for our next activity—and it involves you."

Gerri eyed her warily. "Involves me doing what?"

Mindy opened her mouth, and then seemed to reconsider. "Let me tell you later. I want to build up to it." Then, she switched subjects completely. "Not to be nosy, but what is your relationship with Sven? Friend? Loyal employee?" Her expression turned sly. "Or lover?"

It had been too much to hope for that Gerri could avoid this subject. It had been abstractly embarrassing to talk to Mindy about a skeleton in black peoples' closets—color consciousness. But this was worse because it was personal. She would be admitting her own foolishness in making the promise. But Mindy had been good to her, and Gerri owed her honesty.

She reluctantly recounted that story, from the misunderstanding in South Carolina to her ill-conceived promise to her mother. When she finished, she waited for a scornful comment.

But all she saw was a sympathetic smile. "Your mother sounds like a forceful person."

Gerri rolled her eyes. "She can be."

"And you try to be the good girl and please her."

Gerri looked at her ruefully. "Am I so transparent?"

"Don't feel bad. My mother wrote the book on forceful, domineering, or whatever you want to call it. I've made more than one promise to my mother that I later regretted. I tried to be the good girl, too. Laura didn't have to, of course—she was the glamorous one."

"Tell that to John, 'Grace Kelly,' and see if he believes you." Gerri was happy to see Mindy brighten up immediately.

Just the same, from this and other comments, Gerri had begun to believe that Mindy's childhood was less than ideal. She asked cautiously, "Do your parents still live in Juneau?"

"Yes, and we're on good terms." Mindy paused briefly. "But I don't see them that often. When I do, there are certain topics that are tacitly agreed to be off limits. And I've learned not to make promises anymore."

Gerri nodded. She really didn't want to go further on that subject.

"Well," Mindy returned to the subject. "What are you going to do about Sven?"

"Nothing, for right now."

The disapproval that she had expected earlier was now plain on Mindy's face. "Is that what Sven wants?"

"Actually, yes. He doesn't want me to break my promise casually. We agreed that I will write a letter after Christmas cancelling the promise and apologizing. He said that I'll feel better if I do it that way." She watched Mindy's face carefully as she added, "I guess he remembers— and regrets—some mistakes he made with Laura and with his parents."

A wistful expression appeared on Mindy's face. "Who knows? And I guess Laura made mistakes as well. She could be pretty disagreeable when she didn't get her way." She trailed into silence.

Gerri could guess at her unhappy thoughts and tried to figure out a graceful way to move the conversation off this topic. That proved unnecessary as Mindy spoke up again. "So you two are just friends?"

"For now."

Mindy smiled as if a weight had been lifted from her shoulders. "Just like John and me. Or worse. We're a messed up pair, aren't we?"

Gerri smiled wryly and shrugged. *Not for long, I hope...*

Mindy leaned forward in her seat and grinned. "Here's my plan for our next activity. And it'll help you, too. Both couples want to be together in innocent situations. So..." She slapped her hands on her knees. She was, Gerri noted, in full salesmanship mode. "The hospital is putting on an amateur hour Christmas show for the patients. What do you say the four of us sing some carols in the show?"

"Including Sven?"

"Yes, all four... Oh." She acknowledged Gerri's subtext with a nod. "I've been working on that. The more I open my mind, the more I remember what was decent about him. Neither he nor Laura was ready for the situation they found themselves in... I guess he wasn't really a villain—though you'll never get my mother to think that." She laughed nervously. "But I don't want to talk about that now. What do you think about my idea? It gives us an excuse to get together. Not only for the performance, but for the practices. Of course," she made a face, "I've heard your voice. You'll make the rest of us look bad, but who cares?"

———

The next day, Gerri broached the subject while Sven was washing the dishes in his kitchen after a Gerri-cooked meal. She had offered to cook for him occasionally because she couldn't bear to think of his eating his own cooking. More importantly, it was a means for them to innocently spend time together. She leaned against the kitchen counter as she spoke, watching his face carefully to gauge his reaction.

Sven was skeptical at first. "Why would Mindy be interested in singing Christmas carols? I never heard of her doing that before."

Gerri could see his distrust. Much as she regretted it, rapprochement was going to be a gradual process for both him and Mindy. Crossing her fingers and hoping that Mindy didn't feel betrayed, she decided to share Mindy's real reason. If Sven was upset by Mindy and John's pairing, well, Gerri would be hurt—but at least she would have learned something important about Sven. If Mindy was upset that Gerri had told Sven, well, it was for a good cause.

"Mindy and John are interested in each other. They want excuses to be seen together in innocent contexts. They don't want to flaunt their romance."

She waited anxiously for Sven's reaction—any reaction—but he just continued washing with a distant look in his eye. Finally he spoke. "Wow."

Her heart plummeted. "Do you think it will cause a scandal?"

His eyes snapped back to hers. "Huh? I don't think so. I hope not."

"Then, why did you say 'wow?'"

Now he hesitated briefly and then smiled. "Mindy is, let's say, feisty. You've figured that out by now and, heaven knows, I've been on the sharp end of her temper for years.

"I've only met Dr. Wheeler a few times, but I get the impression that he has that doctor thing going: once he makes a decision it's 'I know best. Just do it my way and you'll see.'"

"Well… They seem to have chemistry when they're together."

He chuckled. "I don't doubt it. I only hope that it's not the kind that blows up the chem lab." Then he looked at Gerri thoughtfully. "Anyway, I wish them the best. I think that they might be being too cautious, but…"

Gerri found his insouciance a bit grating. "Cautiousness is reasonable. A black man chasing a white woman is one of the biggest fears for the bigots, after all. People have gotten killed because of the barest suspicion."

"Emmett Till."

"You heard about that even up here?"

Sven smiled ironically. "We have newspapers, even here." While Gerri was trying to decide whether she should apologize—she didn't want to—he added, "But you're right. I didn't hear about it at the time. That was before I started reading newspapers. I was pretty young." Sven was loathe to admit it, but he had actually not heard of Emmett Till until recently, when he had undertaken his reading project in black history after Gerri had left at the end of the summer. Maybe someday, when he had learned enough about black history so that he needn't be embarrassed, he would tell her—but not yet.

Gerri's anger evaporated; now she was just curious. "You didn't hear it when the TV news was on?"

He chuckled. "We didn't even have TV until 1957."

She could empathize. "My family didn't get a TV until just a few years ago either."

He looked amused and shook his head. "No, I mean that Juneau didn't get TV until 1957. The whole town. I remember when they were building and testing the TV station. People would even watch the test pattern."

Gerri was momentarily speechless. She couldn't remember a time when there wasn't TV in her town—at least for those who could afford a set.

Sven brought her back to the present. "Do you think that we need to be similarly careful?"

Gerri considered this for a few seconds. "I think we should be, umm, discrete. A teacher is a role model, after all. But I don't think that

we would be a lightning rod to the extent that they might. They're such a stereotype—the beautiful blond and the black man."

Sven turned and looked at her thoughtfully. Gerri tried to read his expression but couldn't. "You *do* think she's beautiful, don't you?" Abruptly, she realized her mistake. John's words came back to her. Laura was 'Jayne Mansfield' and 'a lot of people like her.' *Will I ever be out of Laura's shadow?* She blurted, "I forgot. Laura is your standard of beauty, isn't she?"

Sven looked annoyed. He wiped his hands on a towel as he spoke. "Yes, I agree that Mindy is a pretty girl. And no, Laura is not my standard of beauty. In high school, I guess you could say that she was my standard of a lust object. And that of many of the other high school boys. But now..."

He dropped the towel on the counter and rested his hands on either side of her, pinning her. "Now, you're my standard of beauty. If you don't know that, I'll just have to keep telling you. Or find some other way to convince you." He leaned forward, looking at her mouth.

Gerri's heart was racing. She wanted this more than anything. But she had achieved a certain comfort with the notion that she would honor her promise until she was able to disavow it. "Sven," she squeaked—she wouldn't let herself look at his lips, "You said that we should wait until I wrote my mother."

"I lied," he said huskily.

"No, you didn't." She found the strength to put her hands on his chest, pushing gently. "And I think you were correct. We'll both feel better for it."

He took a deep, shuddering breath and straightened up. "You're right, of course. I said we could do it—but I never said it would be easy."

Before he could change his mind, he turned back to the sink. "Of course, I'll sing with you," he said briskly. "I'll do whatever you want. Just don't expect me to have a talented voice."

There was the problem of practice. They just couldn't go in cold. Finding a place to practice was a problem—both Mindy and John had apartments and the noise of their practices, however well-intentioned, would be a problem. Gerri hit upon the obvious solution, but had to convince Sven. She broached the idea during her next visit.

"How about practicing at your place? You don't have any close neighbors."

She could tell that he was none too pleased. She glanced around his living room. He couldn't possibly think that it was not presentable. For a house that he had largely built himself, it was very attractive and very welcoming. And he kept it neat—she supposed that was his nautical influence. One of the first things he had told her on the Glacier Gal was that everything must be secured.

She ran through the house in her mind. She had gotten the tour that she had missed that first night when she cooked him his first dinner there. When she got to his studio, she knew she had found the problem. "You can keep the door of your studio closed. They don't have to find out about your painting."

Sven made a face and looked around. Gerri followed his eyes to one of his paintings hanging in the living room itself. "We can move that when they come if you want. But it wouldn't be that surprising that you might buy a Hush painting."

Once he had agreed, the practices became a regular event. Gerri played the hostess in addition to her role in the group. She liked that. It made her wish that the world were simpler and that she could play that role for real.

———

The day of their performance, Gerri was surprised to realize that she had butterflies in her stomach. The audience was smaller than at her college choir performances and the setting was informal. But somehow, there was more at stake here. She needn't have worried. Their part in the amateur hour show was well-received. It made her realize how much she had missed singing.

After their performance, they returned to Sven's house to celebrate. Gerri watched with a smile as Mindy tumbled out of the car and hurried up to the front door. They were all in high spirits.

Every bit as satisfying to her was seeing Sven and Mindy become more and more comfortable with each other. The anecdotes that Mindy was increasingly willing to share suggested that they had once been fast friends.

"Come on, everybody," Mindy shouted from the porch.

"The door's unlocked. Go on in." Gerri turned back to Sven.

Sven gazed at her, transfixed. Gerri wore an expectant smile and her hair was dusted lightly with snow. She looked adorable. And he couldn't get her voice out of his mind—he would never get tired of listening to her sing.

When she saw him staring at her intently, with a ghost of a smile, her heart accelerated. She had an incredible urge to jump on top of him, throwing him to the snow—just to be in his arms. Probably not a good idea—they would have an audience in a few seconds, if they didn't already. She tried to distract herself. "Sven, you sounded very nice tonight."

He laughed. "I'm glad to hear you say that."

"You were worried?"

"Nah, I know my limitations. I'm glad that you're blinded enough by my charms to think that, though." With that, he grinned and closed the gap between them. Then he tilted up her chin and, slowly and thoroughly kissed her. Gerri didn't even pretend that this was just a friendly kiss. She threw her arms around him and held on. It was Sven who regained his willpower first. "We'd better get inside or we'll be out here for a long time."

After the four of them were settled in and had toasted their success—sparkling cider in deference to the non-drinkers, Sven and Gerri—they sat and rehashed their performance.

"I got several compliments on my singing," Mindy said. "You must have gotten more than that, Gerri."

Gerri shrugged. "A few. What I especially liked though were the compliments on how well we sang together."

"They were right. We did sing well together. Of course, you two girls...uh, ladies...were carrying us guys." John smiled fondly at Mindy as he spoke.

"Sven, what were those children saying to you at the end?" Gerri had been curious at the time, but she had been too far away to eavesdrop.

"They liked 'Deck Us All with Boston Charlie' and they wanted to know if there were more verses. I promised to give them copies of the lyrics." He grinned at Gerri. "I had to tell them that I didn't write it. But I also explained that you arranged it. They were impressed."

"Then they were easily impressed," Gerri said, shaking her head. That had been an inspired idea on Sven's part. These were children who had been in the hospital for a while, and who would likely spend Christmas there. Sven had suggested that a steady stream of sentimental songs could sadden them by reminding them of what they were missing.

'Boston Charlie' was a change of pace. It was a nonsense song that Sven had dredged up from 'Pogo,' a comic strip that he doted on. Actually, Gerri hadn't had that much to do. The song was sung to the tune of 'Deck the Halls with Boughs of Holly.' All she had done was to create an arrangement where it was sung as a duet—Sven and her—with a fast pace and alternating lines between them. Not only had it been fun to practice singing for humor, but it had provided an excuse for her to practice privately with Sven. Gerri had even used that opportunity to sing him a ballad or two. The look of longing on his face had been worth her extra frustration.

"Sven," Mindy asked, "What were you and that old man talking about?"

John frowned. "Mr. Koch? He's a disagreeable old cuss. The nurses can't stand him."

Gerri listened anxiously. She, too, had noticed their interaction. Sven's body language had reminded her unpleasantly of his encounter with Knox and his friend in the Arctic Saloon.

Sven hesitated. Reluctantly, he said, "Yes, he's a nasty one—even though he talked as though he was doing me a friendly favor." Sven mimicked an old man's raspy voice. "He said, 'You'd better be careful. Your girl friend is being mighty friendly with that Negro doctor.'"

Everyone looked at Gerri, who shrugged in puzzlement.

"No, that's the thing," Sven elaborated. "He was looking at you, Mindy."

"So, what did you say?"

"I said 'she's not my girlfriend. Furthermore, she's a grown woman, and she doesn't need anyone's help in deciding whom to like. Don't you agree?'"

"Is that all? He looked awfully scared." Gerri looked at Sven sternly.

Sven looked abashed. "I might have scowled at him a little bit." Gerri shook her head in mock resignation, but she didn't reply.

After the ensuing laughter died down, John turned to Mindy: "Don't worry, nobody listens to what Mr. Koch says."

Mindy reached out and squeezed John's hand. "I certainly won't."

Later, as Gerri was trying to go to sleep, that scene kept coming back to her mind. She was forced to admit that her mother had a point. Even if most people were accepting, being in an inter-racial relationship meant being constantly on guard for the 'nasty ones.'

CHAPTER 40

As the days went on—through the Christmas vacation and into January—Gerri found herself spending more and more time at Sven's house. She wanted to give Mindy privacy, as she and John were spending more time together. She also found that she could usually get work done at Sven's. He didn't constantly demand her attention. If he knew that she was working, he simply turned to one of a variety of other activities, including painting, reading, or just chores around the house.

She had discovered his cache of books on the black experience. When she remarked on them, he seemed somewhat self-conscious, so she didn't dwell on them. They included some that she had not read, so she had asked to borrow some, which seemed to please him.

On this early January day, however, she had a different goal. She had promised herself that today she would finish and mail *the* letter to her family. This was the important one—the one where she disavowed her hasty promise to her mother. Sven was in his studio painting, so this was an ideal time for her to get it done. But it was getting dark already and she still hadn't finished.

She had finished most of the letter, but not the hard part. And, as if composing the message wasn't hard enough, she had to word it in a way that would seem innocuous to her sisters. For they *would* see it. Olivia, as the family scribe, had told Gerri that both Marilyn and Joetta devoured all of her letters. Nor was it gracefully possible to send a separate letter solely to Olivia. Marilyn and Joetta were assigned the task of getting the mail from the mailbox on their way home from school. Any letter addressed to Olivia would double their already intense interest. So somehow the message had to be cryptic—understandable to Olivia, but opaque to her sisters.

She looked back over what she had already written. *You're stalling, girl!* She had written, as always, about her experiences in the classroom and about the kids that she taught. Marilyn in particular was fascinated by this. It was a view into a world so different from her high school experience. One where the students could worry about their grades, their crushes, or about the fortunes of the high school basketball team—without having their lives dominated by the tension of the newly instituted school integration.

She had written about their Christmas caroling. They had enjoyed their experience at the hospital so much that they had looked for other opportunities to perform. A casual remark to Sharon Ingram—who, unknown to Gerri, assisted the music teacher with the high school choir—got them an invitation to join a holiday program after school. That performance had won Gerri considerable praise from the students.

One student's reaction was especially gratifying because it caused a turnaround in her class. Barbara Pruitt, a student that Gerri had been struggling to reach, came up to her and said, "You sing so beautifully." She then paused uncomfortably, and added, "I always tell people that I can't do math because I'm a music person. But after hearing you… I'm going to try harder in geometry, Miss Barton. I really am."

Gerri had written about her Christmas—how happy it was even though she missed them all. She told them how she and Mindy decorated Mindy's apartment and supplied their own Christmas tree (but not that Sven helped to get it). She told them how pleased she was to get their telephone call (but not how relieved she was that she was there to receive it rather than at Sven's).

She had *not* told them about the mistletoe incident: "Come stand here in the doorway," Sven had said with a sly look.

Gerri looked up. "What's that hanging there?"

"Mistletoe. Even friends can kiss under mistletoe."

Gerri felt a thrill of excitement, but she had to make at least a token protest, lest she be thought hopelessly gullible. "That's not mistletoe. It looks like a sprig of spruce from our Christmas tree."

"It's Alaskan mistletoe." Sven did his best to look innocent.

"Mindy, come look at this. What does it look like to you?"

Mindy gave it a glance. "A spruce bough," she said confidently.

"Sven claims that it's Alaskan mistletoe."

Mindy looked at Gerri and then at Sven. "I've heard that."

"Really? When?"

Mindy smiled. "Just now." She turned to go to the kitchen. "Let me know when you're done," she said over her shoulder. "I'll show it to John."

Gerri lay down her pen and, abandoning all pretense of writing, relived that kiss for what had to be the twentieth time. It was not a friendly kiss. It was a promissory note to each other of more to come. As always, Gerri had felt a sense of security in his strong embrace. She had nibbled Sven's surprisingly soft lips until she heard him groan. She wanted to grind her body against his, but she knew that Mindy or John could come back into the room at any moment. Mindy, at least, would tease her unmercifully.

As they broke the kiss, Gerri had whispered, "I'll send the letter right after the new year. I promise."

Now it had come full circle. The kiss that had rededicated her to writing the letter was serving as an excuse to delay it.

She looked out the window again. It was darker, but not completely dark. One of the things that fascinated her about Juneau was how long the twilights were. *Maybe a good candidate for a trigonometry project?* It ought to be possible to derive some formulas…

She shook herself. No more distractions. She would finish this letter before dinner—somehow.

——

As they sat down to eat, Sven debated whether to ask her about her progress. He didn't want to nag her, but each day of 'friendship only' was one more too many. If he was to convince her that she belonged with him, he wanted to get started. He was saved the agony of indecision, as she unfolded a sheaf of paper.

"I finished it—finally. Do you want to hear what I wrote?"

"Very much."

"OK. This is the part to my mother. You remember that I couldn't just come out and say it because of my sisters."

"Yes, yes." Sven could hardly contain his impatience.

She read it aloud:

> So, as you can see, I'm enjoying myself. As I live on my own for the first time though, I try to remember the values with which I was raised. Things look different than they did in South Carolina, and less simple. I've come to understand—and you should as well—that assurances made easily there look different here. Some of those assurances, I realize now, are not appropriate and must be changed. But even as I change them, I will try to keep in tune with my moral compass.

She looked at Sven anxiously. "What do you think?"

He hesitated. He didn't want to be dishonest, but neither did he want to say anything that would delay the letter's mailing. "It is a bit oblique, but I think that she will understand it. And I think that your sisters will think of that passage as simply a bit of soul searching—perhaps brought on by your being away for the holidays."

Gerri heaved a sigh of relief. "Good! You can't imagine how hard this was."

Sven wanted to leave well enough alone, but his conscience came to the fore. "What about your father?"

Gerri shook her head. "I'm not worried about him. If she didn't tell him about my promise, then he'll treat it the same way as my sisters. If she did…" She shrugged. "Contrary to the stereotype about fathers, he's always been a little more laid back about my growing up than my mother has. Anyway, *she's* the one that I made the promise to."

"Great! Do you want me to drive you to the Post Office right now so that you can mail it special delivery?"

Gerri swatted him on the arm. "You awful man. I know why you're in a hurry." *The same reason that I am.* "And you know that the Post Office isn't open now anyway."

Gerri and Sven agreed that Olivia had a right to reply, so once the letter was on its way, they had nothing to do but wait.

Sven had vowed not to nag her, so he had taken to covertly studying Gerri's expression every time she greeted him. Finally, almost three weeks later, she entered his house—he had insisted, in one of their few near-arguments, that she needn't knock, as the door was unlocked anyway. One look at her face and he knew that she had gotten her answer. Her expression was overlaid with worry, so it must not have been good. He waited for her to bring it up.

"Hi, Sven. It's snowy out there."

He smiled and put down the book he had been reading. This was another area of good natured disagreement. "You should buy a car. Even in, what?" He glanced pointedly out the window. "Six inches of snow? It's still extra work walking."

"It's not bad. I like it. And I need the exercise." She put down her book bag and took off her hat and coat. It was also important to her not to be intimidated by the winter weather. Some day, after Juneau was but a memory, she would remember and tell these stories. Reminding Sven of that would only cause sadness for both of them.

She sat down opposite him. "I finally got an answer today." He didn't need to respond. She could see him go still. "She understood me, but she didn't accept it. She assigned Marilyn to write the family letters from now on, but she wrote a preface which was very clear." Gerri recited it from memory:

> From now on, Marilyn will write the letters for all of us here. She had promised to do so some while back and,

as I reminded her, we keep our promises in this family. I'm glad you're doing well and we're all anxious for the school year to be over so we can see you again. Love from your mother.

Sven's reaction was swift. "Guilt trip." *Was this why Gerri was worried? And is this kind of guilt trip really going to work?*

"Yes, it is." Gerri sighed. "But remember, she means well."

"So what are you going to do?"

"Nothing. I've already done it. I wrote the letter. And you were right. I feel better for not having gone behind her back."

Sven expelled the breath that he had been holding. "So we can be more than friends?"

Gerri smiled and patted her book bag. "I hope so. There are clothes and toiletries in here along with the books."

Sven jumped up, grabbed her hands, and pulled her to her feet. "I'm so glad," he said, pulling her into an embrace. "Let me take you out to eat to celebrate."

"I'd love to." But she pulled away. "There's one more thing. I want to get it out of the way now." *So it doesn't spoil the evening...* She sat back down, perching on the edge of her chair, and looked up at him entreatingly.

"My mother means well. And, although she's, um, aggressive, she's not entirely wrong. Marriage, the way things are in South Carolina, would be hard—painful, even. That's why I told you earlier that I don't want to talk about marriage. Can we just enjoy what we have?" She looked at him pleadingly. "Our relationship *is* important to me, even though it may not last for long."

Sven looked at her helplessly. He remembered all too well that she had said that, and he had marshaled arguments against it. The hardest part was keeping his mouth shut. But he had to. It was clearly not open for debate now. They had four months until school ended and Gerri was planning to go back to South Carolina. Four months to convince her to stay. There was no guarantee that he would be able to, of course. Life had not always given him what he wanted. But if he tried too soon, he knew that it would just spoil everything.

He took a deep breath and reached for her hands. "I hear you. And I'll try to shut up on that subject."

Gerri let herself be pulled back into his arms. She wanted to say something reassuring, but nothing would come. Instead, she put her arms around his neck and pulled his head down for a kiss. She pressed herself against him and, opening her mouth to his, groaned as they danced a duel with their tongues. He reached down to her bottom and lifted her ever more tightly against him. When he finally broke the kiss, he had a twinkle in his eye.

"I wanted to start this out on a good note," he said, "I had a special night out planned—a real dinner date." He paused. "But if we don't leave soon, I suspect that we never will."

Gerri was tempted to suggest that they skip the dinner out, but she remembered Sven's desire for an 'old fashioned courtship.' How could a girl refuse that? "We can leave now." She winked at him. *I can't believe I actually did that!* "When we get back, can you help me remember where we left off?"

Sven snorted his amusement. "I think I'll remember."

"Are you going to take me to the Kash Cafe?"

"No. There's a new place that's much fancier. I've never eaten there, but I'd like to try it—to make the night memorable." This was the restaurant where he had met Mindy and John last fall. He could only hope that it lived up to its reputation.

"It sounds lovely." *It'd be lovely no matter where we were...*

CHAPTER 41

He was watching her lips and it was driving her crazy. She blotted them delicately with the napkin and tried to compose herself.

It had been going on ever since they were seated in the largely empty restaurant. It was an unacknowledged contest—who could flirt outrageously enough to break the other's composure. The unspoken rules specified, of course, that no one else be able to detect their game. Gerri was pretty sure that she'd made him sweat a couple of times, but she feared that he was winning now.

"Are you hiding those luscious lips from me?" *Oh yes, he was definitely winning!*

"I don't know what you're talking about." She looked at the napkin as if it were the most interesting thing in the room. "I'm not used to eating in a restaurant with cloth napkins."

"Mmmm."

The cloth napkin gambit certainly hadn't distracted him for long. Gerri glanced around the restaurant and tried to think of another conversational topic. She was jolted to see a woman nearby staring at her. She vaguely remembered the woman arriving as the restaurant filled, but she hadn't paid any attention at the time. Now she wondered—was that a disapproving stare?

She leaned forward. "Sven, be good. There's someone staring at us."

Sven shrugged. "Do we care?"

"I care. There may be some of my students' parents here. They don't expect a teacher to be flirting blatantly in public." *Especially not in an interracial relationship...*

He glanced around covertly, noting the woman to whom Gerri had referred. He had hoped to allay Gerri's concerns with a friendly greeting, but the woman wasn't someone he recognized. Gerri was right, though. Left to his own devices, Sven would be inclined to stare the woman down—to give her the scowl, as Gerri would say—but Gerri's position was more vulnerable than his. It was time to end the flirtation game. "I'll be good," he assured her. He paused to think of another conversational gambit. "Am I allowed to say that I really like your dress?"

"Yes, of course. And thank you."

"The color especially is very eye-catching." It also had a V-neck that had distracted him all evening, but he didn't mention that.

She looked down and inspected it briefly. "It's chartreuse. I kind of splurged on it last fall."

"Whatever you paid, it was worth it."

He looked around the restaurant more openly. "It's a lot more crowded than when we came in. We came early, I guess. This is more like the normal Friday night crowd."

Gerri followed his eyes. "It is a very nice place."

Sven regarded her for a moment. "You know…with all that we've been through, this is our first real, traditional date."

Gerri stared at him thoughtfully. "You're right." Then she dimpled. "Unless you want to count the dance in Pelican."

Sven shook his head. "I enjoyed that…a lot. But I wouldn't call it a date. I was too busy worrying about Ace."

"And little did you know that you had absolutely nothing to worry about." She chuckled as she recalled that night. That was when she had first noticed one of the things that she especially liked about Sven: when his honesty clashed with his ego, he chose the honesty and was willing to sacrifice his ego. She still remembered his admission that he had disliked Ace Artin 'for about five minutes' and she still found that endearing.

They each worked on the remnants of their food in silence for a time. Gerri thought about the dress. It was one of two that she had bought thinking of Sven, the other being the sun dress. They were each more daring than her norm. Her sister, Marilyn, had been with her and had advocated for both of them, expressing pleasure that Gerri was stepping out of her conservative mold. Of course, she hadn't told Marilyn that Sven was a motivating factor… Imagining how he might react, though, had put her in such a good mood that she bought a similar dress for Marilyn—just as bright, but with a more conservative neckline. Thinking of that shopping trip reminded her: "I never told you about the rest of the letter."

"Please do." He had a keen desire to learn more about her family and her life in South Carolina—anything that might help him win her hand.

"You know, ignoring my mother's ulterior motives, I'm glad that Marilyn wrote the letter." She realized the truth of that only as she spoke. "She gives me more news about the school than my mother did."

"She goes to the school where you worked?"

Gerri had to smile. "I live in an even smaller town than Juneau. There's only one high school—with integration anyway."

"So you saw her during the day?"

Gerri made a wry face. "Only when she couldn't avoid it. I guess she thought that it wasn't cool to have a sister working there." She paused. "Or at least a sister working as a lowly teacher's aide."

"Or maybe she was afraid that you would be her mother's eyes and ears."

Gerri cocked her head, feeling unexpectedly cheered. "Maybe. I hadn't thought of that."

"So, how is everything going at the school?"

Gerri hesitated. "As well as can be expected. The first year of integration has been chaotic and stressful, as you can imagine."

He looked at her assessingly. "I noticed that you and blondie didn't get along well."

"That was the least of it. There were fights among the students. I mean, there are always a few, but there were more—and along racial lines. And afterward, the white teachers and administrators invariably believed the white students' versions of events. That sort of thing."

Sven wrinkled his nose. *What a terrible place to work. And this was the place that Gerri wanted to go back to?*

"They even cancelled the football season."

"More fighting?"

"Some, but injuries in practice were a bigger factor. The old black high school had a much better football program than the white school—that was common knowledge, at least in the black community. So, when they practiced together, in that atmosphere of stress and frustration…"

"They took it out on each other—and since the black kids were better at it, the white kids started getting hurt."

"Yes, that's about it. They weren't consciously trying to hurt them, but they didn't realize their own power."

Sven's expression was bleak. "I know that syndrome—all too well."

Gerri did a double take, and then she knew… She put her hand on his arm. "Sven, Ronaldo doesn't hold that against you at all. In fact, Elaine told me that it was lucky in a strange way, because it turned Ronaldo in a different direction into a better, more lasting career."

Gerri studied his face. He didn't look completely convinced. She hurried on. "Anyway, the letter wasn't all bad news. Marilyn said that they're having a poetry contest. She's even thinking of entering."

Sven cheered up markedly. In fact, he looked almost mischievous as he asked, "Did you hear that some poets are demanding to be paid according to the quantity of their output? Isn't that perverse?"

Gerri blinked, trying to cope with the sudden change of subject. "Uhh, it sounds a little unreasonable, maybe, but I wouldn't call it perverse."

Sven grinned triumphantly. "But of course it is! If their output is verses and they're paid according to their output, then it's 'per verse.'"

Caught again… Gerri swatted his hand, but didn't even try to conceal her smile. "To think; just a minute ago I was trying to cheer you up."

Sven looked at her with an almost wistful expression. "Maybe bad word plays are my way of trying to cheer *you* up." He paused and his gaze dropped. "I guess that doesn't work, huh?"

Gerri stared at him as he seemed to study the tablecloth. If Wally was right, then Sven's wordplays meant that he was happy. If Sven was happy, then so was Gerri. She squeezed his hand. "It works, Sven. It definitely works."

———

As they got back to Sven's house, they paused on the porch to look back at the city lights.

"I've never seen so much snow in my life," Gerri said wonderingly.

"This is nothing; there'll probably be a couple of feet by morning. Looks like you're getting your first real snowfall."

"It's so beautiful. And it's so quiet."

"Yes, it is. I think that the heavy snow in the air muffles the sounds."

Gerri continued to stare at the vista. She wanted to memorize all of this magical night. *Maybe someday I'll sit on my porch in South Carolina and remember all of this...* Belatedly, she realized that Sven had left her side and moved toward the front door.

He looked back at her speculatively. "Changed your mind?"

She shook her head vigorously. "No, not at all. It's just..." She wasn't about to tell him about her rather depressing daydream. "It's just so peaceful."

She turned and followed him inside. They had barely closed the door when he swept her up into his arms. She put her arms around his neck and drew his head down for a scorching kiss. She loved the feel of his lips and probed with her tongue. When he felt it, he held her tighter and deepened the kiss. She strained against him, but the thickness of their heavy coats muted the sensation.

She stepped back to remove hers. Thinking about what lay ahead, she wanted to clear the air. "Just so you know, I saw Mindy's doctor and got a birth control pill prescription within a few days after we talked about my writing my mother about the promise."

Sven beamed. "Wonderful."

———

Sven was rather proud of himself as he followed Gerri up the stairs to the master bedroom. He had been a gentleman—mostly—throughout their date. He had needed to prove this to himself: that he had grown up and could conduct himself accordingly, even in the face of severe provocation. And make no mistake—Gerri was just that. It took all of his self-control to wait for the reward that he anticipated at the top of the stairs.

At the same time, he was amused with the whole situation. He was trying so hard to be proper, and Gerri was being so understanding. Or he hoped she was; he would be crushed if she simply didn't share his sense of urgency.

Also amusing to him was the superficiality of his decency. There was no nicer sight to him than the movement of her backside as she climbed the stairs. He had carefully positioned himself four steps behind her. From his carpentry experience, he calculated that this put him a bit more than 30 inches below her—a perfect vantage point from which to admire her. Briefly—very briefly—he wondered if she would be impressed with his putting math to what he considered to be a very practical use, but he decided that it would be exceedingly imprudent to ask her.

Gerri could feel Sven's eyes on her as she climbed the stairs. She was sore tempted to put a little extra wiggle into her motion as she climbed. After all, she was as anxious as he was for the love-making that was soon to come. And she loved knowing (except for the misunderstanding in her parents' yard in South Carolina) that he was truly attracted to her.

But that wouldn't be fair. Sven was fighting his own demons— seeking to prove to himself, if to no one else, that he had matured since his high school days and could behave like a responsible man. He had certainly succeeded in Gerri's eyes. In fact, she might have worried that he was a bit too staid, had she not had such glowing memories of last summer's affair. Oh, yes! The man was more than capable of passion that could set her on fire.

When Gerri stepped into Sven's bedroom, she turned around and looked at him expectantly. He grinned and gave her a self-mocking salute. "Permission to ravish you, ma'am?"

Gerri laughed and ran into his arms. After a kiss that left him breathless, she put her lips up to his ear and whispered, "Yes, sailor. Unless I ravish you first."

Then she nipped his ear and ran her hands up and down his back. She loved the feel of his powerful body. She remembered her first impression of him as a concrete block of a man. That had been wrong. Concrete was too coarse to describe Sven. He was a marble statue of a man—worthy of being displayed in a museum. The thought of Sven on display au natural made her feel warm all over.

Sven had reached the limit of his endurance. All he could think about was Gerri—the way she looked and the way she moved. His hands moved fumblingly to the zipper at the back of her dress.

Gerri pulled away. "No, wait."

"Too fast?"

She shook her head and smiled. This was not one of her sweet, dimply smiles that he so loved. This was a slow, seductive smile. "No, that's not it. But the zipper sticks and..."

Now Sven grinned. "And you don't want me to rip the dress off your body."

Gerri pretended to consider. "Actually, that might be interesting. But I don't want to ruin it." She looked at him with a flirtatious grin. "Especially now that I know how much you like it." She turned around in his arms and said, "Now try the zipper—carefully."

The dress came off without difficulty and Gerri draped it over a chair. Sven pulled her against him from behind. He buried his face in the nape of her neck and ran his hands over the front of her body, with special attention to her breasts. As he caressed her nipples through her bra, Gerri felt the need to feel Sven's naked body. She turned around in his arms, but before she could start unbuttoning his shirt, Sven made a noise deep in his throat and, with one hand, quickly unclasped her bra.

Gerri gasped in surprise. "That was...breathtakingly efficient. Have you practiced that move a lot?"

"Not really," he laughed. "But I'd be glad to start practicing if you'd let me practice on you." He bent his head and closed his mouth over her nipple.

Gerri felt limp as she gave herself up to sensation. "It's been so long," she murmured. She tried to undo his slacks, but the nips, licks, and tugs on her breasts robbed her of her coordination. Sven used one hand to help her with his clothes and then stepped back to finish the job as Gerri did likewise. She was gratified to see that he was breathing heavily and so obviously desired her.

He turned her around again and started caressing her breasts again. Her nipples were hard with arousal, and she sighed in contentment. Sven's arousal pressed aggressively against her, heightening her sense of anticipation.

"You like this?" Sven growled in her ear.

"Mmmm," was all she could manage in reply.

"I'll consider it my sacred duty to accommodate you whenever you so desire."

One of his hands roamed lower, stroking the growing moistness at the top of her thighs. Gerri was impatient now and started to speak. "Sven, let's..." But he had anticipated her urgency and, twisting, tumbled them both onto the bed. She fleetingly worried about her weight landing on top of him, but he didn't seem to notice. They both laughed as they briefly wrestled for a comfortable position. When they had settled—Gerri on her back and Sven on his side next to her—she looked into his eyes as she reached out and squeezed his arousal. *Mine!* She thought with satisfaction.

"Yours," Sven said with conviction. Gerri stared at him. Had she said that aloud? *So much for dignity...* Then coherent thought departed as he again caressed the softness between her legs.

In less than a minute, she could feel herself coming to climax. "Now, Sven," she panted. "I'm ready."

"Soon," he answered, continuing his ministrations to her sensitive core. She could no longer muster a response. Just as she thought that she couldn't hold out any longer, he moved onto her and entered her with one smooth, powerful stroke. She gave a long groan of satisfaction.

He started thrusting in and out, breathing heavily as he did so. Gerri pushed back against him vigorously and ground her hips. Soon, she felt him quicken his pace. She held on tighter and was soon pushed over the edge. As she climaxed with a cry, she felt him release inside her with his own triumphant roar.

They lay, panting and slick with sweat in the aftermath. She clung to him tightly to keep him inside her. After a minute, she maneuvered—ever so carefully—to climb on top of him. "I don't want to lose you," she explained unnecessarily. Once in place, she ground against him.

"You don't give a guy much rest."

"Do you want me to stop?"

"No," he grunted. Sure enough, he was soon matching her stroke for stroke. She looked him in the eye as they moved together. He raised his arms to massage her breasts as they moved, watching with pleasure as her eyes grew unfocused. As she reached another climax, he took her hips in his hands and moved her rhythmically until he, too, was there.

Much later, they lay in each other's arms and waited for sleep to take them. "I've missed this so much," Gerri said softly.

"So have I, my love. So have I."

Later yet, Sven muttered, "I promise that I won't tell anyone that we had sex on our first date."

Gerri snorted as she considered how to respond. *Was that a word play? Not exactly, but he deserves something...* "I'm glad to hear you say that," she finally said. "It shows that you have an important quality for a man living on the last frontier."

"What's that?"

"A well-developed survival instinct."

———

Gerri woke to the sound of the wind howling. She was curious about how much snow there was, but she couldn't bring herself to get up and look out the window—she just felt so snug cuddled next to Sven—the best heating pad ever. Said heating pad moved in his sleep and Gerri moved with him, maximizing the contact of their bodies.

As she lay there, she tried to plan their morning. She would make a special breakfast and then, if the snowfall was impressive, she wanted to go outside and experience it firsthand. That would help with the soreness that she felt after last night's lovemaking. Not that she was complaining—in fact, she wriggled with delight as she remembered…

"You're full of energy."

"Sorry, I thought you were asleep. Did I wake you up?"

"I think that you moving against me will always wake me up—and thank goodness for that." With that he reached for her.

She decided that breakfast and the snow could wait…

CHAPTER 42

The next three months were happy ones for Sven. He and Gerri spent as much time together as her schedule allowed. She became a frequent, albeit discreet, overnight guest. They had even, on that first weekend, made a snowman in his yard. The biggest storm of the season had dropped about thirty inches and Gerri had been mesmerized. He still smiled when he remembered her entreaties. "Come on, Sven. I've made only one snowman in my whole life. And that one was about five inches tall. There wasn't enough snow to make it any bigger."

Still, achieving this happiness required him to adopt a selective tunnel vision. Gerri refused to talk about the future beyond the end of the school year, other than making it clear that she felt the pull of South Carolina—both of her family and of the need to be a part of the struggle for change.

He still had the engagement ring that he had bought with the bonus from the infamous hunting trip. It was safely tucked away and, of course, Gerri didn't know about it. She might well never find out about it. Sven had considered—and still hadn't ruled out—a last minute proposal. But, given her knowledge of his desires and her obvious discomfort with the whole subject, that might simply stoke her resentment and poison their relationship.

That friendship was important to him for its own sake. And it gave him an excuse to stay in touch if Gerri should decide to leave. Who knew? He was almost thirty and he knew his mind, but she was young. Was it possible that someday she would see things differently? That Juneau—and Sven—would seem more attractive in a few years? He could tell that she enjoyed her job. And she had made it abundantly clear that she *was* more than fond of him—even though she had never mentioned love.

A few years. He smiled again, a bit bitterly, as he rolled that around in his mind. Not likely, really. More likely that she would meet some young man down there. Someone close to her age and who shared her interests. *And who was not a jerk*, he added, remembering Thurman. There would undoubtedly be numerous men who would appreciate Gerri as she deserved.

He shook his head to clear it of these thoughts. Brooding wasn't going to help. He picked up his brush and returned to the painting he had been working on, clamping his tunnel vision firmly back into place.

———

What was a life made of? Gerri wondered this, not for the first time. Her work was challenging, occasionally frustrating, but mostly rewarding. Her friendships were satisfying, even though those with the other teachers were primarily 'school' friendships—her busyness and her reluctance to flaunt her relationship with Sven kept the evening socializing to a minimum. Wally and the fishing community had accepted her, especially since the appendicitis episode.

Mindy was a true friend. None of the girls that she had known in South Carolina would she trust more. She missed some of them, but kept in touch with occasional letters.

Then there was the elephant in the room. Sven. Gerri smiled at that metaphor, given his size. But though he might be as strong as an elephant, he was much, much more handsome. Maybe not to a female elephant, but certainly to Gerri. In a simpler world, nothing would have made Gerri happier than to settle down with him and raise a family. But the world of 1970 was anything but simple.

The friends that she corresponded with told her stories of the triumphs and agonies of the Civil Rights movement. She still had access to the major news developments—yes, Juneau had a newspaper. But her friends' tales lent immediacy to it all.

She had joked to two of them (at least they thought it was a joke) that maybe she would stay in Alaska and marry some 'bearded Scandinavian.' One friend had jokingly warned her about jungle fever, and the other had replied in highly scandalized tones that she 'shouldn't forsake the movement' and that 'everyone was needed.'

All of this reminded her of her mother's objections (now delivered in a subtle subtext through Marilyn). Gerri really would be burning her bridges by staying and marrying Sven. Heaven knew she loved him. She had stopped trying to kid herself about that after he came back from that terrifying hunting trip. But would the sweet cream of love curdle in the acid bath of rejection by her friends and family? She had to chuckle at that tortured prose. Now she could appreciate why lovers resorted to poetry. Too bad she couldn't share it with Sharon Ingram, but it was just too personal, too revealing.

Her thoughts circled back to Sven and the notion of a bearded Scandinavian. He looked delicious in a beard. He didn't wear one regularly, but he let one grow when he was fishing. She had convinced him to let his hair grow longer, but she hadn't mentioned his making his beard permanent. It was bad enough to feel the weight of obligations from her family and friends back home. She didn't want Sven to change his life for her, only to have her leave anyway.

And Sven wasn't making this any easier. Thinking about her friend's 'jungle fever' remark one day had led Gerri to impulsively ask Sven, "What do you really see when you look at me?" She should have known that that was a bad idea. He was silent for so long that she wanted to take the question back.

"You don't have to answer that," she finally said. "I didn't mean to put you on the spot. I was just curious."

"I want to answer. I just don't want to mess up my answer. It's a complicated question."

Suddenly, she was convinced that she really didn't want to hear his answer, because it might destroy her illusions. Before she could think of a graceful way to dissuade him, he had started talking.

"I see you in a lot of different ways. As a lover, I see you as a sensual, passionate woman. And one who utterly destroys the notion that a woman can't be sexy, fit, and strong at the same time.

"As a friend, I see you as a solid rock. Someone who's a pleasure to be around. Someone on whom I can always depend, and whom I would trust with my life—and have." He quirked a brief smile as they both remembered his appendicitis. Gerri's heart was pounding already, but he was not done.

"As a man passing you on the street, I see an arresting woman. Someone whose smile, once seen, makes a guy say silly things to try to bring it back. And the dimples..." He smiled and shook his head in mock resignation.

"As another human being observing you, I see someone who is bright, inquisitive, and determined to live a good life.

"As an artist, I see a woman who's a pleasure to paint. Your beauty shines through and your dark complexion gives extra drama to your eyes and your smile."

He finally stopped and looked at her expectantly. She could barely reply. She just shook her head and murmured, "Goodness, Sven!"

No, that didn't make her departure any easier. *Be careful what you ask for...*

———

That was a month ago. Now, at the end of April, the end of the school year was only weeks away. She couldn't put off her private day of reckoning much longer. And no matter what she did, she would disappoint someone terribly. Her relationship with Sven was growing more strained. It seemed as though he was pulling away from her in anticipation of her departure.

Gerri wanted to reassure him, but she could not. She decided that, at the very least, she wanted to be remembered by him as the best first mate that he'd ever had. As she was getting dressed, she smiled in the mirror. He had been so careful to avoid a word play on 'first mate,' even though it must have been tempting. He, in his shy, courtly way, wouldn't have wanted to take a chance on offending her. Not only would she not have been offended, but, in her own mind, she embraced it: Sven had been *her* first mate, and she wouldn't have it any other way.

Which explained—after a fashion—the care with which she dressed today. She had promised to help him do some work on the Glacier Gal. Not only did she want to help him—possibly one last time—but she wanted to spend one more day on the boat that she'd come to love.

She looked in the mirror again. *There. That will have to do.* Her checklist was complete: nappy hair, baggy sweatshirt, and sweatpants. To honor the almost-full-year since she had first walked down the float and met Sven, she had decided to recreate that look. The only place where she drew the line was the breast band. There was no point in hiding her breasts—Sven knew them well. Also, the band was uncomfortable.

"How do I look?"

Mindy thought it was hilarious. "You certainly have an interesting notion of romance. You be sure and tell me what he says." Belatedly, she added, "You look just like you did a year ago. Except…" She looked closer. "You're not wearing the band. Good. You don't want to discourage him completely."

It was a clear day. *A good omen, maybe?* As Gerri walked to the boat harbor, she found herself enjoying the weather and the walk. She lost herself in reminiscence and didn't hear the car until it was passing her. She had just remembered the car which had passed her last year when this one screeched to a stop and then backed up to where Gerri was. It, too, was filled with teenage boys. This time, however, they were familiar.

The driver spoke up. "Hi, Miss Barton. Do you want a ride?"

Someone from the back seat answered for her. "No. Remember, she likes to walk."

"You're, ummm…dressed so casually, I almost didn't recognize you."

"I'm going to be painting today. Can't wear anything that can't get paint on it."

With several farewells from various points in the car, they rumbled off. Gerri suppressed her chuckle until they were out of sight. They had been so diplomatic in commenting on her clothing and, thank goodness, they hadn't remarked on her hair at all.

Finally, she was there. Sven had once said, in an intimate moment, "I didn't know it before, but I must have been prescient when I named the boat. You're the true glacier gal". He was in shirtsleeves, even on this cool day, and Gerri just watched him for a minute as he worked on deck. Her heart filled and her breath caught in her throat. Her man and her namesake boat. She loved them both. As much as she wanted this moment to last, it couldn't. She raised her voice. "Excuse me, Sir."

Sven straightened up slowly and looked her over. Finally, a small smile touched the corners of his mouth. "It's been quite a year, hasn't it?"

Gerri stepped aboard, struck with a feeling of insecurity at his words. He obviously recognized her 'costume.' Was he simply acknowledging that? Or was he acknowledging that the year—and their time—was over? She said, in as upbeat a tone as she could muster, "Yes, it has. The best year of my life."

Sven nodded. "Mine, too." But he turned back to his work.

Feeling a little melancholy, she turned toward the cabin. "I'll get started cleaning up inside."

Sven watched her disappear. He felt like two cents. This waiting was hard. But he knew that Gerri wasn't being intentionally cruel. In fact, it was probably harder on her than on anyone else. She didn't want to talk about it, but he knew that she was being pulled in all directions. Her mother, of course, was a prime manipulator, but Gerri had dropped hints that others—friends from school, perhaps—were joining in the chorus.

His guilt spiked again as he thought of Olivia Barton. It wasn't entirely fair to think of her as a manipulator. Her tactics were manipulative, but that was her only choice, as she saw it. Her motivation was, in large part, a completely sincere concern—no, better to call it a fear—for the welfare of her daughter.

Sven was a long way from understanding this, but the more he delved into his new 'black experience' library, the more he was forced to admit that practically any degree of paranoia on her part was reasonable.

His ruminations were interrupted by a shout. "Sven!"

He couldn't hide his astonishment. Mindy? He couldn't remember *ever* seeing her at the boat harbor. And she was running towards him. "Where's Gerri? I need to talk to her."

He started to gesture toward the cabin, but Gerri appeared in the doorway.

"Gerri." Mindy paused to catch her breath. "Your brother just called."

Gerri erupted in a wide smile; the first that Sven had seen for quite a while. "Wonderful. He was supposed to get back into the country next week. I guess he's early. Did he say he's in Seattle? Did you get his number? I'll call him back."

"No, no. He didn't leave a number. He's at the airport."

That stopped Gerri cold. "The Juneau airport?"

"Yes. He needs a ride. He said he'll take a cab if you want him to, but he doesn't know where to tell them to go." She hesitated. "Do you want me to pick him up? John is waiting for me, but I'm sure he'll understand."

Gerri took a deep breath. "No, I'll pick him up." She turned to Sven, but he spoke first.

"Take my truck."

"Thank you, Sven." She was already off the boat and walking briskly along the float, with Mindy hurrying to keep up.

Sven watched as she disappeared. This was not good news. Olivia was undoubtedly bringing in the backup troops to ensure that Gerri returned home. And her hurried, rather formal thanks—that disturbed him as well. She didn't have to thank him. Whatever was his was hers. Her doing so was a symptom of the increasing distance between them.

Still, if this was the endgame, then he would at least welcome the end of the grinding uncertainty.

CHAPTER 43

As she drove to the airport, Gerri's stomach became knotted. She was excited to see Rich—and *so* relieved that he had returned safely from Vietnam. But she couldn't help but be suspicious. How did he get Mindy's phone number? Her mother's fingerprints were all over this—as if Gerri needed more pressure on her than she already had.

After parking the truck, she paused to make a quick, largely futile attempt to put her hair to rights, then, taking a deep breath, she trotted into the terminal.

Her misgivings were buried at the first sight of him. She gave him a gigantic hug and muttered some words of joy. Then she pulled back and looked at him more closely. He had worn his dress uniform for his flight. "Oh Rich, you look wonderful. You're all right? No injuries?"

"Nothing serious. A few dings here and there." She frowned at that. "Really," he laughed, "I'm fine."

"How long can you stay?"

"I have only a few days." With that reminder, he moved to pick up his luggage. "I guess we'd better get moving."

Outside, he glanced from her to the truck with an amused expression. "Is that yours? Between the truck and your outfit, it looks like you're trying to act like you're still on the farm."

"No, it's Sven's. I borrowed it. And the old clothes are because we were getting ready to work on his boat." To Gerri's relief, Rich hadn't commented on her nappy hair. That would have been much harder to explain.

Rich's smile dimmed a bit. "Ahhh. The famous Sven. Am I going to get to meet him?"

"Of course. I'll take you straight to the boat harbor."

She peppered him with questions about Vietnam as they drove. As he talked, she tried to plan the next few days. *Would Sven be willing to put Rich up?* She decided to ask him privately as soon as she had the chance. Then she had a worse thought. She had been circumspect about staying at Sven's, but not inside the house. There would be numerous traces of her occupancy there. She wasn't ashamed of that, but it wasn't something that she wanted to discuss with her brother.

She parked at the small parking area for the boat harbor. Rich got out of the truck and took a puzzled look around. Gerri gestured. "That's the boat harbor. Let's take your luggage with us." Walking down the boat harbor ramp, Gerri found herself explaining the large tide swing to Rich and how she had made a trigonometry assignment out of it. *Does he even care? Am I giddy, or am I just nervous?*

She needn't have worried about Sven. He was, considering his quiet nature, practically effusive in his hospitality. When he saw them walking toward the boat, he smiled his most endearing smile (Rich couldn't be expected to appreciate it, but Gerri certainly did).

"I'm certainly happy to meet you, Rich. I've heard a lot about you. Gerri, if you haven't made other plans, I insist that Rich stay with me. I have plenty of space and it's no inconvenience."

"That would be great." Rich looked at Gerri for her assent. He certainly didn't have a lot of hotel money in his budget. Also, Olivia's briefing had indicated that Gerri was not logical on the subject of Sven, so Rich welcomed the chance to observe him—and question him— more closely.

"Thank you, Sven," she said enthusiastically. "Are you sure that your house is, uhh, ready for a visitor?" She cast what she hoped was a significant look at him. Sven grinned at her with the slightest of winks—fortunately on the side away from Rich. *Thank heavens, he understands...*

"I keep my house pretty shipshape, but I'll give it a quick onceover before you get there."

Before…? Gerri's look of puzzlement was obvious.

"I'd like to ask you a favor," Sven explained. "I have a couple of errands to run and I'll swing by the house to check on everything. Would you mind fueling up the Gal while I take care of that other stuff? I'm getting ready for a short shakedown cruise, and I thought we could use that to show Rich a bit of our beautiful country."

Gerri blinked. She knew that Sven trusted her to operate the Glacier Gal, but, with the exception of his appendicitis attack, he had always been there with her. Some part of her realized that Sven was trying to send a message to Rich. "Sure," she said as nonchalantly as possible. "Rich, would you like that?"

"Whatever you say, uhhh…" He looked around. "Where's the fuel?"

Gerri laughed. "About ten minutes that way." She gestured. "On the other side of town. I'll show you how pretty the town is from the water. You'll like it."

Gerri enjoyed herself immensely on the jaunt across the harbor to the Union Oil dock. It was such a good feeling to have Rich with her, safe and sound. She took an inordinate amount of pride in pointing out the sights—showing off this town, which was, for the time being, hers. She pulled out Sven's binoculars to point out things such as landmarks. She even pointed out Sven's house. It was partially hidden by the trees on his lot. She also noted—but didn't point out—that Sven's truck was parked at the house. That was good. He had apparently understood her coded message to 'sanitize' the house—removing any sign of Gerri's occupancy—and had wasted no time getting there.

But the best part of the trip for Gerri was the look on Rich's face when she matter-of-factly started the engine, checked that it was running smoothly, untied the lines, and eased out of the boat harbor. This was her big brother, after all. Always older and more knowledgeable than she. Now he wasn't even trying to hide his amazement at her relaxed competence and the casual trust that Sven had placed in her.

"So he just lets you take the boat. Just like that?"

"Why not? I can handle it. In fact, I'm good at it."

"It's a big boat for just one person."

"You mean for a woman." She laughed as she said it, because the last thing she wanted was to start an argument over something silly. She had a feeling that there would be enough contention once he got around to making their mother's pitch—which she was sure he would do any minute. "Wait until you meet my roommate, Mindy," she grinned. "She's a real Women's Libber. She'd give you an earful if she thought you were suggesting that."

"Is she the woman who answered the phone?" Gerri nodded and Rich grinned ruefully. "I'll be careful."

As they approached the fuel dock, Gerri was pleased to see that they were the only customers. She didn't feel like waiting today. Paul Pruitt, the attendant, was out of his shack to help tie her up as she came alongside.

"Just you today?" He greeted her as she came out of the cabin.

"Sven's running some errands." Paul was looking at Rich with frank curiosity. "I got a nice surprise today. Paul, this is my brother, Rich Barton. He's just back from Vietnam. Rich, this is Paul Pruitt. His daughter's in one of my classes."

The two men chatted as Paul fueled the boat. They were comparing services—apparently Paul had served in Korea. When the tank was full and Paul was writing up the receipt, Gerri remembered something else.

"Paul, ask Barbara to remind me on Monday that I have a book for her."

Paul grinned wryly. "Another assignment? She'll love *that*."

Gerri shook her head, untied the boat, and tossed the line back to Paul. "No, not at all. It's a book on music and mathematics. It's just a little gift because she's improved so much."

"I'll tell her. And thank you for working with her." He was talking loudly now, as the boat drifted away from the dock. Gerri saluted him and went into the pilot house to fire up the engine.

Rich pulled a camera from his coat pocket and started fiddling with it. "I just bought this at the PX and I'm still learning how to use it." He took a few shots of the town and then turned to Gerri. "I'd like to take some pictures of you."

"There's probably not enough light in the pilot house," said Gerri hastily. "There will be plenty of time for that later." Rich seemed to be mollified by that and went out on deck to take more pictures of the town. Gerri breathed a sigh of relief. There was no way she wanted her scruffy look recorded on film.

Then Gerri realized that Rich was delaying the inevitable conversation, just as she was. She didn't want this hanging over her head. They could at least lay their cards on the table now, when there was no one else around. *But it could take a while…* She throttled the engine down to just above idling. As long as she stayed clear of boat and seaplane traffic, they could take as long as they wanted getting back to the boat harbor.

Rich immediately came in, looking worried. "Is something wrong? It seems like we just slowed down."

"No, nothing's wrong. I want to talk while we have some privacy." Rich leaned against the door facing her. He looked resigned.

"I know that Ma got you to come up here to talk some sense into me. She's been trying to work on me ever since I left there."

"Gerri, it was my choice to come up here. I wanted to see you."

"I'm glad to see you, too. But that doesn't refute what I said."

He looked uncomfortable. "She's worried about you, Gerri."

Gerri rolled her eyes. "Believe me; she's made that abundantly clear."

"She's concerned that you…" He hesitated, worried that he might offend Gerri and poison the conversation. "That you have a crush on Sven. And afraid that you might do something that you'll later regret."

Gerri laughed—brief and rather bitter. "'Crush.' What an interesting word. Very useful when you want to trivialize the emotion." She paused as she adjusted the boat's heading slightly. "Well, I give you credit for not beating around the bush too much." She gave a slight nod as a salute.

He paused and she could see him searching for words. He was desperate for information, and she decided to help him out. "I'm happy here. I have a real teaching job, which I enjoy. I have a mentor whom I value tremendously. I have friends that I like being with and to whom

I can turn when I need them. Sven is one of them." Gerri decided upon honesty—it would come out anyway. "He is very important to me. He's saved my life—literally—and I've saved his." She took a breath and then puffed it out between pursed lips. "I don't know how to describe everything he means to me without talking for hours."

"You're sleeping with him, aren't you?"

Gerri scowled at him. "That's none of your business. I'm grown."

Rich groaned. That was as good as an answer. He cast around for a way to avoid an outright fight. "Tell me about him."

Gerri smiled beatifically and started talking. She tried to keep it short, but by the time she stopped, it was obvious to Rich: she had it bad. She had also had a much more eventful year than he had ever dreamed. He switched to a different tack. "You'd be cutting yourself off from everyone you know in South Carolina if you comeback flaunting a white lover."

Gerri glared at him. "You don't understand. He won't be a lover. If I decide to stay here, I'll marry him."

"Just like that? What makes you think he's willing?"

"Willing? Sven *wants* to marry me." *At least he did a few months ago...* Gerri worried again about their increasing distance from each other. But she refused to let that show on her face.

Rich made a face. He wouldn't let himself speak, but his skepticism was obvious. Gerri watched him and agonized. This was her big brother who loved her and wanted the best for her, as did their mother. She couldn't stand it if she caused a rift with them.

She reached out and laid her hand on his forearm. "Rich, I want you to know that I'm not taking this casually. I've been agonizing about it for months now. I don't want to disappoint Ma. Or you. Or myself. I don't want to cut myself off from my friends in South Carolina. I want to please everybody. But guess what. That's impossible. No matter what I do, I'll make someone unhappy. Somebody will be disappointed in me."

Rich regarded her soberly, and then his expression softened. "Oh, Gerri, you always did want to please everyone." He hesitated again. He didn't really want to know the answer to this question, but... "What about pleasing Gerri? What would you want if you didn't have to please anyone but Gerri? What would you do then?"

Gerri considered that. Oddly enough, having Rich as her devil's advocate had helped her with her dilemma. Her eyes welled up. She spoke softly so that he could barely hear her over the engine noise. "I'd settle here. I'd marry Sven and raise a family with him. But…"

Rich hesitated. He knew that Olivia would want him to press harder on Gerri, but he couldn't bring himself to do it. Gerri was right—she was grown. Rich had done his duty to their mother. He had a duty to Gerri as well. "And you're sure that he wants to marry you?"

Gerri remembered Sven's 'how do I see you' soliloquy. "I'm sure." Then she remembered their increasingly uncomfortable interactions and smiled hesitantly. "Unless I've turned him off with all my dithering. But what about Ma?"

Rich shrugged, a slight smile playing around his lips. "She'll be angry with you—for about two days. Then she'll get over it and love you both." Gerri smiled, imagining that. "She never had anything to say against him, you know. Only that she was afraid. There was something about a picture…"

Gerri giggled. "Sven painted a picture of me as a gift and showed it to them. It was…"

"It wasn't a nude or anything, I hope."

"No!" Gerri looked scandalized. "Heavens, no. He wouldn't do that. It was just… Never mind. I'll show it to you when we get to Sven's house. Remind me."

With a small smile on her face, she lapsed into silence. Rich almost didn't want to know what this picture looked like. He decided to change the subject. "You talked about being cut off from your friends in South Carolina…"

"Yes?"

"I think that they'll get over this, too. If they don't?" He shrugged dismissively. "People drift apart. Remember, you're the one with the exciting life right now. They might envy you." Of course, he reminded himself, this was all conditional on her having read Sven's intentions correctly. It wouldn't be the first time a woman was wrong about this sort of thing…

"I understand what you're saying. I could live with my friends' disapproval. I like them, but I barely write them once a month—I just don't have time. I really, really hate to disappoint Ma, though."

"She'll be OK. Her heart's in the right place." He stopped and scratched his head. He really didn't want to get into this now, but maybe Gerri needed the distraction. "I'm in her dog house, too, you know."

"Why? What did you do?"

"I'm going to reenlist." Gerri stared at him in shock, but before she could erupt in protest, he quelled her with a raised hand. "They're not going to send me back to Vietnam. I'll be going to school—electronics and maybe that new stuff with computers. I'll have to promise them a certain number of years' service in return, but I'll have some pretty valuable training."

"That's wonderful, Rich. How…"

"How did it happen? I took an aptitude test some time ago. When I got back from the 'Nam, they asked me to take another." He smiled bashfully. "It's just that Barton math knack, I guess."

Gerri digested this. He was right—all four kids seemed to have a knack for math. Even Marilyn, who seemed to care more about being difficult, was good at it when she wanted to be.

Then she considered the wider implications—for the family and her parents. "But they were hoping that you'd come home…maybe take over the farm…"

His smile disappeared. "Yes, and in an ideal world, I'd like to. But…" He made a face. "It's not just the racial problems. You have those, more or less, everywhere. I'll bet you've had some here." He stopped and looked at her inquiringly.

She nodded hesitantly. *A topic for another time…* "Yes, some. But I've always been able to deal with them. And, most importantly, I've always had help and support from others when I needed it."

"Including Sven, I hope."

"Most definitely. *Especially* including Sven," she assured him.

"Good." He made a mental note to ask her for details—but later. "On the farm, you know that tobacco is the crop that brings in the best money. But as I try to look down the road—years ahead—I don't see a rosy future for it. More and more people are talking about the health hazards of smoking. The government's even getting into it. Tobacco will be around for many years, but the golden age of the golden leaf is over."

"If you're right, what'll become of Ma and Dad?"

"Even if I'm right, this isn't going to happen quickly. They'll be retired by the time it gets too bad. And besides," he grinned, "they'll have us, with our supposedly wonderful jobs, to help them out in their old age."

CHAPTER 44

With the Glacier Gal throttled back up to cruising speed, it took only a few minutes to get back to the boat harbor. In this short period of time, Gerri was only too happy to talk about Sven, and Rich was only too happy to listen.

"No, he's not mathematically inclined, but he respects that I am. He…" She paused to decide how to express her thoughts. "He has vision. I think that contributes to his being a highliner—that's a fisherman who regularly does better than others. And I'm sure that's why he's such a good painter. Somehow, he sees patterns and can express them.

"He senses patterns in sound as well. It's as though whenever he hears a word, he thinks of others that sound similar. He likes to make puns—at least when he's happy, according to Wally. Wally's another friend of his," Gerri hastened to add.

Gerri had to stop talking at this point. They had arrived at the boat harbor and maneuvering in the relatively tight quarters required all of her attention. Sven was waiting with Wally at the Glacier Gal's slip. *Does he look impatient?* Gerri hoped he wasn't angry that she had taken so long.

"Let me shut up and concentrate. With everyone watching, this would be a bad time to fumble the docking."

She needn't have worried. Rich threw Sven a line as she turned the boat and backed carefully into the slip. She shut down the engine quickly and, bracing her hand on the gunwale, hopped briskly onto the float. She wanted to say something to Sven to apologize for taking so long to get fuel. But, she realized, she wanted even more to tell him about the decision she'd made.

She put her hands on his arms and looked into his eyes. "Sven, I…" Then she lost her nerve. Her vocal cords froze up as he solemnly returned her gaze. This was tantamount to proposing—to a man who may not be interested any more. With several other people watching. It was such a Women's Lib sort of thing to do. She wished that she were Mindy. Mindy would know what to do.

Sven waited for her to continue. Yes, he had been impatient waiting for her return. But he wasn't surprised. Rich had come up to proselytize for Olivia's point of view. Sven had come back to the float prepared for anything, but now he had to try to read their expressions to figure out where he stood. Before her hesitation, Gerri had seemed happy—that was a good sign. Rich was harder to read. Was that a faint smile playing over his lips?

Sven knew it was a gamble, but he decided that now was the time to roll the dice. He put an index finger against Gerri's lips. "Don't say anything."

Obediently, Gerri stopped talking, but she was deathly afraid. Did he not want to hear? She just stared at Sven, unwilling to catch Rich's eye. After what seemed like forever, but was really just a couple of seconds, Sven smiled. His other hand went into his pocket and he brought out a small box.

Before she knew it, he was on one knee in front of her. "Remember, I said that I wanted to do this the traditional way. Gerri, will you accept this as a token of my love? More importantly, will you marry me? Anytime, anyplace."

"Yes, Sven. I absolutely will. I love you, too." She belatedly became aware of their audience and tugged on his sleeves. "Now stand up and kiss me."

He did so with enthusiasm and, for a moment, the other people ceased to exist. She heard some muted cheers, but she ignored them. She wanted to cling to this moment. Then she heard a click and quickly turned her head.

Rich had the camera to his eye. "Rich, don't you dare take a picture."

"Why not?" He laughed. "This will be part of the family history."

She remembered her baggy clothes. Her hand flew to her hair. "I have to be the worst looking woman who ever got proposed to. At least, let me fix my hair."

"You look wonderful," Sven interjected. "If necessary, I'll buy the picture from him."

She could see that they were all against her. She protested weakly, "I'll get you for this, Rich. I'll push you in the water."

Wally started laughing. "She will, too. You be sure and hand me your camera first."

Rich grinned and looked at them. Sven still had his arms around Gerri's waist. "I'll tell you what," Rich said, "I might be willing to consider making the picture a wedding present." Gerri just leaned her head on Sven's chest. It wouldn't do to have them see her smiling.

Wally approached with his hand outstretched. "Congratulations, Sven. You've been carrying that ring around long enough. I've been wondering when you were going to get up your nerve."

Gerri's head snapped up at that. "When did you buy this ring, anyway?"

Sven looked evasive, but Wally chimed in. "He bought it right after that hunting trip. You remember the one…"

She glared. "That's what you used that big bonus for?" Sven's sheepish look was all the answer she needed. Her hands, still wrapped around him, thumped him in the back. "Oooh! I ought to be so angry with you. Don't you ever do anything like that again. You could have been killed on that trip. Then, where would I be?"

Now, he looked mischievous. "You don't have to worry about my doing that again. This is the last time that I'm going to get engaged. Now, will you try it on so that we can see if it fits?"

This was her perfect day, Gerri reflected. How he had done it, she wasn't sure, but the ring fit perfectly. As she was admiring it, Sven introduced Wally and Rich, and then Wally excused himself to return to his boat.

Sven turned to Gerri. "Why don't we go back to the house and whip up a dinner? Proposing gives me a real appetite."

Gerri stretched up and kissed him again. "Accepting a proposal gives me an appetite, too. But before I start cooking, I want to tell Mindy."

The phone call took some time and was punctuated by considerable squealing. By the time Gerri had hung up, Rich had unpacked and changed out of his uniform. Sven was telling Rich about his impressions of the South.

Gerri interrupted them, her eyes bright with excitement. "Mindy and John want to come over and help us celebrate. Do you mind, Sven? She's already cooking, and she offered to bring the food."

"Of course, I don't mind. Even if I did mind, the food would sway me. She's almost as good a cook as you are."

"Maybe better," Gerri said loyally. "They'll be here in a few minutes."

Sven nodded and turned back to resume his conversation with Rich. "Anyway, it was very interesting, but it was a severe culture shock. I think that's what they call it. And the weather! I couldn't believe how hot it was in November. I guess it never freezes."

"It does now and then," Gerri insisted. "Remember what my father told you about the orange groves freezing?"

"Right." Sven acknowledged her correction. "Practically never freezes."

Rich perked up. "That must be what Dad was talking about. He said to be sure to tell you that they had a freeze a couple of months ago. Cost the farmers lots of money."

At the sound of a car engine, Gerri bounced up from her seat and started for the door. Then, she paused and turned back to Rich.

"Rich, don't jump to any conclusions about Mindy and John. Their relationship started out as a friendship—the romantic stuff started much later. They're not a stereotype."

Rich had no idea what she was getting at, but he had no time to question her. She threw the door open and held her arms out to Mindy.

"I'm so happy for you!" The slender Mindy practically lifted Gerri off the floor. Quickly, though, she stepped back. "Show me, show me!"

The three males watched the display, smiling. Then John stepped around them and extended his hand to Sven. "Congratulations, man. You've got a good one there." He turned toward Rich, but before he could speak, Gerri broke in and introduced John and Mindy to Rich.

Sven watched, bemused, as Rich and John performed some elaborate hand-shaking ritual. *Am I supposed to know this?* No, he decided. He didn't have to *be* black to love Gerri; he just had to respect her blackness. He made a mental note to ask her about the hand-shaking ritual later.

During dinner, Rich learned several things: Mindy really, *really* didn't like the Vietnam War. That was fine with him. He didn't have any happy stories to share about Vietnam, anyway. He also learned that Mindy was not shy about sharing her opinions—and that John was not shy about disagreeing with her. But both of them seemed to enjoy the repartee. He now understood why Gerri had given him the heads-up.

As they were returning to the living room, Rich returned to an earlier subject. "Gerri, you said that you'd show me that picture of you. The one that Sven painted which upset Ma."

It seemed as though the room froze. Sven looked surprised. Mindy and John looked confused. But Gerri looked mortified. Rich realized that he had committed some horrible faux pas, but he didn't know what it was or how to fix it. Sven seemed to be the key, since Gerri was looking at him guiltily.

Sven knew that he should have seen this coming. Of course, Olivia would have mentioned the picture to Rich, and Rich probably asked Gerri about it this afternoon during their private conversation on the boat. And Gerri, preoccupied with Rich's and Olivia's reactions to her romance, had undoubtedly failed to mention Sven's secrecy about his paintings.

What's done is done. Right now, the woman he loved was miserable—and silently berating herself. Sven couldn't tolerate Gerri's misery. After all, he rationalized, his secrecy was a product of his insecurity. It was time to grow up.

"Sure, I'll go get it," he said, throwing a wink and what he hoped was a comforting smile at Gerri. "I like it, even though I probably shouldn't have shown it to your parents."

As he left the room, he could hear the conversational dam break. Mindy said, "Sven painted a picture of you?" in a tone trying to be polite but nonetheless skeptical.

He returned with the picture and handed it to Rich.

Rich's eyes widened. This was 'little sister' all right, but 'little sister' was all grown. "Wow!" He finally said. "It's a great picture," he said to Sven, "but I can see why Ma freaked." He turned to Gerri. "Gerri," he started, "I'm impressed. I promise I'm not going to think of you as a little kid anymore."

Mindy was clamoring for a look, so he passed it to her and John. John was the first to react. He chuckled. "Lookin' good, Gerri. This is the kind of picture that college men put up in their rooms." He extended his hands in a framing gesture. "'Arctic Sistah!' I'm serious, man," he said to Sven. "Somebody could sell prints of this."

Gerri, embarrassed by the praise, felt like hiding her face. Instead, she eyed Mindy, anxious to see her reaction. It was not long in coming.

"Wait a minute!" She was squinting at the signature. "This is a Hush picture. I ought to know. I've looked at enough of them in the window of Taku Books." She looked at Sven almost accusingly. He shrugged.

Gerri was regaining her composure. She was almost limp with relief that Sven seemed not to care about her goof. "It's true, Mindy. Sven is Hush."

"Sven?" Mindy asked incredulously. But she immediately reached out her hand placatingly. "Sven, I'm sorry. I don't mean that the way it sounds. But really?"

Sven moved to the door. "Let me get an older picture. I'll be right back." He returned momentarily and handed another picture to Mindy and John. Gerri peeked over their shoulders and had to swallow her laughter. It was a picture of Mindy looking rather fierce—or was it angry? But somehow, it was a flattering picture.

John reacted first. "I love this. Let me buy it from you."

"No," said Sven, "but please accept it as a gift."

Mindy finally found her tongue. "I look angry," she said in a dismayed tone.

"Ah, but you're beautiful when you're angry," John said with a grin.

Mindy rounded on him. "That's such a male chauvinist thing to say."

"I assure you," John said, undeterred, "you're just as beautiful when you're not angry."

"Thank you," Mindy said, much more cheerfully.

But John wasn't done. "It's just that I haven't had a chance to see you as often when you're not angry." Mindy threatened him with a throw pillow as the rest of them laughed.

Sven watched the horseplay with a smile. He experienced a deep satisfaction that surprised him. Gerri's mistake had been a blessing in disguise. Still, there was one more base to touch. Quietly, he left the room.

When he returned, the noise had died down and they were again examining the pictures. "Here, Mindy," he said. "This one is for you. Or your mother, if you like, but don't tell her that it came from me."

It was a picture of Laura. But not the glamorous shots that were typical of her. This one showed her with a small smile, but looking faintly melancholy. Silently, Mindy stared at the picture. The others, loathe to interrupt her, looked quietly over her shoulder. Gerri thought it was the best image of Laura that she'd seen. Laura came across as a real person—one to whom the world had not always been kind.

Sven watched Mindy's face with anxious fascination. Finally, she took a deep breath and looked up. Her eyes were wet. "Thank you, Sven," said Mindy, blinking to dry her eyes. "This is so true to her. I'll love this." She hastily handed the picture to John, stood up, and hugged Sven with all of her strength. She held the hug for some time until Gerri's eyes started watering. *The reconciliation is complete,* Gerri thought. *How could this day be any more perfect?*

CHAPTER 45

Gerri left Mindy's apartment very early the next morning. Even though she and Mindy had stayed up late talking, Gerri couldn't sleep. She had much to talk over with Sven so that they would have at least tentative plans in place before they broke the news to her family. Gerri was uneasy about that and had already given considerable thought about how to break the news, while causing the least contention.

To put off telling them would only make it worse. The same time zone difference which had allowed Gerri to plausibly defer calling last night would remove any excuse for delay this morning.

Gerri had left the apartment quietly so as not to wake Mindy. This morning reminded her of her first morning in Juneau—the sun was just up, but the streets were still deserted. That first morning was almost exactly a year ago. She had to smile in wonderment. What amazing changes there had been in her life during that year.

When she got to Sven's house, it was quiet. *I'm probably not the only one who stayed up late talking.* As much as she would have liked to let him sleep, she didn't have time to wait. She quietly climbed the stairs and entered his bedroom. Sven was indeed fast asleep. Gerri glanced around quickly. *Curtains! I'm going to have to get curtains.* She buried that thought with a quick grin. It sure hadn't taken her long to develop a proprietary interest in his house.

Her hand had barely touched his shoulder when his eyes opened and he peered at her groggily. He reached for her, saying "You came to join me, I hope?"

Gerri danced out of the way. "No. We can't. Not while my brother's here. But we need to talk. Can you come downstairs?"

Sven stretched and yawned. "I figured that out, believe it or not. After you left, he and I talked for hours. He seems like a tentative ally right now. And we want to keep him that way."

Gerri nodded, grateful for his understanding. "I'll wait downstairs."

By the time Rich came downstairs, they had roughed out their plans. He blinked in surprise at finding them deep in conversation. "You two must not believe in sleeping."

"Hard to sleep when you have a marriage to plan," Gerri offered. "It'll catch up with me later, but there's still a lot to do today."

"Do you expect to get it all planned today?"

"Actually, the wedding plans are already roughed out. I still have some school work to do for tomorrow; we want to show you around, and, last but not least, I have to call home and tell the family. I'm not looking forward to telling Ma."

"I wanted to ask you about that." Rich grimaced. "Let me talk to them first. It's the least I can do—this wouldn't have happened so suddenly if I hadn't shown up yesterday."

"Don't feel guilty, Rich." Gerri cast a mischievous glance at Sven. "You did Sven a big favor by coming."

"I'll say." Sven winked at her. "I've been trying for months to find the right moment to propose."

"Oh, that," Gerri dismissed it airily with a wave of her hand. "I was talking about the fact that we were able to delay painting the boat."

Sven growled and reached for her. "You make light of my agonized waiting, woman?"

Gerri grinned and came into his arms willingly. Then her smile faded as she turned serious. "No. And I appreciate your patience. I'd love you for that even if I didn't have plenty of other reasons."

Rich waited while they kissed. When they didn't seem to be in any hurry to finish, he finally cleared his throat. "Umm, as you said, there's a lot to do today. Tell me your plans so I can tell the family."

Gerri didn't look remotely guilty as she broke the embrace. "We're going to get married after school lets out for the summer. Late May, probably. It'll be a small wedding—just us and a few friends in front of a J.P."

"Ma always imagined your having a big church wedding."

Gerri shook her head. "We don't want to be ostentatious. There are bound to be a few people who are offended. We're prepared to ignore them, but we don't want to rub anybody's nose in it unnecessarily." She paused and winced a bit. "We'd love it if the family could come, but…"

Rich was shaking his head. "That won't happen. You know that Dad can't leave the farm at that time of year."

"How about you, Rich?"

"I'd love to, but my training starts next week. I don't want to screw that up." He saw Gerri's disappointed look. "I'll be there in spirit; you know that."

She nodded resignedly. "When are you going to call?"

"As soon as you two leave. Go run an errand. Take a walk. Something." Seeing Gerri's frown, he elaborated. "You know that the first thing Ma is going to say is 'Put Gerri on the phone.' I want to soften them up first."

"But then she'll think I'm ducking her."

"No she won't. I'm going to tell her that I grabbed the phone when you guys went out on an errand."

Sven turned to Gerri. "You want to take a walk?"

"I guess so. It's not like I have a choice."

———

It took some time to calm Olivia down. Albert was accepting from the start and Marilyn and Joetta were excited. But Olivia was a harder sell. In the end, Rich reminded her about the high rates for long distance calls—there was no direct dial between Alaska and the other states—and summarized his argument quickly. "From what I've seen, Sven loves her, he respects her, and he likes her. Those are three distinct things, and each one is important.

"They're aware that not everybody will approve, but they have a core of supportive friends. I've met some of those friends and they seem very nice."

Olivia sighed. "I hope so."

Rich got an inspiration. This was a bit beyond his mandate, but… "They realize that you can't leave the farm to attend, but Gerri and Sven would love it if you could come up later in the year."

He waited while she relayed that to Albert. "We'll see," she finally said.

When Gerri and Sven got back to the house, Rich was standing on the porch. Gerri tried to read his expression without success. "Well?"

"I can't believe that you two are out here without coats on."

"Quit stalling, Rich."

"It went well—eventually. They want you to call them, but Ma promised not to give you any grief. And, of course, the girls think that this is the most exciting thing ever."

Gerri sagged against Sven. "Thank heavens. And this was the easy one."

Sven was only too happy to put his arm around her. "What do you mean?"

"They're family. Even if Ma disapproves, she still loves me. The harder thing is going to be telling the people at school. I think most of them will be fine, but there are bound to be a few… I just hope that the few—the nasty ones—don't make too big a fuss."

————

Gerri arranged her notes on her desk in preparation for her first period. The nervousness was bubbling beneath her calm exterior. She had come in early this Monday morning to sign her contract for next year. It had been waiting there for several weeks while she had been agonizing about her future. Nobody in the office had noticed her ring.

That ring was a ticking time bomb. She wouldn't know what to expect until the news was out. Momentarily, she regretted being right-handed—if she had been left-handed, they would surely notice the ring the first time she wrote something on the board. Still, somebody—some girl, no doubt—was bound to notice it during a visit to Gerri's desk before the day was out.

She didn't have long to wait. At the end of the first period, Barbara Pruitt had a question on her homework paper. Her discovery was marked by a squeal and a total loss of interest in the homework question.

"You're getting married?"

"Yes, I am." Gerri smiled and gently attempted to return to the homework question. But that was a lost cause. Barbara and several friends clustered around, hoping for more gossip.

"Does that mean you're leaving? Please say 'no.'"

Gerri smiled. "No, I'm not leaving."

"Who are you marrying? Is it someone from Juneau?"

Gerri thought she heard the name 'Dr. Wheeler' mumbled in the second row of girls, and she tried not to cringe. "He's from Juneau," she said firmly. "Sven Halvorsen is his name."

This met with some recognition. A couple of the boys, having joined the periphery of the group, pantomimed boxing motions. Barbara overrode any other comments, saying triumphantly, "I thought so. My dad said that he thought you two liked each other."

Gerri was finally forced to push them out to make way for her next class. As she did so, she reflected on how lucky she was that Barbara had been the first to notice—someone friendly to Gerri and whose family was friendly to Sven.

The rest of the morning was predictable. The news of Gerri's engagement had spread quickly, so Gerri had to take a minute at the start of each class to acknowledge it and answer a few questions. Student reaction varied. Most took it in stride, some appeared delighted, and a few frowned. Of course, Gerri reminded herself, some of the latter might have been in the 'Laura Schumaker' camp—disapproving of Sven more than the marriage per se.

As Gerri approached her usual lunch table, Sharon Ingram was ready. "I've been hearing about this all morning. Show me your ring."

After Gerri obligingly displayed it, Sharon asked, "Sven Halvorsen? How did you even meet him?"

Gerri gave a quick explanation of her summer job. Jake interrupted at this point. "Is he local? I don't recognize the name."

Sharon nodded. "He was before your time. He graduated about ten years ago. I had him in one of my classes. He…" She cut a glance toward Gerri, who nodded.

"Yes, I know all about his troubles." She summarized quickly for Jake. "He got married too young and, when his wife was killed in a car accident, some people really resented him."

Sharon looked relieved to be spared that explanation. "I liked him. He was an engaging young man. He had a lot dumped on him in his last year of high school. And I don't think his wife's family has forgiven him to this day."

"Mindy has."

Sharon blinked in surprise. "Oh! I'm glad to hear that. If anybody in that family is capable of forgiveness, it would be her."

The comic relief came in the last period of the day. Unsurprisingly, it was orchestrated by Frank Arquette. Frank was one of Gerri's most frustrating students but, at the same time, one of her favorites. He was universally acknowledged to be one of the brightest students in the school, and he was definitely the best math student that Gerri had ever taught.

He was frustrating because he grew bored easily when class went too slowly for him—which was more often than not. Gerri had taken to suggesting challenge problems at the beginning of class for the students to think about. She never mentioned Frank explicitly, but rarely would anyone else touch one of them.

He was also something of a cutup. His sense of humor reminded her a bit of Sven's, except that it leaned less on wordplays and puns and more on baroque (and generally bogus) math calculations. He, like Sven, seemed to revel in his audience's groans.

Gerri had won Frank's admiration with an offhand remark. After hearing one of his frivolous calculations, she told him about the Drake Equation for estimating the number of galactic civilizations. It had been told to her in much the same offhand fashion by Dr. Kuznetsov, and she had never imagined that she would use it, but something about Frank's elaborate calculations reminded her of Drake's ambitious attempt to quantify—however roughly—the unknowable.

Today, Frank came into class announcing that "This marriage is going to cause a lot of trouble."

If it had been anyone else, Gerri would have been alarmed. With Frank, she waited until he settled into his customary seat at the back of the room—he had always liked elbow room and didn't want anyone whispering next to him. Then she cocked her head and gave him an inquiring smile. Wild horses couldn't stop him from elaborating.

He consulted a sheaf of papers that he had in his hand. Ostensibly, these were calculations, although Gerri knew full well that they were just there to look impressive—whatever he was about to say, he had memorized. "You probably get addressed by students around 100 times a day." As usual, he was willing to fudge his numbers for maximum drama. "And there are almost 200 days in the school year. So that's 20,000 times that your name is spoken.

"Now, 'Miss Barton' is three syllables and 'Missus Halvorsen' is five. That's two extra syllables every time we call your name. So, in all, there's a total of 40,000 extra syllables in a year. If each syllable takes a quarter of a second, then there will be 10,000 extra seconds—almost three hours that are taken away from our learning."

He stopped with a triumphant grin, and the rest of the class reacted in their usual fashion—a stunned silence while they tried to process his math, followed by objections from those willing to joust with him.

"She could use 'Ms.' instead of 'Mrs.' Then there'd only be one extra syllable." Gerri grinned—Mindy and the Women's Libbers would be pleased.

"She could keep her own name," another girl piped up. "That'd save another syllable." Even better—Gerri would definitely have to tell Mindy about her acolytes in this class.

A boy spoke up. "She could ask us to call her 'Teach.' That's only one syllable."

Gerri decided that it was time to stop this. "OK, class. Just so you know, I will be taking his name. And it'll be perfectly all right to call me 'Ms.'" That was the least she could do for Mindy. "But," She gave the last speaker a stern look. "Nicknames such as 'Teach' are not acceptable."

Now she had one last task—to shut down this discussion. Frank fully expected it, and the other students wouldn't want him to have the last word. "I'll tell you what I will do, now that this problem has been pointed out. I'll be glad to keep each class in session one minute longer next year to make up for it."

That elicited a chorus: "No, no." "Don't listen to Frank." "We'll talk faster, we promise." Frank just laughed.

At the end of class, Frank came to the desk. "Seriously, Miss Barton, congratulations." He paused. "Of course, my sister says that you're supposed to congratulate the guy and offer the gal condolences." He grinned engagingly. Gerri could see why—beyond the obvious academic reasons—the girls sought him out for help.

Mrs. Kallek had unobtrusively observed the class. She also sat in the back, well away from the other people. As the room emptied, she got up and slowly made her way to Gerri's desk.

"Hello, Mrs. Kallek," Frank said cordially as he prepared to leave. "You're looking well."

"Hello, Frank. Still performing your wild flights of mathematical imagination, I see."

As he left, he nodded cheerfully over his shoulder.

Mrs. Kallek smiled at Gerri. "He's a very personable young man, considering how cheeky he is."

Gerri had to laugh. Mrs. Kallek was so modern in her ideas that she occasionally caught Gerri by surprise with her rather traditional use of the language. "He is that," Gerri agreed. "Both of them. I thought you weren't coming in today."

Mrs. Kallek gave her a reproachful look. I had to make a special trip to hear what's happening. You never mentioned a word." With that, she took Gerri's left hand in hers. "Very nice, young lady. Well, I for one am perfectly willing to offer congratulations to both the bride *and* the groom. And very sincere congratulations at that."

"Oh," said Gerri, flustered. "I… It just happened this weekend. It's been very hectic. My brother came to visit and…" She waved her hands.

"And you haven't had time to sit down and relax. Do you have a few moments to sit down and tell me about it? Or are you rushing home to your brother and your fiancée?"

"I have some time. Rich—that's my brother—could stay for only two days. We spent yesterday showing him around and Sven took him to the airport this morning." Gerri gave her a quick summary of her weekend. Then, because she was dying of curiosity, she asked, "How did you find out if you weren't coming to school?"

Mrs. Kallek gave her an amused look. "You mean, 'How does the gossip network function around here?' Very well, thank you. My spies in the principal's office phoned me at home with the news."

"But they didn't even notice when…"

"And they were quite annoyed about that. Not with you—they know that you're a bit on the shy side. They found out about it later when *their* spies—quite a number of them, as it turned out—reported it." She paused and looked smug. "So if you plan to keep secrets, you'll have to do a better job."

"I'll remember that." Gerri had noticed that the news spread quickly among her students. Apparently, it went through the whole school with the same speed.

"Tell me about your plans," Mrs. Kallek continued, "When and where is the wedding? Most importantly, am I going to get an invitation?"

Gerri's jaw dropped. "I hadn't even thought about that," she confessed. "We're planning a very small, quiet wedding." She thought quickly. How to say this without spoiling the mood… "We're not completely sure how people will react. I mean, I'm sure that almost everybody will be fine, but there will probably be a few," *The nasty ones…* "Well, we don't want to be ostentatious and rub people's noses in it."

Mrs. Kallek nodded as she gave that some thought. "I understand," she finally said. "Perhaps better than you know. My late husband was a Gentile. That wouldn't seem so significant now, but forty-some years ago…" She wrinkled her nose. "Those were different times—uglier times. And, yes, there were a few comments. And a few people stopped doing business at his grocery store. Not many, but a few.

"So I do understand your caution. But I really think that everything will be OK. If anyone tries to make a fuss to the school system, Herbert will squash it quickly. He's pretty good at doing the right thing."

"I've always felt that he supported me," Gerri agreed.

Mrs. Kallek smiled, glanced at the classroom door, leaned her head toward Gerri, and lowered her voice. "Of course, as we saw with the 'hair interview' on your first day, sometimes he first has to be told what the right thing is."

Chapter 46

By the time Gerri finished at school, it was evening. She decided to go straight to Sven's house, imagining her first private time with her fiancée—and with no relatives to behave for.

When she arrived, however, Sven was on the phone. When he saw her, he smiled mischievously and said, "Here she is. You can tell her yourself." With that, he handed the phone to Gerri, ignoring her inquiring looks.

When she answered it, the first thing she heard was a sing-song, "I told you so, didn't I?"

"Who? Oh, Elaine. How are you? And, yes, you certainly did."

"I'm so happy for the both of you. And so is Ronaldo. Now, give me all of the details."

Gerri didn't know what Sven had already told her, but she decided that Elaine would be very willing to hear it all again, so she gave her the summary of the weekend and of their wedding plans.

When she finished, Elaine's only reaction was "Huh! Have you picked out a wedding dress yet?"

"Well, no." Gerri mentally went through her closet. She hadn't acquired much of a wardrobe—just enough to keep her going at school. "I'm sure I can find something in my closet," she said hopefully. "It's just going to be a small wedding.

"Yes, you mentioned that. But still, it's a special day and you want to wear something special."

"That would be nice, but..." Gerri didn't know what the Juneau clothing stores had to offer and didn't want to spend the time or the money to shop in Seattle, which is what she suspected that Elaine would suggest.

"Then it's settled. I'll make you one. I'm a pretty good seamstress. It'll be our wedding gift."

"Really? Thank you, I..." Gerri wasn't sure how this could be accomplished from afar, but she appreciated the thought.

"Good. Let's get started. I have a pretty clear mental image of you, but I have a list of measurements that I want." Elaine read Gerri the list, making sure that Gerri wrote it all down. "You can call me back tomorrow with the results."

This was all moving very fast for Gerri. "What did you have in mind for the dress?"

Elaine summarized quickly. "I see you as a young professional. I see a white, knee length dress—demure but a bit sexy. I'll make a sketch and mail it to you. If you don't like it, then we'll talk. Then I'll bring it up a couple of days early and we'll try it. That'll give me plenty of time to make alterations."

Gerri's head was spinning. "So you're coming up for the wedding?"

"Wouldn't miss it. Neither would Ronaldo, even though he won't admit it."

After Gerri hung up, she just sat there for a minute. She could feel her heart pounding. This was starting to feel so real.

Sven watched her, gauging her reaction. "I invited the Whites. I hope you don't mind."

"Of course not! I'm delighted. I really like them. And of course, you should invite whomever you want."

Sven smiled ruefully. "I don't have that many friends, but those I do have are important to me."

"If they're important to you, then they're important to me," Gerri assured him.

———

Gerri got one more happy surprise before her wedding. Mindy came bustling up to her after school one day. "Good, I caught you before you left."

"You came here just to see me?"

"No, we just finished a meeting of the Future Office Workers. Lately, you're a hard person to catch. I wonder why?" Mindy's smile said that she knew exactly why.

With all that they had shared, Gerri was beyond being embarrassed around Mindy. Nonetheless, it was with a slight blush that she confessed, "Yes I know. Sven and I have been spending a lot of time together." She briefly debated tossing out some remark about 'making plans,' but decided that it wasn't worth it. Mindy wouldn't believe it anyway. And it would have been moot—Mindy was impatient to share her news.

"We're planning a wedding reception. It should be very nice."

"Oh? Where?"

"At Mrs. Kallek's house. She called me and offered. She lives in one of those big old houses on Seventh Street. It sits on a ridge above downtown and it has a great view. She's not strong enough to help much with the setup, but she helped me find some people who will."

"Thank you, Mindy. Thank you so much." Gerri had been resigned to making compromises to keep her wedding inconspicuous, but her friends were making sure that she had the full experience and she was very grateful.

———

The days leading up to the wedding were both the longest and the shortest days of Gerri's life. They were short at first as Gerri commenced her preparations while still taking care of her teaching chores. They were long toward the end—most of her preparations were done and the school year was over.

On the morning of the wedding, she had a bad case of butterflies. She went to one of the unfinished rooms of the house where Sven was working. Did he have butterflies? It was hard to tell. He was making the room into a guest bedroom—to make room for visiting in-laws, he had explained. *But today?* Is this his way of dealing with stress? Or was he simply not very anxious? "Goodbye, Sven. I'm going to Elaine's hotel room. I'll change there and Elaine and Mindy are going to do my hair. I'll see you at the J.P.'s office."

Sven leaned in and gave her a kiss. "I can hardly wait. And by the way, your hair looks nice as it is."

Gerri gave him a look. "You always say that. I want it to be a bit different for the wedding."

He nodded, knowing that he would never win this exchange.

"You'll be there on time, won't you?"

"Of course I will. I'll be there early. And I'll be wearing my suit."

One part of her wanted to wait and go with him, but Mindy and Elaine had decreed otherwise. When she was with Sven, she seemed to be less nervous. She eyed him for a minute. "Are you nervous?"

Sven favored her with a twisted smile. "Nah! See my hand? Steady as a rock." His hand rested, unmoving, on a dresser.

She looked at it suspiciously. "I don't think that's how it works. You're supposed to hold it out in mid-air."

He lifted his hand with a chuckle. It shook slightly, but noticeably. "OK, you've got me. I'm scared to death."

She asked, not entirely in jest, "Are you having second thoughts?"

"Good grief, no. I'm the luckiest guy in the world. I just... I don't want to end up disappointing you." He reached out and brushed her cheek with the back of his fingers. "I'm too dirty to give you a hug, but I'll make up for it later. I promise."

She reached up and brushed a kiss across his lips. "Just don't drop the ring during the ceremony." His laughter followed her out of the house.

It turned out to be Gerri's hands which trembled during the ceremony as she put Sven's ring on his finger. She glanced at him to see if he had noticed and received a wink. For some reason, that steadied her.

Sven felt like he was floating from the moment he saw Gerri in the wedding venue. She looked gorgeous, dressed all in white except for a broad headband which pulled her 'fro back into a puff similar to what she had had during the Pelican dance. The headband was bright magenta in perfect contrast to the rest of her outfit. She looked like a confection—good enough to eat, yet precious enough to cherish forever.

He could tell that she was a bit nervous and tried to reassure her with a wink. She reacted with a slight smile and seemed to settle down.

——

The reception looked very fancy—almost as if it had been professionally catered. Yet, Gerri knew that it was all volunteer work. She reminded herself that she had some heartfelt thank you notes to write.

There were two people arranging a buffet spread. They looked very official in their matching white shirts and black slacks, but when they turned to Sven and Gerri, she did a double take. It was Barbara Pruitt and Frank Arquette. Her astonishment must have shown, because Frank cracked "Yes, we're free labor, but if you want you can pay us in grades next year."

Gerri just laughed and gave him a look. "I don't think so. But thank you both."

As they mingled and nibbled, accepting various congratulations, Gerri marveled at Mrs. Kallek's house. It showed its age a bit, but it was grand. With a touch of sadness, Gerri realized that there was probably more life in the house today than there had been for years.

The only negative moment came when Gerri found herself momentarily alone with Barbara. "Where's your boyfriend? I haven't seen him for a while."

Barbara frowned and leaned in to speak quietly. "We broke up."

"I'm sorry to hear that. Or should I be?"

Barbara gave a little sigh. "No, you shouldn't be. We had a fight over my helping here. He…he disapproves of your marriage. As if it's any of his business," she added with disgust.

Gerri didn't know quite how to respond. She knew there would be some negative reactions and she was prepared to deal with them. Still, it didn't seem fair to have Barbara's life disrupted over this. "Well," she finally said, "I'm sorry for you, at least."

"Don't be," Barbara assured her. "I'm glad I found out about his views before things got really serious between us. Sometimes you think you know someone and…" She shrugged.

Sven approached Elaine and Ronaldo. "You two look pretty impressive. I think this is the first time I've seen you in a suit, Ronaldo. And Elaine...you always look glamorous."

"What do you think of your bride? Mindy and I worked on her for two hours this morning."

Sven turned and followed Elaine's gaze to Gerri. "I think you're a genius. But I also think that she would look beautiful in anything she threw on."

While Sven was occupied, Gerri sidled over to talk to Mindy. "We'll be leaving soon. We have a lot left to do today." Seeing Mindy smirk, Gerri poked her discretely. "You have a dirty mind," she laughed. "*Besides that,* we have to go home, call my family, change our clothes, and get down to the Glacier Gal. And with the time difference, the phone call has to be soon, or my sisters will be asleep."

Mindy pretend-pouted. "So I won't see you for a while."

"Not for a while. We'll go directly from the honeymoon trip to the fishing grounds. But we'll be in town off and on. And of course I'll call."

"A honeymoon on a fishing boat? I don't know about you guys."

Gerri chuckled good-naturedly. "We've got a lot of good memories on the Glacier Gal—and we'll make more. And as far as the fishing goes, well, we're going to have a lot of bills to pay. My family's coming up at the end of the summer and we're going to help them pay for the trip."

"Oooh, that's great. You never told me."

"It was just decided last night. It turns out that their school year starts about a week after the harvest—and a week after our school starts."

"That is so cool. I can hardly wait to meet them."

Gerri caught Sven's attention and they made ready to leave. As they said their goodbyes, she took that opportunity to whisper to Mindy. "I can't thank you enough. This was far beyond any of my expectations. And," she nudged Mindy for emphasis, "maybe you're next."

Mindy just blushed.

Then they were in Sven's truck waving to the people assembled on Mrs. Kallek's porch. Frank had insisted on escorting each of them to the vehicle and formally opening the doors.

Sven started the engine and Gerri settled back to enjoy the ride but, as they started moving, there was a terrible cacophony behind them. Gerri looked back in alarm, trying to imagine what they might have hit. Sven swore. At that moment, Gerri saw the assemblage of people cheering and Frank making a victory sign. She quickly touched Sven's arm. "It's OK. I think Frank tied cans onto the rear bumper."

Sven snorted. "Now I know why he escorted us to the truck. He wanted to make sure we didn't go around the back." He couldn't help a grudging smile. "Sneaky kid."

Gerri smiled to herself. "I think it was sweet." She thought about their day. "You know, with the help of our friends, we really got the whole wedding experience."

"Mmmm. Even the corny part."

At Sven's house, they changed quickly—they had agreed to consummate the marriage on the Glacier Gal—and Sven gestured Gerri to the phone.

Gerri gave the long distance operator her parents' number and said, "I'd like to make a person-to-person call to Mr. or Mrs. Robert Barton."

The operator asked who was calling. "Mrs. Gerri Halvorsen," Gerri answered proudly.

Sven watched her affectionately as she talked to each in turn. There was some repetition—each member of her family wanted to hear the details firsthand. Gerri didn't seem to mind, though, and Sven surely didn't mind watching her. Her animation and expressive hands were weaving their usual spell on him.

Then he perked up his ears. "He's right here. He did fine—he didn't drop the ring and he didn't even faint." Sven scowled at her without conviction. "You should see how nice he looks in a suit," she continued. "Yes, just a second."

She held out the phone to him. "Ma wants to talk to you."

Sven wiped his hand on his pants and cautiously took the phone. This made him almost as nervous as the ceremony itself had. "Hello, Mrs. Barton. You certainly have a lovely daughter."

"Hello, son." Olivia's voice seemed softer and more hesitant than Sven had remembered. "You can call me 'Ma' or 'Olivia,' if you prefer, 'Mrs. Barton' seems too formal for family."

"Yes, Ma'am; I'll remember that."

There was a snort of amusement from the other end of the line. "That wasn't one of the choices, but that's OK. You'll get used to it." She shifted topics abruptly. "So, when are you two going to make me a grandmother?"

Sven froze and then he looked to Gerri for rescue, but she was examining some invisible spot on her dress. "Uhhh, we're not sure, but not right away. We'd like to get used to living together for a while first." Gerri's head jerked up at his answer. Was that the right thing to have said? Or should he have dissembled?

"Don't wait too long. I want to be young enough to enjoy them."

"You'll be young for a long time. We're not waiting that long."

Gerri reached for the phone. "Don't put him on the spot, Ma. For now, we have to work hard and make enough money to pay all of our bills. And we want to prepare for your visit." With that, she moved smoothly into a discussion of the upcoming visit.

Sven breathed a discrete sigh of relief. His answer had satisfied Gerri at any rate, and that was the most important thing. As their conversation continued, he relaxed in his chair. He loved looking at her. He could feel a painting coalescing in his mind. As he tried to fix the details, he realized how happy he was. It had been years... No, he'd never been this happy. Something that had been tickling his brain for some time suddenly came to the front, and he grinned. *I'll have to remember to tell Gerri...*

She finished the conversation and hung up. "Our first phone bill as a married couple is going to be pretty scary."

Sven just shrugged. "It was worth it."

"So what were you smiling about there at the end?"

He looked embarrassed. "I thought of a story. Just a joke, really. It's not important."

Gerri recalled Wally's words. *When he's happy...* "Tell me."

"I thought of how to deal with those orange grove freezes that your father talked about."

Gerri kept a straight face with difficulty. *And when he's happy, I'm happy.* "And how is that?" She prompted dutifully.

"Fill up railroad coal cars with soil and plant the orange trees there. You can move them around. If there's a freeze predicted in Florida, then take them to Texas, and so on."

That almost—*almost*—made a weird kind of sense, Gerri thought as she waited for a punch line.

"I've even got a name for them."

"Oh?" *Here it comes...*

"Meanderin' Oranges." He looked at her with an expectant grin.

She made as if to throw a book at him, and then dissolved into laughter. "That's terrible."

CHAPTER 47

As the Glacier Gal motored along, the twilight deepened. The sky was crystal clear. Sven was at the helm with Gerri leaning against him, nestled in his arm. Conversation proceeded in a desultory fashion—each of them thinking back on the day and occasionally pondering the future.

Gerri snuck a look at him, trying to process her good fortune.

Sven caught her staring and grinned. "It's too late to change your mind."

She nudged him. "That's the last thing I want to do. It's just…hard to believe that all this is real." She leaned more snugly against his side.

Sven gave her a squeeze. "I'm an incredibly lucky guy." If anything, he decided that was an understatement. This was how he should feel on his wedding day: euphoric.

"Everyone…" Gerri paused for a brief sigh. "Everyone was so nice to us today. It made the day even more special."

"Mmm."

"If Mindy and John end up getting married someday, I want to do something extra special for her."

"I agree. And I'm sure you'll think of something."

After several hours of travel, they stopped in a small harbor to spend the night. Sven dropped the anchor and motioned for Gerri to cut the engine and the running lights. Then, unexpectedly, he stuck his head into the pilot house door and gestured peremptorily, "Come outside and look at this."

Gerri was surprised. It was too dark to see much—there were no lights outside and no other boats in the harbor. Moonrise was still an hour away and the shore was only dimly visible. But when she stepped outside, she looked up and caught her breath. There was a dazzling blanket of stars. She'd never seen them more brilliant. And to cap it off, there was a dim, but colorful display of northern lights. "Oh, Sven. It's beautiful."

He pointed skyward. "The Big Dipper." His finger moved. "And the North Star."

This wasn't the first time that Gerri had been made aware of the special significance of that constellation to Alaskans. "Alaska's flag," she murmured. From now on, she thought proudly, it would have the same significance for her. She, too, was an Alaskan.

Sven grinned in the darkness. "I choose to believe that it's an omen—a sign of good luck for our marriage."

With that she tore her eyes from the sky and pulled his head down to hers. "I like the way that sounds," she breathed. Then she captured his lips in a long, tender kiss.

———

Sven was lying on the bed in what he used to call the captain's cabin. He smiled as he reminded himself that it needed a name change. Co-captain's cabin? Master stateroom? Whatever—they'd come up with something. With his fingers interlaced behind his head, he looked up at the ceiling. Gerri was in the head—probably wishing that she had a normal bathroom. He was patient. After all, he had waited a long time for this day. Gerri would come when she was ready, and whenever she came, she would be magic. Sven had no illusions that he was an expert on women, but even he knew that you don't hurry a bride on her wedding day.

This knowledge came from intuition, not from experience. In his first marriage, any sense of eagerness or anticipation had long since been washed away by their mutual guilt and stress. He took a moment to regret Laura's sadly truncated life, but then put that out of his mind. While he earnestly wished that Laura had lived to move on and, perhaps, find a real love of her own, that was the unchangeable past. Gerri was the present—and the future.

It seemed a bit lighter. He glanced at the window in the cabin. The moon was rising and its tendrils of light were peeking into the cabin. A barely audible noise caught his attention. Gerri was easing quietly through the door, naked under a short, diaphanous robe. He caught a tantalizing whiff of something—a perfume that he didn't recognize, but one that he hoped he would smell again.

"Sorry I took so long. Are you still awake?"

Sven laughed out loud. "You underestimate yourself. I would stay awake all night for you."

Gerri lowered herself to the bed beside him and ran her hand over his chest. As she touched him, Sven rolled toward her. His hands quickly found the sash of her robe and untied it. His left hand moved slowly—tortuously slowly—up her torso, stopping at her right breast. He paused there, rubbing her nipple until it hardened deliciously. She gripped his arm and pulled him closer for a much-wanted kiss.

The kiss lingered, their tongues dancing together, and Gerri moved her hand to his chest. She felt a faint vibration and realized that he was humming almost inaudibly—a sound of his male satisfaction.

He then abandoned the kiss and moved his head downward, tugging lightly on her other nipple. She arched her back and gave an involuntary hiss of satisfaction. Then his hand moved back down her body and caressed her at the apex of her thighs. She knew that she wouldn't last long under this treatment, so she rolled up to sit on top of him. With both hands, she kneaded his torso, then quickly fixated on his now rampant manhood.

She rubbed its tip against her sex and positioned it for entry. Sven didn't need any more encouragement. With a sudden movement of his hips, he sheathed himself in her. His inaudible hum changed abruptly to a pleased growl as he moved rhythmically—and Gerri moved with him. Their first climax happened quickly, and Gerri rode the waves of sensation, which seemed to go on and on.

Much later, with the moon high in the sky, they lingered near sleep—too tired to stay awake, but unwilling to say goodbye to the day. Gerri roused herself one last time. "You know what? This bed was the start of our romantic life and now it's the start of our married life."

"Mmm," said Sven. Gerri almost felt the vibration in his chest rather than hearing him. "I like that." That was his last waking statement.

When they got underway the next morning, Sven still wouldn't name their destination. He had promised to take her to a 'secret place' which he assured her was magical. Gerri couldn't resist taking this as a challenge, and she followed their progress on a chart. At one point, she looked up from the chart and laughed. "Sumdum? I'm surprised you haven't made a pun out of that."

Sven put on an injured look. "That's too easy. I have standards, you know."

Gerri feigned astonishment. "Oh, really? No, I *didn't* know that."

He chuckled. "Watch out, wench. You're going to get what you deserve."

She leaned into him and fluttered her eyelashes. "Oh, I hope so."

He put his arm around her and held her there. As she rested comfortably against him, she reflected on another of the many reasons that she loved Sven. She felt able to be bold around him, knowing that he found her beautiful—and respected her completely at the same time.

They were working their way slowly up a long arm of the sea. And there were icebergs—more than Gerri had ever seen. They were so thick that the Glacier Gal had to creep along, sometimes barely above idling speed, to avoid damage to the boat.

Another look at the chart and she knew their destination. She teasingly protested. "Ford's Terror? That doesn't sound magical to me."

He was obviously pleased with her deduction. He grinned happily and said, "But it is. You'll see. And very few people ever come here."

She believed him completely—his judgment was impeccable in these matters—but she wasn't willing to stop teasing. "I suppose that Ford didn't find it too magical."

"I suppose not. I'd love to know how it got its name. Evidently, Ford wasn't properly prepared." He turned serious momentarily. "As we've both found, Alaska has an abundance of magical places which can kill you if you're not prepared."

Soon they were anchored and Sven announced, "We're going ashore for a picnic." Their anchorage was near one of the only flat areas in sight. A landing, let alone a picnic, would be impossible anywhere else, as the mountains rose steeply from the sea.

Gerri knew that there was more to this than just a picnic, but she resolved to let his surprise unfold on his terms. "It's very pretty. The steep mountains remind me of the pictures of Norwegian fjords."

Sven nodded and gestured vaguely. "It's even better further in. We'll see that later." They walked through a grove of trees and came to the bank of a rushing river. He made a fire and brought out hotdogs and marshmallows. "See if you can figure out anything strange about that," he said, gesturing to the river rapids in front of her.

Gerri accepted the puzzle and studied the rapids. To her right—upstream—she could see what appeared to be an extension of the inlet where they had anchored. To her left, a towering cliff forced the river into a right turn, after which (ahead of her) it flowed into a large still body of water. *A lake?* "Wait a minute! How can a river be flowing downstream from sea level?"

"Excellent! You've found the strangeness. You'll figure out why soon. Now come and eat." Gerri enjoyed being spoiled—it was rare for Sven to cook for her nowadays. She enjoyed even more what came afterwards. Sven spread out a tarp on one of the rare patches of soft sand and put a folded blanket on the corner nearest to his head. They made slow, sweet, passionate love and then snuggled under the blanket to relax. This was an excellent part of the adventure; she would never have imagined that she would ever make love outdoors.

But the puzzle still intrigued her. After they had relaxed for a while in a post-coital glow, she took another look at the 'river.' To her astonishment, it had slowed its flow dramatically. There were only a few eddies of slow moving water where before there had been rapids. While she was processing this, Sven finished cleaning away the traces of their presence and came up behind her.

"I think it's OK for us to go through now."

That clicked in her mind. She turned quickly toward him. "This isn't a river at all, is it?"

Sven smiled. "No, it's not. But what is it?"

She thought furiously. He had said something last summer... "It's the tide, isn't it? And it's trying to fill the inlet behind it."

Now he grinned happily. "Right! And it's so strong, that the Glacier Gal would be thrown against that cliff if we'd tried to pass through before." He gestured to the right angle. "Now we can get in, although it still won't be easy."

"And getting out again?"

"We'll wait for another slack tide tomorrow."

The wait was worth it. Once they were inside, the mountains became outright cliffs. It was the most spectacular scene she had ever seen. Surely none of the national parks could be more so. Between the scenery and the peaceful quiet, Gerri felt as though she and Sven occupied their own dream world.

But the real world could not be denied for long. The following day they left Ford's Terror and headed toward the main channel. The icebergs were less thick, so they made good time. When they were back in familiar waters, Sven looked at Gerri and raised his eyebrows. "Time to start paying the bills?"

Gerri nodded and, just that simply, their honeymoon was over and it was time to start fishing. By now she knew that, contrary to Mindy's belief, Sven was not cheap. He just hated being in debt. If he couldn't pay for something, he would do without, but he was willing to plan and work tirelessly for those things which mattered. Now what mattered to both of them was to make enough extra money to help pay for her family's visit.

———

They had a good season. They worked hard for it, but they were able to set aside enough extra money to finance the Barton's entire visit. Gerri didn't think of herself as greedy, but it gave her immense satisfaction to see how healthy the 'Halvorsen family accounts' were. Sven, citing her math talents, had asked her to be the official family accountant. Gerri suspected that he could have handled it just as well, but she was happy to help.

Two events stood out during the summer. The first occurred after several weeks of fishing, when they decided to attend the Pelican town dance again. They attended partly to create a new family tradition, but partly because they had genuinely enjoyed the last one. There was a considerable difference in people's reactions to Gerri this year. Last year, she had gotten a lot of curious looks, but, other than Ace Artin and Edwin John, no one actually attempted to say hello. This year, there was a steady stream of people who introduced themselves and offered their congratulations. The bush telegraph, as she had come to know it, was operating with its usual efficiency.

But the most welcome introduction of all came when they saw Edwin John sitting at a table—apparently babysitting the crew of his boat again. Next to him was a woman whose brown face was wreathed in smiles. Edwin waved Gerri and Sven to his table. "Come on and sit down. Gerri, meet my wife Ellen. Ellen, this is Gerri *Halvorsen*." He emphasized her last name with some amusement.

When the greetings were over and everyone was comfortably seated, Gerri teased Edwin. "I'm surprised you remembered me after seeing me only once and that a year ago."

"Oh, I remembered. Sven was guarding you so carefully. We laughed about it later." He gestured to include Ellen. "So we weren't really surprised to hear about your marriage."

Sven smiled shamefacedly. Had he been that obvious? He turned to Ellen to change the subject. "It's good to see you again. So you've taken to the fishing life?"

Ellen laughed gaily. "No, but he promised me a short trip. I just wanted to come to this dance."

"Really?" Gerri looked around the hall. She enjoyed the dance, but in no way was it worth a trip all by itself.

Ellen laughed again. It seemed to be her most natural expression. "Not for the dance itself. I came to meet the woman who tamed Sven."

Gerri looked down at the table. She couldn't meet Sven's eyes because she knew that he would say something outrageous. "I don't think that he's capable of being tamed, but…" Now she found the courage to peek at him and smile mischievously. "I guess I'll find out." He didn't reply, but the look that he gave her made her face get hot.

"So," Ellen continued, "are you starting a family?"

"Not yet." Sven answered quickly. "We want to live together alone for a while. Get to know each other before we pile on any added stress." Gerri nodded her agreement. Her reasons were a bit different—she wanted to get a better feeling for what life would be like for a mixed race child before they committed themselves.

Ellen moved on to lighter subjects. She was an easy person to talk to. By the end of the evening, Gerri felt as though she had known her for years. Ellen provided an interesting perspective for Gerri, as she was living in a town which made even Juneau seem like a big city. Before they left, she extracted a promise from Gerri to visit.

The second event of note came about a month later, at the end of a long and hard, but very profitable, stretch of fishing. They had used the long summer daylight and had worked several 18 hour days in a row. It wasn't masochism driving them—the fish were biting in such large numbers that they couldn't resist augmenting the family finances. After they had sold their latest catch, Gerri couldn't think of anything but her sore muscles and rest—lots of it. When Sven left the dock, she assumed that he was headed back to Juneau.

Gerri was soon disabused of that notion when Sven turned into a channel leading back to the ocean. She looked at him in puzzlement. "We're not going back to Juneau?"

Sven got one of his mysterious looks and said, "Let's take a little detour. It'll be part of our adventure."

Sven was not autocratic, either as a boat captain or as a husband, so Gerri wasn't offended. Clearly, he was planning some sort of surprise. She tried to summon the energy to play along. The surprise didn't last long. Soon she realized that the landmarks were familiar. "Aha!" She looked at him triumphantly. "We're going to that hot springs, aren't we?"

He laughed and said, "Right you are!" Then he sobered up and asked, "You don't mind, do you? I know that your memories of the place aren't pleasant."

Gerri considered that. No, they weren't pleasant, but that was her fault, not Sven's. He obviously felt that this was a special place. She squeezed his arm affectionately. "No, I don't mind. We can make new memories, better ones."

———

As they walked out of the woods, Gerri looked at the now familiar pair of shacks with an increasing sense of anticipation. *Unlimited hot water for my aching muscles—I can hardly wait.* She cast a sidelong glance at Sven. *And skinny dipping with the most handsome guy around!*

Still, she looked around carefully before she started undressing. Sven saw this and chuckled. "Don't worry. There's nobody within miles."

"My brain knows that, but I'm not used to undressing in public."

She gathered her courage and they stripped quickly. She stole a peek at Sven. *Lookin' fine!* Then Elaine's words in Seattle came to mind: 'that's a lot of man there,' and Gerri started giggling.

Sven pretended to be hurt. "You're not supposed to laugh when I undress. That's bad for my ego."

"I was just reminded of something. And if you could read my thoughts, your ego would be just fine."

Sven waited, but it was clear that she wasn't going to elaborate. He dismissed it from his mind and stepped into the larger of the shacks. "Let's get these tired bodies in the water."

The interior was filled with a rectangular pool, about ten feet square four feet deep. As she slid into the water, Gerri's breath caught involuntarily. "It's hot, all right."

Sven was already in the water. "Ahhh, this feels good." He was sitting on an underwater bench, relaxing, but the sight of Gerri's curvy body beside him took his mind in another, distinctly non-relaxing direction. He could feel himself beginning to get aroused.

They sprawled there for some time, enjoying the feeling of the hot water. Gerri leaned her head back and half-closed her eyes. After a companionable silence of several minutes, Gerri glanced at Sven. His body betrayed his interest. "Whoa!" She reached for his arousal. "I suppose you're going to say that this is all my fault."

He pulled her into his arms. "Absolutely. Although I don't think that 'fault' is exactly the right word."

She presented her lips for a kiss. He took advantage of this to start stroking her abdomen and downward. She stood it as long as she could and then got up to straddle him. He surged deep within her and she rode him until she was seized by an intense orgasm. Sven's hoarse yell filled the air as he came with her. Afterwards, she rested, her body still joined to his, as he sprawled on the bench.

"Do you realize that we've been married for only a couple of months, and that during that time, we've made love in public places twice? This is not the way I envisioned my life unfolding."

She felt Sven's chest jerk as he chuckled. "Complaining?"

"Not a bit."

"This could be a good cure for sore muscles, but I don't know how we'd market it."

"Let's don't."

Later, having stayed in the water for as long as their bodies would allow, they went outside—still naked. Sven suggested that they sit on one of the rocks next to the shack, but Gerri insisted on first scanning their surroundings with their binoculars. Finally she was satisfied that they were truly alone and sat down beside him.

He eyed her with appreciation. "I could watch you like that all day. You look gorgeous—and as sleek as an otter."

She cast him an amused glance. "Is that some obscure Alaskan compliment, or do you have some obsession with otters that you want to confess to me?"

He took a few seconds to try to think of a clever retort, but finally settled—with a chuckle—for, "Not the latter."

Gerri was reminded of her vision of Sven as a marble statue. Emboldened by his remark, she offered her own. "I could watch you all day, too. You remind me of those statues of ancient heroes in museums."

"Nude statues?"

"Mm-hmm. Maybe you could have a career as a model."

He snorted in derision, but a sidelong glance gave Gerri the sly satisfaction of seeing his face suffused with a reddish tint.

After that, they sat in silence and just contemplated the ocean. Gerri could see steam coming off of them as the water evaporated. Sven had been right—her soreness was gone.

As they walked back to the boat—now fully dressed—Gerri put her arm around Sven. "Thank you for thinking of this. Now I have *excellent* memories of White Sulfur Hot Springs."

CHAPTER 48

Gerri had been standing for some time, shifting her weight impatiently from foot to foot as she scanned the sky, but predictably it was Sven who saw the incoming jetliner first. Gerri had never been able to discern the secret of his amazing vision, let alone duplicate it. It wasn't just acuity. It was, she was convinced, related to his ability to find fish and his talent as an artist.

Still, she was stubborn enough to mutter, "How do you do that?"

He shrugged. "I guess it's knowing where to look." But he had no real answers; it just seemed natural to him. "Let's go inside and meet them."

Not only was this the culmination of their extra hard work this summer, but Gerri hadn't seen her family for most of a year. She quickly walked ahead.

They still had to wait interminably while the plane landed, taxied, and finally started to disgorge passengers. The Bartons were, thankfully, among the first ones off the plane. Gerri paid special attention to their clothes. She wanted to be sure that her family had taken her seriously about the weather. Now, in early September, it was probably in the nineties in South Carolina, whereas it was in the low sixties in Juneau. If they were constantly cold, the trip would be a disaster.

And there was no reason for it. Sven and Gerri had saved enough money to finance a small shopping expedition—guided by the ever-willing Elaine—to get them appropriate outerwear.

Sure enough, they all wore jackets. Marilyn managed to look particularly fly. Then Gerri stopped worrying about that as they ran squealing into her arms.

"Joetta, you look so big. You must have grown six inches. And Marilyn, you look very elegant."

The chattering was nonstop as they collected the baggage and loaded it into their borrowed car. Olivia looked at Gerri quizzically and said, "I thought you said that Sven had a truck."

"He does, and I bought a Volkswagen beetle, but neither one will hold everybody unless someone rides outside in the back. So we borrowed this for a couple of days from one of the other teachers."

"You bought a car?" asked Joetta excitedly.

"You bought a bug?" asked Marilyn scornfully.

Gerri laughed. "Yes, I bought a car. I still walk to school sometimes, but if I have a heavy load of books or if the weather is awful, it's nice to have an alternative." She turned to Marilyn. "A bug may not be the coolest car around, but it gets good traction in the snow." As she expected, mention of snow quieted Marilyn.

That first day, a Saturday, was spent sightseeing around Juneau. On Sunday, Sven and Gerri took them out for a short cruise on the Glacier Gal. Gerri especially wanted to give them at least a taste of life on the water. They weren't favored by any porpoise visits, but they did see a whale sounding—pivoting vertically with its tail in the air to start a deep dive—only about a hundred yards away. Gerri had seen this behavior a number of times, and it never failed to impress her. It certainly impressed the Bartons.

Sven, to Gerri's amusement, pulled a similar trick to that which he had when her brother visited. When they were ready to leave the float, he arranged to be the one untying the lines, leaving Gerri to start the engines and guide the boat out of the harbor. Gerri appreciated the subliminal message being delivered, although she was amused.

The gesture was not lost on her parents. While her sisters were out on deck talking to Sven, Olivia and Robert were with Gerri in the pilot house. Olivia—never the reticent one—asked, "He lets you run the boat?"

Gerri smiled at her predictability. "He doesn't *let* me. We're a team. Whoever's most convenient will handle it." Robert just raised his eyebrows, smiled, and shook his head.

They made sure to get back to town in time to have Mindy and John over for dinner Sunday night. It was supposed to have been a joint effort on the part of Gerri and Mindy, while the others relaxed. Olivia, however, insisted on making the effort a threesome.

Monday went a bit off script. Gerri had to teach, since the Juneau schools were already in session. They had planned for Sven to chauffeur her family around. The agenda included visiting the bookstore—Sven knew Rosie would want to meet them—and a drive to the end of the road. Sven had looked askance at the latter, but Gerri assured him that it would intrigue them, especially if they arrived there without warning.

To Gerri's surprise, Marilyn approached her Sunday night and asked, "May I come and visit your school tomorrow? Maybe sit in on some classes?"

"I suppose so. Do you mean one of my classes?"

Marilyn shrugged. "Maybe. Maybe some other classes as well."

"I don't see why not. Let me check with one of the other teachers."

Sharon Ingram not only approved, but invited Marilyn to start the day in her first period English class. The next morning, Gerri drove Marilyn to school, introduced her to Sharon, and left to go to her own class.

She expected to see Marilyn after first period, but she didn't appear. When lunchtime rolled around, Gerri still hadn't seen Marilyn. When she sat down with Sharon, she asked about Marilyn's visit. "I haven't seen Marilyn since I left you. Did her visit go OK?"

"It went very well. She was quite a hit. My students had an assignment to write a poem, so some of them were read to the class. Turns out that Marilyn had written some herself. With a little gentle persuasion, she shared them.

"One was a sweet one about growing up on a farm. The other one was pretty bleak." Sharon grimaced at the memory. "It was about being a black student in a newly integrated school. You could have heard a pin drop after she read that one."

"I'm surprised that she had the nerve to read them." *She didn't even share them with me...*

"Yes, it must have taken some courage. But the students were very supportive. In fact..." Sharon gestured. "She's over at the corner table eating with some of her new friends."

Gerri craned her neck. The group around Marilyn seemed to be having a good time. "Silly me. I kept expecting her to appear in my doorway wanting to go home."

"No... I don't think you'll see her again. When they left my class, my students were competing over which classes she should visit."

But she did see her. Just before the start of her last period, senior math class, Marilyn walked in, chatting with Frank Arquette. Gerri looked at her warily. Would she observe the proper decorum? Or would she perform as an entitled little sister?

It was a relief to have her stop at the desk and ask politely, "Mrs. Halvorsen, may I sit in on your class today?"

Gerri couldn't find a trace of sarcasm or disrespect in her voice. "Certainly," she smiled. "You may sit in any of the empty seats."

Marilyn sat in back, next to Frank, who was in his accustomed chair. As the class progressed, Gerri kept an eye of them. They paid only partial attention to Gerri, but they were quiet and not at all disruptive. Gerri couldn't complain about their lack of attention—it was normal for Frank to be working on his own or on one of her challenge problems, and she could hardly demand the attention of someone who was just visiting.

Whatever they were discussing involved scribbling on a piece of paper—it might even have been math. Gerri would have loved to look over their shoulders to find out. She even considered giving the class a problem and circulating, but that would have been too obvious.

At the end of class, the two of them came up to her desk. "Thank you," Marilyn said. "It was very interesting."

Gerri was tempted to say, 'Did you even notice the class?'

Marilyn sensed her skepticism and hastened to add, "Yes, I listened to your lesson—some. But Frank was showing me your latest challenge problem. I wish that my teachers had given those."

Gerri nodded. She should have thought of that. Frank had been working in a desultory way her latest offering, which was the classic Königsberg Bridge Problem. He believed—correctly—that it was impossible, but the challenge was to *prove* that, which had so far eluded him.

She stole a glance at the clock. "Marilyn, I have some papers that I have to look at. Would you mind waiting? I shouldn't be more than half an hour."

Marilyn furrowed her brow as she considered that. "Maybe I'll walk home. I think I remember how to get there."

Frank spoke up. "I'll give you a ride. I think I know where you live." He turned to Gerri and gave an address. "The long driveway just across the bridge. Right?"

"That's right. And thank you, Frank. Now I can get my work done without having to worry about her getting lost." Marilyn rolled her eyes at the implied slight of her geographical sense, but was happy to accept the ride.

Sven had intended to take the Bartons on a walk around his property Monday afternoon. It wasn't as big as the Bartons' farm, but it was pretty and had some nice views of the city and the mountains. Satisfied that everything was under control at home, Gerri worked for a little longer than she had intended. When she finally got home, Olivia met her.

Gerri recognized the signs that Olivia was annoyed, and immediately sought to calm the waters. "Hi, Ma. Did you have a nice day?"

Olivia allowed herself to be sidetracked—temporarily. "Yes, mostly."

"Did you take a walk around the property?"

That was the opening that Olivia was waiting for. "No, we didn't. We were waiting for Marilyn. When she finally came, she was with some white boy. And then they sat there yakking for about five minutes."

"It's OK. That was Frank. I asked him to give her a ride home. I had some work to finish."

"Hmmph."

"Did you ask her about her day? I hope she had a good time."

"I didn't have to ask. She's been talking about it ever since. She had a ball. And every other sentence was 'Frank this' or 'Frank that.' Are you sure you trust this boy?"

"Absolutely. I can't think of any of my students whom I would trust more. You'd like him if you met him. He's very friendly—and very smart."

Olivia frowned, not entirely ready to be mollified. Gerri moved on smoothly. "Would you guys like to eat out? Or should I get started on some dinner?" After they decided to eat in, Gerri and her helpers made quick work of the meal preparation.

The dinner conversation was dominated by Marilyn's adventures. And, yes, Frank's name came up frequently, but so did those of several other students. Joetta had been charmed by the book store. Robert and Olivia were bemused, as Gerri had predicted, by the notion that you couldn't drive out of Juneau. After the 'end of the road' was simply—wilderness.

———

As they were getting ready for bed, Sven and Gerri compared notes. "I'll try to get home earlier tomorrow. Do you have anything special planned for them?"

"I'll see what they want to do. We might take the hike that we missed today. And, if they'll sit still for me, I'd like to sketch your parents. I'll turn it into an oil painting later and give it to them as a Christmas gift."

Gerri paused as she was undressing. "That sounds great."

"By the way, does Marilyn draw? While you were cooking, she borrowed a bunch of paper from me."

"Not that I know of. Of course, I didn't know that she wrote poetry either." Gerri thought about Marilyn. She seemed to have matured in the months since Gerri had left South Carolina. Olivia, her worries notwithstanding, had to be relieved. As she slipped her dress off, she thought again about Sven's day. "You know, I'm sorry that I'm putting so much of the entertaining on you."

Sven moved up to embrace her from behind. "Don't worry about it, I don't mind. We're a team, remember? And we'll be alone again soon."

The next morning, Gerri left for school early, determined to avoid staying late. Only Sven saw her off. The others were still in their rooms. They shared a quick kiss as she went out the door. "Goodbye. Love you."

"Love you too."

It was a routine day for Gerri until her last class. As it was about to start, she heard a murmur from her students. Looking up, she saw Marilyn standing in the doorway looking at her inquiringly. Gerri hadn't expected to see her today, but she had no reason to object to her presence. She nodded her approval and Marilyn walked to the back of the room.

As Gerri watched her progress, she realized that Marilyn had matured in more ways than one in the past year. Today's outfit was a knit dress which—while completely tasteful and within the dress code—was much more striking than yesterday's. Gerri would have to compliment her later—she looked really good. The murmuring of the class was testimony that they had noticed as well. But Marilyn showed no interest in the general reaction; she was focused on the back of the room. Gerri angled her head in time to see Frank looking transfixed. He quickly recovered, moved the chair next to him up close to his, and patted it hopefully.

Gerri couldn't help but think of Olivia. She would have kittens if she could see this. But it didn't matter—one more day and they'd be gone. Maybe they could be pen pals. That would be nice.

The class proceeded similarly to that of the day before. Frank and Marilyn had limited engagement with Gerri's lesson, spending their time scribbling and quietly discussing something. Maybe there were a few more shared looks and smiles than the previous day—yes, Gerri was keeping an eye on them—but they didn't disrupt the class.

She was even a little impressed. First, that Marilyn had chosen a nice guy like Frank for her little flirtation. And, second, that she seemed to have caught his eye in two days when a number of girls in school had tried for much longer than that with no success. Now, if Marilyn could only keep her mouth shut about this around Olivia...

At the end of the class, when most students eagerly left to get on with their post-school day, Frank and Marilyn lingered in the back.

When they were the only ones left, they came to the front looking pleased. "We think we've solved the Königsberg Bridge Problem," said Frank. "May we give you our solution?"

"Really?" Gerri looked at them both. "Go ahead. I'd love to hear it."

Gerri didn't give them an easy time of it. She had previously made it plain to Frank that a clear, convincing argument was required. She questioned them and demanded more details on several points, but in the end, she had to concede that they had a valid proof of impossibility.

"This is excellent! I'm very impressed. With both of you," she added with a look at Marilyn.

Frank was grinning happily. Gerri had never seen him so ebullient when he had solved one of her previous challenge problems. *That's OK. They earned it!*

He turned to Marilyn and asked, "They've got a soda fountain downtown. Have you got time to go get a milkshake to celebrate?"

Marilyn looked pleadingly at Gerri. Gerri couldn't throw a damper on their last day. "I think you have time. Just remember to be back in time for dinner. This is your last night here." She reached for her purse. "Do you have money?"

Frank shook his head. "No. Your money's no good here." Gerri stifled a laugh. One of the things that she liked about him was his ability to be self-mocking as he uttered a cliché.

Marilyn gave him an arch look and a small smile. "You mean you don't use American currency out here on the frontier?"

He leaned toward her and tapped her on the arm. "No. I mean that I want to treat my research partner to a celebration."

Gerri got home late and tired, but happy for Marilyn. Her experiences at the high school would definitely make the trip to Alaska a roaring success for her. Gerri hadn't decided how much detail to share with Olivia, but she looked forward to telling Sven all about this.

She didn't get a chance to enjoy it for long. As she opened the door, she saw everyone sitting in the living room looking solemn. Olivia jumped up and intercepted her. "You've created a monster," she hissed.

CHAPTER 49

Gerri groaned and started to walk toward the living room. Olivia followed her and continued her diatribe. "She's so crazy about this boy that she wants to stay here."

Gerri looked more carefully at the people. Marilyn looked miserable—tearful and defiant. Robert looked concerned. Olivia looked outraged. And Joetta looked somehow smug. Lastly, she looked at Sven. He was not happy.

Joetta piped up with barely disguised satisfaction. "She kissed him!"

Marilyn rounded on her. "I kissed him on the cheek, you little brat. And what were you doing spying on us, anyway?"

"Ma told me to come out and get you so you wouldn't spend all afternoon out there with him." Gerri now understood Joetta's smugness. It wasn't pretty, but Gerri had seen it before—she had even, heaven help her, done things like this when Rich was home. It was the younger child feeling satisfaction and power by ratting on the older child to their parents.

She was just trying to figure out how to bring some rationality to the proceedings when Sven abruptly stood up and, with an unreadable look, walked out of the room. Seconds later, Gerri heard the front door close. She was beset with guilt. Sven hadn't asked for any of this drama; she had brought it to him. Not the actions of a good team member.

Marilyn made another appeal. "This isn't just because of Frank."

Olivia overrode her. "I don't believe you. You've been talking about nothing else since yesterday."

Gerri couldn't concentrate. What must Sven be thinking? She couldn't shake the feeling that he was disappointed in her. She held up her hand to stop the conversation. "Can you all just hold it for a minute? I want to talk to Sven." Somewhat to her surprise, they stopped. Maybe they realized that this was Gerri's home in which they were arguing.

Sven leaned against the porch railing and stared absently across the channel at Juneau, as he silently berated himself. He shouldn't have left. He knew that—especially when he might have something to contribute if the discussion became rational. It was cowardly of him to abandon Gerri, but it reminded him so vividly of his own fights with his parents before their final estrangement.

He heard the door click shut behind him and turned. Gerri was in his arms immediately. "I'm so sorry," she said.

"Why are *you* sorry? You didn't start it. I'm the one who should be sorry—leaving you on your own in the middle of a fight."

"Don't call it a fight. It's a discussion."

"It sure sounded like a fight."

"OK, a *spirited* discussion." She felt Sven snort in amusement. "Didn't you have family discussions?"

Now, he was really amused. Somehow, Gerri had managed to make it seem as though he had done nothing wrong. He leaned back so he could see her face. "No, we didn't. If a discussion means a give and take, where each party listens to what the others have to say, then we definitely didn't. Family fights, yes. Family harangues, certainly. But not family discussions."

Gerri looked into his eyes. Someday, she wanted to learn more about those days—but not now. She sighed. "I really should go back in there before it really *becomes* a fight."

He took her hand. "And I should go in beside you. But before you go…" He took a breath. "I drove her to school this afternoon."

"You didn't have to do that."

He shrugged and made a dismissive face. "It was no problem. Plus, it looked like rain and she had fixed herself up and everything."

"I noticed." *Was this really all about a crush on Frank?*

"She was excited about the class. Not just about Frank. That paper that she asked me for last night? She was using it in her room last night, scribbling and working on some problem. Something about bridges?"

"Really?"

"Yes. I think that we should hear her side of this."

"Really?" *Do I sound like a broken record?* "Does that mean that you would actually consent to this?" This was the last thing Gerri would have expected.

"Let me put it this way. If you're against it, then so am I. If you're in favor, then we would have to reach an understanding with her, but I wouldn't fight it."

"Whew! That's the last thing that I expected to hear. What about us wanting to live alone together?"

"I still do. And in an ideal world, we would be—starting tomorrow. But I think she hates her high school, and, from my impression of it, I can't say that I blame her. I wouldn't want you to be stuck in that situation, and she is your sister. Let's see what she has to say—what kind of a case she makes."

Gerri reached up and brushed his lips with hers. "I love you, Sven. OK, let's go and talk."

Eager to make up for his earlier cowardly flight, Sven sought to take the initiative. "If you don't mind, I would like to hear what Marilyn has to say." Marilyn shot him a grateful look.

Olivia looked as though she wanted to object, but she couldn't. Sven was, after all, their host. And he and Gerri were the people whose lives would be the most disrupted by Marilyn's plan. "Go ahead," she finally said.

"Thank you," Marilyn said, looking at Sven. She took a deep breath and gripped her thighs. Gerri could see where her hands had been shaking. "This is not just about Frank. Yes, I like him. But I think everybody likes him." She looked at Gerri for support. Gerri nodded her agreement.

"I would love to have a study partner as smart as he is. But it's not just that." She looked around beseechingly. "They actually think I'm smart. They make me feel a part of the classes. Do you have any idea how good that feels? Back home, half the time the teachers won't call on me, even if I raise my hand. And if they do, the white kids will roll their eyes, and half the black kids will look disgusted, as if I'm trying to get over or something.

"If I were in school here, I'd feel like I was a part of things. And I'd work harder because I'd want everyone to *keep* thinking that I'm smart." She turned to Gerri. "I studied that challenge problem last night. Do you know when the last time was that I spent a vacation evening working on a math problem? Hah! Try 'never.'"

After Marilyn's plea, the tone of the discussion started to change. Sven didn't know whether it was Marilyn's persuasiveness or the fact the Sven and Gerri didn't reject the idea out of hand. Her parents still had questions and concerns, but Olivia calmed down, and it seemed as though she and Robert were starting to consider the idea seriously.

When the tide seemed to have turned in favor of the idea, Sven counseled caution, asking Gerri, "There are lots of things to think about on our end, but do we know whether the school would even allow this?"

"I think so. Students do transfer in after the start of classes." She thought for a moment. "I'm not sure about transcripts and records and such." She stood up abruptly. "Let me make a phone call or two."

While she was out of the room, Sven thought about all of the things which could go wrong with this. He remembered—reluctantly—his own tumultuous senior year. "Marilyn," he began, "You should consider that this might be hard on you even beyond school. *If* your parents give their consent, then you'd still have to live in this house. We'd have responsibility for you and you'd be answerable to us. That means that you'd have to accept that Gerri and I have parent-like authority over you. Having Gerri acting like your mother is not something that you're used to, I'm sure. And having me acting like a father when you barely know me... Are you sure that you can live with that? Because if you make Gerri's life miserable or if you embarrass her at school..." He even threw her one of his patented scowls, thankful that Gerri wasn't in the room to laugh at him. "I'll have you on a plane out of here so fast that your head will spin." *I can be the nice guy later; I need to know how Marilyn will react to adversity now.*

Marilyn hesitated for only a couple of seconds. "I understand and I accept that. I'll try to be good." She paused and he could see the wheels spinning in her head. "I'll help around the house—whatever you need."

Gerri returned just in time to hear Robert's observation. "Olivia and I'll talk about this, but I must say that it's very generous of you to even consider it."

Sven looked at Gerri. Then he smiled and replied, "I have it on reliable authority that Gerri has tamed me."

The Bartons looked at her with fascination, and she glared at Sven. *Note to self: slap Ellen next time you see her!* She settled for a quick disavowal: "Pay no attention to him. Here's what I found out…"

The school, it turned out, would present no major obstacles. Paperwork would be required, but Marilyn could enroll and attend classes before it all arrived. The evening dragged on, though, with Gerri, Marilyn, and their parents getting the logistical details hammered out. There would be boxes of clothes and the like to be mailed from South Carolina. And there would be some shopping trips here to augment Marilyn's wardrobe in the meantime.

Sven found himself irrelevant and decided to get some dinner for everyone—carryout food would have to do, since the women were too busy to cook. He turned to Joetta, who was wearing a long face, and asked, "I'm going to pick up some food. Can you come with me to help carry it?"

Once in his truck, she turned weepy. "I don't want her to stay here. Then I won't have any sisters."

How am I supposed to deal with this? Sven didn't know, but ignoring it wasn't an option. *I'd better practice acting like a parent.* "You can still write each other, just as you did with Gerri. Anyway, she won't be gone forever. And while she's gone, you'll be the big girl of the family. You'll have your pick of bedrooms." That seemed to mollify her a bit. Then, on an inspiration, he asked her about her friends back home.

That worked. She apparently had many and she was looking forward to telling each of them all about this exciting trip. She was still talking about them as they sat and waited for their pizza—which she helped to choose. *Crisis averted...*

———

Gerri was late getting to bed, but Sven was still awake. "Did you get everything worked out?"

"As much as we could think of." Gerri slid in beside him and put her arms around him. Sven shifted so that he could hold her. "Let's just cuddle," she warned him.

"OK," he responded. "You must be tired."

"I am. But I'm also afraid that we could be heard if we..."

He chuckled. Her sisters' bedroom was right next to the master bedroom. "Once your family leaves, we'll put Marilyn in the bedroom in the back. Any noise you make won't carry back there. Besides, don't teenagers play music a lot?"

"Maybe." She thought about that and then dug him in the ribs. "But maybe she'll play it too quietly to block the sounds."

Sven grinned, amused by her discomfort. "We'll get used to it. Or she will." He paused. "Or maybe she'll be the first teenager in history to get yelled at for having her music _not_ loud enough!"

Gerri giggled, already starting to feel drowsy in his arms.

Sven thought about the evening. It hadn't been the disaster that it could have been. And, best of all, there was no lingering ill will between him and Gerri. "Now I know what a family discussion is," he muttered.

Gerri roused herself. "Good. Did you like it better than a family harangue?"

"Much better." He shifted again to see her better. "Did I ever tell you about the butler whose boss always yelled at him?"

Gerri looked at him warily and shook her head.

"The butler really hated the verbal abuse, but he was afraid to say anything openly for fear of losing his job. So the next time his boss rang for him, he drew himself up and responded with all of the dignity that he could muster, 'You harangue, sir?'"

Gerri studied his face. He looked pleased with himself. *He's happy!* "I love you," she said with a smile. "And that was terrible!"

CHAPTER 50

September, 1971

Gerri and Sven sat out on their porch and just relaxed. The long days of summer were over, but today had still been uncommonly warm for this late in the summer. Gerri looked across the channel at the city and the sunset on the mountains. She didn't think that she'd ever get tired of this view.

Sven glanced over at her. "Well, we made it."

Gerri felt a satisfied smile growing, but she just nodded.

"And all year long, we never once had to tell her to turn her music up."

She reached out and nudged him with her toe. "Stop being bad. Marilyn would have been so embarrassed..." Gerri thought for a while. "She's matured a lot since I left South Carolina. I'm proud of how well she did this last year in school. Of course, I can't help but worry a little about college. She's a long ways from home at the University of Washington. Either one of her homes, for that matter."

"I think they'll do well. She and Frank will watch out for each other."

"Just like they did this past year."

"Do you think they'll end up together? Romantically, I mean."

Gerri considered that. "I don't know. I don't think that even they know. But it definitely amuses them when people speculate about them."

"Fortunately, neither one of them is in a hurry to get married. I remember Marilyn saying once that she wasn't getting married before she was 25."

Gerri remembered that as well. She also remembered that Frank had previously claimed that he wouldn't marry before he was 30. When Marilyn had made her proclamation, however, he had responded with, "Yeah, maybe 25 is a good age." Both he and Marilyn had found that to be hilarious. Gerri had understood Frank's sense of humor well enough by that time to catch the sly reference: they knew that Frank was exactly three days older than Marilyn, so he was subtly suggesting that he and Marilyn might be getting married at the same time.

"I feel a bit sorry for your mother. She must feel like she's losing her family."

"She did want Marilyn to apply to colleges closer to home, but I think she's satisfied with UW—especially since they offered Marilyn a really good financial aid package."

"Did you ever tell Olivia that Marilyn and Frank applied to the same schools?"

"No. That would have just made her worry more, especially if she heard about Stanford." Frank had gotten accepted at Stanford—he had gotten accepted everywhere that he'd applied—but he declined because Marilyn didn't get accepted there.

"Umm," said Sven. "It's strange to have an empty nest before you even had a real nest." He shot her a sly smile. "I mean, whenever I thought about bringing a third person into our home, I just assumed that we would start out with a little teeny person." He gestured with his hands a couple of feet apart. "And it would grow gradually into a full sized person. But we started out with a full sized person."

Gerri had to smile, but that didn't stop her from teasing him. "It?"

"Now don't go all Mindy on me. I admit that, in an ideal world, English should have a word for 'he or she,' but 'it' isn't a bad substitute."

She smilingly nodded her acceptance and changed the subject. "When we do decide to make a little person, I think that you'll make a good father." With that, she leaned over for a kiss.

When they finally broke the kiss, Sven stared at her, drinking her in. "I love you," was all he could say.

"And I love you."

Sven reluctantly checked his watch. "How soon do you have to leave for Mindy's wedding shower?"

"I have a few minutes yet. But remember, I'm helping with the setup."

"You always said that you wanted to do something special for her when she got married." He paused. He didn't want to bring up any unpleasant subjects, but... "Did she ever say whether she had any trouble with her family about marrying John?"

"She said that they accepted it more easily than she had expected. They might have been against it initially, but they've met him several times, and they like him. Or, as Mindy says, 'He charmed them, and we always avoided arguing around them—they wouldn't have understood.'"

"Does her mother know that I'm going to be at the wedding?"

Gerri cast him a glance. "Yes. Mindy sat her down and talked to her about that. She told her mother that you'd be there as the husband of the matron of honor, and she got a promise that there wouldn't be any scenes. When Mindy gave her that painting, that might have helped."

"She didn't tell her that I painted it, did she?"

"No. She left the impression that you had had it commissioned. But that still convinced her mother that you cared about Laura."

"Good."

They were silent for a minute. Sven was glad that the toxic residue of that chapter of his life seemed to be dissipating.

Gerri had already moved onto another topic. "There's only one more loose end that concerns me."

He grinned. He had a strong suspicion as to what it was. Sure enough, she enlightened him.

"Do you have your parents' address? I'd like to write them and introduce myself."

Sven smiled fondly. "Ahhh, Gerri the peacemaker."

"Well? I think it's only polite. And if it gets you and them closer together, that would make me happy."

"I'll give you the address. But I worry that they might be unkind to you—especially if they find out that you're not white."

"I certainly won't hide that. In fact, I'll enclose a picture. If they react badly, then I'll be disappointed, but I won't be crushed. And at least I will have tried."

Sven was silent, lost in his thoughts—or perhaps in his memories. Gerri thought back on the last two and a half years of her life. She had gone from a college student with a rather provincial outlook—she had hardly even considered a life beyond South Carolina—to a respected teacher comfortable with travelling thousands of miles to the opposite end of the continent. Even more amazing, she had gone from an insecure girl in a relationship that she had come to suspect was merely manipulative, to a confident woman who had found the love of her life in the most unexpected place.

Add to that, the fact that she had helped to bring two people dear to her, Sven and Mindy, back to a friendship that they had lost years before.

And of course there was the satisfaction of having helped in some small way, through the example of her 'adventure,' to turn Marilyn's life around.

Sometimes, it seemed to her as though anything was possible. She looked at Sven and smiled. "I'm optimistic," she said.

Made in the USA
Monee, IL
12 March 2020

GERRI BARTON has lived a dutiful life, never straying far from her home in South Carolina. It took a scornful, cheating boyfriend to make her realize: at least once in her life, she wanted an adventure. Her parents, though of limited means, try to provide this as a college graduation gift--a trip across the country to visit her brother.

In this year of 1969, such a trip is not without danger for an unaccompanied young black woman. She makes it to her brother's Army base in Washington State unscathed, but her adventure is cut tragically short by his deployment overseas.

Stubbornly determined to extend her adventure somehow, Gerri, unknown to her parents, takes a side trip to Juneau, Alaska. There, her inexperience catches up with her and she runs out of money. Her search for a temporary job leads her to a fisherman, Sven Halvorsen. Depending upon whom you talk to, he is either a nice man with a tragic life--or a monster.

Sven lives a quiet life in a town where many still blame him for his wife's death. Against his better judgment, he hired a persistent, but inexperienced, Black youth as a deckhand. What he got was an attraction which was utterly unexpected.

Pursuing this attraction took him to places that he never imagined. He yearned to make a life with her. Can he convince Gerri of this? And can he convince her to uproot her life in the face of hostility from her family and friends?

ISBN 978-1-4949-5281-5

9 781494 952815